Matchmaker,
Matchmaker

To Barb —
   I'm "Farklempt" that
you came tonight. I'm so
lucky to call you friend.
Grand County Women are
it! I hope you like this...

   Love,

   Joanne

Matchmaker, Matchmaker

Joanne Sundell

Five Star • Waterville, Maine

First Edition
First Printing: January 2006

Published in 2006 in conjunction with Tekno Books.

Set in 11 pt. Plantin by Elena Picard.

Printed in the United States on permanent paper.

Library of Congress Cataloging-in-Publication Data

Sundell, Joanne.
    Matchmaker, matchmaker / by Joanne Sundell.—1st ed.
      p. cm.
    ISBN 1-59414-411-7 (hc : alk. paper)
    1. Women physicians—Fiction. 2. Jewish women—
Fiction. 3. Colorado—History—To 1876—Fiction. I. Title.
PS3619.U557M38 2006
    813'.6—dc22
                                                    2005027050

I have three amazing children,
but this is dedicated to my daughter, Zoe.
I never finished her baby book or her baby blanket.

This is her story.

Chapter One

Philadelphia General Hospital—1867

Too exhausted at three o'clock in the morning to do anything but find her dormitory bed, Zoe-Esther shuffled by the second-floor women's ward, relieved that all appeared calm. The night attendant looked up from her desk and nodded. Zoe-Esther managed a weak smile. Four long hours of isolated study in the anatomy lab had left her drained. Her eyes burned. She blinked hard several times and checked to make sure she had replaced her spectacles in her skirt pocket. One turn now down the long, darkened corridor, then only a short walk past the men's ward, and she could climb the narrow stairs to her own quarters. She quickened her step. The male patients were off limits.

Only weeks until her graduation from The Women's Medical College, Zoe-Esther mustn't let anything interfere with the completion of her clinical studies. Philadelphia General allowed the female medical students from the nearby college to work in their hospital, but only with scrupulous male supervision. Under no circumstances were they ever to work with male patients by themselves. Fortunate to be one of the three women that would graduate out of an original class of eighteen, she'd worked too long and too hard to have anything go wrong now.

As she padded past the restricted area, her head began to fill with thoughts of her upcoming exams. She wondered about the order of her searching examinations in anatomy, physiology, chemistry, and materia medica, and pondered which parts would be written and which oral. She knew she'd have a dissection in anatomy, a litany of questions in pathology and histology, and experiments to conduct for physiology. Determined to review all her notes, both laboratory and lecture, she would get little, if any, sleep over the next two weeks.

Someone coughed.

One of the male patients.

Zoe-Esther stopped and listened. The coughing worsened. Then she heard a voice, a man's, perhaps the attendant on duty. She waited a moment before leaving to make sure the patient settled. When she heard nothing more, Zoe-Esther believed all was well and began to climb the stairs.

Just then the attendant came running out of the ward and caught up with her. She knew most of the hospital staff, but this young man was a stranger to her.

"Have you passed any doctors tonight, miss?" he gulped breathlessly. "Do you know if any are still in the hospital?"

"No, I've not, and I do not," Zoe-Esther replied, a little indignant at the nervous orderly's assumption that she was not a doctor.

"I see you're on your way upstairs. Would you wake up one of the medical students for me then?" He ordered more than asked.

Though accustomed to this lack of respect on the part of the staff, it still irked Zoe-Esther that most men didn't accept women as physicians. This wasn't the time to let a small slight affect her, however.

"Young man," she said stiffly. "I am a medical student, second year, soon to graduate. Lead the way to your patient."

Even in the dim gaslight from the overhead fixture, she could see disbelief written all over his gaunt features.

"You . . . a doctor? A wom—?"

"Yes, yes, I'm a woman," she interrupted. "Now that we've gotten that out of the way, would you please lead the way?" Annoyed with the attendant's hesitancy, Zoe-Esther feared the patient would be dead before either of them got to his bedside.

For one fleeting moment it occurred to her that she would be attending a male patient. The fact that it might not be the wisest of actions didn't deter her. She pulled her stethoscope out of her coat pocket, retrieved her spectacles, and all but shoved the poor, penitent orderly forward.

Mute now, he led her into the men's ward.

She followed the wiry aide between the rows of patients. Some slept despite the ragged coughs coming from the back of the ward.

"Turn up the lamplight here and pull that screen around the bed." Zoe-Esther snapped out her orders the moment they reached the patient.

The attendant obeyed immediately.

With enough light now to better assess the situation, Zoe-Esther's heart lurched. She sucked in a breath. *Why he looks . . . he's so like I've imagined . . . could he be?*

Eyes closed now, his breaths laborious, the ashen-faced patient lay flat in bed, his chest and surrounding bedclothes soaked in bright red blood. Without even examining him she could tell the blood came from his lungs and not his stomach. His obvious youth, as much as his handsome appearance, took her by surprise. *Why, he can't be much older than my own twenty-two years.* Each time he coughed, more of the frothy liquid bubbled out of his mouth. Coughing or spitting of blood, hemoptysis, she repeated to herself. He'd kicked off the remainder of his covers, but that's not what troubled Zoe-Esther just now. She made an immediate diagnosis.

But his name. She had to know.

"His name?" She demanded of the attendant at her side.

"Wh—"

"It's a simple question, young man. What's the patient's name?" She struggled to sound matter-of-fact while her insides did flip-flops.

"Well, it's . . . just a minute, miss." The attendant stepped to the foot of the bed and grabbed the clipboard that hung at the man's feet. "Collins. It's George Collins," he read aloud.

George. George. She relaxed a little. *Of course, George. Not . . . he's not . . . him. Zoe-Esther Zundelevich, get hold of yourself,* she silently chastised. *Such ideas in your head. It must be the lateness of the hour that has hold of me. Yes, that's all. I'm just tired.*

"Miss? Miss?" the attendant repeated.

"Yes? What is it, young man?" she replied, agitated with herself.

"The patient." He nodded toward the infirm Mr. Collins.

"Wait a moment. Just give me a moment." She closed her eyes to help sort out her confused thoughts. In a few seconds she reopened them, knowing she had to put all her attention now on the sick man in front of her.

Tuberculosis. Consumption. Pulmonary Phthisis. The White Plague.

Put in the corner to die.

She had no doubt that Mr. Collins had been relegated to the back of the ward and left to succumb to the invasive lung-destroying disease, since his case probably wasn't interesting enough to the hospital physicians and medical students. With no known cure or effective treatment for tuberculosis, the patients warranted little attention as medical or surgical cases.

Feh! If any of the hospital physicians were lying in this bed and suffering from the same ailment and invalidism, no doubt they would be interested then!

Zoe-Esther closed her eyes and concentrated hard, trying to remember everything she ever learned about tuberculosis.

Known by many names for centuries, tuberculosis, still commonly referred to as consumption, only recently was identified in medicine as a specific disease by the French surgeon, Jean Antoine Villemin. Before Villemin, tuberculosis only described the symptoms of pulmonary phthisis or consumption; and not the disease, itself. The term "tuberculosis" came from the discovery, in the 1600's, of small tubercules or inflammations and scars on the lung known as tubercula. The same surgeon, Villemin, proved tuberculosis to be infectious.

Unfortunately there was still no known cause for tuberculosis. Contrary to the popular wisdom about the disease—as some in the scientific community refuted Villemin's work while many in the lay community had no idea of it—Zoe-Esther supported Villemin's evidence that tuberculosis was infectious, and not inherited. She also, in fact this very night, had just finished re-reading the work of Joseph Lister related to antisepsis in surgery and the importance of a germ-free environment to promote wound healing.

11

Two immediate problems faced Zoe-Esther: to save the patient and prevent herself and the attendant from contamination by the patient's lung infection.

"Get me two clean laboratory coats, a fresh gown, phenol, and a basin of hot water," she delegated in an even tone to the attendant.

This time he didn't move.

"Do it. Now," she ordered.

Relieved when the frazzled young man left to do her bidding, she realized that she didn't have time to wait for his return before she approached the dying man. Mr. Collins was drowning in his own blood. She would exercise caution. She had no choice but to act. The only thing she could do for herself at the moment was to avoid his coughing directly in her face. As for the blood, she'd have to clean herself afterwards as best she could.

Usually with a patient in shock from so much blood loss, the head should be lowered and the feet raised. But with such labored breathing and certain blockage of the air passages in his lungs, she elevated his head and chest instead. She grabbed the stack of pillows from the foot of the empty bed across the way and placed them behind his upper back.

The repositioning had an immediate effect. Her patient could take in a deep breath, however moist and rattled. His coughing subsided, and with it, the bleeding. Certain he'd ruptured blood vessels in his lungs, she was relieved when his hemorrhaging slowed and then stopped. He quieted. Zoe-Esther was grateful. His body and mind needed the relief that only a cessation of symptoms could offer. He had to be in shock, but by some miracle, he was maintaining. With great care now, she removed the pillows from under his head and back then slid them under his lower legs and feet. Pulling out her stethoscope she placed it against his bloody chest and listened, first to one side and then the other. Both were full of fluid.

Pulmonary congestion. Impending heart failure.

At this point, with his case so advanced, Zoe-Esther knew little could be done. The moment she pulled her stethoscope away, his labored breathing resumed.

When he opened his dark eyes, ever so slowly, yet ever so deliberately, she looked into the shadows of his death. *He will not go alone. I will stay with him.* If she could bring him any ease, she would.

"Here you are, ma'am." The attendant finally re-apeared.

First I was a miss and now I'm a ma'am. Suppose it would be asking too much to be called, "Doctor," she thought to herself.

"Thank you. I wonder if you'd be good enough to tell me your name?"

"Amos, ma'am. Just Amos." He appeared embarrassed at her query.

"Well, Just Amos, thank you. Now if you'd get some fresh linens, you can help me get our patient cleaned up and comfortable."

"Course, ma'am. Right away," he replied, then disappeared again behind the screen.

She didn't wait for him to return before she set to work. First she had to bind her hair out of the way. It was forever coming loose from its tie at the back of her neck, and she was forever re-gathering the mass of long coppery tresses up again. Natural curls. Whoever invented such a useless thing? Then, as quickly as she could, she removed her white laboratory coat, soiled now beyond recognition, and put on a clean one. She buttoned it up as high as it would go before she reached behind her patient's neck and untied the wet strings of his gown. After lowering the gown to his waist she collected the basin of hot water and towels and began washing all the blood from his face, neck and trunk. She took as much care as she could not to get any of his blood on her. Then, as soon as Amos returned, she instructed him to put on the other laboratory coat before having him help her remove the bloody linens, then replace them with clean bedding. Once this was done, Amos assisted her in getting their patient into a clean gown and covered with several warm blankets.

Grateful for all their sakes that Mr. Collins no longer coughed, she instructed Amos to sit with him while she went to fetch the medicines she needed. She took the bottle of phenol with her to scrub her hands and arms and to wipe down her stethoscope. In the operating room, along with phenol as a method of sterilization, carbolic spray was being introduced for germ-free surgery. Zoe-Esther knew the tremendous import of this discovery, as patients often "passed" due to wound infection, or sepsis, after surgery. Now their chances for recovery would be greatly improved.

With the appropriate dose of morphine for pain relief and comfort, a measured amount of amyl nitrate for the heart if need be, and an effective dose of chloral to assist in the prevention of coughing, Zoe-Esther made her way back to Mr. Collins' bedside. It was almost dawn, but she paid little mind. No one else appeared to be up and about yet. *So, today I'll be exhausted. Why should today be different from any other,* she mused more lightheartedly than she felt.

Mr. Collins was asleep when she returned. Good. *Rest and quiet are the best medicine.* Amos was asleep, too, snoring away in a nearby chair. Quietly as she could, she set down her medicines, then turned to look for a chair herself. Her head ached and her eyes burned. She pulled off her spectacles and rubbed her eyes, then replaced the wire rims in her skirt pocket and started for the empty chair.

"And wh . . . what . . . is your name?"

The rich timbre of the weakened, dying man's voice shook her from head to toe. She wheeled around, surprised he even had the strength to talk. Amos was still fast asleep.

"My name?" she repeated, still somewhat shaken.

"Yes," he managed despite his labored, congested breaths.

"Please." She came closer and put her hand on his arm "Do not talk. You must conserve your strength. There'll be time later for conversation."

"No," he wheezed. "No time . . . later. Tell me . . . now. Tell me . . . your . . . name."

Her heart went out to him for she knew he spoke the truth. If he lived another day it would be a miracle.

"I am Zoe-Esther. Zoe-Esther Zundelevich," she answered softly.

"Such a beau . . . tiful . . . name. Un . . . usual." He smiled in between his difficult words. "And . . . and a doctor. I'm . . . impressed."

"Well, not yet, actually, but in two weeks. In two weeks I'll be a doctor."

"No two . . . weeks. Now. You're . . . one now." He began to cough.

Still, Amos slept on.

"Please, Mr. Collins," Zoe-Esther implored and grabbed a clean linen towel to place lightly over his mouth. "You mustn't talk. You must rest. Please." She selected the chloral from the bedside table and poured a little into a spoon, then put it to his lips.

He took the medicine and closed his eyes. When he settled a little, she did the same. She was ready with the mor-

15

phine, should he need it. At best, she could help him be comfortable. How she wished she knew what caused his lung infection so she could help him; so he would not have to die so young.

For only a second, he opened his eyes, and raised his hand to her. When she took it in hers she could feel the strength still pulsing through his disease-ridden body. He closed his eyes once more. She thought she saw a glimmer of a smile. At least, thanks to God, he seemed at peace.

Mr. Collins died with his next breath. His hand dropped from hers, his life force gone forever.

Outwardly Zoe-Esther was the picture of calm, but inside she cried for George Collins. She grieved not just because of his dying, without the benefit of family and friends around him, but also because he could have been the one.

Amos finally woke.

"Is he a goner, ma'am?" His simple question was barely audible in the quiet stillness of the ward. "Yes, Amos. He's a goner," she said as if unruffled by the experience. With a coolness she didn't feel, she pulled the bed coverings up over Mr. Collins' serene face. She swallowed hard before speaking again. "Well now, Amos, you'd best help me get him prepared and down to the morgue." The difficulty of the moment must be ignored, Zoe-Esther knew. There would be other moments just like this one in medicine. She would never have enough schooling to prepare her to lose a patient. Feeling helpless, she prayed one day there would be a cure for tuberculosis and the many other diseases that killed so many, so young.

Zoe-Esther woke with a start. The clock chimed eight bells. Eight o'clock! She pulled her pillow out from under her head and pushed it against her face, groaning all the while. There was no need to check her classmates' beds. Morning lectures began at seven. Cassandra and Jane were long gone. "Punctuality. Punctuality. Punctuality." Professor Marsh's warning rang through her head. She groaned again. Maybe she could sneak into the back of the physics lecture hall. Perhaps no one would notice. Another groan. Since there were only three females in the group of students, it was unlikely she could sneak in.

With dread oozing inside her, Zoe-Esther sat up, put her feet on the brick-paved floor, and sent her pillow flying across the little dormitory room.

"What's to be done? Nothing. That's what's to be done," she answered aloud. "You're late and you're going to really catch it from old Professor Marsh."

Like her pillow, Zoe-Esther began to fly around the little space to which the female medical students had been assigned. The room contained three single iron beds, one washstand and chamber set, one old, rickety, straight-backed wooden chair, and two small, paned windows without the adornment of curtains. The floor was always cold and the wallpaper always drab. Right now their appearance matched Zoe-Esther's gloomy mood.

The only thing she could be grateful for at this moment was that at least she was already dressed. In the recesses of her addled brain she remembered falling into bed around six. She hurried and poured fresh water into the cracked basin to wash her face and clean her teeth. Checking for her spectacles in her pocket with one hand, she dabbed her face dry with the other. Of course her hair wouldn't cooperate this morning.

"Is it too much to ask that you fall into place just once!" she muttered as she ran her brush roughly through the long, coppery mass, then struggled to collect the errant tresses in a black ribbon at the back of her neck. She thought of Cassandra and Jane, who both wore their hair in sensible buns at their napes. Cassandra's well-behaved blonde locks never flew every which way, and Jane's brunette curls were always in order, as were their clothes. Unlike her own current dishevelment, Cassandra's tall, neat thinness was equally matched by Jane's short, tidy, roundness. Zoe-Esther took a moment to study her image in the small oval mirror over the washstand.

Hmm. Bloodshot eyes. Dark circles under them indicating too little rest. Coloring a sickly pale yet cheeks flushed. Perhaps a slight fever. Rest, proper fluid intake, and a nutritious diet highly recommended.

Zoe-Esther laughed out loud at this.

If she wanted to be a doctor, she'd have to do without "rest, proper fluids, and a nutritious diet," for the next two weeks, at least. Out of habit, she ran quick hands over her high-necked, long-sleeved white blouse to bring some order to it, then smoothed the folds of her charcoal-gray wool skirt. The tips of her black-booted feet showed under its edges. In the next moment she sped out the door, and somehow managed to grab the books and lecture notes she needed for class.

"Jake, what in tarnation are ya doin' up at this time of the mornin'?"

"Well, you know the old saying, Matthew," Jake quipped in his usual gravelly tone. "There's a sucker born every minute. What if one of them has a mind to pass through the Golden Gates right now? I can't afford to miss them, can I?"

Matthew shook his balding head, then ran a hand over his wrinkled face, once, then again.

"Shoot, Jake. The day ya cain't afford somethin' is the day I throw in my towel," Matthew replied, holding up the bar rag to emphasize his words. "Ya already got most folks' money here in Golden City, not to mention half the territory. I think ya can afford a lil' extra sleep."

"I'm not sure I like the sound of that, Matthew. Makes me seem low down and downright greedy. I think I need a drink to soothe my wicked soul." Jake gave Matthew a quick wink and bellied up.

"Makin' me say it again, are ya?" Matthew frowned at the younger man, the small bits of color left in his once-dark eyes sparking their disapproval. "It's too dang early for liquor and ya know it. Your innards are gonna rot afore you're thirty."

Jake grinned at his old friend. "Let's see. I reckon that gives me two more good years. How about you letting me worry about my innards and you just worry over pouring me some Jack Daniels?"

"Harrumph," the old man growled.

Jake grinned again. Matthew sounded like a mean bear dragged out of hibernation a little too early. But when no glass or bottle of whiskey was placed in front of him, Jake's insides began to rumble, too.

"Listen, Matthew. You're not my ma or my pa, so don't be acting like them. I've done all right so far. Own my own place and my own faro tables, which, by the way, put a roof over your cussed old head. So I don't think I need you telling me when I can or can't take a drink." No sooner were the words out of his mouth than Jake regretted them. Matthew didn't deserve them. Hell, he was more of a ma and pa than Jake had ever had. Too few in Golden City, Jake knew, cared if he lived or died. But Matthew . . . Matthew did.

19

"Old friend," Jake began in earnest. "Don't pay me any mind this morning. Got up on the wrong side of bed is all. I didn't mean to take things out on you, but I sure could use a drink, Matthew." He hated having to be so honest, but he needed that drink.

If Matthew had any more to say about Jake's penchant for alcohol, he didn't let on. Turning his back, he took a glass down from the shelf and set it down hard on the smooth mahogany in front of Jake. Without so much as a look for Jake, he placed a half-empty bottle of the Tennessee whiskey next to the glass and left Jake by himself at the bar.

Alone now, his six-foot-two, well-muscled frame more slumped than upright, Jake rested one elbow on the wood of the bar while he filled his glass to the brim with the other. His hand was steady, not a tremor. In his line of work, he couldn't afford the shakes, not at the faro table. He tilted his head and threw back the whole drink in one gulp. Ready to pour another, he caught his image in the ornate, etched mirror over the bar.

Didn't think much of his looks. Never had. Never would. He stared at his full, shaggy head of salt-and-pepper hair he wore cut straight across at the back of his neck. He'd started turning gray at seventeen, and sure got more attention from women than he bargained for because of it. They were always pulling off his black Stetson and wanting to run their fingers through it like he was some kind of store-window dummy. Clean-shaven except for a thick, smoky mustache, Jake peered into the mirrored gray shadows of his own eyes, but only for a fraction of a second. He never wanted to look too deeply and see what lay hidden there.

"Hell," he muttered, then turned his dark expression

into a slow grin and poured another drink. "To us, old partner." He lifted his glass in a toast. "To lucky cards, beautiful women, good liquor, and the almighty dollar." He slammed back the second drink quicker than the first.

Most every day began this way for Jake. Had for years. In fact, for as long as he could remember he'd downed a few every morning. There wasn't any particular reason for it. He'd just always done it. Maybe he wanted to live up to his namesake of Whiskey. He was known throughout Missouri and the Colorado Territory as Jake Whiskey. Chose the name himself and damn well liked it. Some didn't. The gamblers, gunslingers, cowpokes, and tinhorn hustlers who'd tried to cross him, and were lucky enough to live to regret it, cursed the name of Jake Whiskey.

"Mornin', honey."

Jake knew that velvety voice and heavy scent of rosewater only too well. *Belle.* He didn't turn, but waited for her to appear in the etched mirror next to his own image. The moment she did, he threw a lazy smile at her still-sleepy reflection.

"What are you doing up, Belle? No customers yet?" he teased into the mirror.

"Jake Whiskey," she chided and rapped him hard on the shoulder.

He turned toward her and looked down into those blue pools, brim full with fury at him. God, she was beautiful, even with her soft red mouth set in a hard line now and her delicate, fisted hands planted on the small curve of each voluptuous hip. The action made her ruby satin robe fall open, just enough to reveal the tops of her full breasts. Long blonde hair shimmered over them like a silky curtain of gold that played hide-and-seek.

"Just what," he drawled in a husky tone, "has your

21

feathers all in a flutter? The Golden Girl of Golden City has no call to get so riled up over nothing." He couldn't resist kidding with her. Besides, she could take it, and then some.

"I wish you wouldn't talk about other men, especially when . . . when we've just . . . all night. I don't give a damn about the men who pay me, no matter how much. You do realize, don't you, that I never charge you? Ever wonder why?"

He knew she wanted an answer. Hell. She deserved an answer, but he couldn't give her the one she wanted to hear. They'd had this conversation before and it never went anywhere.

"Listen, Belle, let's go back upstairs and finish this little talk." The corners of his mouth twitched into a slight grin, but stayed hidden under the droopy sides of his mustache. He reached for her arm and gently clamped his hand around it.

"C'mon, Golden Girl. C'mon."

As soon as he spoke he could see she wanted the same thing he did. Embers of desire already burned in those fiery blue pools.

"But, Jake, I want—" She tried to concentrate on her words while he led her upstairs. "I want you to make me a respectable woman . . . a *somebody* . . . a wife."

"Belle, you're already a somebody and have more respect from the men in this town than any hundred—hell, than any thousand—women in the West."

He stopped on the stairwell and pulled her hard against him.

"There's nobody that respects you more than me," he whispered low into her ear. "Nobody," he repeated then trailed gentle kisses across her cheek and found her mouth. He couldn't wait to get her back to his bed and make her forget all about needing to be anyone's wife. Especially his.

of any further contemplation instantly evaporated when the lecture hall door slammed shut at her back.

"Well?" Daniel's anxious question greeted Zoe-Esther the moment she'd left Dr. McGriff's office.

"Well, what, Daniel? You sound just like Professor Marsh," she returned, knowing full well what he meant. Just then Cassandra and Jane rushed up.

"Oh Zoe-Esther," Cassandra managed, breathy and in obvious distress over her friend's plight. "What did . . . did Dr. McGriff . . . are you out?"

Appreciative of Cassandra's concern, Zoe-Esther was amazed Cassandra didn't first gush all over Daniel. Jane, too, seemed to restrain herself.

"I don't think it's fair at all, Zoe-Esther," Jane said. "You're smarter and work harder than any of the rest of us. It's just not fair that stodgy old Dr. McGriff can toss you out of the hospital and out of school. It must be because you're a female, Zoe-Esther."

Daniel looked suspicious.

"All right, Little Miss Mystery, want to tell us what happened in there before we've got you packed and out on your ear? You wouldn't want us to waste all this sympathy on a needless cause, now would you?"

"Why, Daniel Stein. Do you think for a second I'd keep any of you in suspense on purpose?" Zoe-Esther couldn't resist dragging out the moment.

Now Jane and Cassandra appeared suspicious, too.

"Very well," she smiled at them. "I'm not out on my ear, or any other body part. You simply won't believe it. Of course Dr. McGriff was upset with me. You should have heard him. 'Young woman, do not forget that you are a woman.' " She tried to copy his gruff declaration without

27

laughing. " 'Females are not permitted to attend males without careful supervision. You overlooked this steadfast rule when you attended the deceased consumptive.' Humph," she interrupted her own litany. " '*Deceased* consumptive.' He should have said 'Collins, *George Collins*'. The deceased was a person with an identity."

Daniel, Cassandra, and Jane all nodded their agreement.

"Go on, then," Daniel encouraged. "What did he say next?"

Zoe-Esther's mood was dampened at the thought of Mr. Collins' death, and it was difficult for her to begin again.

"Yes, well, let's see, oh yes. Dr. McGriff made all the usual comments about males and females in medicine and the importance of following rules; and how I'm the first student under him who has disobeyed the rules; and how this doesn't speak well for Philadelphia General, much less The Women's Medical College of Pennsylvania." She paused and sighed. "Of course, just when I thought he'd boot me out the door, he said, 'this time I'll make an exception, young lady, seeing as how you've demonstrated exemplary behavior in your tenure here, and seeing as how you no doubt only had the patient in mind. Just don't let it happen again, Miss Zundelevich.' "

"Oh, Zoe-Esther, I just knew it," Jane said, not giving anyone a chance to refute her suddenly changed opinion. "Certainly, they couldn't toss you out, what with your exemplary behavior and all."

Zoe-Esther, Cassandra, and Daniel all burst into laughter. Then Jane and Cassandra each gave her a quick, congratulatory hug. Daniel's wasn't so quick. Caught up against him, Zoe-Esther peered over his shoulder at her roommates. The corners of their smiles turned downward.

Oh for pity's sake, they're jealous. Ridiculous. Jealous of

Daniel and me. Could anything be sillier? When she tried to break free, Daniel's arms didn't loosen, but pulled tighter around her. For the first time in a very long time, Zoe-Esther didn't know what to do. To be captured in Daniel's awkward grasp and to have Cassandra and Jane stare at her with such mournful looks on their distraught faces sent her own nerves into an anxious tangle.

The tangle worsened.

Daniel put his cheek against hers, then brushed a whisper against her ear. "I won't let Dr. McGriff or anyone else in this hospital hurt you. Now or ever, mina lieber." His warm breath unnerved her every bit as much as his words.

Mina lieber!

My love!

Zoe-Esther couldn't believe what he just said, in Yiddish or in English. For one thing, and one thing only, was she grateful at this moment. Since Cassandra and Jane weren't Jews, like Daniel and herself, they wouldn't understand the Yiddish endearment. Many east European Jews spoke the handed-down mixture of German, Slavic, and Hebrew. Though not fluent in Yiddish, she knew some bits and phrases from her papa.

Oy gavalt, unterzogan!

Oh mercy, and to whisper so in my ear!

Daniel is my friend, my best friend. Not mina lieber! *Not my love!*

More than Professor Marsh, more than Dr. McGriff, Zoe-Esther dreaded looking at Daniel. Afraid of what she'd see and with no idea what to say to him, she closed her eyes a moment to collect herself. When she opened them, Cassandra and Jane had disappeared. She was alone now in the cleared corridor, alone with Daniel.

As suddenly as he'd grabbed her, he let go. He appeared as shaken as she felt. She'd never seen such a serious expression on Daniel's handsome face, so pensive yet decided.

"I'm going to get this out, Zoe-Esther." He spoke in a rush. "So don't break in like you always do."

Too befuddled to be insulted she kept quiet.

"I was planning on waiting until after graduation, but now seems like a pretty good time to tell you, to ask you—"

His strange gaze and unexpected words forced her to interrupt.

"Then, Daniel, I think that whatever it is you wish to say should wait until after graduation," she replied, hoping with all her heart he would agree. That would give them both time; him to realize he should take back his mistaken declaration of affection, and her to choose the right words so as not to cause him injury. She held herself perfectly still in the tense silence, crossing her fingers behind her back while she waited for his answer.

His features softened.

She released a small sigh of relief.

When his full grin returned, when her old friend seemed to return, she dared another breath, this one deeper and more soothing.

"All right, Zoe-Esther, you win," he capitulated, then placed his hands on her shoulders.

She felt his cool fingers splay down over her upper arms. Perfect surgical fingers. She'd always told him he had the hands of a surgeon. Little did she imagine he'd ever want to use them on her!

"I'll wait two weeks, but only two weeks," he said, his grin gone now. "Then we'll talk, you and me. All right?"

"All right," she parroted, and held her body rigid while her thoughts did somersaults.

30

"All right then. Two weeks," he reiterated, as if to seal their commitment. "I'm due in anatomy now and you're late for your *materia medica* lecture, Miss Zundelevich," he teased.

She flashed him a smile, this time less worried about being tardy than about her unavoidable upcoming talk with him.

He smiled back, then turned and left.

The corners of her mouth drooped, much like her room-mates' did, the moment he was out of sight. Cassandra's and Jane's affections for Daniel, however, were quite the opposite of her own. On any normal day, Zoe-Esther would dash to make the next lecture on time, but this was not a normal day. Right now, she longed for boring and ordinary over surprise, and all her nerves tingled. It took every effort to induce her sluggish feet to turn in the right direction and begin to walk. The day was already horrendous. How could her being a little late make things any worse? Besides, the problem that faced her now had nothing to do with medical school, and everything to do with Daniel.

"Copper all your bets, gentlemen," Jake announced to the four other men seated at his faro table, then shuffled the deck and placed it face up inside the box, the shoe that housed the cards. All thirteen denominations of the spade suit, Ace through King, were displayed on the cloth table board. The men placed their even-money bets, much like Roulette, on more than one card at a time. A quick look and Jake knew exactly who bet and exactly how many bets each man made. When play started he pulled off the soda, the top card, and discarded it next to the betting board.

One card followed another onto the soda pile as play went round the table. On successive turns, loser cards went

31

one way and winner cards the other. When loser and winner cards were the same denomination on a turn, Jake declared a split and took half of all bets placed. It was fair game to give the house an edge in faro. And so it went round the table, with Jake settling bets on winning and losing cards. Chips passed from one hand to another, from one stack to another, so fast that anyone observing might find it hard to follow the play.

"Damn you, Whiskey, I won the hand, you son of a bitch. Give them chips over. Won 'em fair and square. No way in hell I halved my bet and took away my copper." His pockmarked face red and sweaty, the big cowboy reared out of his seat and backed clear of the table.

Chair legs scraped across the polished plank floor as other players hurried to get up from their play. The piano music stopped. Voices hushed.

In a matter of seconds, everyone around the snarling cowboy had scattered.

Everyone but Jake.

Looks just as mean as the snake he is, Jake thought, *and just as deadly.*

"C'mon Wooster, simmer down. Sit down." Jake spoke slowly and deliberately. He was careful to keep both his hands on the table, in plain view of the upset card player. "Quit your rattling and have a seat." *Damn.* It was in the eyes, always the eyes. All glazed over like a mad dog. This one wasn't any different from the others who'd accused him of running a dishonest faro table. *I'm a lot of things in this sorry life,* Jake admitted to himself, *but a cheater ain't one of them.*

"Get up, you yellow-bellied cheat!" Wooster shouted.

Jake didn't budge.

No doubt encouraged by Jake's lack of response, the

cowboy spoke even louder this time.

"I said, get yerself up, you lily-livered, lyin' son of a bitch!"

Jake sat motionless. There wasn't any point in trying to talk to Wooster, not with those eyes and that spittle dripping out of the corners of his crooked mouth. Jake would wait for him to draw the first card.

Wooster looked all around the large gambling hall, seeming to puff out his chest a little more with each face he encountered.

Must be he thinks he'll win this hand. Still Jake waited. So far the hell-bent cowpuncher hadn't gone for his gun.

"Say, Whiskey," Wooster began, his tone more quiet and cunning now. "You shore remind me of that faro dealer from Virginia City. What was his name? Oh yeah, Black Jake he was called."

Jake knew the name and the story.

"Seems that ole' Black Jake had a faro set-up just like this a' one. Big man in Nevada, yessir. Like you. But I guess he wadn't as big as he thought since he done lost all his money in one night. Near eighty thousand smackers. Cleaned him out. Know what he did then, Jake Whiskey?"

Slowly, Jake eased his gun hand off the table and down over the holster at his side. He put his sure fingers around the handle of his Colt .45, and he waited.

Wooster took another gander around the room. Apparently satisfied that he had everyone's attention, he kept on.

"Well, he done just like others I've come across. Shot hisself dead, he did. Yessir."

He was close, real close. Jake tightened his fingers around his gun.

"Don't reckon you'd do us all a favor and put a bullet in

yer own head now would you?"

Any time now.

"Reckon then . . . yer makin' me up an' have to do it!" Wooster yelled then drew his gun and fired.

But it was the cowboy who lay dead on the floor, blood seeping from the gaping hole in his chest.

The smoke from Jake's Colt settled and disappeared as quickly as his draw. He walked over to the dead man and knelt down.

"You stupid son of a bitch," he said in a low voice. "You didn't have to die tonight." Then he rose to his full height and looked at the bar to find Matthew.

"Get the sheriff," he said.

"Bliss, pure bliss," Jake nuzzled into Belle's ear before he eased off her.

Belle, still under the spell of his expert lovemaking, needed a few moments to calm her stirred body. Her breasts rose and fell softly with each difficult breath. Beads of perspiration covered her nakedness. Little droplets began to trickle, slowly and sensuously, and formed wet trails to her loins. The rhythm created anew there pulsed into tiny rivers of excitement. She luxuriated in the sensation, and her desire again heightened.

Only one man ever, ever made her feel this way.

Jake Whiskey.

"Well then, how nice and convenient, darlin'," she purred to Jake while turning on her side to face him. "My name just happens to be Bliss." Like Jake, she'd picked her last name, too. Only Jake didn't know that she knew about him. Oh, she knew a lot about him, all right. She'd made a point of finding out everything she could. After all, she was going to marry him.

Harder to catch than she'd thought, Jake wasn't like any of the other men she knew in Golden City. She'd had dozens and dozens of proposals since she'd started working at the Golden Gates, but not the one she wanted. In the business five years now, since she was twenty, Belle knew she was the best, the Golden Girl of Golden City. The envy of most, she had all the fancy outfits and money any girl could want. Her lifestyle, though, wore on her more and more each day. She'd begun to worry.

What will I do when my looks are gone? When my waist has thickened and my face isn't smooth anymore? What happens then? I won't end up dried up on opium or dead in some shriveled-up old stranger's smelly bed!

Before that happens, I'll marry Jake.

Besides, she'd always wanted him over all the rest. Of course, she had one little problem. He didn't seem to want her or any woman, permanent-like. She'd make sure to change that, soon as she could.

Jake grabbed his tobacco makings from the nearby washstand, rolled a smoke and lit up. After a satisfying inhale, he stared out the paned window of his second-story room into the April dawn. He let out his breath and watched the smoky stream fade into the morning stillness. He took another puff, but what he really could use was a drink. Liquor helped take it all away; all the things he never wanted to think about, to remember.

When he first woke in the morning, at the moment when sleep hadn't quite let go and the day had just begun its hold, he was agitated awake by the same gnawing urge to climb out of his skin and into somebody else's—anybody else's. But he never would, never could.

Ah hell. Jake attempted to redirect his thoughts. *What in Blue Blazes do I have to complain about? I got it all, don't I?*

35

Money. This place. Belle next to me. You're a damn fool, Whiskey. His thoughts took another sudden turn. *Yeah, fool is right. I got everyone fooled. Even Belle. They all think they know me. But they're wrong.*

Dead-as-Charlie-Wooster wrong.

Chapter Three

"*Nu,* Star, what did that nice young Daniel Stein want?"
Yitzhak Zundelevich asked the moment they were alone.

Zoe-Esther turned from the door she just closed behind
Daniel and faced her beloved papa. All her life he had
called her Star, and not Esther, "Because you sparkle like
Queen Esther. Like the brightest star in the heavens." And
so, every year during the holiday of Purim, she felt a special
connection to good Queen Esther, who had helped the Jews
defeat evil King Haman long ago in Persia.

Despite being sixty-five years old and withered around
the edges, Yitzhak stood straight and proud. He never bent
or stooped. He always wore his skullcap just at the back of
his full head of white hair. The little black yarmulke never
slipped off. A miracle itself, Zoe-Esther always thought. His
wiry limbs and robust zeal for each new day made her almost forget what she knew to be true. She wished he were
as strong and indomitable as he appeared.

Her whole world, her entire life, centered round him,
only him. She never knew her beloved *ema.* Her mother had
died soon after Zoe-Esther's birth, and not a day went by
that Zoe-Esther didn't feel the pain of it, or the guilt. *If only
one of us was to live, it should have been my ema.* Yitzhak
never spoke of his feelings, but from the moment Zoe-

Esther sensed how much he missed his *lieber,* she determined to make it up to him. His happiness would always come before her own. Always.

Nothing can ever happen to Papa.

It can't. I won't let it.

The day she helped take George Collins to the morgue, she realized Yitzhak had come down with the same illness. In denial, ignoring his coughs and bouts of fatigue, she blamed his symptoms on cold weather and overwork. Now she couldn't afford to do so; not with his life at stake.

Time had run out.

Today. Now. I must talk to him. I must tell him.

Taking in a deep breath for courage she searched for a way to begin. She smiled at the mischievous twinkle in his faded blue eyes, and knew full well where his thoughts had wandered.

To me and to Daniel.

"Such a nice young man, a nice Jewish boy. And a doctor, too." Yitzhak spoke before any words came out of her mouth. "Mind you, your old papa has said nothing. Two years, and have I said anything to you about the nice Daniel?"

"No, Papa," she replied.

"Child," he took one of her chilled hands in his warm ones.

Nerves made her palms cold and sweaty.

"*Oy gavalt,* Star. What makes you so cold? Come. Sit and we will have a fire." He motioned for her to take a seat in one of the two straight-backed wood chairs by the small, stone fireplace.

Except for a few tiny embers, the flame had gone out.

"I'll just put a nice . . . piece . . . of wood here," his voice was muffled as he reached for the kindling and laid it atop the smoldering embers. He reached for the poker and stoked until the fire relit.

"Papa," she implored. "You must keep yourself warm. You mustn't let the fire die down so."

"You want I should waste good wood and good money when you are not home? And here it is the summer?"

Zoe-Esther cringed inside. She hated that they had to economize. She hated the pathetic little stack of wood by the crumbly fireplace, their even more pitiable lack of furnishings, and their poor store of food. Yitzhak should have an ever-present warm fire, soft pillows at his back, and a kitchen full of *milchig* and *fleishig*. Along with meat and dairy there should be mounds of noodle pudding, full bowls of borscht, and piles and piles of fruits and vegetables. Their apartment, a two-step walk-up off the muddy street in the middle of the most teeming, run-down section of Philadelphia, was too small and too cold and too damp. She hated it, now more than ever. Now because all of it was killing her papa.

Zoe-Esther knew exactly what she had to do to save him.

"Papa, I have to talk to you."

"Yes, yes Star, I know. About Daniel. Already I tell you, yes. I approve."

"You approve?" She was dumbfounded. "Of what, Papa?"

He settled back against the hard wood of his chair, folded his stiffened hands in his lap, then threw her a broad smile.

"Of you, you and Daniel."

Oh no, Papa. Don't, she begged in silence.

"You have both been busy with school but now you can stand under the *chuppah* and join together in marriage. You and Daniel, kalah and chassen. Such a proud papa, I'll be.

39

Such a proud *zayde,* I'll be."

Oy vey, Zoe-Esther's heart plunged to her feet. *I just graduated from medical school and already he has me married under the wedding canopy to Daniel, and a mother!*

"Daniel Stein will make me a good *eydem,* a good son-in-law. He is a doctor, like you, and he is a Jew, like you. You will both carry on the traditions of our people in this great country of Amerika." Then his smile disappeared and he leaned towards her, just a little. His voice was more hushed. "You know, Star, now I can confess something to you, my beautiful, smart daughter. This is a great country, yes, but not so many Jews. I was worried you might take up with *goyim,* with a Gentile. This, I must tell you, has been on my mind. But now, now you have chosen Daniel Stein, and my worry is gone." He smiled again. "Thank you, Star. You are a good daughter to take such worry from your old papa." In obvious satisfaction, he leaned back against the wooden slats of his chair.

Zoe-Esther got up and knelt at Yitzhak's feet, then took his hands in hers, agonizing over a way to begin.

"What is this, Star?" he asked with the gentleness only a father can impart to a daughter.

"Papa," she began. "There's something else now, more important than my standing under the canopy with Daniel or anybody else."

His look of bewilderment gave her pause, but she continued.

"I worry, too, Papa. I worry about you."

"Me? Star, pl—"

"Hush, Papa, and let me finish." She gave his fingers a gentle squeeze. "I worry because you have a cough that grows worse every day."

"A little cough, such a *tzimmes.*" He took his hands

away and tried to get up.

"No, Papa. I'm not making a fuss over nothing! You must sit and you must listen to me," she begged. Grateful when he eased back down, she folded her hands and rested them on his knees. "Papa, I believe you have an illness you've developed here in America. I don't think you brought it with you from our village when we left Russia." She hurried now; she didn't want to stir up painful memories of Kiev or the *shtetl*. "The sickness has a name. It is tuberculosis."

His eyes held no trace now of the twinkle she'd seen in them only moments before.

I'm sorry, Papa. So sorry, her troubled thoughts turned to her *ema* in heaven. She glanced up. *Forgive me for having to bear him such news.*

"Star," he broke into her silent plea. "You are not in *shul* in prayer. You do not have to *davnen* or light the *yartzite* candle yet to mourn my death. Now get up off your knees and sit down like a good daughter."

She obeyed and stood up, then pulled her chair close to sit across from him.

"Pa—" She didn't have a chance to say more.

"My beautiful Star, so much like my Sarah," he smiled now as he spoke. "Eyes soft like the doe yet full of spark and mischief, and hair that outshines the brightest morning in autumn. All shimmer and goodness, your mama was—just like you. I look at you and I see my Sarah, little Star. You're so much like her, right down to that tiny sweet cleft in your chin."

Zoe-Esther couldn't believe it! He never talked about her *ema!*

"So much like your mama." *Oh, Papa.* Her instincts told her to press him further now and explain the impact of his illness, but her heart had already shut everything inside her down, to hear more.

How she'd longed for Papa to speak of her *ema,* but he never did and she never dared ask. What she did know she'd learned from the villagers in the *shtetl* where she was born. She remembered every word.

Your mama was a good, kind person. And mefunitse! Fastidious! How she worked to prepare everything for Shabbas. Such a table she would prepare. Her challah was the most delicious egg bread, the very best. And you can't imagine, there was not even a speck of dust anywhere in the house when the Sabbath began! The polished Shabbas candle holders and menorah in your house were the envy of our village. Your mama was so proud to have them. Your papa is the best silversmith in all of Russia. He made her the most beautiful things to keep our traditions. How he loved her. How she would have loved you, little Zoe-Esther. Such a shame she did not live to see you grow up.

Whenever Zoe-Esther would ask why or how her *ema* died, the villagers kept silent. Their silence, along with her papa's, made her believe, to her child-like thinking, she must be the reason her mother had died. After all, she was alive, and her *ema* was not.

"Your mama—"

When Yitzhak began to speak again, Zoe-Esther snapped out of her reverie. Her heart skipped so in her anxious chest, she placed a hand over it, unaware she'd even done so.

"Your mama, she should rest in peace, was happier than she had ever been in her life when she found out she was going to have you. We both were. The day you came into this world was such a blessing for us. Your mama held you and held you. 'My one true *mitzvot,*' she said to me. 'My one true good deed in this life is to bring our beautiful little Zoe-Esther into the world.' "

Yitzhak fell silent.

Zoe-Esther could see how difficult this was for him, even before tears spilled down his cheeks.

He started to cough, then drew out his handkerchief to cover his mouth. Another cough, this one deeper.

She reached out to him.

"Child," his wheezing finally stopped and he settled. "Sit, sit. I am fine." He replaced his handkerchief as if to underscore his words.

She obeyed, but she knew he wasn't fine. Numbed by his illness and his revelations, she sat still.

"In the whole village, your mama and me, we knew we were the happiest, the luckiest. Each week we said a blessing for the *schadchen,* such a good match she made. I can see, my daughter," the tiniest of smiles twitched at the corners of his dry, thin lips. "I can see this is a surprise to you, that I married my Sarah because of the matchmaker."

Zoe-Esther thrilled to see the twinkle again in his watery blue eyes.

"Like you, little Star, perfect, just like you. So much love and happiness . . ." His voice faded and his mood darkened. "The week after you were born, your mama got sick, very, very sick. No one in the village knew what could be wrong. We were poor. We had no doctors. We asked the rabbi, but he could do nothing. Now, you are a doctor, and I can speak to you of these things. Your mama got a bad fever, very bad. It took her life, from me and from you." Unable to go on, Yitzhak buried his head in his hands and cried.

Zoe-Esther put her arms around him. The worn wool of his homespun shirt scratched against her cheek.

"Oh Papa," she crooned. "I'm so sorry, so very sorry. So much you had to bear, so much."

Yitzhak's sobs turned into tortured coughs. He reached again for his handkerchief.

Zoe-Esther sat back in her chair, resolved to follow through with her plans.

"Listen to me," he said, his tone clearer and his lungs calmer.

She read embarrassment in the familiar wrinkles on his dear, tear-stained face. He had nothing to be embarrassed about. Nothing.

"I am sorry, Star, for many things. Mostly, I am sorry I never talked to you before about your mama. It was wrong of me—"

"Hush now, Papa," she interrupted. "Don't worry so. It's all right."

"No, child. It was selfish of me. I was afraid, afraid to say her name, afraid to think of her, afraid to remember the pain of losing her. For this, my daughter, I am ashamed."

"Please, Papa. It's all right," she quietly reassured him. "I understand. I do. I understand."

Grateful when he appeared to accept her words, she wanted to change the subject and raise the matter of his illness, and was very surprised when he did it for her.

"Maybe, too, the reason I say such things to you now is because I am sick. Your old papa will not be here forever. This I know. You do not have to tell me about this consumption . . . this . . . what you call . . . tuber . . . tubercu . . . losis. I have known this, and I accept it. My only regret is that I will leave you, my daughter. But you, you have made my happiness on this day. You will marry that nice Daniel and all will be well."

"Oh, Papa," she said, unable to control her sudden frustration with him. "Yes, you have symptoms of tuberculosis, of consumption," she corrected for his benefit. "But Papa,

44

you are not going to die, not if I have anything at all to do with it! And this isn't the time to think of Daniel or anybody else but you, Papa. You must get well, and you will."

Yitzhak smiled at her.

"Only just made a doctor and already you think you can do the impossible. I know about this consumption," he tapped his chest several times then gestured in her direction. "I know nothing is to be done."

"You're wrong," she argued. "Yes, if we stay here where it is cold and damp and every day brings a new chill to your bones, you will not get well. The air here is not good for you. The climate is not good for your lungs. The infection will only get worse. You need to live where the air is better, cleaner, and where it is dry. This is what I meant to speak to you about today, Papa. We have to leave. We have to go west. I've decided we should go to the Colorado Territory."

"Oh, so you have decided, have you?" he said. "Star, my life means little. It is your life that is important. I will not have you leaving Daniel Stein or the hospital you love so much to schlep across the country to live in some wild place, and lose everything that you have worked for. *Mekabets zayn gas!*"

"Papa, we will not have to go begging on the street. I have heard about the West. It will be full of opportunities for me as a doctor and your health will improve there. I know it. Please, please do as I say."

Encouraged when Yitzhak seemed to soften and ponder her plan, she decided to save the details of their move until she'd made him a good strong cup of tea. They would both feel better after a cup of tea.

Zoe-Esther rolled onto her stomach and buried her face in her pillow. She held it there for long moments. When that didn't soothe her ruffled thoughts, she flipped onto her back again and stared at the designs in the fractured ceiling above her. Tonight all the cracks formed the pancreas. Last night they had shaped a perfect kidney. Tomorrow, another body part would loom over her head and assault her slumber.

Tomorrow. Yes, what of tomorrow?

Restless and overcome with worry, she sat up in her little iron bed, nearly identical to the one in her quarters at the hospital. She wanted to get up and brew another cup of tea, but she didn't want to chance disturbing Yitzhak, who slept in the next room, the only other one in their tiny apartment. Her shoulders sagged. She needed more than tea now. She needed a miracle.

But maybe, just maybe, their meager savings would be enough for their journey west. A master at economy, she'd saved every penny she could. From the moment Yitzhak became weak and unable to do enough bit work as a silversmith to support them, she'd put a little away here and a little away there. Despite being a member of the less-favored sex, the hospital allowed her to work a set amount of hours each week as a medical student. Her tasks were limited mostly to housekeeping instead of medicine, but she didn't mind. It brought in money. Blessed money. Needed money.

She had not forgotten that Yitzhak had sold the family menorah he made in Kiev for the tuition to send her to medical school. Carefully crafted from the best silver in all of Russia, it was beautiful. Over her protests, he'd sold it. *For me. So much he's sacrificed for me.*

Her gaze shot across the darkened room to the candlesticks they kindled every Friday at sunset to usher in the Sabbath. A sliver of moonlight danced first across the little table and then playfully tiptoed over the familiar silver. *I cannot let Papa sell them, too. Not for me. I cannot. He's already lost too much.*

This resolution set firm in her mind, she went down the list of anticipated expenses. They needed train fare out of Philadelphia and payment to join a wagon train from Missouri to the Colorado Territory. Ever practical and prepared, she'd already checked into which route they would take, how long it would take, and what supplies they'd need for such a pilgrimage. Satisfied with her plans, she decided to save her wished-for miracle until they arrived in the West. She'd need it then to find work so she could take proper care of Yitzhak. Certain it wasn't a good thing to pray for money, she prayed for guidance instead.

Feeling a little better now, Zoe-Esther lay back down, but the sleep she wanted eluded her. Her thoughts strayed to the malady she was sure had taken her *ema.*

Puerperal fever.

If only medicine had known then what it did now about germs and their deadly transfer. Recent studies had shown that the unclean hands of those delivering the baby transmitted germs to the mother, causing fever, and often death. Hand washing, simple hand washing, could have saved her *ema.* Though the reason for her mother's death was doubtless a clinical one, Zoe-Esther still felt the emotional burden of it. For that, there was no fix, no recent study.

Forcing her thoughts to a happier subject, she warmed to the news that her parents had been brought together by the *schadchen,* the matchmaker. *So many years,* she marveled, *and I didn't know.* But then again, it shouldn't be such a surprise. The matchmaker of her recollection was ever busy. That her parents were matched in a loving marriage made her realize all the more how right the *schadchen* must be!

Knowing only too well how hard life was for Yitzhak without his Sarah, Zoe-Esther had asked God, so many times, why He took her *ema* from Papa. And why Yitzhak had to suffer. It seemed so unfair. She should accept God's will, but in her heart of hearts, she could not.

It was far easier to accept the will of the matchmaker in making a match for her parents. This she could accept. This she could understand. Not for a second would she fault Yitzhak for harboring such a secret.

How can I when I have one of my own?

She'd kept her secret since she was nine years old, just before her papa took her to America.

"And, I'll keep it until I'm ninety-nine," she vowed, then sat straight up in bed. The clock struck four. Zoe-Esther flopped back onto her stomach and nestled her cheek against the frayed muslin. "You have two hours, Zoe-Esther Zundelevich, now go to sleep," she ordered. "And no more wasting time on such girlish foolishness."

The moment she'd said it, she knew that very same girlish foolishness would keep her awake the rest of the night.

Chapter Four

"You have to go then, Zoe-Esther?" Daniel asked again. "What you want to do for your father is a risk. If you stay here, I'll help you treat him. Together we can make him better. I'm sure of it."

"Daniel, I have made up my mind. You know what that means. I will not change it. It is more of a risk to keep Papa here in this cold, damp climate. His tuberculosis will only worsen." She could tell by Daniel's expression that he knew she was right. She could also tell that he wanted her to stay in Philadelphia for another reason.

As she stared into his soulful, dark eyes, how she wished she saw her old friend in them, instead of this stranger. If only the Daniel she had known for the past two years would reappear. And, with all her heart, she wished her papa hadn't made up his mind that she should marry Daniel. To make matters worse, she'd lied to her papa, and said she would.

How could she choose otherwise, and cause her papa to be as melancholy as Daniel appeared to be? How could she disappoint Yitzhak and bring him any more grief than he already bore? She could not, and would not. As much as it went against her own wishes and desires to lie, she had promised her papa that after he got well, she would marry

Daniel. Of course she'd keep this promise to herself, and not, under any circumstances, tell Daniel. In fact, she hoped the distance she was about to put between herself and Daniel might make him change his mind about his affections for her.

Yes, that would solve everything.

Her spirits improved. She was certain that Daniel wouldn't want to wait so long for her. He would surely grow weary of waiting and fall in love with somebody else. *I won't have to break my pledge to Papa. Daniel will do it for me.*

"Daniel, don't worry. I'll write when we arrive at our new home."

"Zoe-Esther, tell me that you won't keep things from me. If you have trouble, any kind of trouble, you must let me know. If you need me to help with your father, I will come. I will help."

"No, Daniel." She tried to keep her voice calm and her demeanor cool. The very last thing that she wanted was for Daniel, or any man, to go chasing across the country, worrying and fussing over her. She did not need to be rescued. She needed to be left alone. If only she thought Daniel would understand, she would explain things to him. A modern American woman with modern American ideas, she would never be content, even if she were madly in love with Daniel—which she was not—to love, honor, cherish and obey him, or any man. It just wasn't in her nature. For the present, between Daniel's sorrowful countenance and Yitzhak's, she dared not say a word.

"I thank you, Daniel, but do not worry over me. I'll be fine. I'm sure of it. I'm a doctor now and I know there will be more work for me out west than I can handle," she said, all the while praying it would be true.

The skeptical look Daniel shot her annoyed her.

"I know exactly and precisely what you're thinking, Daniel Stein. You think that because I wear a skirt, I won't find employment as a doctor. Well, you couldn't be more wrong," she all but yelled at him.

"Zoe-Esther." Daniel, sounding frustrated, raised his voice to a level with hers. "It's hard enough for a woman to work in medicine here in Philadelphia. We're far more ahead of times than people out on the frontier."

She knew he was right, but she'd never admit it.

"Daniel." She swallowed her anger and softened her tone. "Let's not quarrel. Papa and I are leaving in a few minutes. *Thanks to God, Papa isn't listening to this. Thanks to God, Papa hasn't spoken to Daniel about any of this.* She knew Yitzhak had not, since she'd never left the two of them alone. Their brief exchanges had consisted mainly of "hello" and "goodbye." *What would I have done if Papa had actually said something to Daniel about my promise to marry him? Oy Vey!* "Daniel," she wanted to get going as quickly as she could. "Can't we say goodbye as friends?"

"Of course, *mina lieber.*" Daniel took a step closer. His mood changed. "But not as friends."

Don't say it again, Daniel. Please don't. No matter how much she wished he wouldn't, she knew he would.

"I don't want you for my friend, Zoe-Esther, and you know it. I want you for my wife."

Yes, she did know it, but she didn't have to like it.

His words and intimations had the same effect on her now as they had two weeks earlier, outside Dr. McGriff's office. Only this time the churning in her stomach was worse, much worse, as if she had mistakenly ingested a thick, slippery measure of rendered chicken fat. Where was her old friend? Not this schmaltzy one. Where was that Daniel? This Daniel made her insides sick and her head

51

spin with regret. This Daniel wanted her to be in love with him. Her feelings for Daniel could never go beyond friendship. She sighed in resignation. Now more than ever, she was certain that God hadn't put her on this good earth to fall in love with Daniel or any man.

No. Just as "to love, honor, cherish, and obey" isn't in my nature, neither is romance. I'm quite happy to leave those feelings to others.

Zoe-Esther carried her resolve never to fall in love with her on the train out of Philadelphia and onto the prairie schooner she and Yitzhak purchased, then boarded, in Independence, Missouri. Here they joined a group of immigrants and settlers heading west on the Santa Fe Trail. If they'd wanted a shorter route, more to the north, on the California-Oregon Trail, they would have had to wait at least two weeks for the next wagon train to gather. Both she and Yitzhak wanted to press on rather than wait.

Neither the passage of time, the distance involved, nor the hardship of travel had any effect on Zoe-Esther's steadfast resolve to leave Daniel and his foolhardy, romantic notions about her back in Philadelphia. Besides, worry over her papa's ability to tolerate their journey took precedence over everything else. Every day the great steam locomotive sent its full complement of black smoke sparking and spitting through the passenger cars. A fine sooty mist settled on their clothes—and in their lungs. She fretted over every one of Yitzhak's coughs, and rued the day such an unhealthy conveyance was ever invented! Relieved when they switched to the prairie schooner, despite the occasional clouds of kicked-up dust on the Santa Fe Trail, at least the air was healthier for Yitzhak.

His little complaints increased as their journey wore on. If he didn't miss *Mikvah Israel,* his synagogue in Philadelphia, he missed having a nice glass of hot, steamy tea by his little fireplace. Zoe-Esther didn't mind that he kvetched about this and that. In fact, she welcomed his complaints and would have worried more if he didn't have any. So far he'd held up remarkably well, in spite of the obvious toll each mile of the journey took on his health. After a long day of rigorous travel over uneven terrain, and after all the wagons pulled into a protective circle to guard against any possible Indian attack, Yitzhak would climb down from their wagon and hunt for pieces of wood for the evening campfire. Try as she might, Zoe-Esther couldn't discourage him from this task. His coughing spasms increased, not unexpectedly; she knew they were partly due to fatigue from hard travel. As for his weight loss and ensuing night sweats, she read these as clear signs of his advancing disease. The sooner they reached the end of the trail, the better. She prayed she'd made the right decision in putting her papa through such an ordeal. On those days when weather permitted, she opened the back flap of their schooner so he could rest out in the open. The dry air would improve his health. It had to.

Two months to the day after they left Pennsylvania, with money low and spirits lower from worry over her papa, Zoe-Esther pulled her team to a halt behind the larger wagon in front of her and secured the heavy reins. They had reached Fort Garland in the Colorado Territory. She examined her hands. The hide straps had worn them red and raw. No matter. More important was the miracle that she'd learned to drive the double team of horses in the first place. There were so many things to learn. Now that she had embarked on a whole new way of life on the frontier, she had better get used to it.

Soon after their arrival at the fort, she sold their team and prairie schooner back to the wagon master. Then, after gathering up what belongings she and Yitzhak had, she promptly made a decision on where they should settle.

Golden City.

It had sounded perfect to Zoe-Esther the moment she heard about the territory's capitol, a mining supply boomtown. Located some ten miles west of the much larger Denver City, Golden City rested in the foothills up against the great Rocky Mountains. There she and Yitzhak surely could lead the golden life. Patients would line up in scores to see her, and her papa would quickly regain his health.

Her spirits improved.

Good fortune smiled down on them when the Pollards, a middle-aged clerical couple they'd befriended on the wagon train, offered to take them to Golden City. Since they dressed plainly in black from head to foot, Zoe-Esther wondered if the Pollards were Quakers. Not wanting to open any discussion on religion and draw unnecessary attention to herself, she didn't ask. Nor was this the time to turn down the Pollards' charitable invitation, especially with their savings already so depleted. She and Yitzhak had forty dollars left to their name. She had no idea how much they'd need to find a place to live, but the forty dollars would have to do until she established herself in medicine. That could take time. Time neither she nor her papa had.

Time and money.

Right now both were in short supply.

Never one to wallow in self-pity or self-doubt, Zoe-Esther straightened her shoulders and held her chin high as she sat on her makeshift seat in the back of the Pollards' wagon. Yitzhak—she turned a moment to check him again—lay on a pile of quilts toward the front of the wagon, and slept. With the flaps of the schooner pulled up, Zoe-Esther had a front row seat to all the sights and sounds of the frontier. As the untamed landscape rolled by, a sense of adventure overtook her apprehension. She let all her worries of the past months disappear from her thoughts, if only for a few moments. So many new people and new places. She'd already seen an Indian. Or had she? She thought of the young woman she'd examined before leaving Fort Garland: her very first patient in the West. Even though the young woman's skin was white, everything else about her was Indian. Perhaps she'd been a captive to one of the many tribes in the West. Zoe-Esther had heard stories of such things. She didn't hesitate to help the poor creature when she saw the young woman being harassed and assaulted by a half dozen soldiers.

Stupid brutes! Criminals, each and every one of them!

Luckily, the maid had escaped unhurt. At least physically, Zoe-Esther thought. The emotional healing from such an assault wouldn't be as easy. Living in a wild land among savages, many of whom, Zoe-Esther concluded, were no doubt white, she prayed the young maid's fate would be a good one.

The crisp September morning held a chill despite the bright sunshine. Zoe-Esther pulled her gray knit shawl closer about her and shut her eyes. When she opened them, the spectacular vista before her took her breath.

She'd had a glimpse of the Rocky Mountains as the wagon train pulled into Fort Garland, but she hadn't appreciated their vast expanse until now. As far as the eye could see, to the north, west, and south, the great peaks rose up from the flat plains like impenetrable walls, daring anyone to try and cross them. Zoe-Esther couldn't imagine it. Why, the very spot on which she now rode had to be at least five thousand feet above sea level. She wondered what sort of individuals would even try to carve out an existence in such rugged territory, at such formidable heights.

"I guess I'm about to find out," she quipped, while the heavy-laden schooner creaked and bumped its way over the rough wagon track toward Golden City.

When the wagon party arrived at the intersection of two roads, one turning off to Denver City and the other pointing to Golden City, dusk fast approached. Zoe-Esther could barely make out the letters on the signposts in the dim light. The moment Reverend Pollard giddy-upped his team of horses on past the signposts, the wagon jolted hard. She turned around and saw that Yitzhak still slept. She was glad for it; knowing how much he needed rest. As for herself, she'd fought sleep all day, not wanting to miss any part of the journey. She hoped they would reach their destination before nightfall. Only a few more miles and they'd be there. Only a few more minutes and it would be dark.

When the Pollard wagon party arrived on the outskirts of Golden City, Reverend Pollard picked a spot for them to set up camp for the night. "The town can wait until morning," he'd said. Busy helping Yitzhak get comfortable, Zoe-Esther prayed in silence as if she were in *shul,* bowing before the open Arc.

Please, Dear God, let Papa get well in this city of gold. Let him know your healing hand. Guide me in all that is right. Amen.

After she helped Mrs. Pollard prepare a simple meal of cold biscuits and fried potatoes, Zoe-Esther bedded down for the night on the hard ground beneath the schooner. Above her, inside the wagon, Yitzhak was quiet; his sleep, blessedly, uninterrupted by spasms and coughs. Zoe-Esther pulled her covers up below her chin and tried to get comfortable, but the rapid fall in temperature made her shiver. With no extra blanket, she would have to think of pleasant thoughts to keep warm.

Only one came to mind—the same one she'd had many times before.

Nine years old again, bathed in the afternoon sunshine, she stayed hidden as she made her way around the back of her village to the door of the matchmaker. She didn't want any of the other kids to see her and tease her. When the other girls went to see the matchmaker, she'd scoffed at them and told them she never would do anything so foolish. Grateful that the cottage door opened at her first soft rap, she didn't hesitate and stepped inside.

The matchmaker's smile warmed Zoe-Esther every bit as much as the Russian sunshine. Her round, jolly features were framed in a blue cotton babushka. Here and there, strands of gray hair peeked out from under the edges of her scarf and blended into the patchwork of tiny wrinkles etched on her face. The faded striped dress that covered her ample frame reminded Zoe-Esther of the gypsies she'd read about in one of her papa's books.

"Come, come in little Zoe-Esther. I will get you a cool drink of water and some cakes. Sit. Sit, and we can have a nice visit."

Nervous, yet determined, Zoe-Esther obeyed and sat down at the simple wood table.

The matchmaker returned from the kitchen and set her plate of cakes on the table. She pulled out a chair and collapsed into it.

"Here, have a little something, child. You are all skin and bones. Eat, eat."

Zoe-Esther stuffed a cake in her mouth and tried to think of how to begin. She could leave and not ask the matchmaker. But then, if she did—if she left and went to Amerika and didn't ask—she'd never know.

"Schadchen, *I . . . I—*"

"*Tish, tosh, child, I know why you are here. You do not have to say a word. I have been waiting for you to come. I have much to tell you.*"

"*You have? You do?*" *Zoe-Esther answered, mystified by the matchmaker's words.*

"*Of course, child. You have come for the same reason all the others girls do. You have come to find out his name, haven't you?*"

"*His . . . name?*" *Zoe-Esther whispered, gripped with panic and regret over her visit.*

"*Yes. His name. You do want to know* who *your match will be when you grow up, don't you?*"

Zoe-Esther nodded mutely.

"*Excellent. Now be a good girl and have another bite of cake and then I will tell you all about the one you will marry.*"

Zoe-Esther took another bite of cake, but she couldn't swallow the sweet confection. How could she eat when she was about to hear his *name!*

Less chilled now, Zoe-Esther finally fell asleep under the Colorado sky, with one name on her lips and one image against her heart.

Jake stepped into the morning rain. Soon enough, the rain would turn to snow. He walked across the muddy street toward the Clear Creek stables. After a good ride, in spite of the dreary day, he'd get to work. Since he spent his afternoons and evenings inside at the faro tables, a ride on Missouri always got whatever things he needed to get out of his system out. He and Missouri had been together a long time. Since Independence. Jake counted on his horse's companionship and trusted Missouri more than he did most humans.

"Hey there, fella," Jake cooed to the handsome animal as he walked inside the stable.

The big chestnut whinnied and pawed at the straw in his stall. The other stabled horses stirred a little at Jake's appearance, but soon settled.

"Ready to go are you, big guy?" Jake opened Missouri's enclosure and pulled his blanket and saddle from their perch on the rail. "It's a little wet out today, old friend," he spoke as if the animal understood his each and every word, then placed the saddle on Missouri's back and pulled the cinches taut. When he turned to reopen the stall latch, Missouri bumped him square in the back with his muzzle.

"Hey boy. Not so fast. We're going," Jake laughed, then let the horse nibble at his hand. "Oh, I see. Think you might talk me into that biscuit first, do you? Don't worry, you'll get it later. Like always." Jake's tone turned serious. "Yeah, like always," he rubbed Missouri's muzzle. "It's just you and me. Huh, big guy?" He gave the horse a last pat and led him out of the stable and into the morning rain, then mounted up.

The downpour showed no signs of stopping. Jake drew the flaps of his tan slicker close together and pulled the brim of his Stetson low on his brow. Despite the inclement weather, the streets were already jammed with loaded supply wagons headed for the gold fields in the mountains. Work here didn't come to a halt just because of a little rain. As long as there was gold to be found, there would be plenty of miners around to find it.

Good, Jake thought. *Good for me, and good for business.* Miners liked to gamble, and they didn't seem to care if they were much good at it. If he happened to be there to take their money, then so much the better. If the miners had to lose to somebody, it might as well be to him. So far Golden City had treated him pretty damned well. In the seven years he'd been there, he'd made a very profitable living as owner of the Golden Gates. He'd made a lot of money and money said it all. He wasn't complaining, even on a morning like this, and he welcomed the deluge the same way he welcomed most days. Each day was pretty much the same as the next. Didn't expect anything different. Didn't want anything different.

A strange sensation trickled down Jake's neck when he turned the last corner out of town. He didn't know what it was, but it didn't feel like rain. He scanned the street to see what could have grabbed his attention. Nothing looked out of the ordinary.

Just a few cowboys on horseback and an old prairie schooner.

His eyes narrowed and fixed on each rider and then the wagon. He'd passed hundreds of wagons like this one: immigrants and settlers all looking to strike it rich. The mountains and plains were full of them. Had been since '59. All pretty much came west for the same reasons. Maybe that's what threw him off. The driver of the wagon, dressed in a black frock coat and hat, didn't look like most men he'd seen come into town. Must be a preacher, Jake figured. He hadn't seen too many in these parts. Not too many bothered with Golden City.

As the wagon lumbered by, the wind picked up. The same unfamiliar sensation he'd experienced only moments before hit him again. He checked his collar. Dry as a bone. Damn, he didn't like being off his game. He thought he saw something out of the corner of his eye. Wagon flaps. He could have sworn someone jerked them shut. Turning around full in the saddle, he glanced behind him but saw nothing.

Must be the wind playing tricks.

Inside the wagon, dry for the time being, Zoe-Esther tied the strings of the flaps together and listened to the rain as it pelted the heavy canvas. Instead of being soothed by the sound, she began to panic. For the briefest of unreasonable moments, she imagined that if she and Yitzhak set even one foot outside the schooner, they'd either drown or be buried alive in all the mud!

Two thousand miles and it's come to this. More rain and cold. Oh Papa, what have I brought you to? What have I done? Golden City looks anything but golden!

Riddled with guilt over her decision to come west, the confidence she'd had when she left Philadelphia drained away. Nothing was left but fear. Zoe-Esther started to tremble. How she hated to be afraid. It always made her remember. And, she didn't like to remember.

Like the torrential rain outside the wagon, she could hear the Russian soldiers of her childhood charging down on her village with their sabers drawn, ready to strike. Screams of death were all around her. She ran as fast as she could to escape the soldiers' wake of destruction. She was one of the lucky ones, she and her papa—this time. The soldiers did not kill all the Jews in the village. Only some. Enough to keep everyone afraid.

Would she always be afraid? Afraid that she wasn't one of the chosen, but one of the despised. Cast out from all acceptable society. And that any day . . . any time . . . the soldiers could come. Zoe-Esther straightened her back and raised her chin. She refused to entertain any more frightening thoughts or to bow her head as if she were one of the downtrodden. She was part of a proud and faithful people. She was proud to be a Jew. It was only her childhood fear that had momentarily caught up with her. She shed her fear as quickly as she could. Though she had no idea what this new day, in this new place, would bring, she determined to meet it head-on. She had to, for her own sake, and for her papa's.

Several hours passed. The storm showed no signs of letting up. Zoe-Esther couldn't afford to wait any longer to look for a place to stay. The Pollards wanted to help her find a hotel, but Zoe-Esther swallowed her pride and told them that it would cost too much. Instead, she hoped to find a rooming house. It would be cheaper. Over the protests of Yitzhak and the Reverend and Mrs. Pollard, she climbed down from the wagon, determined to make her own inquiries.

Prepared to get wet, but not for her feet to be sucked into nearly foot-deep mud, she grabbed hold of the schooner's closest wheel and tried to steady herself. Her blouse and wool shawl were already soaked through to her skin. Her hair came loose from its tie and immediately plastered against her back, like heavy hands unwilling to let go. Chilled and shaky, she blinked hard and struggled to see through the oppressive rain.

She managed to make out the letters over the building across the street: The . . . Gold . . . en . . . Gates. Certain it had to be a mercantile with shopkeepers who would know where she could find a rooming house, she decided to ask inside. With great effort, she freed her feet from their muddy snare and began making her way toward the store. Each step through the thick mire was hard-taken. The relentless torrent pounded against her back as she maneuvered her way past a surprising number of wagons and riders on horseback. She knew why she had to trudge through such weather, but couldn't imagine why on earth anyone else would be out in the heavy rain.

When she reached the porch in front of the Golden Gates, her burdensome, drenched, mud-spattered clothes felt like shackles. It took all her strength to step onto the planked porch. Once there, she sought immediate shelter under the porch roof and tried to shake off some of the mud. She didn't want the shopkeepers inside to think ill of her. Her efforts were useless. Mud lashed itself to the hem and folds of her soggy blue skirt. Try as she might, she couldn't remove any of the splotches from her once-white sleeves or the front of her blouse. She ran cold, tremulous fingers over her wet hair and across her cheeks. There wasn't a thing she could do about her appearance. No matter. Her looks paled in comparison to the task at hand. Intent on securing a safe shelter for her papa, she pushed through one of the heavy swinging doors of the mercantile.

Careful to stand just inside the entrance, Zoe-Esther hugged her arms against the shivers and clenched her jaw to control her chattering teeth. As soon as her eyes grew accustomed to the light inside, what she saw surprised her. It didn't look like any kind of mercantile she'd ever seen.

Instead of shelves of dry goods and counters laden with bolts of cloth, at least a dozen round tables and chairs filled the huge space. A large mirror spanned one entire wall. Beneath the mirror stood a dark wooden breakfront; the kind she'd imagined rich people owned. The red and gold striped wallpaper made her think of sheets of shiny, streaming hair ribbons. The carved rail and stairway could rival those in the most elegant of homes back East. She looked up. Three glass-bowl chandeliers, suspended strate-gically from the room's high ceiling, had drawn her atten-tion. She hadn't expected to see anything like them in a rough western town. Only one of the chandeliers, directly overhead, was lit. Mesmerized by the flickering, gas flames—her only companions in the apparently empty hall—something inside her began to warm and stir. What-ever it was, it made her uneasy. She hugged her arms tighter and looked back down.

The moment she did, what she saw unsettled her far more than the gentle dance of the lamplight overhead.

Chapter Five

"Help you, lady?"

Startled by the sudden appearance of a man, Zoe-Esther stepped back. One more step and she would be out the swinging doors of the Golden Gates.

"Come on in. I won't bite."

From the looks of the stranger, she wasn't sure. His shadowy eyes, dark clothes, and salty voice unnerved her. So did his shaggy mane of prematurely gray hair. She had heard of the occurrence but never met anyone who had started turning gray so young. This man couldn't be out of his twenties. Zoe-Esther studied his thick, smoky mustache; fascinated by the way it swooped down at each corner of his mouth and framed his handsome chin. On impulse, she wanted to reach up and brush the bristled hair from his lip to see his entire mouth. She did not. Another impulse hit her—this one was more disturbing to her than the Westerner's rough good looks—and harder to fight.

Zoe-Esther felt as if she'd stood in this very doorway before, with this same man, and heard the exact same words. The French called the sensation *déjà vu*. She called it ridiculous, unacceptable, and impossible! The idea that she might have shared some sort of past life experience with this shadowy primitive, or had some kind of acquaintance or remembrance of him, struck her as entirely illogical and foolish. Then what could be the reason for her uneasy feelings? *It has to be the rain and cold. Yes, that's all. Only the storm,* she told herself and calmed a little. Her shivers and shakes, however, didn't calm. She rubbed her hands up and down her arms and tried to get warm.

"Here, put this on," the inscrutable stranger said.

Before Zoe-Esther could stop him, he had removed his coat and draped the heavy garment around her.

"Come on," he urged. His deep, rich tone lulled her every bit as much as his strong fingers at her elbow. His touch wreaked havoc with her already-frayed nerves, and all her well-trained discipline and logic deserted her, along with her control. She could feel her control ebb and scatter into vulnerable little puddles. It frightened and excited her.

Zoe-Esther followed the compelling stranger's lead and let him guide her away from the door. A voice inside her said not to—that each step was risky—but she didn't listen. The stranger's gentle yet firm touch and gritty command invited her to a place she'd never ventured before. This unexpected assault on her senses put Zoe-Esther on the edge of a dangerous precipice. Any moment she could slip and fall into its inviting depths.

A pleasant mist wafted in the air around her. Zoe-Esther thought of fresh-made musk soap just as it lathers. Instinctively, she chased after the alluring fragrance and breathed in deeply. Accustomed to men that smelled of formaldehyde, antiseptic, or lye, she wasn't used to men who smelled so good. The heady effect aroused her womanhood from its lifelong slumber.

"Wait here," the stranger said before he disappeared through a doorway behind the bar.

Zoe-Esther stood still, amazed at her very much out of

character, mute obedience to the tall, muscled stranger. She had the oddest sensation. As if her will, her thoughts, and her entire body had suddenly come under a magical spell. *Is it this place? This man?* Shaken, yet rooted to the spot, Zoe-Esther waited for him to return. She pulled his jacket close around her and welcomed the warmth the black broadcloth offered. Bathed now in the scent of aromatic musk from his jacket, her nostrils flared slightly at the trace of something else, something new. She breathed deeper.

Him.

It was the stranger's male scent that was new to her. It enveloped her. It seduced her. Instead of being repelled by such an intimate realization, she reveled in his seductive, clean smell—like nature itself, yet laced with a hint of leather and new tobacco.

"Here, let's get you dry."

The stranger's sudden reappearance startled her. Zoe-Esther's arms flew out and his jacket dropped to the floor.

Oy gavalt!

"I'm sorry, forgive me, I'll—" Flustered, she bent down and scooped up the fallen broadcloth. "I'll wash this and get it back to you right away," she gushed, wishing she were outside in the safety of the Pollards' prairie schooner. She wished she had never entered this lion's den. The stranger said he wouldn't bite. Then why did she feel he could, at any moment, if he wanted?

"Hold on there," Jake said, taking his coat from the shuddering female. He put it back around her shoulders. But when he tried to wipe away the wet and grit from her face with the towel he'd fetched, she stepped out of his reach.

"Look lady, I'm just trying to help. I won't bite. I already promised. Remember?" He couldn't help teasing the skittish female. He wasn't used to a woman being so squea-mish around him. In fact, he was used to exactly the oppo-site.

When he first set eyes on the rain-drenched female, she reminded him of a little girl lost in a storm. Now that he had a closer look, he could see she definitely wasn't a child. Those trim curves could only belong on a woman. Her wet clothes gave her away, clinging to her body in a manner that revealed far more than they covered up. Pulling his gaze up over well-proportioned hips and small, but ever-so-shapely breasts, he looked into a pair of the most intriguing, sloe-brown eyes he had ever seen.

Mesmerized by the tiny flecks of copper and gold spar-kling in their depths, Jake thought of precious metals, yet to be mined. He thought of the one thing that he valued most in the world. Money. Despite her drenched appearance, this peculiar creature was the color of money. He couldn't tell now, but when dry, her hair must shine just like her eyes. Her skin, too, must be dusted with the shimmer of rich minerals. She looked like an undiscovered gold strike, all full of virginal passages and priceless secrets.

Damn.

Jake put his hand to the back of his neck. There it was again. The same uneasiness hit him, just like earlier when he was riding out of town. He felt off his game. Out of the blue, an image of wagon flaps pulling shut in the downpour hit him.

Damn.

Always on the lookout for trouble, he remembered that at the time he didn't think he'd seen anything unusual. Nothing but a few riders and a covered wagon.

"Lady, where did you just come from?" Jake didn't ask. He demanded. He didn't feel like being so polite anymore.

"Where did I just come from?" Zoe-Esther parroted, uncomfortable with his question. She wanted to protect her privacy. She slipped his coat off her shoulders and held it out to him.

He didn't take it.

"Listen, lady, will you keep the damned coat around you? Hell, I don't want you freezing to death in my place."

"Your place?"

"Will you stop repeating everything I say and just answer me?" he bellowed, not bothering to hide his growing irritation and frustration with the situation.

Reflexively, Zoe-Esther took a step back. It wasn't like her to be timid, but something about the stranger tied her tongue and knotted her insides.

"Look lady, I'm not trying to scare you." Jake didn't want any woman, even this one, feeling like she had to run from him. He softened his tone. "I'm just curious, that's all. Where did you come from?"

His change in manner untied her tongue. Her heart skipped faster.

"I'm from the East," she told him.

"No," Jake said. "I mean just now, right before you came into my place."

"I came from the prairie schooner across the street. I arrived here this morning."

Now Jake knew what bothered him about the woman, and he didn't like it one bit. He gave her the once-over again—this time through a suspicious gambler's eyes—and found her wanting. Maybe her rosebud, sensual mouth and the tiny cleft in her comely chin didn't attract him. Maybe her eyes didn't shine so, and her figure wasn't to his liking. She talked funny, too. Had some kind of accent, like a foreigner.

The Queen of Hearts flashed across his thoughts, plain as day. It was Jake's turn to step back. Edgy, he wanted the intrusive female out—out of his place, and out of his life. It's in the cards, always in the cards. No gambler could afford to press Lady Luck, and Jake didn't want to start now. It was asking for trouble to play with the Queen of Hearts. He couldn't win. No one ever did.

"Lady, if you don't mind, I've got work to do. You can keep the coat. There's the door," he finished.

The stranger's curt statement broke whatever unexplained hold he had on her. Zoe-Esther was confused by his words and distressed over her unusual behavior. She took a step toward him.

"I'll go, but here," she removed his coat from her shoulders, again, and held it out for him to take.

This time he accepted the garment without a word.

"If you don't mind, Mr.—" She waited to hear his name.

"It's Whiskey."

"Mr. . . . Whiskey," she repeated, taken aback by such an unusual name. "Mr. Whiskey, would you be kind enough to direct me to a rooming house?" No matter how much this man upset her, she was determined to get the information she'd come for in the first place. At least her teeth no longer chattered, and her shudders were almost gone.

"Lady," Jake said, not a bit interested in learning her name, "there's a rooming house a few streets over. Mrs. Bartlett's."

"A few streets over," Zoe-Esther repeated. "Which way?"

Damn, Jake wanted this hand done.

"South."

"South. A few streets south," Zoe-Esther said again.

"Well then, thank you, Mr. Whiskey." She looked down at his white shirtfront, avoiding his eyes. Unless she was very careful, she could get lost again in his slate gaze: an inviting, dreamy maze, all silver and shadow. She must not lose her focus. She must concentrate on her purpose. She must not pay any more attention to Mr. Whiskey's rough-hewn good looks or breathe too deeply of his unbridled, masculine scent.

"Thank you. Good day, Mr. Whiskey." Zoe-Esther tried to sound nonchalant as she turned to leave the Golden Gates. She was afraid now. Not of Mr. Whiskey, but of her own feelings. She hated what just happened. She had no explanation for her behavior. Never, ever had she behaved so oddly. In all of the textbooks she had studied, she had not come across this phenomenon. In fact, in the whole of her life she had never felt so exposed, invaded, and overpowered. Unexpectedly, she thought of George Collins. This meeting unsettled her more. What possible connection could there be between the deceased George Collins and this very much alive, primitive beast of a man? For the life of her, Zoe-Esther couldn't imagine.

By the time Zoe-Esther secured rooms for herself and her papa at the Bartlett Rooming House, the rain had ended. They said their goodbyes to the Pollards, appreciative beyond words for all their kindness, and wished them well. Anxious for Yitzhak to get warm and dry, Zoe-Esther guided him up the rooming house stairs, noting how tightly he grabbed the wooden rail with each step taken. There was a third floor but, blessedly, their rooms were on the second. This would be better for Yitzhak, especially since his room had a little porch balcony off of it. The room was expensive at six dollars a week. Hers would be a dollar less. Before they reached their respective rooms, she calculated exactly how far their money would take them.

Three and a half weeks! That's how far!

At least the room rate included food, though she knew they probably couldn't eat most of the fare provided. No pork. Never pork. Nothing of the cloven hoof. No scavenger foods. No shellfish. Zoe-Esther and Yitzhak no longer ate strictly kosher—meats symbolically drained of blood and slaughtered by proper ritual by a *sh'hitah*—since they'd arrived in America, but they still observed many Jewish dietary laws and ate only those foods permitted. Nothing *t'refah*. Nothing prohibited must be eaten. And no serving dairy and meat dishes at the same meal. According to the traditions of Judaism as specified in Talmud Torah, the study of Jewish Law, "Thou shalt not mix the meat of the kid with the milk of the mother." Though more Orthodox Jews followed every daily ritual, Yitzhak and Zoe-Esther upheld their devout belief in the Ten Commandments, upon which their religion is based and upon which Jews believe that all life is subject to Moral Law.

Maintaining their Judaism had been a challenge since leaving their village in Russia. Religious observance remained a challenge in Philadelphia, and would be an even greater challenge on the frontier. What choice did Zoe-Esther have? None, she decided. If she hadn't uprooted her papa and brought him west, his death from tuberculosis would have been a certainty. She could not let that happen.

"Number four, Papa. Here's your room," Zoe-Esther unlocked the simple, paneled door and opened it.

Yitzhak, moving heavily, went inside. He looked, to Zoe-Esther, every bit of his sixty-five years. Her heart broke yet again for him.

Do not worry, Papa. You will get well. You will have your

life back, she vowed in silence.

"A nice room, Star. And dry. Thanks to God we found such a place in time. I thought we might have to build an Ark in this Golden of yours," Yitzhak said and grinned.

Her heart mended a little at his wit, at his good humor.

"Come, Papa, you need your rest," she said and took hold of his elbow to guide him to the oak, high-backed bed. It was a feather bed. A thick, multicolored quilt rested at its foot. Though simple, Zoe-Esther thought the room was quite elegant. A white chamber set rested atop an oak washstand in one corner, while a comfortable looking, slatted rocker had been placed in the opposite corner. The small bedstead had a kerosene lamp on it, and a box of matches. The walls were papered in a light, floral print, adding to the room's cheery appearance. The best feature, to Zoe-Esther, had to be the little porch balcony just outside, to the back of the rooming house. The door to the balcony opened by the room's only window. As soon as Zoe-Esther got her papa settled, she'd go out on the balcony and check the view for him.

She took a quick look at her watch-pin, which by some miracle, still worked. Four o'clock. "Supper is at six," Mrs. Bartlett had informed them. Yitzhak could rest for two hours.

"Star. Star, do not be in such a rush." Yitzhak reached inside his coat pocket. "I must put our *mezuzah* on the doorpost to mark our new Jewish home. He pulled out the tiny, rolled parchment encased in metal, inscribed with the *Sh'ma* proclaiming the love of One God, and the blessings of obeying the Commandments, and walked over to the main door to his room and opened it.

"Papa, can't this wait until tomorrow? Until we find a hammer and nails?" Zoe-Esther wanted him to rest.

"Wait, why should we wait?" Yitzhak said, grinning, and took two small nails out of the same pocket he'd gotten the mezuzah. "Hold these," he told Zoe-Esther, handing her the *mezuzah* and the nails. He reached inside his carpetbag for his tools. Although he no longer worked as a silversmith, he always kept the implements of his trade with him. "*Danken,* Star," he said, retrieving the needed items from her outstretched hand. In no time he hammered the *mezuzah* to the outside portion of the doorpost. "We must never forget our symbols, child. Remember what the Commandments tell us: 'You shall write them on the doorposts of your house and on your gates.' "

"Yes, Papa," she said then stepped into the comfort of his frail arms. "I love you so, Papa. You are so good, and in all things I will obey you."

"Little Star, as your papa all I can do is teach. The rest is up to you and to God," he said, and gave her a quick kiss on her forehead. "Now I can rest," he announced and slowly sat down on the edge of his bed.

Zoe-Esther helped him remove his ankle-high work shoes, glad they had purchased the ready-made brogans before coming west. She was not, however, glad for all the caked mud on her papa's shoes. Her serviceable, worn boots were equally damp and muddied. They both must have tracked a lot of dirt up the stairs and onto the floor outside their rooms. She quickly slipped off her boots. If she hurried she could clean up any muddy trails before Mrs. Bartlett discovered them.

Yitzhak's eyes closed. By the time Zoe-Esther reached the door to the balcony, he'd fallen asleep. She opened the first door, and then the hinged, screen door. *Perfect,* she thought the moment she went outside. *Just right.* She'd pull the rocker from Yitzhak's room onto the balcony and he could sit, take in the fresh air and sunshine, and enjoy the view of the foothills and distant peaks. Even better for her beloved papa, the balcony overlooked what appeared to be a busy street. There would be plenty for him to see and kvetch about. She had something to kvetch about herself at the moment: cold and wet stocking feet. Hurrying back inside, she gently closed the balcony doors, scooped up her dirty boots, and then pulled the door to Yitzhak's room shut behind her.

"*Oy vey!*" Zoe-Esther exclaimed, nearly tripping over her trunk and the rest of their possessions piled in the hallway. It wasn't much, really. Another old carpetbag, a basket of linens she'd embroidered since childhood, a wooden crate filled with personal items of value, including their treasured silver candlesticks, their copper tea kettle, her medical bag, and, of course, as many books as they could bring. Zoe-Esther wasn't about to go anywhere without her medical texts and Yitzhak would never part with his volumes devoted to religious study.

"*Bentshn,* Mrs. Bartlett," Zoe-Esther spoke quietly to herself. "Bless her for fetching our things. Such a *mitzvot.* Such a good deed." She looked for her room. Number three was located at the end of the hallway. Good. Right next to the water closet.

"How convenient," she quipped. "To be so close to the convenience."

Fumbling inside her wet skirt pocket, she retrieved the skeleton key to her room. Then she checked her other pocket for her spectacles. Thank heaven they hadn't broken on the journey west. She ran her fingers over the expensive case she'd bought before leaving Philadelphia. Five dollars. She still winced when she thought of the price. But, if her wire rims broke because she didn't have them safely encased, she wouldn't be able to see things clearly or work with any ease. Her wire rims had been special-ordered, and she wasn't about to risk anything happening to them. Besides, she couldn't afford to order another pair.

Voices downstairs spurred Zoe-Esther into quick action. She darted for her door, unlocked it, and deposited her boots, cradled precariously under one armpit, on the plank floor in her room. Without so much as a look at the rest of her room, she rushed back into the hallway and dragged her heavy trunk along the carpeted runner, and inside her room. She did the same with her basket and crate.

Glad to have her things inside before anyone saw her clutter in the hallway, Zoe-Esther closed her door and leaned against it. She glanced around her room, her home, for the present. Tears welled in her tired eyes. Home. Not since her childhood village, not since she lived with her papa in the secure embrace and comfort of their simple little cottage, had she been in such a place as this. The room made her feel at home. Before she collapsed where she stood, she made a beeline for the bay window seat, the room's only window, and eased down onto its soft, needle-point cushion. She ran shaky hands over the floral design of the cushion, admiring such handiwork, then swiveled enough in her seat to look outside.

The sway of the evergreen trees in the late afternoon breeze made her smile. *I could sit here forever.* Since she didn't have forever, Zoe-Esther pulled her gaze back to her room. Along the wall opposite her stood a maple, floor-to-ceiling wardrobe with a washstand fashioned out of the same wood, next to it. A small, square, beveled mirror hung above the washstand and a basin and pitcher, painted in colorful wildflowers, rested on its gleaming wood surface. A matching chamber pot had been set on the floor beneath.

The room had a full-size bed! In the whole of her life Zoe-Esther had never slept on such an extravagance. She quickly hopped off the window seat and onto the bed.

Even with her arms stretched out full atop the crocheted coverlet, she still couldn't reach the edges of the bed. She closed her eyes and reveled in the feeling, in the pure luxury of it. Giggling, she rolled from one side of the bed to the other. She felt like a girl again, living in the *shtetl*. Why, she could be tumbling in the first spring grasses or frolicking in the early snows of winter. She lay still now, and stared at the ceiling. There were no cracks. No irregular shapes to keep her awake like the ones on her ceiling back in Philadelphia. Instead, narrow strips of natural wood fit together, each one tongue in groove, each one smooth, each one perfect. She closed her eyes again.

"Yes, perfect," she whispered into the quiet of the fading afternoon. "And so much room, enough for two."

All of a sudden the unexpected image of him—Mr. Whiskey—took shape in her mind's eye. She bolted upright. Disturbed by the unwelcome appearance of the handsome stranger, she had no idea why he entered her thoughts now. Why did his intruding image come to mind when everything was perfect? She lay back down and shut her eyes. She stretched her arms out and tried to think of any reason she'd be thinking about Mr. Whiskey. When the answer hit her, she scrambled off the bed as fast as she could.

Room enough for two. For two!

"Oy vey! Oy gavalt!"

Zoe-Esther had never, ever had such thoughts before.

To think . . . to imagine him next to me . . . in my bed—

Flabbergasted and frightened, she had to think of something. She had to find a remedy for such unexplained thoughts.

Think of medicine, Zoe-Esther. Think of logic.

Yes. If she could put her scattered thoughts into some kind of scientific perspective, she could identify the problem and fix it. But the longer Zoe-Esther paced back and forth in her cozy room looking for answers, she realized that she couldn't fix anything at all. Needing to make some sense of her thoughts, she settled on the probability that Mr. Whiskey's sudden apparition had to be an idiosyncratic phenomenon: an unusual, unexplained occurrence, wholly unlikely to happen a second time.

There. Now she felt better. She tossed the unwanted image of Mr. Whiskey right out her second-story bay window.

Chapter Six

"Baruch ataw Adonoi, elo hay nu melech ha olam, ha motzie le hem men ha'aretz. Amen." Yitzhak said the blessing over the bread, as he always did before beginning each meal. Unmindful of the stares around Mrs. Bartlett's crowded supper table, he reached for the basket of bread in front of him.

Zoe-Esther noticed all the eyes now fixed on her papa—all ten pair of them. *No doubt,* she thought, *they've never heard a Hebrew blessing before, much less seen a yarmulke on a man's head instead of a cowboy hat, especially at the supper table.* Among all the men seated, Yitzhak wore the only head covering. Zoe-Esther wanted to explain and tell everyone that observant Jewish men always wore yarmulkes. That they were not considered hats, but a symbol of being under God. Except for one woman, who wore a solemn expression, all the other residents of Mrs. Bartlett's rooming house were men. Locals, Zoe-Esther guessed, judging from their western clothes. And, judging from their collective, pointed stares, most of them were none too pleased that she and Yitzhak sat at their table.

On the wagon train west it had been different. Everyone worried over surviving the exhaustive trip; not over who sat next to whom around the cook fires. Funny, Zoe-Esther hadn't given much thought to their being Jews since she and Yitzhak left Philadelphia. Religious differences between herself and her papa and the rest of the folks traveling in their wagon train, had not come up as an issue before. Now, all the other differences between herself and the rest of the world—not just that she was a Jew and a foreigner, but twenty-two, unmarried, and a physician—a female physician—stared her in the face.

She stiffened in her chair, refusing to give in to worry or self-pity.

Daniel's warning came to mind, and she didn't like it. She didn't agree with Daniel's assumption that she couldn't make a good life for herself and her papa in the West. She didn't agree that she couldn't find work as a physician in the West. One thing she and Daniel hadn't talked about tugged at her. They had not discussed the possibility of religious prejudice. Zoe-Esther immediately put this from her mind, certain that she could prevail in this wild territory. She turned toward Mrs. Bartlett, the only one who seemed to favor their company.

"Mrs. Bartlett," Zoe-Esther directed, determined to pull attention from her papa any way she could. "Mrs. Bartlett, this all looks delicious. And . . . and our rooms . . . why, they're very nice indeed. Very comfortable, too." She felt like a babbling idiot and hoped that Mrs. Bartlett would say something and save her.

"Why, thank you, dear. I'm that glad," Mrs. Bartlett rejoined.

Zoe-Esther liked Mrs. Bartlett from the start. She seemed a little eccentric, which, of course, made her all the more interesting.

Like the schadchen, *the matchmaker in our village.*

Zoe-Esther put down her forkful of mutton and took a

sip of water. Right now wasn't the time or the place to think of the matchmaker.

"Mrs. Bartlett," she started over, anxious for distracting conversation. "Does it rain here often? It certainly was quite stormy this morning."

"You'll get used to it, dear," Mrs. Bartlett replied with a smile, then got up and fetched the platters of vegetables and meat from the nearby buffet.

Zoe-Esther's spirits plummeted at such news. The climate in Golden needed to improve, so her papa could.

"Here now," Mrs. Bartlett said to everyone. "Who would like more?"

The others at the table, engaged in animated chatter between one another, stopped talking long enough to heap seconds onto their plates.

Yitzhak declined more food. He had not touched any of his; not even the bread he blessed at the beginning of the meal.

If Mrs. Bartlett took note, she said nothing and returned the serving platters to the buffet. Grateful for her silence, Zoe-Esther worried over Yitzhak. His poor appetite alarmed her. He needed good nutrition, rest, and dry, clean air. She thought of the rain again, evidently a common occurrence, and felt low-spirited herself.

"Now, as I was saying—" Mrs. Bartlett stopped mid-sentence and looked at Zoe-Esther. She tilted her head toward Zoe-Esther, as if she were waiting for something.

The pause in conversation made Zoe-Esther uncomfortable.

"Oh." She suddenly realized what Mrs. Bartlett wanted to know. "It's Zoe-Esther."

"Yes, well, as I was saying, Zoe-Esther. You have a lovely name, dear. Most unusual," she said, her curious brow less furrowed now.

When Mrs. Bartlett said nothing else, Zoe-Esther took the opportunity to study her new landlady more closely. A whole litany of description came to mind: round, jolly, pleasant looking, expressive, watchful, and, a little nosy. In her mid-fifties, Zoe-Esther guessed, Mrs. Bartlett's once-brown hair was pulled into a floppy graying bun at her crown. Her brown eyes still retained their rich color and youthful gleam. Wearing what Zoe-Esther felt must be a ready-made, Mrs. Bartlett's green and white, striped cotton reminded her of dresses back East—the ones without crinolines, of course. For the life of her, Zoe-Esther couldn't imagine why anyone would ever want to wear the cumbersome, bothersome, accidents-waiting-to-happen hoops in the first place. She decided that Mrs. Bartlett had to be quite sensible not to wear such a nuisance.

"You happened to arrive on an exceptional day, you and your papa." Mrs. Bartlett smiled at Zoe-Esther, then at Yitzhak.

Snapped back to the moment, Zoe-Esther hoped Mrs. Bartlett had something good to say this time about Golden City.

"Of course the first exception is that I had any rooms at all," Mrs. Bartlett smiled again. "The second is, of course, the weather. Ordinarily we have sunshine here, nearly every day. At least three hundred a year I'd say. You've arrived on a most exceptional day. Mind you, we have our rain in the warmer months, like today, and we have our share of snow in winter. But more often than not, we're fighting sunburn and dry, chapped skin."

Zoe-Esther's spirits lifted. Dry and sunny three hundred days a year! She'd take dry and sunny over damp and cloudy Philadelphia, anytime. Encouraged by Mrs. Bartlett's words, Zoe-Esther thought that now she might just have her golden miracle in Golden City after all; and her papa would get well.

A quick glance at Yitzhak and she could see he needed to get upstairs and in bed. Any minute he could seize with coughing, and she didn't want anyone to know how ill he truly was—and give everyone a chance to dislike her and Papa any more than they did already.

Zoe-Esther rose from her chair.

"Thank you for the meal, Mrs. Bartlett. It was the best I've had in months," she said before realizing everyone else could hear her. She wanted to kick herself for saying too much. None of these unfriendly faces needed to know her business. So why didn't she hold her tongue? Miffed at herself, Zoe-Esther went around behind Yitzhak's chair, and whispered to him that it was time to leave.

"We'll say goodnight," she said under her breath to Mrs. Bartlett, then hooked her arm in Yitzhak's to slowly guide him upstairs.

"What's wrong, honey?" Belle whined softly; then trailed light kisses down Jake's chest and over his belly.

"Nothing's wrong," he answered half asleep, slipping a hand under her chin. He gently pulled her back up, and on top of him. To convince her nothing was wrong, he drove his tongue deep into her mouth while he splayed his fingers over her bare backside. He pressed her against him in an erotic, rhythmic motion. His loins grew hard, but the rest of him felt lifeless and strangely disconnected from the moment. When Belle broke their kiss, then sat up and straddled him, he felt numb as she eased over his erect manhood. For the first time in his life he lay passive while a woman rode him. His body went through all the right motions but any desire he felt drained away and left him empty inside.

Damn.

He couldn't afford to be sick. Never missed a day at the faro tables. Must be he was just dog-tired.

No other reason for it. Couldn't be.

He always lusted after Belle the way a starving man reaches for that first bite. Hell, having a sensual, pleasurable woman in his bed meant more to him than most things in this life. It was high on his list, just behind money and Jack Daniels. The truth was he didn't think he would ever have enough of either of them: money or Jack Daniels. In the mood for a stiff drink and a quick game of faro, oddly, he wasn't in the mood for Belle.

Jake hadn't been with another woman since he took up with the "Golden Girl of Golden City" over a year ago. Why should he want another woman? Belle was beautiful, passionate, skilled in bed, and only wanted to please him. A man would be an idiot not to want her. Besides, she was from his world. She was like most of the women he knew growing up: women from saloons and dancehalls. The fact was he never even noticed anybody outside the business. He had never been with a woman who wasn't from his same world. Never had. Never wanted to. The thought of being with somebody from a different world made him uncomfortable. He didn't have to think about the reason. He already knew it.

Sam Hill. Here he was in the middle of it with the most desirable damned woman this side of the Rockies, and he wasn't even enjoying their lovemaking. Bad hand. Bad luck for sure. The instant he thought about the poor cards dealt him now, the image of the slender, rain-drenched, coppery female appeared before him. The Queen of Hearts. He didn't need any reminders to stay away from her. Not only was she bad luck, she wasn't from his world. Golden City was a big enough place that their paths shouldn't cross again. He didn't know much about the strange female, but of one thing he was certain—she wasn't his type. She wasn't any saloon or dancehall girl. He didn't take to her anyway. *No sir. Little Queenie doesn't have a thing I want.*

When she was finished and spent, Belle rolled off Jake. She asked the same question she had before.

"Jake, tell me what's wrong," she cooed rather than demanded. Not a stupid woman, she had to take care with Jake. She wasn't married to him—yet.

"I told you. Nothing," Jake answered, his voice low and even. "Get some sleep," he said, then drew her naked shape against his and shut his eyes.

Belle knew better than to press her question. She would wait for the right time, the right opportunity to find out who was on Jake's mind. It had to be another woman.

She could sense it. Smell it. Taste it.

After all, hadn't it been her business for the past five years to know men inside and out? She relied on this natural-born skill; it kept her at the very top of her game. No, Jake didn't have to tell her a thing.

For the first time since she'd been with Jake, Belle believed she had a rival for his attention. And for the first time in her life, she was jealous. Rage crept up and over her like a blanket of stinging ants. The pain of her jealousy fueled her anger. Until this moment it had never occurred to her that anybody else could interest Jake. *I swear,* she promised herself silently. *No other woman will ever get him.* He was hers. He was her ticket to respectability and out of the saloon and dancehall life.

Belle settled even closer against Jake and pressed her lips

to his chest, sealing another self-made promise. No matter what it took, she would find out who the bitch was who dared interfere with her plans to become Jake's wife. Nuzzling his warm skin, calmer and more confident now, her lips curved into a vengeful, determined smile. She'd watch and wait, and when she discovered the identity of her competition, she would make her move.

Upset when Yitzhak didn't feel like going to breakfast in the dining room, Zoe-Esther hurried downstairs to fetch him some tea and toast. Her thoughts raced ahead of her. Yitzhak's last coughing fit had been the worst. *Thanks to God, no blood yet,* Zoe-Esther told herself prayerfully. But his condition was deteriorating fast. Fearful, despite the bright, morning sunshine, Zoe-Esther hoped beyond hope that her beloved papa would survive the winter. If he could make it through the next months, then he might make it through the precious years ahead. Another thought plagued her as she passed inside the empty dining room to the kitchen. If tuberculosis were contagious, by staying at the rooming house, all of its occupants would be exposed. Despite their unfriendly reception last evening, she knew she shouldn't place the other boarders at risk. For now it was best that Yitzhak remain isolated in his room. But only temporarily. Zoe-Esther needed to find a place for them to live—a place far enough from town to prevent the spread of the morbid lung disease. The question was how? How was she to afford such a move? Just as in Philadelphia, time and money ran short. The hourglass had already overturned.

Tray in hand, Zoe-Esther climbed the stairs, stopping just outside Yitzhak's room. It broke her heart to see her strong papa so weak. She fought off tears. Instead of crying, she resolved to find work. Today she would, she must, secure work in one of the physicians' offices in Golden City. There had to be several doctors, and surely one of them would need her help. She steadied her hands and gently opened Yitzhak's door and went inside.

Two doctors hung out their shingles in Golden City and neither one of them wanted to hire Zoe-Esther. Feh! Neither of them, she decided, could have possibly attended medical school. No doubt they were both frontier-trained instead. Disappointed and frustrated by their disapproval of a female doctor with "citified notions," Zoe-Esther tried to remain cool and collected while she made her appeal for work. She told them both that she received her Doctor of Medicine in Pennsylvania. The moment she said it, she realized it was a mistake to mention her medical degree, judging from the resentful looks that both doctors had given her. Almost to the letter, both doctors said the same thing: "If a woman were to work with me, I'd lose all my patients."

"Why, not a one would come," one said while the other only laughed in her face. If she didn't know before, Zoe-Esther certainly knew now, how frontier doctors felt about an educated woman. Whatever would they say if they discovered she was also a Jew!

Unable to convince either Dr. Pritchard or Dr. James, either "Doc," that a third pair of hands would be "a help and not a hindrance" in Golden City, especially with the growing number of miners, ranchers, and settlers coming into town, Zoe-Esther turned a deaf ear to their warnings:

"Best not to try anything on your own."

"If you do, you'll be crazy."

"No one will come to you for help."

"If you know what's good for you, you'll git back East."

"Feh!" Zoe-Esther mumbled the Yiddish exclamation of disgust under her breath and stomped down the planked walkway towards the rooming house. She was furious with herself and with the so-called "docs" in town. *Me crazy? They're the ones full of mishegaz!* If they were serious about providing good health care to the townspeople, they could have fooled her. She refused to think about Daniel's warnings. Now wasn't the time for it. She couldn't afford to wallow in self-pity or over-worry, not with Papa so ill.

Solutions. She needed to find solutions. Ideas tumbled over in her mind but, like loose rocks, they rolled downhill and not up. She and Yitzhak could move to Denver City, but she would run into the same set of problems. There was no reason to think Denver City, some ten miles away, would provide any opportunity for work either. If she took the few dollars hidden in her room and tried to open her own office, not only did she not have enough money, but she now knew it would take time for the townspeople to trust a woman doctor. It would probably take months for her to see any decent earnings. She thought of being back in Philadelphia, back in the corridors of the hospital where she was accepted and could practice medicine. But then she thought of her papa, dying in that very same cold, damp city. No, the best choice for Yitzhak had been to leave the East. When he was well, then they might consider returning to Philadelphia. But not yet.

Zoe-Esther stopped to collect her thoughts. The moment she did, she realized that she wasn't on her way back to the rooming house. Instead, she had managed to wander into a part of town set up as a tent city, bustling with people, horses, wagons, and makeshift shops and eateries. It must be where a lot of the miners and their families lived.

She thought of the teeming section of Philadelphia she'd left behind. The differences between the two cities outweighed any similarities. Here in Golden City, the air was dry and clean, the creeks were filled with mountain spring water, and the pioneers struggled to carve out a new life for themselves.

Back East, she heard about the California Gold Rush of '49 and the Colorado Gold Rush of '59, but never imagined such a sight like the one before her. Obviously many, many Americans had come west to seek their fortunes. Though she'd come to the Colorado Territory for quite another reason, Zoe-Esther felt strangely akin to these people. From the looks of most folks, they had about as much money as she had: near to none. Dressed mainly in *shmata*, Zoe-Esther thought of the old clothes worn by the villagers in the *shtetl* in Russia. A whole ocean away and still the world is much the same. People change very little from one continent to the next, she acceded silently.

Surrounded by so much activity amid so much need, her spirits picked up a little. These hearty souls didn't appear too deterred by the fact that they hadn't struck it rich just yet. Of course she had no way of really knowing this for certain, but judging from the smiles most folks wore, and the liveliness in their step, Zoe-Esther made the assumption. The tented encampment went on for a half dozen blocks. Zoe-Esther threaded her way through all of them, eager to absorb some of the energy and tenacity she sensed from its inhabitants.

Urchins played, running this way and that, while dogs chased after them. Some of the children didn't have shoes on. Zoe-Esther hoped that they would get some before winter. Dirty-faced boys in patched britches shot past her, while giggling girls in worn prairie skirts tried to catch up.

She wondered why the children were not in school. Many looked to be of school age. As in her village, perhaps work came before study. In her village only boys studied and read books. Girls learned how to become good homemakers. Zoe-Esther's back bristled at such injustice. Boys and girls, men and women, should all have the same opportunities for a good education and to make a good wage. It wasn't fair that life wasn't fair. In some things, Zoe-Esther realized, America and Russia were not so different. But, she had to acknowledge, she would not be a doctor now if she were still in the old country.

Nu? What good is it to be a doctor with such a barrier keeping me from my patients now like the one put up between men and women in synagogue? How to overcome such a mechitzah? She had to find a way. She must.

As she wandered through one tented block after another, Zoe-Esther wondered if the people who lived here had any medical care; if they had the money, enough *gelt,* to go to Doc Pritchard or Doc James; if they were good enough to be seen by the so-called docs.

Feh! Good enough for medical care!

Quite unexpectedly she thought of George Collins—who hadn't been good enough, who had been left to die of tuberculosis, alone and forgotten as his case no longer interested the medical community! Anger over it still caught in Zoe-Esther's throat. She swallowed hard. Until this very moment, she hadn't thought about the incidence of tuberculosis out West. Looking around her, she realized there could, indeed, be cases among all the people living in the canvas shanties and mud-caked alleyways. It defied logic to think her papa was the only victim of tuberculosis in the territory. Papa. Her shoulders drooped and her feet dragged under the weight of her thoughts. She forced her attention elsewhere, reading the signs hanging on the flaps of many of the tents, signs advertising everything from a two-bit shave to a two-dollar bath to a ten-dollar miner's pickax. A good bowl of stew cost one bit while a basket of laundry was worth a dollar.

One dollar for a basket of laundry.

Zoe-Esther began computing her potential earnings. At a dollar a basket, if she washed a dozen baskets a week, she would have enough to pay for a roof over her papa's head. Not here among the needy, but elsewhere in Golden City, she could try to get enough customers to make the money she needed. Her heart sank when she realized she'd be taking the very bread out of these poor people's mouths if she took their work. *I'd rather starve.*

But Papa. I can't let Papa starve.

Didn't she have any other skills to put to good use, skills that wouldn't take anything away from these struggling families? For so long all her attention, all her effort, had gone toward becoming the best doctor she knew how to be. Without that, little seemed left. She would much rather stitch up a gaping wound than sew buttons onto clothes.

That's it.

I can embroider. I can stitch designs onto linens instead of repairing the human body. For now. Only for now.

Encouraged, Zoe-Esther picked up her step and turned in what she thought was the right direction to get to Mrs. Bartlett's Rooming House. There were hotels and saloons plenty enough in Golden City, and she would visit each one of them, inquiring about embroidering fancy, personalized stitching on their linens and wares. She computed what she needed to charge for each finished design. Piece by embroidered piece, she would keep food on her papa's table and a roof over his head.

★ ★ ★ ★ ★

Two days later Zoe-Esther approached Mrs. Bartlett, having made the decision to trust her. At this point she had little choice. Yitzhak's condition progressed instead of improving. Seized with consumptive fits, he often coughed up blood-tinged mucous. Zoe-Esther was afraid he could hemorrhage. She was also afraid of the spread of his infection to others, and needed to get her papa isolated as soon as she could. To make matters worse, so far she hadn't found any customers for her embroidery work. Not even one.

"Good morning," Zoe-Esther said in a quiet voice, pleased to find the proprietary, Mrs. Bartlett, alone in the front parlor. "I wonder if I could speak with you?"

"Come in, Zoe-Esther," Mrs. Bartlett smiled. "Sit. Sit and we'll visit. First, child, let's get you a nice biscuit or a piece of cake," she coaxed and turned towards the kitchen. "I'll be right back."

Why she sounds just like the schadchen *from my village!*

For a split second Zoe-Esther was a child of nine again in the matchmaker's cottage, with the name of her betrothed echoing in her head, as if she heard it just yesterday instead of over thirteen years ago. Then an obscure image, his image—the one she'd tried to conjure and imagine ever since the matchmaker revealed his name—began to clarify in her mind's eye. Zoe-Esther scooted closer to the edge of the settee and concentrated as hard as she could, in an attempt to get a closer look at her match.

It didn't work, and if she moved forward another half an inch, she would be on the floor.

Mrs. Bartlett returned with a tray of sweets.

"Have one, my dear. Have two," she insisted and put the inviting fare right in front of Zoe-Esther. "If you don't mind my saying it, child, you could use a little more meat on your bones. Why, you're thin as a rail," she pronounced and removed the tray only after Zoe-Esther took a slice of teacake.

Zoe-Esther took a bite. It was delicious but she wasn't a bit hungry. Anxious over her papa, over their draining finances, not finding work, and needing to search out another place to live, she forced the bite of cake down. Her stomach rebelled right away. Since she really hadn't eaten much for the past few days, nothing was about to go down easy. And the thought of her match didn't help. Frustrated with herself for thinking of her intended, unrealistic and nonsensical match in the first place, she grew even more frustrated when she tried to make out his features. For so long it didn't matter what he might look like, but for some strange reason, it did now. In fact only since—

Only since I've been in Golden City.

"Child, child," Mrs. Bartlett drew Zoe-Esther back to the moment.

"Oh yes, I'm sorry. My goodness, this is very good. Yes, very, very good." Zoe-Esther forced down another bite of cake.

"I'm that glad you wanted to chat dear, because . . . well because . . ." Mrs. Bartlett hesitated. "The truth of the matter is that I know your papa is ill. All of us here know."

Zoe-Esther didn't get mad; she was too worried to waste energy on anger.

"I've not said a word to the others mind you, but I know he's most probably a lunger."

Nor did Zoe-Esther get angry at Mrs. Bartlett's nonmedical description of her papa as a lunger. She was right.

"Mind you, I don't care about the coughing, but my customers, well . . . they've been complaining. I've a business to run here, dear. I hope you understand."

If she hadn't already made up her mind to leave the

rooming house, Zoe-Esther wondered just how understanding she would really be about Mrs. Bartlett discussing her papa's condition. Mrs. Bartlett's anguished brown eyes stared at her, eyes filled with sincerity and regret. It was impossible for Zoe-Esther to summon any ill will towards the plump, kindly woman. Besides, Mrs. Bartlett reminded Zoe-Esther of the *schadchen*. How could she be angry with the matchmaker?

All pretense of sociability was gone now. The facts about her papa's illness were out in the open. Zoe-Esther held her back erect and spoke frankly.

"You are right. Papa has tuberculosis." She read the question on Mrs. Bartlett's face and corrected herself. "Consumption. Papa has consumption."

Mrs. Bartlett nodded in apparent understanding.

Zoe-Esther continued. "I've brought Papa west to try and cure him." Tears welled up from her gut. If she didn't keep talking, she might not be able to finish what she had to say. "We'll leave this very day, but I need to . . . to . . ." She had to swallow any pride she had left. "I need to ask you, Mrs. Bartlett, if you could suggest a place for Papa and me to live. I'll pay, of course. I'll pay the same as we're paying here: eleven dollars a week. If there is anything cheaper, it would be better."

Zoe-Esther waited to see the expected pity and disapproval on Mrs. Bartlett's face, but none came.

"Go on. I'm listening, dear," Mrs. Bartlett encouraged.

"If you could think of a place away from town that we could rent, I'd be most appreciative. It doesn't have to be anything special. Papa and I aren't accustomed to fancy things. In fact, quite the contrary."

This disclosure didn't seem to faze Mrs. Bartlett in the least. Heartened, Zoe-Esther kept on.

"I'm still looking to find work and until I do, money is tight, very tight. Is there anything at all, any place at all, you can think of?"

"Dear, if things were different, I'd let you stay—"

"Please don't worry yourself. It's all right. I understand. I truly do," Zoe-Esther reassured.

Mrs. Bartlett wrinkled her brow. She appeared to be concentrating hard.

"There might be something. Yes, the Claims Office might have a place for you. I've heard about unoccupied miners' cabins scattered here and there in the foothills, standing empty because of dried up claims. You should check with the Claims Office, child. I wish I could offer more."

"I'll go straight away, Mrs. Bartlett." Zoe-Esther got up immediately. "Thank you," she said and smiled. "Where is the Claims Office?"

The moment she got the directions Zoe-Esther was out the front door and hurrying down the street.

Chapter Seven

Jake was in a bad mood. He'd been up half the night trying to convince Belle to go to sleep. She wouldn't say what it was that troubled her, but he knew something had to be wrong the way she was behaving. It wasn't just when they were in bed. She acted strangely when they were up and about, too. She hadn't let him out of her sight for five minutes in the past five days. Belle said she didn't want to be alone. She wouldn't say why. He would tolerate her strange behavior until he found out the problem. Hell, maybe she was acting funny because of him. After all, he hadn't wanted to exactly linger in bed with her lately. He ignored the obvious reason for it: that he might be losing interest in her.

At Jake's signal, Missouri picked up his step. The only peace Jake could get, what with Belle constantly underfoot, was on these morning rides when he could be alone. Once he cleared the town, nothing but solitude lay ahead in the foothills, solitude and winding trails up mountain slopes. A little farther, up Clear Creek Canyon, the terrain got steeper and rockier. But here, two miles outside of Golden City, the trail was still easy. Jake wasn't going as far as the canyon. He didn't have any desire to head up to the high mining camps of Blackhawk, Central City, or Breckenridge.

Hell, he got gold nuggets aplenty at his own faro tables. His daily take at the Golden Gates was pretty damn good.

Missouri pricked his ears and snorted. Jake pulled Missouri to a stop and looked all around to see what spooked his horse. Something was up ahead. Damn if it wasn't a woman coming down the trail, right at him. Relieved it wasn't Belle, and unless his eyes played tricks on him, it was—little Queenie—on foot! What in Blue Blazes was she doing here? He pulled out his tobacco makings to roll a smoke. He'd wait and find out.

The draw on his cheroot tasted good. It took away some of his uneasiness over this unwelcome run-in with Lady Bad Luck. He figured her to be clear of the Colorado Territory by now, her being a greenhorn from the East and all. Pretty obvious to him now: he'd figured wrong.

Up most of the night embroidering linen towels for the Gilpin Hotel, the only hotel that had said "yes" to her so far, Zoe-Esther was dead-tired but she didn't care. The important thing was that she had found a customer, and that meant money. At a dollar a napkin, she already had twelve dollars in her basket. Half of the order was done. Tonight she would start on the second dozen. Twenty-four dollars would pay a month's rent, with enough left over to buy the embroidery threads she needed to finish her order.

The agent at the Claims Office would charge her five dollars a week to live in the cabin on the vacated property. Zoe-Esther didn't care how run-down the agent said the deserted cabin was, or how far from town; she took him up on his offer right away. He wanted to show her the log-hewn cabin first, but she declined. She didn't want to reveal her reason: that she was desperate for a place to shelter her papa; that she would take just about anything at this point.

What she needed instead, she told the claims agent, was a ride for both her and her papa to the cabin, and help in moving their belongings. Thanks to God, the agent complied. By nightfall she and Yitzhak, too ill to protest, were out of Mrs. Bartlett's Rooming House and in their new home.

To Zoe-Esther's pleasant surprise, the cabin sat at the top of a rise, against a cropping of evergreen trees and right next to a swift, mountain stream. Fresh, dry air, and pure, clean water. *Just what Papa needs!* It would definitely take some work before Zoe-Esther could call the tar-pitch-roofed cabin home.

The claims agent hadn't lied when he said the cabin was run-down, but it looked sturdy enough to Zoe-Esther. Thick log walls enclosed two puncheon-floored rooms, one larger than the other. An old, rusty, iron bed frame had been left in the smaller room. Zoe-Esther would clean this up for Yitzhak. It would do as a nice little bedroom for him. Happy for the stone hearth in the main room, she examined the scratched, well-worn table in front of the hearth. Dilapidated benches were pushed beneath the table. A broken rocker lay on its side under one of the cabin's two, small, oilcloth-covered windows. The small bedroom had one window, an exact match to the windows in the main room. The rocker Zoe-Esther would fix, and the windows she would get used to. She tried one of them. The latch worked and it opened easily. She intended to keep the windows open all the time in nice weather, since the oilcloth allowed only partial light inside. The moment she opened the window, bright morning light poured into the cabin. Zoe-Esther stepped outside to examine the windows from the other side. When she went around the side of the cabin to check the bedroom window, she discovered a large, built-in, wooden bench just underneath the window.

An idea popped into her head. A good idea, she hoped. Grabbing two quilts from their belongings still packed on the buckboard that brought them, Zoe-Esther arranged the quilts, just so, over the rough-hewn bench. *Here Papa can rest and be comfortable. Here Papa can fill his lungs with fresh, mountain air.*

Zoe-Esther checked her watch pin. Eleven-thirty. The claims agent was about to leave. Zoe-Esther asked him if he would please drive her back to Golden City, and then back to the cabin. She needed to purchase a mattress for Yitzhak, a kerosene lamp, and food. She had little money left but she had no choice but to spend it on the vital items. Relieved when the kind agent agreed to her request, Zoe-Esther thanked him profusely before finding her papa.

Yitzhak had wandered around to the back of the cabin. She heard him coughing and rushed to his side. It didn't take much convincing for Yitzhak to allow her to escort him around to the bench. She helped him lie down on one quilt and covered him with the other. After reassurance from the claims agent that her papa "should be just fine" while she was away, Zoe-Esther approached Yitzhak. He lay quiet and peaceful. She knelt down by his side and whispered to him that she would be back very soon. He smiled and quickly fell asleep.

With her papa safely asleep and the sun still high over-head, Zoe-Esther made sure she had her money first, then climbed onto the buckboard for the trip back down the mountain into Golden City.

A week passed. Zoe-Esther and Yitzhak managed to get along, considering how ill he had become, and how little she knew about frontier life. Just as she did with her embroidery work, Zoe-Esther decided to take things piece by piece. Once the cabin was scrubbed clean, all her energy and effort went toward caring for her papa, and, if there was any time left, she spent it bent over her needlework. Today, basket in hand, she made her way down the foothills trail toward Golden City. The walk there and back should only take a couple of hours. After she collected her pay for her stitchery, she intended to go to the mercantile and purchase what she could for her papa: fruit, vegetables, and a nice chicken. Tonight she wanted to make him a pot of chicken soup. She hurried down the path. She didn't want to leave Yitzhak alone for very long.

"Oy vey."

Zoe-Esther stopped in her tracks. She saw something— someone—down the trail. She should put her wire rims on to see more clearly, but for some strange reason, she did not, and left them in their case in her skirt pocket. Squinting hard, trying to focus on the figure up ahead, and taking cautious steps, she started down the trail again. Her heart raced. She hated to admit it, but she was a little scared. *Why surely there can't be any danger up ahead,* she thought, all the while praying it was true. Her feet didn't want to keep going, but she made them. A frontier woman now, she must be brave and keep walking.

From what she could see of the man up ahead, he looked harmless enough, just sitting on his horse. There had to be lots of people who routinely traveled back and forth in the mountains. She couldn't get upset every time she passed one of them. She began to relax, chastising herself for being afraid. But when the stranger's face became clearer, when she saw exactly who he was, she got scared all over again.

Mixed up and befuddled, even more *farmisht* than she

was the first time she met Mr. Whiskey, Zoe-Esther, completely out of character for her, checked the hair ribbon at her nape to make sure none of her wild tresses had escaped from under it. Her stomach turned somersaults. In a panic, she looked to either side of the pathway, hoping to see another trail, one that didn't force her to go right by Mr. Whiskey. She didn't see one. Should she stop and *kibbitz* with him? *No. How can I chat with him when I feel all . . . all* farmisht *inside? I can't. I won't.* Besides, she hadn't forgotten how he'd shooed her out of his saloon like so much chopped liver. No matter what her feelings were when she was around him, or her opinion of him, Zoe-Esther kept on walking.

As she drew closer, watching the way he sat on his horse, staring at her, all dressed in black, blowing gray puffs of smoke as if he were lying in wait for her like a wily, nocturnal lion ready to pounce on its prey, the more annoyed she became. She forgot her fear. He was not in his lion's den and she was not in any mood to be pounced on. Working herself up into a good irritation by the time she reached Mr. Whiskey, she didn't stop, but stepped off the trail and headed into the scruff and wild grasses.

"C'mon, lady. You don't have to go off and do that," Jake hollered behind her, aggravated with the maverick female. He slid off Missouri and crushed what was left of his smoke under his boot. "Of all the stubborn . . ." he mumbled low under his breath. "Yeah, stubborn and pretty," he had to admit. Her hair, even bound at her neck, caught his eye. The coppery waves of curly hair reached clear down to her waist. And the way her slender hips swayed just beneath her hair . . . She sure was a looker. Even from the back. Especially from the back, he thought, as he watched her trim shape storm away. Even so, he was tempted to let her keep on going. *Playing with the Queen of Hearts isn't in the cards for me—today or any day.*

"Ah hell." Jake realized she would probably go off and get herself lost. It didn't take him long to catch up with her.

"Listen, lady. You're not going to get too far in this territory if you run off half-cocked every time things don't suit you."

Zoe-Esther stopped and turned around to face her unwelcome company.

"Hell. Don't you know you can get all turned around out here quicker than you can skin a damned jackrabbit?" Jake demanded. "The vultures will be swarming over you before anybody from town will find you," he warned. "And that temper of yours—it'll get you into more trouble than you need be in, Queenie."

Zoe-Esther didn't respond. Queenie? She stood rooted to the spot, staring at him.

Closer now, Jake could see he had been right. In the morning sunshine her face, her hair, she sparkled like a cache of costly ore. He'd never seen such skin, all creamy and dusted with tiny flecks of copper and gold. Her nut-brown eyes twinkled with the same natural shine, the same shimmer. He remembered how he'd likened her to an undiscovered mine, filled with secret tunnels and virgin passages, all soft and just inviting him to enter. Damn.

Jake took a step back but couldn't take his eyes off her.

From the top of her burnished head to the tips of her boots, she interested him all right, and he couldn't do a damned thing about it. He didn't want her to leave. Not yet. If she weren't the color of money, maybe he wouldn't care. If she didn't make him feel like he had a stack of chips in front of him higher than all the rest of the players at the faro table, maybe he wouldn't care. If her hair didn't shine like copper and invite his touch, maybe he wouldn't care. His fingers twitched at his sides. He itched to run them over and through the length of her hair, and over the silky curve of her cheeks. Was she as smooth and compliant as the soft metal he likened her to? Under that high-button blouse and clear-down-to-her-ankles skirt, was she? His fingers twitched again.

Hell. Right now he couldn't shuffle a deck of cards, much less run his hands over the mysterious creature in front of him. Bad luck for sure. The day he couldn't shuffle a deck of cards was the day he stood to lose it all. Everything, his whole fortune, depended on the game. He had to stay in it with a steady hand.

"And just who do you think you're looking at?" Zoe-Esther demanded, her anger suddenly refueled.

"Why you, Queenie. I'm looking at you."

The moment he spoke, her anger vanished. She wasn't prepared for what he said, and for the way he said it, or for the invasive effect of his rugged good looks. Only moments ago she'd had a basketful of complaints to rail at him, but she couldn't think of one of them now. He undressed her with his words and left her exposed, *farmisht,* and terrified. The longer she looked up into the gray shadows of his penetrating eyes, the longer she was drawn into the warmth emanating from his powerful physique, and the longer she breathed in the heady combination of musk and tobacco, the more terrified she became. Why couldn't she pull her eyes from his and walk away? She would be safe then. Isn't that what she wanted? Didn't she want to get away from him?

She thought so.

Yes, of course. I know so.

But her heart refused to obey. Much as she wanted to leave, she didn't.

"Mr. Whiskey." She had to say something, do something, to get herself out of this impossible situation. "Mr. Whiskey—" Nothing else came out. She panicked all over again.

"Yep," he said. "That'd be me."

"Mr. Whiskey," she tried again. "I'm heading toward town."

"Is that a fact?"

He chuckled and she tried to re-muster her anger, but she failed. When she saw a smile escape out from under his shaggy, gray mustache, all she could rally was a slight pique. His concealed grin gave little away. She wished she could see what was under his mustache. She thought she glimpsed white, even teeth and smooth lips. When he pulled off his hat and ran a quick hand through his full head of salt-and-pepper hair several times, something about his hand caught her attention. Fascinated by his fingers, she watched as Mr. Whiskey ran his hand through his hair in deliberate, deft strokes—hands like a surgeon.

Like Daniel's, but not like Daniel.

Except for their hands, Daniel and Mr. Whiskey had little else in common. Where Daniel was an academic, this man probably never even opened a book, much less read one. Where Daniel was gentle and refined, the roughened Mr. Whiskey had manners, but of a very different kind. The westerner's words held nothing but sarcasm, intimidation, and insinuation. Daniel never made her feel the way *this saloonkeeper . . . this gambler . . . this probable hard-drinking debaucher*—Zoe-Esther censored the rest of her wicked thoughts. What was she doing? Not just sizing up Mr. Whiskey, but what was she doing standing here in the middle of nowhere with him? Papa would be furious with her. *Alone with a* goy: *a non-Jew.*

She'd arrived at the biggest difference between Daniel Stein and Mr. Whiskey: one was a Jew and one was not. Daniel was Yiddish, Jewish like her. She could only guess about Mr. Whiskey. Whatever he was, he was not a Jew. She wondered if Mr. Whiskey had any religion at all? Unable to imagine a life outside Judaism, Zoe-Esther tried to put her unexplained interest in this salty frontiersman in some kind of reasonable, logical perspective. She made up her mind, then and there, to consider him just another male specimen, another somatic type, a psychological sample worthy of her study. *Yes, that's all Mr. Whiskey is to me.* Having convinced herself that she had no interest other than pure academia in Mr. Whiskey, she decided nonetheless, that any further contemplation of him would be most unwise. Besides, didn't she have important business in Golden City? Rather than standing here dissecting unwanted notions about a man who was her opposite in every way imaginable, she needed to get to town.

What if her papa awakened and seized with coughing, or worse, started to hemorrhage?

Jake didn't even try to pursue the crazy female when, without so much as a word, she darted past him, regained the trail, and hurried down it.

"What are you looking at?" He tossed at his loyal horse when he reached the big chestnut waiting for him on the trail. Missouri whinnied and bobbed his head. *I'll be damned,* Jake swore to himself when he realized his companionable sorrel's coat was the same color as Queenie's coppery mane. The horse whinnied again.

"Hey, old pard, I'm sorry. I got no cause to take anything out on you." Jake softened his tone and rubbed the animal's muzzle before he took up the reins and climbed into the saddle. He glanced down the path. Queenie had disappeared quicker than the sure-footed mountain sheep that combed these ridges. Much as he didn't want to, Jake felt a grudging admiration for the greenhorn easterner. Why in tarnation was she out here, alone, on one of the trails leading up to Blackhawk and Central City? The mines were some thirty miles up in the hills, and she sure as hell couldn't have gone that far, leastways on foot, even for someone as spry as she. He turned Missouri off the path and headed for the wagon trail a half-mile away. He'd rather take that, than stay on this one: the same one Queenie was on.

He would turn back toward town in a bit, but not yet. Faro wouldn't start up until the afternoon. He needed more time out here by himself.

Yeah, right.

Ruined his morning, running into that gal. The problem was that he couldn't get her figured, and worse for him—now he wanted to.

Elated when Yitzhak ate his entire bowl of chicken soup, Zoe-Esther got up from the table and went outside to fix his bed for the night. Earlier in the day, on her walk back from Golden City, the idea struck her and she intended to put her theory to the test. The idea hit her a week ago, but only now had she reasoned it through. Her treatment method could mean life or death for her papa. If she implemented something risky, he could die. If she didn't, he would surely die of tuberculosis before winter's end. His symptoms grew worse. Yes, he ate all of his chicken soup, but it would take more than chicken soup to save her papa. Zoe-Esther was more scared for him now than ever.

Thanks to God the outside bench was large enough to serve as a makeshift bed. Before supper she pulled the straw mattress she had bought in town off Yitzhak's bed, re-arranged its contents to better fit the bench, then placed the mattress along the bench's surface. Whoever built the cabin had gone to a lot of trouble to make the expansive wooden seat and for that, Zoe-Esther would be eternally grateful. It was wide enough and long enough to serve as a temporary bed. She piled the quilts back on top of her papa's "new bed" and hurried inside to get Yitzhak. Soon it would be dark.

"Little Star, what is it . . . you want your . . . old papa . . . to do?" Yitzhak managed to say in between gasps for breath.

Alarmed by his weakened condition and his increased shortness of breath, Zoe-Esther did her best to hide her fears from him.

"Such a ridiculous idea to sleep . . . outside! This is *mishegaz!* I don't want—" He began to cough, so much so he almost fell to the floor. Zoe-Esther caught him and helped him sit back down at the table, realizing all over again how very ill he had become. She gently rubbed the back of his neck until his coughing completely stopped. It pained her to see him so weak, so ill, with death pursuing ever closer. Feh! She would not let death catch up with him. Not Papa. Death might just as well go knocking some-where else, for she would stand in its way no matter what! She would help her beloved papa thwart death. This very day she'd found the way to do it using the wondrous power of Mother Nature, itself.

Hadn't they traveled all this way, two thousand miles, for the altitude; in search of dry, clean, and healthy air to fill Yitzhak's failing lungs? Why, then, should she keep him inside, away from the sun's warm rays, the stars shining wonder, and the fresh, crisp air flowing across the prevailing winds like a healing infusion of God's miracles? Determined to follow through with her plans, she needed to convince Yitzhak to agree. In his present state, she didn't think he would protest too much about anything she suggested. Standing behind his seated, exhausted form, she kissed the top of his head and hugged his shoulders.

"Dear Papa, please trust me. I have my reasons for wanting you to be outside in the fresh air. It will be healthier for you. I believe with all my heart that this will help you, and maybe cure you. I just know it will, Papa." She choked back sobs. "It will not be so comfortable all of the time for you outside, but Papa, I will stay with you and God will be with you. Your lungs will fill with His gift of pure, healing air. We must try, Papa. Together, we must try."

Yitzhak slowly raised his hand from the table and reached behind him, lightly patting his daughter's hand that still rested on his shoulder.

It was all Zoe-Esther needed to tell her that he agreed to her plan. She knew he was too weak to do much but comply. Her heart went out to him. Unable to hold them back any longer, hot tears rained down her cheeks and neck and soaked the collar of her blouse. *Thanks to God, Papa can't see me cry.* Taking a few moments to collect her emotions, Zoe-Esther squared her shoulders, stood tall, and took in a deep breath. There was no more time to waste.

"Come, Papa," she gently urged and helped him to his feet.

"Child . . . I bring you . . . nothing but . . . *tsuris*," Yitzhak rasped breathlessly.

"Hush, Papa. You do not bring me troubles. You bring me only blessings and joy," Zoe-Esther cooed to Yitzhak, as if she were trying to soothe a child to sleep. She wished she could lift away the heavy burden of illness from her papa's stooped shoulders.

A cool October wind greeted father and daughter the moment the pair stepped outside. Zoe-Esther was glad her papa wore his reliable *gatkes,* his winter underwear, when she saw him brace against the wind. Quickly now, she needed to tuck him under the pile of warm quilts. The temperature had dropped markedly since before supper. Exposing her papa to the cold worried her, but not enough to stop her treatment plan for him. She had no intention for the treatment to be worse than the cure, but for a moment, she wondered if it might be. Brushing this worry aside, she vowed that she would make sure her papa stayed warm. She would sleep outside herself to keep watch over him and make sure that he did.

Thankful for the clear night and for the bright moon, Zoe-Esther had Yitzhak tucked under the mound of quilts in no time. She refused to think of his outdoor bed as a sickbed. Satisfied when Yitzhak fell asleep quickly, and content to see him so peaceful, Zoe-Esther hurried inside the cabin and dragged the rocker she'd repaired outside. Though rickety and splintered, the rocker was made of sturdy wood. It should do just fine for her.

In her full set of clothes—blouse, skirt, cotton chemise, stocking feet and all—Zoe-Esther pulled the latch to the cabin door shut behind her and rearranged the rocker, just so, right near Yitzhak. Grateful for the moonlit night, she curled her legs up beneath her and settled under the weight of her quilt. Thanks to God she and Papa had brought all the family quilts with them from the old country. Her *ema* had sewed the pieces of the quilt covering her now. Zoe-Esther ran her hands over the precious flowers and patchwork as if they were portions from the sacred Torah scrolls.

She considered the quilts as important as the other reminders of their traditions, of their Jewish family life: their
Shabbas candlesticks, their *mezuzah,* obedience of dietary
laws, and, most important of all, their keeping of the Sabbath. It pained her still that her papa sold their menorah because of her. One day she would find a way to replace the
silver menorah with another, so they could again celebrate
the joyous Festival of Lights in all its brilliance. She looked
heavenward. How the stars twinkled, so luminous now, as if
kindled for all eight nights of Hanukkah. For the first time
in as many days her heart, her spirit, found solace and con-
tentment. She closed her eyes and leaned her head back
against the wooden pillow the rocker provided, and
breathed in the fresh, mountain air. Long, deep breaths
meant to soothe and comfort.

Something screeched in the distance. Zoe-Esther's eyes
flew open but the rest of her didn't make a move. Too
scared to budge, much less to think, she sat in numbed silence and discovered the night was anything but silent. Like
a burst dike, her frightened thoughts raced in every direction. What was out there?

Mountain lions! Wolves! Coyotes! Bears! Indians!

On the wagon train west, she heard all the talk about
keeping a vigilant watch for all sorts of wild creatures, and
for Indians. If she had to pick, she would rather confront
Indians than wild animals. At least with Indians she might
have a chance to reason with them. The same welcome
breezes that she prayed would heal her papa brought with
them unwelcome calls of the wild. Zoe-Esther swallowed
hard. She knew she wouldn't get any sleep tonight. No
matter what, she wasn't about to leave her papa, and no
matter what happened on this night, tomorrow she would
get the largest ax she could find to chop wood, to keep a

protective fire going, and to use as a weapon against—God only knew.

The weather grew colder with each passing day. Now the nighttime temperature often dropped to freezing, giving Zoe-Esther little choice but to change her treatment regimen for Yitzhak. If she kept him outside at night with winter coming, he could die from exposure before tuberculosis killed him, despite the little blaze she kept going and her sitting vigil over him with her ax handy. The daylight hours would have to suffice.

Yitzhak's symptoms worsened. He was very weak. Zoe-Esther had expected improvement before now. Instead, his coughing persisted and his night sweats increased. He hardly touched a bite of food. Even her chicken soup couldn't entice him to eat. He never complained, talking very little at all. His quickening downhill turn frightened her, but Zoe-Esther meant to hold steadfast to her belief that his cure depended on being outside in the fresh, clean air. Soon his condition had to improve. She decided to add more supportive measures to Yitzhak's treatment. *Please, God. Let them help Papa.* She would make sure her papa received good nutrition—finding some way to get him to eat—and add fresh milk to his daily diet. Exercise, too. Daily exercise would strengthen his failing body.

Miracle of miracles, over the next days, Yitzhak began to improve. *Thanks to God for such a miracle!* Zoe-Esther wasn't sure if Yitzhak's improvement was due more to the fresh, mountain air or to the addition of milk to his diet and their short, daily walks, but she didn't care. Together, they had beaten tuberculosis. Well, maybe not beaten, but at least Papa was getting better. Just how long his improvement would last; she had no idea. She would keep encouraging him to eat well, get proper exercise, and breathe deeply of the fresh mountain air. Keeping up her trips into town every day to fetch milk from the mercantile was top on her list. If only she had a dairy cow. But how could she afford such a luxury when she didn't have enough extra money to purchase a much-needed horse? There was nothing to be done for it, she knew. She would travel on foot to Golden city, whether for milk or to sell her embroidery.

At the mercantile only the day before, Zoe-Esther had overheard a conversation about the capitol of the Colorado Territory being moved to Denver City and away from Golden City. It could happen any day now, the men had said. Maybe one day, when Yitzhak was stronger, they would make a trip to Denver City. Maybe it would hold more promise for them than Golden City.

Promise.

For some unexplained reason that particular word stuck in her head. It puzzled her. Why should *promise* bother her? She hadn't made any promises to anyone to be of any concern—or, had she?

Papa. I made a promise to Papa about Daniel. I promised him we would return one day to Philadelphia and that I would marry Daniel. Oy vey! What have I done?

Now that Yitzhak was getting better, her thoughts could turn toward such things.

Meshuga! Never can I marry Daniel!

Of course, she would straighten everything out with her papa, but not yet. When he was stronger, then they could kibbitz about her foolhardy promise to marry Daniel. Right now was not the time. She dare not do or say anything to cause her papa to become agitated and possibly fall ill again.

Zoe-Esther's mood dampened with each step toward their cabin. The whole matter of her promise to her papa unsettled her. She didn't like to keep secrets, especially from Yitzhak. Just then she thought of another secret she kept: one since childhood. Her mood worsened.

Promises.

Feh!

I will never meet the man "promised" to me by the schadchen. *Talk about foolhardy. I'm the fool.*

Chapter Eight

Jake raked in the chips from his winning hand and declared the game over. He got up from the faro table and so did all the other players, all but one: Silas Preston. Jake never missed a name, a face, or a bet. A down-on-his-luck-miner, Preston had thrown a claim title into the pot on the last hand. Preston had lost the hand, and his claim. Jake already had the claim in his pocket, not yet bothering to read the document.

"Game's over, Preston," Jake reminded the still-seated man.

Preston's expression was glum, emphasizing years of hard work etched on his craggy, weathered face. The miner finally looked up at Jake, as if just realizing someone spoke to him.

"Yeah, over," Silas repeated in a mindless tone.

Jake read the man's weary eyes and knew Preston wasn't going to pull a gun. What he saw instead was disappointment, despair, and even fear. Too bad. In the game of cards, just like life, sometimes you win and sometimes you lose. Jake had learned the lesson only too well, and Preston would have to do the same. Needing a smoke and another shot of Jack Daniels, Jake left the man alone at the deserted faro table.

"Yeah, who is it?" Jake snapped in an agitated tone through the closed door to his office, knowing full well that it had to be Belle. In a few minutes he was due to get another game started but he still had some paperwork to finish.

Another knock.

Damn.

"Well, come on in," he growled and swiveled around from his roll-top desk. He leaned back in his chair and prepared to shoo Belle right back out.

"It's me, Mr. Whiskey," Silas Preston said and pulled off his dusty, dilapidated hat as he entered. "I . . . I need to—"

"Close the door," Jake interrupted, relieved it wasn't Belle, but not exactly pleased to see the unlucky card player either.

"Yessir," Silas said and obediently closed the door.

Damn. Jake didn't need anyone calling him sir. He never used the word and didn't like it when anyone else did. It reminded him of all those down-and-out days when he had to say "sir" to get a bit of work or a little food or a place to sleep. Silas Preston looked down—and out. Jake wanted to get rid of him as quickly as he could.

"I gotta talk to you, Mr. Whiskey. It's real important."

It was obvious to Jake the man was nervous.

"So talk," Jake said and watched as Silas rotated his scruffy hat in his hands.

"My claim, the one I just done lost, it's all we got in the world, Mr. Whiskey. I cain't go back to my wife an' young'uns with nuthin' to show for all a this. You see, Mr. Whiskey, this was our last shot, our last hope to get us a stake to live on. I just figured that if I could get me some lucky cards then we'd have enough till our claim shows pay dirt."

Jake really didn't like hearing this.

"Our claim, it's all we got to show for the years we done been here. I was thinkin', Mr. Whiskey, if you could see your way clear to givin' me my claim back, then my young'uns an the wife, we'd all work for you for as long as it takes to make it up to you."

Jake really, really didn't like hearing this.

"Sit down, Silas." Jake snagged the corner of a straight chair with his booted foot, and scooted the chair in front of the miner.

"Yessir. Thank you, sir," Silas said and sat down.

"Let's get one thing straight, Silas. Don't call me sir. If you say it once more, you're outta here."

"Yessi . . . I mean . . . Yes."

Silas Preston's story struck a nerve with Jake.

Jake didn't want any man beholden to him, much less any man's entire family. It was one thing to win or lose at cards with the players at the table—it happened every day— but it was a whole other thing to put a man's family and children on the losing side. Used to caring only for himself all of his life and surviving the best way he knew, in all these years Jake really hadn't thought about how the losers at his faro table might have families at home waiting for them.

Yeah, and he knew why he didn't.

He'd never had a family.

"Tell you what I'm going to do, Silas," Jake spoke low and even. "I'm giving you back your claim, but on one condition. If you ever speak of this to anybody, I mean anybody, I'll get it back from you quicker than you can spit and holler howdy," he warned, and he didn't wait for an answer before he turned back to his desk. He hadn't filed the claim away yet and easily retrieved it from the loose stack of papers in front of him. Then, for no reason at all that he could think of, he pulled a hundred dollars from the roll of bills in his pocket.

"Here," Jake shoved the document and the bill at Silas.

"I don't know what to say, Mr. Whiskey. I just don't," Silas whispered, marveling at the contents in his callused hands.

"Just take it and get out of here. And remember. Not a word. I can't have folks around here thinking I'll go all lily-livered at every hard-luck story I hear," Jake warned again.

Silas Preston got up.

"Thank you. I'll never forget whatcha done here, Mr. Whiskey."

"Good luck to you and to . . . your family, Silas."

Silas put his hat back on, nodded to Jake, and then left.

Jake leaned back in his leather swivel and wondered if he'd just done something right or something very, very stupid.

Zoe-Esther's neck ached. No amount of rubbing or warmth took away the stiffness. She knew why she had the problem but wasn't going to change her routine of sleeping every night in the rocker next to Yitzhak's bed. Even though he was much better, she wanted to be there in case he needed something should he awaken. Besides, she used the time to complete her embroidery orders. The flickering kerosene lamp gave off just enough light for her to see what she was doing. She pushed her spectacles back on her nose, having to squint a bit for such close work. Such a *brochah.* Such a blessing, that she had orders in the first place. Four now—two hotels and two saloons—had her stitching monograms onto hand towels, pillowslips, and linen napkins. It wasn't the practice of medicine, but it brought in money, enough to live on. And, that's all that mattered.

She had yet to approach the Golden Gates, by far the most elegant and successful gambling establishment in Golden City, to ask for work. The idea of asking Mr. Whiskey for anything upset her in ways she still refused to recognize or, at least, accept. There was enough to worry about what with caring for Yitzhak, adjusting to frontier life, and sewing piece work, without adding the disturbing effect Mr. Whiskey had on her when she was with him. And even more disturbing was the effect he had on her when she wasn't.

In those rare moments when she wasn't ministering to Yitzhak, scrubbing the cabin, chopping wood, embroidering, hurrying to and from town, cooking, mending clothes or, God forbid, trying to sleep, Zoe-Esther sought the comfort of her childhood imaginings. She would let her thoughts travel back in time to the matchmaker's cottage in the *shtetl* and hear his name—her match—and try to conjure his image.

But only one image appeared before her now.

Mr. Whiskey!

She tried to force his image from her mind, but she failed. She tried to stop her imaginings of him, but she failed there, too.

Slate, shadowy eyes embraced her, while strong arms pulled her against his rock-hard chest, their hearts beating as one. She pulled away to run her fingertips over his smoky mustache, down its sides, and then to touch the smoothness of his gentle lips, and wait . . . wait for his kiss.

"Feh! Meshuga!"

Worse than having these crazy and ridiculous thoughts was the sudden, jolting realization that the fanciful child inside her had grown into a woman, a woman with desires and longings for—Mr. Whiskey! Never could there be such a match with a man like Mr. Whiskey. He was not a Jew, and he swore more than anyone she'd ever met, was a gambler, a saloonkeeper, a probable drinker, a roughened frontiersman, and . . . and . . . uneducated! To help fight her unwelcome feelings for Mr. Whiskey, Zoe-Esther silently repeated the name the matchmaker had given her so long ago:

Yaakov.

Not Mr. Whiskey.

Uncertain whether or not she felt relief or disappointment that Mr. Whiskey's name was not Yaakov, Zoe-Esther did everything she could to dismiss, from her mind and body, unwanted notions about a man who *will never be my match*.

Again, she failed. Mr. Whiskey's image refused to disappear from her mind's eye.

One area where she would not fail had to do with her papa. Never would she mention a word of her crazy notions about Mr. Whiskey to her ailing papa. Yitzhak would condemn any such union. For a Jew even to consider marriage to a goy is forbidden, and Zoe-Esther would never do anything to send her beloved papa to an early grave.

Zoe-Esther had to laugh at herself. *Such a fool. Such a golem I am.* To worry over nonsense when Mr. Whiskey had absolutely no interest in her. Anyway, she'd already made her vow never to vow to love, honor, cherish, and obey any man. Not even Daniel, who was not a *goy* but a Jew like her, and from whose lips she'd never heard a curse word, and who wasn't a gambler, a saloonkeeper, a rough frontiersman, or uneducated. If she ever, under some *mishuga* circumstance, agreed to marry anyone, it would

119

have to be to a man like Daniel: a man to whom her papa would give his absolute approval and blessing.

But the matchmaker said Yaakov, not Daniel.

Neither Daniel's nor Mr. Whiskey's name had any similarity to Yaakov. Zoe-Esther took comfort from this. Didn't she? For the briefest of moments, she wondered if she did. She shook her head and took a cleansing breath to chase away any lingering doubts about Mr. Whiskey not being Yaakov.

There.

She felt better now.

She no longer needed to worry over her unwanted, unexpected, and upsetting feelings for Mr. Whiskey. He was not in her future. She'd be wise to ignore him completely, and the unwanted stirrings he caused inside her.

"Mrs. Bartlett," Jake drawled and tipped his black Stetson her way as soon as he stepped inside the foyer of her rooming house.

"Come in, Jake Whiskey," she invited, her pleasant, apple-cheeked face all smiles.

Jake followed her into the front parlor and took a seat after she did. He pulled off his hat and began to fidget with its brim. The settee cushion seemed too soft and the back too hard, and he shifted once, then again. His eyes finally met Mrs. Bartlett's watchful ones. She sat across from him, wearing a bright smile. He did his damnedest to smile back. The problem was, he didn't feel much like smiling, or even talking. Then why the hell was he here?

He knew why. He just didn't know how to say it.

Mrs. Bartlett broke the silence.

"Some coffee, Jake Whiskey?" she offered, the corners of her mouth twitching, trying her best not to laugh at his obvious discomfort. "It's all made. I'll just get some for us," she added, not waiting for him to answer.

Jake watched her disappear from the parlor, glad for a few moments to shake off his nerves.

Back in no time, Mrs. Bartlett set her tray of coffee and cakes down on the little table in front of Jake. She poured him a steaming cup of coffee. He wanted a smoke and a shot of his favorite Tennessee whiskey instead, but took the offered brew all the same. Before Mrs. Bartlett sat back down, he'd finished half of his cup; no matter that the hot liquid burned his mouth and throat going down.

He watched Mrs. Bartlett sip her coffee. She said nothing. He had the feeling she would sit there until the cows came home, waiting for him to state his business. He'd sure known her long enough to know that she would. Liked her a lot. Always had. When he first came to Golden City, she'd let him stay a spell in her rooming house, delaying the rent until he could pay. The two struck up a friendship. He'd trusted her from the start, odd ways and all. The only other person he trusted in town was Matthew. In Jake's line of work it didn't pay to befriend too many folks. Trust could get a body killed quicker than a pointed and loaded Winchester.

"I came to ask you something," Jake at last said. "There's a woman—"

He shut up. The knowing look on Mrs. Bartlett's face the moment he said *woman* made him keep quiet. Damn if he didn't have the feeling she knew all along just why he'd come. Sam Hill. This wasn't easy for him.

"Like I said . . ." He'd get this out now if it killed him, and it pretty near might. "Like I said there's a woman who arrived in town some time ago. A little freckle-faced thing with long rusty hair and an attitude that won't quit. She needed a place to stay and I sent her here. The next time we met up she was hotfooting it down the hills outside of town, pretty as you please, all hell-bent to get to Golden City. Never said why or what to me and I'm curious is all. Yep, just curious about her. I'm sure you remember her, Mrs. Bartlett, with that foreign sort of accent of hers that she's more than willing to let loose on a body."

Mrs. Bartlett set down her cup, sat back in her chair, and folded her hands in her lap. She smiled to herself.

"I know just the one you're referring to," she said, her eyes twinkling as if she were about to reveal a well-kept secret. "The little freckle-faced thing with 'long rusty hair and an attitude that won't quit' has a name, a beautiful name. It's Zoe-Esther Zundelevich. Must be a Russian name, I expect."

Queenie, was all Jake heard.

Mrs. Bartlett went on.

"Poor thing arrived here with her sick papa. He suffers from the consumption, I believe. No sooner were they settled here at my place, than they up and left. I'm ashamed to admit it, but with all her papa's coughing, my other boarders . . . well, they all wanted Mr. Zundelevich to leave. Zoe-Esther understood, the sweet thing, and left with her papa as soon as she could."

Jake's chest tightened. He knew what it felt like to be turned out in the cold.

"She found a cabin to rent," Mrs. Bartlett continued. "An empty miner's cabin two miles outside of town in the direction of the gold fields up Clear Creek. She has stopped by to see me once since then, and tells me she and her papa are getting along just fine. You know, Jake Whiskey, I don't know that I've ever met such a brave, devoted, selfless young woman." Mrs. Bartlett paused and stared straight at

Jake as if to underscore her words. "And don't you know she's doing stitch work for some of the hotels and saloons to make ends meet. Won't take a penny of charity. I tried, but she's a proud little thing."

Damn, he didn't want to feel anything about Queenie. He didn't want to *want* her, but the more he heard about Queenie from Mrs. Bartlett, the more he was drawn in.

"There's one more thing, Jake Whiskey. Something I think you ought to know."

He waited for the other shoe to drop.

Here it comes. The Lady Bad Luck part, where I find out Queenie is really a gold-digger. Or wanted by the law. Or an opium addict who needs to get married because she's gone and gotten herself knocked up.

"She and her papa, Jake Whiskey, they're Jewish. I think that's the other reason, I'm not proud to say, that my tenants—good Christians all," Mrs. Bartlett intoned, her voice dripping with sarcasm. "I don't think my boarders wanted Zoe-Esther and her papa here because they're different."

Jake expected just about anything to come out of Mrs. Bartlett's mouth—anything but this.

His surprised expression must have given him away.

"Jake Whiskey, do you even know what a Jew is?"

He shook his head in admission that he did not.

"Let's just say then, that they don't believe what Christians do. You know, in the resurrection of Jesus Christ," Mrs. Bartlett clarified.

No, he didn't know—about Jews or Christians or Mormons or Quakers or any of the others he ever heard about. He never paid any mind to religion, the same way he never paid any mind to family; and he wasn't about to start now. None of them had anything to do with him.

Jake had heard enough, and listened long enough, to

know he didn't like what he just learned about Queenie. He learned that he was already more interested in her than he bet on. She didn't sound like any of the women he usually fell for. *So why in Blue Blazes am I wasting my time with Queenie?*

His gut wrenched.

He didn't have to wonder what the reason was. He knew, deep down, that he would never be good enough for somebody like Queenie, somebody in respectable society with a family and religion. Two things he knew absolutely nothing about.

Without another word, Jake stood up and nodded goodbye to Mrs. Bartlett, determined to stick to his own kind: the Belle Blisses of the world—a world he knew, a world where he belonged.

The bitter cold November nights forced Zoe-Esther to spend much of her day gathering and chopping wood to keep a fire going in the hearth. Her papa needed to stay warm.

Two months of living in the West, and of fear for Yitzhak, had now given way to the probability that her papa soon would live a normal life again. The decision to come west for a change in altitude, climate, and the air her papa breathed was the right decision. The Colorado Territory had been kind to her papa. It had cured, or at least had slowed and interrupted, his tuberculosis. If the progression of his tuberculosis had been interrupted . . . maybe . . . just maybe . . . other invalids who suffered from tuberculosis could benefit from this same high altitude, with its dry, unpolluted air. Ever the physician, Zoe-Esther wondered if her papa's treatment could, indeed, one day, help others in the same way it had helped him.

This morning she had another twelve dollars' worth of embroidery in her basket to deliver to the Silver Spur, a saloon not far from the Golden Gates. The time would come when she would be forced to enter the Golden Gates and ask for work from Mr. Whiskey. If not for her papa, and keeping him well fed and healthy, she would rather starve than have to see Mr. Whiskey again. She didn't mind being humbled or the humiliation of being poor, but she did mind having to be in Mr. Whiskey's presence. If only she were accepted as a doctor in Golden City by the established doctors—*both men,* she fumed silently—there would be no need to live on piece work, begging door-to-door, *mekabets zayn.*

Mekabets zayn.

Papa's exact words to me before we left Philadelphia. I said we would never have to go begging door-to-door, and that's just what I'm doing.

Zoe-Esther gave her stiff neck a shake.

She wasn't *exactly* begging door-to-door. She was, after all, doing honest work for an honest dollar. Yes, she had to knock on doors to do it, but it was work for pay, and not begging. How very much she would prefer to work in her field of medicine. There had to be a way. She determined to find one, sooner rather than later.

After finishing her business at the Silver Spur, Zoe-Esther walked in the direction of the mercantile. She needed to find warm coats for herself and Yitzhak. Maybe something like the long oilcloth greatcoats she'd seen men wearing around town and on horseback. The coats looked durable, and no doubt could withstand wet, cold weather just fine. She wondered if they were terribly expensive. Zoe-Esther's worn, wool shawl didn't keep out the cold. She wore *gatkes* like her papa, but the winter underwear didn't keep her warm enough, either. The fact that *gatkes* were for men and not women didn't bother her a bit. They added warmth and that was all that mattered. Besides, no one would ever see underneath her clothes to know she donned the scratchy, unattractive *gatkes*. If only she could afford a pair of winter boots and thicker stockings. The western brogans she wore, men's boots like her papa's, didn't keep her feet as warm and dry as she'd hoped. Ordinarily the boots should protect her and keep her warm and dry. She knew why they didn't.

I'm always walking in the rain and mud, and soon I will be walking in snow. I don't have a horse to ride, and that is that.

"Feh," Zoe-Esther muttered, disgusted with herself for, yet again, complaining about not having a horse to ride to and from Golden City when the snows come.

If she and her papa lived in town, she wouldn't need a horse. But for now, they must stay in their mountain cabin. Yitzhak needed to take daily walks in the fresh air, and he had long weeks of recuperation ahead of him. Perhaps even more important now, she wasn't sure the danger of the spread of tuberculosis had passed. What if Papa could still infect others? No, it wasn't worth the risk to Yitzhak's health, or to the health of others, for her to move them to Golden City.

Out of habit, Zoe-Esther walked in the direction of the miners' tented section of town. She enjoyed threading her way down the busy, muddy corridors, with all the sights and sounds of children playing and hard-working people going about their business. Here she didn't feel so alone, so singled out by society. Why, none of these good people would care if she were Jewish or not. She hadn't forgotten the looks on the faces of the boarders at Mrs. Bartlett's supper table that first night. The looks were not just because her papa was ill, and she knew it. The looks were because they were Jews.

The horrific image of soldiers, with their sabers high in the air, chasing down the hillside toward the village of her childhood in Russia, ready to single out and kill Jews, flooded before her.

She hated being afraid.

In America, Zoe-Esther knew, she need not fear the soldiers. Only shunning from others. Shunning might have a sharp sting, but it cannot kill like the razor sharp edge of a soldier's blade.

She felt better. A little bit, anyway.

Zoe-Esther heard a child cry out. She quickly scanned the crowded street, looking for the injured youth. Then she saw him. A little tow-headed urchin not more than five or six years old, with his arm dangling unnaturally at his side as if it had fallen off and been stuck on backwards. A group of children surrounded the urchin, but she saw them scatter the moment the child cried out again. A thin woman with tarnished yellow hair rushed to the child. Zoe-Esther guessed she was his mother. The woman threw her arms around the child and began to cry, too.

Zoe-Esther rushed to the mother and child, breaking through the circle of onlookers to reach her patient.

Chapter Nine

No wonder the poor little fellow cried so. Zoe-Esther realized the moment she saw the position of his arm that the child's shoulder had separated. She would have to examine him to find out if he had any breaks in his arm, in the humerus, radial, or ulnar bones.

"Ma'am. Ma'am." Zoe-Esther looked straight at the sobbing mother. "I need to examine the boy's arm. Is your tent near?"

The upset mother paid Zoe-Esther no mind, and cradled her child closer.

"Ma'am, I'm a doctor and I want to help your son," she had to yell over the cries of both mother and child.

"You're a what?" The woman stopped crying and stared, dumbfounded, at Zoe-Esther. "Ain't no docs round here except Doc Pritchard and Doc James," she said in an accusatory voice.

"Yes," Zoe-Esther replied. "Well, now there's another one." She wanted to help the boy instead of having this needless exchange with his mother.

"I may be poor, but I ain't no fool," the woman shot back. "So don't go tellin' me you're a doc when I know ain't no women doin' doctorin'. Now leave me be to take care of my boy." She stood up, helped her boy to a stand,

and then led the child away, pained cries and all.

Frustrated, Zoe-Esther watched the two disappear through the door flaps of a nearby tent. She hurried to catch up with them.

"Ma'am, please. I *am* a doctor, I swear to you. I would like to help your son, if you'll let me." She felt a little silly talking through a layer of canvas, but her heart went out to the hurt child on the other side. While she waited for the mother to reconsider, Zoe-Esther heard—no, felt—the presence of others gathering behind her, no doubt curious about all the fuss. She didn't turn around to see the group of onlookers.

Ever so slowly, the tent flaps parted and the worried mother peered through the opening. She motioned for Zoe-Esther to come inside.

"You shore you're a doc?" the mother asked, her tone softer.

Zoe-Esther understood the mother's fears and suspicions; it made her appreciate the mother's consent all the more.

"I gotta say right up front then, Doc—"

"It's Zundelevich, Dr. Zoe-Esther Zundelevich," Zoe-Esther broke in.

The lines in the woman's tight brow relaxed and she let out a heavy sigh.

"Like I said, Doc Zoe, I gotta say right away I cain't pay nuthin' to you. I don't have the money to pay you. I cain't pay Doc Pritchard or Doc James no way, neither. So if you're expectin' pay, I—"

"*Oy vey,*" Zoe-Esther broke in again. "If that's all that's stopping you from letting me treat your son, then put your worries to rest. I'm not asking for any payment. I just want to help the child," she said and placed her hand over the anxious mother's clenched fingers.

The woman appeared stunned by what Zoe-Esther just told her.

"Then, all . . . all right," she whispered, all suspicion and tension in her voice gone. She stepped aside to allow Zoe-Esther access to her son.

The child lay writhing on a cot at the back of the tent. Zoe-Esther set her basket of embroidery down on the empty cot next to the boy's, wishing the basket were her medical bag instead. Quickly now, she pulled her spectacles from her skirt pocket and put the wire rims on.

"Here now, young man," she kept her voice gentle as she began to examine him. It was best to examine a child as quickly as one could, not just because of the child's suffering and pain, but also because, if given enough time, a child was likely to protest and not cooperate in the examination. Right now, however, the boy seemed oblivious to her ministrations, rolling from side to side in obvious pain. Zoe Esther, as gently as she could, tried to keep the little fellow still enough to let her slip off his thin, shabby coat. She took special care with his injured arm. Once his coat was off, the boy calmed somewhat, though his good arm continued to flail. To prevent the child from further injuring himself, and her, Zoe-Esther indicated to his mother, to come close and keep her son's uninjured limb from moving.

The mother complied immediately.

With the little fellow's good arm secure, Zoe-Esther could begin.

"Let's just fix you up, young man." She tried to reassure him while she examined the boy's shoulder and arm. Her initial diagnosis had been correct; the boy had a separated shoulder. Though no bones had broken through the skin, she discovered his forearm was fractured. By observation and palpation, she found the slight break in the radial bone. A simple fracture, she determined. Even if she'd had any laudanum with her, she wasn't sure it would help, or if she would even use it. Administering potent drugs to a child, unless absolutely warranted, couldn't be too good for their growth and development. Though many doctors prescribed laudanum for children for many reasons, Zoe-Esther remained skeptical, sure such drugs harmed more than helped.

"Ma'am," Zoe-Esther looked at the boy's mother. "I'm going to re-set his shoulder first. It's been pulled out of its socket and needs to be put back in place. Keep a good hold on him," she instructed, and then in one quick, expert move, she straightened her patient's shoulder.

"Mama! Mama!" The child squealed in pain.

Poor little fellow is scared and exhausted, and hurting. Zoe-Esther wanted to finish what she needed to do, so he could sleep.

"Ma'am, do you have any bed sheeting or cotton I could tear into strips? And, I'll need two sturdy sticks or pieces of board. And, and a large kerchief. Could you get them? I'll see to your son while you do," she smiled at the concerned, attentive mother.

In no time the requested items appeared on the empty cot next to her basket. Zoe-Esther worked quickly to secure the boy's fractured arm in a splint to help him heal properly. She took care to tie the knot under his elbow, just so. The little fellow sat up when she was finished, studying his new sling. He didn't cry anymore. Glad the boy's pain had evidently subsided, Zoe-Esther wished she had a peppermint or a rope of licorice to offer him now. He'd been such a good little patient. He smiled at her. All the payment she needed was in his adorable, gap-toothed grin.

Lemuel, she found out, was the child's name.

Lemuel's arm, Zoe-Esther instructed his mother, would take weeks to heal. He would need to keep his arm in the splint the entire time. She left more instructions for fluids and rest and said she would be back tomorrow to check on the child.

With my medical bag and peppermints.

Zoe-Esther hurried up the mountain trail toward her cabin. Her step was light and her spirits lighter. The evening turned bitter cold as she made her way home. The wind picked up, making her shiver. Her thin wool shawl offered little protection. She'd not bought her needed coat as yet. Zoe-Esther didn't care. She was happy as could be. It had been months since she'd practiced any medicine, except caring for her papa. She'd had no idea how much she had missed being a doctor—until little Lemuel. How she looked forward to her house call to see him tomorrow.

Her one house call turned into more than she'd bargained for. The moment she finished her check-up of the boy and stepped outside his tent, a young woman approached her. The woman carried a small child in her arms. The little girl's cough sounded to Zoe-Esther like the croup. Right behind the mother and child, a man stood and waited patiently. The collar of his soiled shirt was unbuttoned, exposing the festered boil on his neck. And behind him was a middle-aged woman with a bandaged hand, then an old man with his boot off, then a young man with a child in tow, and then another and then another. Zoe-Esther couldn't believe so many were waiting in line to see her. She would gladly see each and every one of them, privileged and happy to practice medicine again.

It was nightfall before Zoe-Esther reached home, utterly exhausted. She had seen patients all afternoon. On the way home she didn't think how dangerous it might be to wander up the mountain trail at dusk, just when animals begin their ritual prowl. In such a hurry to share her good news about practicing medicine again with her papa, she literally threw caution to the wind. This time she had been lucky not to encounter any wild animals. She had so much to tell Papa.

Zoe-Esther felt well paid for her services. She considered a "spankin' " clean red bandanna, a loaf of "fresh-made" soda bread, a "lucky for shore" rabbit's foot, and a copy of *The Golden Transcript*, "hot off the presses," adequate payment, indeed. As for the rest of her new patients, IOU's would "have to make do 'til we can pay you, Doc." Of course, Zoe-Esther refused to accept any monetary payment. It wasn't the smart thing to do, but she didn't feel like being smart today; she felt like celebrating.

She would have to find just the right thing to say to Papa, since she had no money in her pocket to show for all her work today. Surely her papa would understand and be happy for her. *He will not have forgotten the* shtetl. *He will remember how hard life can be. He will understand how the poor mining families in Tent City have very little to their names.* She was sure he would.

Money.

Thinking about how little money she and Papa had, took away some of her good mood. She knew what she had to do.

Now she would have to go to the Golden Gates and ask for work. With the supplies and medicines she needed now to restock her medical bag to care for the indigent patients in Tent City, she had to earn more. When she added this newest expense to all the rest, she'd little choice. Besides, she'd promised to run a clinic once a week in Tent City. Money, not finding time, was the problem.

Since Yitzhak was getting around better and was very close to a full recovery, Zoe-Esther felt she could accommodate a busier schedule. If she organized her sewing and running a clinic and caring for Papa and their home, she could manage everything sufficiently. It made her feel good to think of working as a doctor again. It also made her feel good to think she would be providing care to those patients "not worthy enough" for the likes of Doc Pritchard and Doc James.

A bullet in the shoulder wasn't something Jake had planned on when his second faro game of the day broke up. He hadn't seen it coming. The group at the table seemed friendly-like, but he hadn't paid close enough attention to them, and he knew it. His concentration lately turned more toward rusty-haired females with a scattering of coppery freckles and a sassy tongue, when he should have been concentrating on the players at his gaming table.

Damn. The pain shot clear down his right arm to his hand, his playing hand. Hell, he hadn't figured on killing anyone today, even the cheater he'd just shot. During the game, Jake knew the bastard was cheating. Why he hadn't called the man on it then and there bothered him almost as much as the pain shooting up and down his arm. He shouldn't have given the stupid bastard a chance to pull a gun on him.

Jake didn't have to look at the man he'd just shot to know that he was dead. He looked at Matthew instead.

The trusted barkeep got two men to remove the body and get it to the undertaker.

It could just as easily have been him going to be measured for a pine box, and Jake knew it. The throbbing on his right side grew worse and he made for the bar. He took one shot of whiskey, then another.

"Jake, darlin', are you all right?" Belle rushed up.

"Sure am," he said then poured himself another drink with his good hand.

"Jake, you've been shot!"

"Yeah."

"You need a doctor. Not whiskey!"

Matthew returned. One look at Jake and he didn't need Belle's prompting to send for a doctor.

And Jake didn't need Belle snapping orders at him. What he did need was more Jack Daniels and his head in the game, nothing but the game. He'd let his guard down and flat-out invited bad luck to walk right up and sit at his faro table.

"Oh, Jake." Belle began to cry.

"Don't waste your tears on me, Belle," Jake said, then poured more whiskey.

The sheriff showed up and walked toward the bar, and Jake.

"Sheriff, wait just a minute," Matthew brushed past the stone-faced lawman, to reach Jake first.

"Cain't find any of the docs, Jake. No sign or nothin' sayin' where they gone," the worried barkeep finished in short, uneven breaths.

"Matthew . . . settle down." Jake spoke through stabs of pain. "Hell, you're gonna need a doc if you don't," he chided his old friend. "I don't need anything . . . that a little more of this can't help me with." When he turned to pour more whiskey he saw the sheriff's reflection in the mirror over the bar.

"Join me, Sheriff?"

Jake didn't bother to turn around to face the lawman, and belted down another drink.

"Jake," the sheriff said, coming to stand right behind Jake. "After you get all fixed up, I'm coming back and we can chaw over this. Don't like anyone dead in my town, legal or otherwise. No, sir. But I've already heard from folks how it all went. Won't be no charges. I'll tell you what, Jake Whiskey," the sheriff added, his tone less serious. "If you down any more of that stuff, I just might have to cite you for drunk and disorderly."

"I know where a doc is." A stranger, a miner judging from his looks, spoke up.

"Where?" Matthew and Belle asked in unison.

"Over in Tent City is a doc. Comes every week and I know the doc is there now."

"Go get the doc, stranger. Will ya?" Matthew said.

"Shore will," the miner agreed and hurried out through the swinging doors.

"And you, Jake Whiskey," Belle pulled his good arm around her shoulder. "You're going upstairs to your room so the doc can tend to you when he comes."

Jake didn't protest. He was getting drunk. Hadn't meant to. He just figured alcohol would kill the pain. Alcohol always did.

Matthew stepped up and took Jake's arm from Belle. The sheriff came up on Jake's other side and the two men grabbed hold and helped Jake upstairs.

Belle was right behind them.

"Clear everybody out," Matthew yelled over his shoulder to one of the dealers downstairs.

Jake wasn't so drunk now that he didn't comprehend what Matthew had just said.

"No," he spoke harshly to Matthew. The pain in his arm

hadn't let up. "Keep the tables going. The liquor . . . poured. The piano . . . playing. And the . . . girls dancing. Old friend," Jake's voice dropped to a whisper, "keep the money . . . coming in . . . all right?"

Amazed at how much liquor the man could drink and still not slur his words, Matthew turned his head and looked behind him, at Belle.

"Keep things goin' 'til I get back."

"Then I'm coming up, Matthew. Soon as you get back," Belle promised, and reluctantly went downstairs.

Zoe-Esther hastily tidied her makeshift examination room inside the tent provided her, gathered up her instruments, medicines, and bandages and replaced them in her medical bag, and then pulled her shawl close around her shoulders. Glad she was finished with her last patient for the day in Tent City, she hurried outside into the brittle November afternoon. The man who had summoned her to the Golden Gates waited for her. She quickly followed him. Instead of it registering in her brain that she actually was being called to minister to somebody outside of Tent City, all Zoe-Esther could think of at the moment was Mr. Whiskey. She hoped against hope that she would not have to see the handsome Westerner again. By the time she reached the Golden Gates and stepped onto the planked porch in front of the saloon, she had convinced herself that Mr. Whiskey was definitely out of town and would not be inside.

"A woman doc?" Matthew didn't even try to hide his surprise and displeasure.

"Yes," Zoe-Esther answered, distracted, and quickly scanned the large, crowded room. She breathed a sigh of relief. Mr. Whiskey was nowhere in sight.

"Well, got no choice," Matthew came up to her. "You'll hafta do."

Free now to be incensed, she was. She made a guess, from the looks of the man's advanced years and his attire, that he might be a bartender here. His vest and the towel stuffed in one of its pockets gave her the hint.

"Lest you lose sight of it," Zoe-Esther said, glaring at the aged barkeep, "I was called here. And you *do* have a choice." The man's words made her mad. She shouldn't stand here and argue with him. She should be attending her patient, but she couldn't help herself. "You can ask me to leave, and I will," she announced, all the while knowing she would not; not before taking care of her patient.

"Don't go gettin' yourself all in a dither, missy. We need ya upstairs," Matthew explained and took hold of her elbow. "This way now. Up ya go."

Zoe-Esther thought of Professor Marsh. This man reminded her of her old professor back in medical school. Professor Marsh had no trouble telling her what to do, either.

Zoe-Esther followed the barkeep upstairs, stopping when he did, in front of a closed, wood-paneled door. The barkeep turned the glass knob and eased the door open.

"The doc's here," the older man announced and kept his hold on her elbow until they reached the patient's bedside.

Oy vey!

Him!

Zoe-Esther couldn't believe it was Mr. Whiskey! He wasn't supposed to be here. He was supposed to be out of town—indefinitely. Scared to death, she didn't know what to do. For a moment she lost sight of why she was there, in his room, and wanted to turn and flee. She was about to do that very thing when someone spoke, drawing her back to the moment.

"Matthew, we need a doctor here, not some . . . not her."

Zoe-Esther looked at the honey-haired, attractive woman. She should be offended by the woman's insult, but right now she warmed to the distraction of it—distraction from Mr. Whiskey. But, Zoe-Esther knew there was nothing to be done for it. She had to deal with this situation and get things over with as fast and she could, and get out.

She watched the way the woman hovered protectively over Mr. Whiskey; so close that the ends of her long hair fanned out over the blanket covering his chest. She looked up and gave Zoe-Esther a disapproving once-over. Her look of disapproval spurred Zoe-Esther to action.

She walked over to the, thanks to God, sleeping, Mr. Whiskey and pulled her wire rims from her skirt pocket. Ignoring the offensive blond woman, Zoe-Esther put on her spectacles. Odd, she thought of George Collins just now; handsome George Collins who lay dead; whom she once thought, for one fleeting moment, could be her match. Odd indeed to think of George Collins at a time like this, at Mr. Whiskey's bedside. What possible reason could there be? When she thought of the reason—that she didn't want Mr. Whiskey to die like George Collins—the notion frightened her.

"What happened to him?" Zoe-Esther asked the blonde, fighting to control her fears. She did her best to sound composed and professional.

The blonde said nothing.

"He was shot about an hour ago," Zoe-Esther heard from the man behind her.

Shot! Maybe he is . . . dead! Zoe-Esther panicked.

But the instant she saw the rise and fall of Mr. Whiskey's chest under the layer of covers over him, she began to calm down. She had to get hold of herself, and keep hold of herself. She looked down at her sleeping patient. His eyes were closed, without so much as a flutter. His hair was rumpled. She wanted to touch it. Her heart began to race, forcing her to remind herself that she was a doctor, here to administer care to her patient. She continued her cursory examination of her patient, of his lop-sided grin under that thick slate mustache, and then smelled . . . alcohol.

Her patient, Zoe-Esther now realized, was dead after all—dead drunk!

"This man has been drinking," she declared.

"Yep, he shore has," the barkeep behind her agreed. "But he's shot an bleedin' all the same."

"Where was he shot? How many times?" Zoe-Esther demanded, and quickly pulled the blanket covering him down to his waist, bared to her now. She ignored his nakedness, anxious to examine him. She found the bullet wound in his right shoulder. Blood seeped out the small hole. Relief washed over her. *Thanks to God, it's not worse.*

"Just once. He was only shot once. Right where you're lookin', " Matthew answered.

"Thank you," Zoe-Esther responded, only now remembering she had asked the question. "Thank you . . ."

"Matthew. Name's Matthew."

"Thank you, Amos," she said, before she could catch herself. "I mean Matthew. Thank you, Matthew." She looked away from Mr. Whiskey and turned around to toss Matthew an apologetic smile.

The blonde hadn't budged.

"Ma'am, I'm afraid you'll have to move," she instructed in her most business-like manner.

Still, the woman didn't budge.

"Belle," Matthew spoke up. "Do as the doc says. Don't worry, she'll take real good care of him."

That's just what Belle was afraid of. She didn't want any woman taking real good care of Jake, except her. From the moment the redhead had set foot inside Jake's bedroom, Belle was on her guard. She wasn't sure against what—yet. But she was determined to stay and find out.

"Matthew, I'll need two basins of boiling water, quick as you can," Zoe-Esther gently commanded.

"Right away," he said and left.

Uneasy, but not unprepared, Zoe-Esther set her medical bag down on the small table by the bed, and opened the black case. She withdrew a clean towel with dressings rolled inside of it, scissors, her packet of instruments, and the items needed for stitching. Lastly, she removed her precious store of phenol. She left the ether in her bag; she didn't need it, since he certainly did not. Even if she had to perform full surgery on him now, he wouldn't need ether to put him out. If he were any more out, he could be dead.

Focusing only on her patient, and on removing her first-ever-bullet without causing her patient further injury, Zoe-Esther, for the moment, forgot about the woman still standing by the bed. She mentally went over the exact steps she needed to follow in order to safely remove the bullet. All of a sudden the heavy scent of rosewater assaulted her, and mixed with the medicinal smells from her medical bag. She looked up, feeling sick. Where on earth . . .

The blonde.

Zoe-Esther didn't think she would ever again favor the scent of rosewater.

"Here ya go." Matthew set the basins of water on the bedstead.

"Thank you, Matthew. Could you bring that other table over here," she asked, nodding in the table's direction. "I need it next to me."

As soon as she had everything set up to her liking, Zoe-Esther was ready to begin. She studied her patient's face, *Mr. Whiskey's face.* She'd conveniently forgotten just who her patient was.

Still sleeping.

Feh . . . still passed out!

A shadow crossed the room and settled on Mr. Whiskey's features.

"No, no, this won't do," Zoe-Esther muttered, once again conveniently forgetting exactly who her patient was. Even with her wire rims on, she needed better light. She looked up. There were two wall sconces, one on either side of her patient's bed. They were already lit, and the light was too dim. She asked Matthew to turn the gas lamps high. As soon as he did, the light was perfect for her to see what she was doing.

Zoe-Esther unbuttoned and rolled the sleeves of her blouse up to her elbows. She took a bar of surgical soap from her medical bag, scrubbing her hands in one of the basins of water provided. She didn't want to introduce any infection to her patient. Clean hands for a clean wound, she reviewed mentally—the work of Pasteur and Lister set firmly in her mind.

First, she cleaned around the injured area, then took great care to examine and ever-so-carefully probe the wound. The bullet was lodged straight in, about an inch and a half. Her patient was lucky it hadn't shattered, or turned, or penetrated major blood vessels. She selected the required instrument from the set of instruments she'd arranged on the nearby table, then expertly removed the

142

bullet. It took her little time. The area looked good and her patient shouldn't have any problems with healing. Satisfied with her work thus far, only one task remained. A few stitches should suffice to close the small opening. The stitches would need to be removed in a week.

After she secured a clean, dry dressing in place over the wound, Zoe-Esther collected her instruments and placed them in the basin of now-tepid water. Taking a clean square of cotton she wiped each instrument with phenol and then returned them to her bag, with a reminder to herself to rewash them later, in boiling water. Busy collecting her things, and finished with her patient, Zoe-Esther was ready to leave. She didn't want to wake her patient. He needed rest.

"Queenie?"

Mr. Whiskey!

Mr. Whiskey is my patient! She quickly sobered to the realization.

Zoe-Esther dreaded turning around to face him. What was wrong with him? Why wasn't he asleep? Under normal circumstances, the turn of her words would have made her laugh—these circumstances were anything but normal.

She finally turned to face him. Her eyes met his slate, heavy-lidded gaze.

"Damned if it isn't you . . . freckles and all." Jake tried to keep his eyes open. He must be good and drunk. He had to be. There wasn't any way Queenie could really be at his bedside. He had to be drunk as a skunk; dreaming her up. Hell, he couldn't remember right now. Shutting his eyes again, he wondered if he were still asleep. But when he reopened his eyes, Queenie was still there. Damn. Did he bring her up to his room? It was a devil of a thing to forget if he had. He sure as hell had thought about it enough since he'd met her. Just then a pain shot through his shoulder, forcing him to remember he'd been shot. Sam Hill. He was having trouble keeping his eyes open. Feeling himself slip, he did his best to stay awake . . . to remember . . .

"Queenie." He wanted her near. "Stay with me," he begged, before everything turned black.

Belle was furious with Jake, and with herself. She'd known something was up the way he ignored her lately, and now she knew the reason: this meddlesome bitch. Angry at the situation, Belle swore she would do something about the redhead. No way would she let this pathetic newcomer invade her territory and take what was hers. *Jake is mine. He's going to marry me.* Jealousy—a first for Belle—welled up inside her. Her clothes suddenly felt too tight, suffocating, in fact.

Embarrassed and shocked by Mr. Whiskey's drunken comments, Zoe-Esther had to get out of there. She mumbled something to Matthew about coming back to check on Mr. Whiskey in a week, and added that Matthew should give Mr. Whiskey lots of broth, and make sure that his bandage stayed clean and dry. Zoe-Esther had nothing to say to the antagonistic blonde and ignored her. She didn't like the unfriendly woman. Quickly now, Zoe-Esther shut her bag, took off her wire rims and replaced them in their case in her pocket, rolled down her sleeves, retrieved her shawl from the chair back, and was out the bedroom door, down the stairs, and away from the Golden Gates in two minutes' time.

All Zoe-Esther wanted was to get home and put as much distance as she could between herself and the Golden Gates. If she hurried she might make it home before dark. The early evening air was freezing. She didn't care, refusing to admit the real reason she needed to flee: Mr. Whiskey.

Frightened by her encounter with Mr. Whiskey—by the fact that she liked him—it frightened her just as much to think what Yitzhak might think if he found out.

Papa wouldn't like it.

She would never tell Yitzhak, or anyone, that she liked Mr. Whiskey. She would forget about him soon enough, she told herself. She would forget her feelings for him and the way goose-flesh rose all over her when he'd called her Queenie.

How did Mr. Whiskey know that she was named after Queen Esther? How could he possibly know? He wasn't a Jew.

There it was—the very reason she should have no thoughts whatsoever about Mr. Whiskey—he was not a Jew.

Chapter Ten

"Papa, what are you doing?" Zoe-Esther hurried inside the cabin and pulled the latch closed.

"Doing, what do you think? I am making a nice glass of tea," Yitzhak answered then stoked the fire under the kettle suspended over it.

"Papa, let me do that." Zoe-Esther rushed over and took the iron poker out of his hand. "You sit now and rest. I'll get your tea."

"Star, I can get my own tea," he told her, then sat down in the nearby rocker. "Rest, rest. It is all I have been doing for weeks. Rest inside, rest outside," he went on. "Watching you work yourself to death running down the hillsides to town and then back up with a pail of milk for me and more sewing orders so you can stay up all night and work on them. And now, now you take care of the poor miners and their families, for nothing. Feh! So much *tzedakah*, so much charity for everyone but yourself."

Happy to learn he had so much breath left in him and to hear him kvetch again, she wasn't happy to hear what he complained about: her. She didn't like that he worried so much. Better he should worry over himself than over her.

"Papa," she rose from the bench but couldn't look him in the eye. "I'm fine and you know it. A little hard work never hurt anyone," she tossed out matter-of-factly and began busying herself around the cabin, hoping he would drop the subject.

"Sit, Star. Sit and talk with your old Papa. The water, it will boil without you. Now sit."

"Yes, Papa," she said reluctantly and pulled the bench out from where she'd just pushed it under the table.

"Child," he paused and waited for her to sit. "I am well now. It is time that I helped you."

His faded blue eyes held a twinkle. Yes, he was improved, but not well.

"Things would be easier for you, better for you if we found a little place in Golden City. What kind of life do you have here, alone in these hills with your papa? You should be with Daniel now, not me. And work, work, work. All you do is schlep back and forth, up and down. *Kayn*, Star, this is not good for you."

"Papa." Zoe-Esther didn't know what to protest first. She couldn't believe he'd brought up Daniel. She had thought so little about Daniel since their move west, and had assumed Yitzhak had done the same. Obviously, her papa had not forgotten Daniel. But more pressing now, she must make sure her papa's health continued to improve.

This conversation wasn't going to be easy.

The water in the kettle boiled.

Zoe-Esther got up and fixed Yitzhak his glass of tea, and then handed it to him.

"It wouldn't be wise to move to town yet, Papa. It's too soon. Yes, you are better, but you are not fully recovered. This pure mountain air you breathe every day and every night is working its wonders. You need more time to recuperate. Please, Papa," she implored.

Yitzhak seemed to listen to his daughter. He took another sip of the steaming tea.

"If I stay in these hills, then I work, Star. I will do things to help or I will not stay," he said emphatically.

"All right, but only light chores."

"All right," Yitzhak smiled over his glass. "Now we make progress. Now we can talk of Daniel."

"Daniel?" She tried to hide the strain in her voice.

"Of course, Daniel," Yitzhak said. "Daniel Stein, your future husband, my future *eydem*. Who else should I bring up? What other nice young man have you met? What other young man have you agreed to stand with under the *chuppah*?" he asked in a good-natured, fatherly manner.

Zoe-Esther's insides warred between two names: *Mr. Whiskey and Yaakov.*

Only one could stand with her under the marriage canopy, and it could never be Mr. Whiskey. She tried her best to conjure Yaakov's image, but the image of Mr. Whiskey, with his rugged good looks and tall, muscled frame, came to mind. Feh! Disgusted with herself for pondering the idea of ever marrying any man, even her Yaakov—a man who in all likelihood didn't even exist and whom she would never meet anyway—Zoe-Esther tried to dismiss both Yaakov and Mr. Whiskey from her thoughts.

"Star," Yitzhak said, picking up where he left off as if there had been no pause in the conversation. "I think when Daniel comes we can have a kosher wedding, even out here in this wild country. Some of the immigrants on the wagon trains are Jews. Surely God will include a rabbi or two among the flocks," he smiled at her.

When Daniel comes! Oh, Papa. God forbid you are serious!

"Papa, when is Daniel coming?" she asked, trying to cover her utter panic at the idea that Daniel really might come west.

"Oh," Yitzhak looked straight at her now, as if to underscore his intent. "When you send for him, then he will come and you can marry."

Relief washed through Zoe-Esther so forcefully, she needed to sit down again.

Yitzhak's brow furrowed. His tone turned serious.

"Only one tradition, little Star, would I have wished for. That the *schadchen* could have made the match between you and Daniel."

She knew Papa thought now of his beloved Sarah, and not of her and Daniel.

"It is a tradition we had to leave behind in the old country," Yitzhak sighed, his shoulders slumping. "But with your Daniel," he said, brightening, "with your Daniel you will have a nice kosher marriage and your mama will smile down and bless you both."

Zoe-Esther didn't agree—on the nice kosher marriage or that her *ema* would bless such a union—a union without love.

"Do not make it so long before you send for your Daniel," Yitzhak added in light-hearted admonition. "I am not getting any younger, and who knows, I could get sick again."

Zoe-Esther watched him watch her as he spoke and refused to feel any guilt over his plea to her, to hurry and summon Daniel.

"You know children would bring such joy and *naches* to this old man. A *zayde*, a grandfather, I would like to be."

"Papa, how late it gets, and me with no supper on the table." She tried to make light of his last comment, doing her best to hide how upset she was over what he said. That he worried over grandchildren, and that he expected grandchildren, she had never thought of such things: of having children. *Oy vey, Papa!* It grew dark in the cabin, despite the kerosene lamp on the table she'd lit only moments before. Zoe-Esther hurried outside to get more wood to place on the ebbing fire in the hearth, glad for something to do to take her mind off her papa's worries over her being married and giving him grandchildren.

"*Nu?* What shall it be, Papa? I think borsht and a little potato would be nice," Zoe-Esther decided and pulled down off the nearby shelf the covered Mason jar of beet soup she'd made earlier in the week.

"Star," Yitzhak said behind her.

He wasn't finished with their conversation, she suspected. She took the cover off the Mason jar and listened, not wanting to hear anything more about Daniel.

"Star. Soon. Soon, send for Daniel."

"Yes, Papa," she answered him with a lie. *Please forgive me, Papa. I am not a good daughter to tell you such a lie.*

"Doc will be here in a few minutes, Jake. Sit tight," Matthew ordered.

Jake didn't feel like sitting tight and he still didn't believe Queenie was a doc. As soon as Matthew told him, he knew his old friend was pulling a fast one on him. Any moment it would be Doc Pritchard or Doc James coming through the swinging double doors to his place.

Not Queenie.

His shoulder was still a little sore, but considering he'd been shot less than a week ago, he felt pretty damn good. The hangover he'd had from trying to dull all the pain hurt worse than the bullet. Seated now at his faro table, he lit up a smoke and shuffled a fresh deck of cards.

"How many you letting in your first game, Jake?" Belle

sauntered up and placed a possessive hand on his uninjured shoulder.

The heavy scent of rosewater cut into his enjoyment of his smoke. The two didn't mix as well as they used to.

"Hello, Belle," Jake said, but didn't look up from his cards.

"Don't you mean Golden Girl, Jake? I'm still your Golden Girl, aren't I, Jake?"

Less in the mood for this conversation than a session with the local doc, Jake knew he had to end things with Belle. Soon as the doc left, he'd sort it out with her.

"You're still the most beautiful Golden Girl in Golden City," Jake said, and pushed his hat brim back, and looked into her teary blue eyes. Damn, he'd never seen her cry. *Hell, she'll be crying later, too, I reckon.*

"Jake," Belle sniffled. "I need to know if—"

"Doc's here," Matthew called out from the bar and interrupted Belle.

Just in time, thought Jake.

The moment Jake looked from Belle toward the front doors of his saloon, he felt like he'd been gunshot all over again.

Queenie!

Zoe-Esther nodded at him and began to make her way, medical bag in hand, through the crowded saloon.

Jake rose from his chair and tipped his hat in her direction.

Belle didn't miss Jake's immediate reaction to the dowdy, skinny, trespassing redhead.

"How are you doing, Mr. Whiskey?" Zoe-Esther spoke first, her nerves all jittery and on end. She knew her voice was shaky. When she looked into the gray lure of his eyes, she fought to keep steady and remember her purpose: a house call, and nothing more.

"I'm good," he finally said.

"Good?" she parroted.

"Yeah, Queenie," he drawled in a hoarse undertone.

Embarrassed, flushed, and feeling goose flesh crop up all over, Zoe-Esther looked down at her hands, her feet—anything but his handsome visage. He was her patient, for pity's sake, and not some beaux. Swallowing what little pride she had left, despite her schoolgirl behavior, she raised her eyes to meet his gaze once again.

"Mr. Whiskey, I need to examine you," she said, hoping her voice didn't quiver as much as her insides did.

"Is that a fact?" The corners of his mustache worked into a slow grin. "Well now I just don't know if I oughta let just any woman touch me," he teased.

"I'm not a woman, I'm a doctor," she blurted before she could stop herself.

"I'm afraid I can't agree on that, Queenie," he said, his voice low and intimate. "I don't know about the doc part, but you're a woman for sure."

His last words vibrated up and down her spine. She felt warm and flushed. No matter, she was here to see him as her patient. She must keep that foremost in her mind, she told herself, all the while praying her face hadn't turned crimson. What else was it Mr. Whiskey had just said? That he didn't know about the doc part? It piqued her anger, enough to help her control her attraction to him.

"Mr. Whiskey, if you choose to think I'm not a doctor, then perhaps you should make another choice. Whether I should stay or leave."

"Hold on, Queenie, I didn't say that," Jake's smile went away. "I want you to stay."

She'd heard him say that before. A week ago, to be precise. Only this time, he wasn't *shikeh;* he wasn't drunk. Her heart began to hammer in her constricted chest. She couldn't find a good breath. The more she studied him—held to the spot by the tantalizing twitch at the corners of his mouth, the invitation in his heated gaze, and the magnetic pull of his powerful, masculine frame—the more undone she felt.

"Let's go upstairs," Jake said.

Unprepared for his salty command, Zoe-Esther froze. She wasn't ready for . . . for *that.*

"Come on, Queenie, unless you want to look me over down here, I think we oughta go upstairs to my room," he teased.

Of course. The exam. Of course.

She felt ridiculous for thinking he meant anything else.

"Yes, your room will do." It took everything in Zoe-Esther to sound nonchalant. This was awful. How could she get through it? How could she hide all she felt for this man who was her opposite in every way? She drew her shaky fingers into little fists against her already cold, clammy palms.

Belle had heard enough and had had enough.

"Yes, let's go upstairs," she said coolly.

"I don't need you," Jake said too quickly. "Belle, you don't need to, that's all. I'm fine and I know you've got better things to do right now."

It hurt like a slap across the face and a punch in the stomach—both at once. Belle fumed inside. *Doesn't need me? We'll just see about that, Jake Whiskey. We'll just see.* Belle watched as the skinny, prudish, interloping doc followed *her* man up the polished staircase.

Something would have to be done about the Doc, and soon.

★ ★ ★ ★ ★

Zoe-Esther followed her patient up the steps and tried to concentrate on anything but him, to help ease her frazzled nerves. Once inside his room all she saw, at first, was his bed. The last time she saw the Victorian, mahogany, four-poster, he was in it—passed out, *shikeh*—and she wasn't alone with him then.

The door shut behind her.

Startled, she whirled around so fast she bumped right into the hard muscled wall of his chest.

"I'm sorry," she whispered and quickly backed away, almost tripping over her own feet.

"I'm not," he said.

"Oy vey," she muttered, unaware she'd even opened her mouth. This was the single worst moment of her life, and perhaps the best. Shaggy hair, slack mustache, rough edges and all, Mr. Whiskey affected her in ways she shouldn't be thinking.

"Well?" he broke into her disturbed thoughts.

"Well what?" she said, her mind blank.

"Where do you want me?" He took a step toward her.

She took one away from him.

He took a second one.

So did she.

"Queenie, you afraid of me?"

"Afraid of you?" she tossed back her reply as if his question were the silliest thing in the world. Scared to death, she felt like a trapped animal and wanted to escape. Or did she? "I've never been afraid of anything or anyone in my life," she lied to him.

A slow, unnerving grin came over his handsome features.

Zoe-Esther wanted to be irritated and angry with Mr. Whiskey, but she wasn't. Instead other feelings, pleasurable and warm, pulsed through her. Her head felt light, but her arm, the one holding her medical bag, felt heavy; so heavy that any moment her bag would drop to the floor.

Oy gavalt!

Utterly embarrassed at her unprofessional behavior, Zoe-Esther stiffened her spine and gripped her medical bag hard, determined to focus on something other than Mr. Whiskey.

Turning a trained eye to her surroundings, and away from Mr. Whiskey, she realized she hadn't noticed how elegant the room was last week when she had been here. From its marble-top bedsteads, plush burgundy draperies, and ornamental carvings on the large wardrobe, to what she thought might be saber designs on each chair leg, the room dripped with opulence. Specific details eluded her, no matter how hard she tried to bring their fuzzy edges into focus. Unfettered by a lifetime of fuzzy edges and poor vision, Zoe-Esther narrowed her eyes for a closer look: crystal decanters . . . velvet bed coverings . . . beveled mirrors and paintings in gold frames . . . a fine china chamber set . . . and etched glass sconces. Her intense scrutiny of the room began to give her a headache. Thinking better of it, though she couldn't reason why, she set aside her inclination to don her wire rims for a better look at the exquisite room, and instead continued to squint at the craftsmanship of each work of art, crystal design, and graceful stick of furniture.

"Which will it be? My room or me?" Jake lashed out. He'd seen women give his money the once-over before. Hell, he hated that Queenie was just like all the rest. He'd read her wrong, and had thought she was different. No denying it though—the way she sized up everything like she was taking his measure. Under all that book-learned, fine

155

talking, buttoned-up-past-her-neck get-up, he realized Queenie was nothing more than a gold-digger. Disappointed in Queenie, and in himself for letting her get this close, he wanted to get her out of his room, now.

"Oh, I'm sorry, Mr. Whiskey," Zoe-Esther said, puzzled by the change in his tone and self-conscious that he caught her staring at the things in his room. "You, Mr. Whiskey," she tried to answer his question, even though she didn't understand what he meant by it. If only she didn't know how stupid and silly she must sound. Intent on maintaining some degree of decorum, Zoe-Esther squared her shoulders, and gripped her medical bag even tighter.

"Please," she spoke quietly. "Sit here on the edge of the bed, Mr. Whiskey, and remove your shirt so that I may have a look at your wound."

Zoe-Esther turned her back to him and set her medical bag down on the bedstead, and opened the heavy case. She couldn't help but wonder what caused the change in his expression and demeanor. His icy treatment upset her. All of the delightful warmth she felt only moments before, vanished. Disturbed by his moodiness, and her reaction to him, she had to escape this lion's den as soon as she could. Working quickly, she took her suture removal scissors and a fresh dressing from her bag, then turned around to tend to Mr. Whiskey's wound.

She thought she was prepared to minister to him, but she wasn't.

The moment she turned around, the impact of what she saw overwhelmed her. With his shirt off, naked to the waist, Mr. Whiskey looked wonderful—more than wonderful. She didn't need her wire rims to experience the heady impact. His body seemed sculpted right out of the pages of her prized anatomy books, whose drawings, like him, were perfect. She'd never imagined the beauty of the male in a flesh-and-blood man. Not like this. Not with toned muscles in such faultless proportion, hardy, pulsing veins in all the right places, an exact distribution of dark bristled hair over his chest, a powerful neck, a regal head, and sheer male prowess emanating from every cell and pore. She could only imagine the rest of him.

The way Queenie looked at him just now—Jake really wanted to get her out of his room. When a woman eyed him the way she did, he usually had her in his bed, not standing next to it. He fought the urge to encircle her tiny waist in his fingers and pull her to him.

"Hurry up, I've got business downstairs," he didn't try to hide the edge in his voice, or the hostility.

"Yes, of course," Zoe-Esther knew she'd been caught staring again, and winced inside at the unwelcome, unmistakable flush on her face.

"Just let me, just let me—" She fumbled in her pocket to find her wire rims, very relieved when she finally did. "I just need to put these on." Zoe-Esther held up her spectacles for him to see. "It's a strain to see clearly without them," she added, right away upset to have said so much.

He looked more curious to her now than annoyed.

"You need to wear those?"

"Yes, it helps to see things clearly, Mr. Whiskey, especially in my profession," she answered his indignant question, a bit irked by it. On top of everything else, she didn't need to hear criticism over needing to wear spectacles.

He smiled now.

The room warmed up, and so did she.

Zoe-Esther didn't understand the sudden change in him: one minute cold, and the next friendly. What changed his mood? Surely it couldn't have anything to do with her spectacles. Yet, he seemed so interested in the fact that she needed to wear them. What could her vision, or lack of it, have to do with anything? Whatever the reason for his change in attitude, and the grin that he wore now on his handsome face, she was grateful Mr. Whiskey no longer seemed upset with her.

"Okay, Doc," he said in a teasing voice, "I'm all yours."

Zoe-Esther swallowed hard, then set to work.

The wound looked good. No redness, swelling, or signs of infection. The stitches appeared clean. No problems with circulation to the area.

"Mr. Whiskey, please raise your right arm for me, very slowly," she advised, concentrating so hard on her examination, she was unaware she'd taken hold of his arm to help guide it. "Good, very good. You're healing nicely and have no restriction in the use of your arm." She let go of him, oblivious that she'd touched him yet again. "Let me get these sutures out," she said, then snipped the knots of the sutures in a matter of seconds. "There, all done. You won't need a dressing. Just keep the area clean and dry and continue to exercise your arm. If you detect any change in the wound or develop pain upon movement, please send for me."

"Oh, you can bet I will," Jake said, his voice ragged and low.

His words had the same effect on Zoe-Esther as an open vial of ammonia under her nose. So did his smoky scrutiny. Desperate to escape both, she looked away, remembering now who he was and where she was.

"I have to go, Mr. Whiskey," she whirled around and grabbed up her supplies and shoved everything into her medical bag. Usually she meticulously collected her things, washed them, and replaced them with care. Nothing, Zoe-

Esther recognized, was at all usual about this situation.

"Wait, Queenie. Please."

She clamped her bag shut but didn't turn around. If she did, she'd have to look at him again and she wasn't sure right now if she could and keep her feelings for him a secret. The professional barrier that existed between them only moments before, the barrier that kept him at a safe distance, tumbled away and left Zoe-Esther with nothing but her unmistakable attraction for him.

He mustn't know.

Papa mustn't know.

No one must know.

"Please, Queenie," Jake urged and put his hands on her shoulders, turning her around to face him.

She'd forgotten to take off her spectacles.

Cute. Those spectacles were damn cute on her, Jake decided. Suited her. They'd moved down her little freckled nose, and he gently pushed them back up.

Zoe-Esther yanked off her wire rims and fumbled in her pocket for her case to put them away.

"Queenie," Jake forced himself not to touch her again. "You don't have to do that. Those spectacles are about the most beautiful thing I've ever seen on a woman."

"You're a joker, Mr. Whiskey," she managed to say, despite her tight throat.

"I don't joke, Queenie, not about that."

"About what, Mr. Whiskey?" She wished she knew his meaning. And she wished he'd put on his shirt. "I have to go."

"No. Not yet," his husky command stilled her.

"I'll stay a moment if you'll get dressed, Mr. Whiskey," she said, bewildered by her own reply, and gave him her back.

Jake liked this woman. A lot.

"All right," he conceded.

"All right, then," she slowly pivoted until she faced him again.

"Queenie, where did you come from?"

"From Philadelphia," she offered.

"No, I mean—"

"Before Philadelphia?" Her nerves made her interrupt him. "From Russia. I came from a village outside of Kiev."

"No, Queenie, I mean you. How did you, a woman, a doc and all, get here, in my room, in my life?"

Mr. Whiskey's low, whiskey-voiced question threw her insides into turmoil. Except for a sip or two of ceremonial wine at each Shabbas meal, she had never partaken of strong drink. Why did she feel as if she just had?

"I hardly think, Mr. Whiskey—" Thrills shot through Zoe-Esther. She dared not acknowledge what he'd just said to her. No one, not even Daniel had ever said anything so intimate.

"Don't think, Queenie. Just tell me," Jake urged and took a step closer.

Zoe-Esther couldn't move. She didn't want to. It went against everything she stood for in life to be in his room now, no longer doctor and patient, but man and woman. If she stayed only for a moment, would it be so wrong?

Jake took her heavy bag from her, and set it down on the table nearby.

Zoe-Esther had nowhere to look, to turn now, but to him. Pulled in by everything about him, his slow smile, his male scent, his powerful physique, she felt herself submitting to him.

"Queenie, I'm gonna kiss you now," he warned in a thick whisper.

The excitement of his intimate promise vibrated all up and down her spine. At that moment she knew that no power on earth—not her papa or the matchmaker—could stop him from kissing her, or her from wanting him to.

Chapter Eleven

Swept up in currents of desire, with anticipation and excitement riding on each pleasurable wave, Zoe-Esther tried to imagine what Mr. Whiskey's kiss, his touch, would do to her.

She had never been kissed.

Hypnotized by his penetrating slate gaze, as if he already touched her, her eyes didn't leave his. But the moment he lowered his head to kiss her, she struggled to keep her lids open. When he hesitated, holding his mouth just over hers, she gave in to his power and shut her eyes, waiting—for what, she had no way of knowing.

Her body wanted this. *She* wanted this. Suddenly anxious, Zoe-Esther realized Mr. Whiskey would find out one of her secrets: that she didn't know how to kiss a man! What if he found her wanting? She wasn't beautiful like the haughty blonde woman downstairs. She wasn't experienced in the ways of men. She didn't know what men wanted or needed. Maybe she didn't want this to happen. Maybe this *shouldn't* happen. Panic and doubt made Zoe-Esther open her eyes. His mouth on hers made them close, chasing away all panic and doubt.

Tiny rivers of excitement sprang anew from every virgin nerve in her, creating a tide that could not be turned, and giving Zoe-Esther the answer she needed. She did want this to happen. Her heart raced faster. Her quick breaths matched his. The soft brush of his mustache tickled her face. Magnetic, strong fingers under her chin kept her mouth steered to his. Drawn to him, unable to stop herself even if she had wanted, she opened her mouth to him—and, all the rest of her.

Caught up in the sweet sensation of his demanding warm lips, at first she barely felt his splayed fingers on her back. He tasted wonderful, like ginger tea spiced with mint and tobacco leaf. The savory pleasure spread through her. She wanted more. The gentle, driving force of his tongue guided hers to imitate him, and when she did, any control she had left, left her. Now a hungry lioness in the lion's den, willingly trapped, no one and nothing else could compare to this moment.

Zoe-Esther felt alive, reborn in Mr. Whiskey's arms. Here she could live and here she could die. Each touch of his masterful hands brought new arousal to her already stirred mind and body, and all previous existence ceased to exist.

The same pulsing rhythm she felt at the touch of his guiding lips and tongue circulated ever downward, each pulse building into its own crescendo of agonized sensation. Her body kindled and flamed. Unbidden, her arms tightened around his neck. She stood on tiptoe and melted into his kiss, into him.

When he pulled the grosgrain ribbon from her hair, she didn't care. When he lowered his hands down her back, using slight, then more forceful pressure, she didn't care. When his hands found her derriere and he pressed her to him, there, she didn't care. Despite the thick layers of her skirt and gatkes, she felt his stirred manhood against her, and still, she didn't care.

Only one worry gripped her now: that any moment he might stop.

Any moment the sensual caress of his lips, the delicious pain in her breasts, the wanton desire in her female center, the intense emotion consuming her, might end. Somewhere in her mind Zoe-Esther knew it had to be wrong to feel like this, to behave like this, to covet a man she hardly knew so much she dare not let go.

"Jake, ya in there?" Matthew called out, and rapped on the door.

"Jake," he rapped harder. "Belle's right behind me and havin' a cat fit."

Jake heard Matthew, but he didn't want to.

He had to let Queenie go, but he didn't want to.

Not now. Not yet.

He'd never kissed, or been kissed, like this. Something inside of him burned all hot, raw, and unleashed. Not just where her honeyed mouth molded against his, or where her passionate curves pressed against him, but all over. Damn. This hand he'd just been dealt—this game, this woman—he hadn't bargained on.

Never play with the Queen of Hearts.

The familiar warning flashed across his brain, but it was too late. Queenie wasn't just in his arms, but already in his blood, warming it and heating it to a boil. Instinct told him that only she could put out the wildfire raging inside him now. One sip, one drink from her soft lips, wasn't enough, not enough at all. Good luck or bad, he had to take this faro hand, and her, to his bed.

"Jake," Matthew called out again.

Jake finally broke their kiss, but kept Queenie's yielding body pressed against his. It felt like the most natural thing in the world to be doing this, to be with Queenie. The way she held onto him, leaning into him like she was a part of him, made him ache in places he hadn't before. Damn. He wished he could answer the question he read in her misty eyes and on her sweet, flushed face, with his kiss, with his body. Right now, right here, in his room, in his bed. He wanted, no, he needed to be inside her. He'd burn up and go crazy if he couldn't, and he knew it.

"Jake, c'mon. Belle's here and there's a fella downstairs that needs to see the doc," Matthew yelled now.

Damn Matthew. Damn Belle. And damn everybody else.

Jake wanted to yell, too—for Matthew and Belle both to go away. But he didn't feel like saying anything yet and break his hold on Queenie.

The thunderous bellow outside the door penetrated Zoe-Esther's aroused state and jerked her, cruelly and without mercy, back to the real world.

Instant and utter humiliation over what just occurred between her and Mr. Whiskey circled and twisted inside her shaken body and bound her forever to this impossible moment. Embarrassed beyond anything, ever, in the whole of her life, she didn't know what to do or say. What had come over her? What had suddenly possessed her to throw herself into this man's arms? What had taken such control of her that she had lost all of her own? One thing she did know: Mr. Whiskey had some kind of power over her, the kind that robbed her of all rational thought and rational behavior.

A wanton, a strumpet, a harlot, a loose woman! *Drek! Trash! Shmootz!*

Every description that she could conjure applied to her immoral behavior. Worse, on some level in her troubled thoughts, she couldn't reconcile the fact that Mr. Whiskey had awakened the woman sleeping inside her—each kiss making her impatient for the next, each caress stirring her desire for the one to come. Oppressive guilt took firm hold. She had to get out of there, and away from Mr. Whiskey. Willing herself not even to think what he must be thinking about her, she looked toward the door and her escape.

"I have to go." Zoe-Esther wrenched out of his arms and backed away. "Mr. Whiskey, I—" She couldn't think straight. Completely *farmisht* and confused, she made a dash for the door.

"Queenie, no. Don't go."

This time Mr. Whiskey's words didn't stop her.

"Queenie, please," Jake begged.

His plea fell on deaf ears.

She reached for the glass knob.

He caught her hand before she could turn it, and whirled her around to face him, then let go.

With her back only a hair's breath from the door, Zoe-Esther pressed against the unforgiving wood in a vain attempt to keep a safe distance from him—as if there could ever be such a thing—ever again.

"You come out or I'm coming in," Zoe-Esther heard, no felt, the unfriendly vibrations against her backbone. A woman's voice this time.

The blonde.

Zoe-Esther's response was visceral and immediate. She shot an accusing glance at Mr. Whiskey, her accusation rooted more in jealousy, than in his preventing her departure just now. On top of everything else, on top of her degradation and humiliation in expressing such blatant desire only moments ago, she was jealous! How could this be? How ever did she get herself into this *mishegaz?*

The longer she stared up into Mr. Whiskey's handsome,

intense visage, the longer she met his magnetic slate gaze, felt his quick, warm breaths on her face, and took refuge in the shadow of his powerful body, she knew exactly how and why she'd gotten into this fix. And she'd have to pay for it for the rest of her life—sentenced to dreams of him, only him.

"Queenie," Jake whispered and reached for her.

"Don't. Don't touch me, Mr. Whiskey."

Her words stopped him.

Relieved when they did, she rushed with her next.

"This, this was a mistake, Mr. Whiskey. I should never have come. It was wrong of me."

He straightened and backed away, his features unreadable now.

Zoe-Esther should have been glad for it, but she was not.

The blonde hammered on the door again. The knob rattled against Zoe-Esther's spine. Unable to brave another look at Mr. Whiskey, she clamped her fingers on the knob, unlocked the door and yanked it open, hurrying past the man and woman who stood just outside. She refused to brave a look at the two of them either, and ran down the stairs and out the front doors of the Golden Gates.

Not until cold winds slapped her in the face and stung her back to her senses, did Zoe-Esther slow down and realize she did not have her shawl or her medical bag with her. And she hadn't checked on the patient supposedly waiting downstairs in the saloon to see her. A block away from the Golden Gates now, she wasn't about to return. But then, shouldn't she?

A man shouted at her back.

My patient?

She stopped.

"Doc. Doc."

She quickly turned and recognized right away who it was.

Matthew. The barkeep.

He held her shawl and medical bag in his outstretched hands.

"Here ya . . . go . . . Doc," he offered in-between breaths. "Oh, and that fella . . . who was wantin' to see ya . . . said he'd catch ya next time."

Zoe-Esther accepted her things, glad no one required her immediate services, and tried to smile at Matthew's kindness. It was hard to summon a smile. Dejected and embarrassed, she managed to find her voice.

"Thank you, Matthew."

"You're shore welcome, Doc," he replied.

His faded blue eyes reminded her of someone: Papa. Zoe-Esther sensed Matthew had more to say to her, but he kept silent. Puzzled by his behavior, she smiled at him.

"Goodbye," she extended her hand.

Matthew shook it.

"Real glad ya fixed Jake up, Doc. Yessir. I mean yes ma'am," he corrected, sheepishly. "If anybody in this town could use fixing up, it's Jake for shore."

Zoe-Esther retrieved her hand and flexed her fingers. They felt numb, just like her head.

She didn't register what Matthew said, about how Jake could use fixing up. All she heard was his first name.

Jake. *His name is Jake.*

Disappointment piled onto everything else. Of course his name wouldn't be, couldn't be—*Yaakov.* Never would the *schadchen* tell her to make a match with anybody named Jake Whiskey.

Never.

Zoe-Esther wondered how she could have ever wished,

even in the secret recesses of her soul, that Jake Whiskey could have been her intended match. Impossible. Ridiculous. *Mishuga.* Yet somehow she must have done so, otherwise she wouldn't feel so awful now. Why else would she have so willingly given herself to him?

Oy vey! Would I have? If he had wanted me . . . would I have?

Her answer scared her worse than anything else had scared her on this horrid day.

"Ya all right, Doc? Is somethin' wrong?"

Matthew's question pulled her back to the moment.

"Why no, I'm fine. Thank you," she lied, then quickly turned away from Matthew, and hurried along the muddy street. Paying no mind to the darkening day, with dashed hopes as her only escort, Zoe-Esther trudged up the lonely path toward home, unfazed by cold winds and the distant howl of wolves.

Jake's attempt to clear things up with Belle turned into a disaster. Even before her rants and raves over Queenie, he'd known that what he and Belle had shared together was over. *Damn.* If he'd wanted her out of his life before, he sure as hell wanted her out now.

Belle hissed and spat like a wounded animal ready for a fight.

"You're a son of a bitch, Jake. A no-good son of a bitch."

Belle paced back and forth in his room. He'd let her get this off her chest, and then he would get her out. She didn't seem pretty to him anymore; her looks faded with each ugly word that came out of her once irresistible mouth.

"A year. A whole year we've been together and you turn away from me for that . . . that plain, skinny excuse for a doc. You don't even know if she is a doc, any way. My guess is she ain't."

"Belle, hold on," Jake walked toward her. She was wrong on all counts.

Belle set her feet squarely apart, put her balled fists on her hips, and faced him.

"Belle, you got no cause to put the doc anywhere in this. This is between you and me, and has been for weeks. We were through before. So don't go blaming the doc."

"I don't believe you, Jake. I won't listen to this. We were . . . we were supposed to get married, you and me." Tears began falling down her unhappy face.

Damn. Don't Belle. Don't.

"Oh Jake, I'm sorry."

She thrust herself against him and threw her arms around his neck before he knew what hit him. Out of instinct he pushed her clammy, clinging body from him.

"It won't work, Belle, not your tears or your words. There was never any plan between us to get hitched, and you know it. Damnit, Belle, neither one of us is meant for love or marriage. You got your profession, one that brings you respect and money, and I got mine. Gives me the same thing."

When she began to calm down, he assumed she'd heard him and agreed with him. She didn't seem to be spoiling for a fight anymore.

"Well fine, Jake. If you say so, then fine," Belle said all smooth and easy, like fresh-churned butter.

Her tears dried and her mood changed.

Jake didn't know what her change in mood meant, but he knew he didn't trust it.

"Yes, fine," she cooed as she stiffened her back and put her hands to her hair and tidied it. "I'll just go now. I've got a hundred things to do and a hundred men to do them with."

Her strange laugh didn't ease his building mistrust. And if she meant to hurt him with the mention of other men, it didn't work.

"Papa, please. It's late and I'm tired. We can talk tomorrow." Zoe-Esther scooted her bench out, rose from the table, and cleared the cups and bowls as fast as she could. If she hurried to clear the table, then her papa might not press this conversation. She hadn't wanted to have this discussion before, and she definitely didn't want to have it tonight.

"Star. Child, sit back down. The dishes they can wait. I know you are weary, but I also know you have troubles. I can see *tsuris* written all over your beautiful face. Come, tell your old papa what brings you such a heavy heart?"

Blessed, wonderful Papa.

To say anything to him now, to confess how she had just thrown herself into the arms of Jake Whiskey, a saloon owner and a gambler, and worse—not of their faith—and to reveal what a fool she'd just made of herself, would only bring distress to her papa. He was doing so well, in remission from tuberculosis, she hoped, and she dared not do or say anything to upset him and cause his symptoms to recur.

Zoe-Esther did what her papa wanted and sat back down.

"Star," Yitzhak reached across the table and took one of her hands in both of his aged, fatherly ones. "I know when my daughter is unhappy. I see how hard you work, for little or nothing, caring for me, and for the poor in the town. I see you walking, day in and day out, so many miles, no matter the weather. I see all of this and I do not like it,

171

child." Yitzhak released her hand and put an endearing finger under her chin. "My beautiful daughter," he tilted her head up. "Such circles under her lovely eyes, such worry on her little forehead, and such a grim line that hides her smile."

Zoe-Esther brushed his hand away, uncomfortable under his close scrutiny. The last thing she wanted was for Papa to worry over her.

"Papa, you're mistaken. I haven't been sleeping enough. That is all. As for exercise, I get plenty on my travels between here and Golden City, which is very good for my health. As for my smile, here it is, Papa . . . all for you," she grinned mischievously and got up to give him a big hug and a kiss on the cheek. "Now I'm going to bed, Papa," she announced. "And so must you."

Yitzhak rose, bade his daughter goodnight, and headed toward his room. Sleep, however, would have to wait. He must make a plan: a plan to help his little Star. Before his head touched his pillow, the idea came to him—and he knew exactly what he had to do.

Mad at herself the moment she awakened, Zoe-Esther sat up in her little corner bed and glared at the basket of unfinished embroidery at her feet. Why hadn't she made herself stay awake and finish her work? The order was due today.

"Feh!"

Disgusted with herself, she had succumbed to nervous exhaustion last night, and since she had, she wouldn't get paid today—and she needed the money. Only one thing to do. She would sew all day and get the order to town before nightfall, and before the Sabbath. In no time she'd dressed, tidied her bed, and made breakfast for Yitzhak. As soon as she was finished, she plopped down in the rocker and began stitching C-C-H onto linen toweling. Maybe the Clear Creek Hotel would give her an extension, but she couldn't afford to count on it.

The more Zoe-Esther tried not to think about Jake Whiskey, the more she did. Her usual artistry with her embroidery was turning into a jumble of loose threads and uneven knots.

"Feh! Feh! Feh!"

Exasperated, she dropped her needlework in her lap and glared hard out the oilcloth-covered window, wanting to enjoy a bit of needed morning sunshine. "Feh!" She pushed the window out and then propped it open. The air was cold but she didn't care. Papa was in his bedroom, and wouldn't feel the chill. Zoe-Esther let the sun bathe her face, and took a deep, cleansing breath to help wash away any thoughts of Jake Whiskey.

Jake sat uneasy on Missouri, wondering if he would ever have a decent, peaceful ride again. After yesterday with Queenie, his food tasted bad, his drink tasted worse, he couldn't get his head into faro, and he'd slept little. He gave no thought to his sore shoulder.

" 'A mistake,' Queenie said. 'I shouldn't have come. It was wrong of me,' " Jake mumbled to himself, and gave the reins of the bay mare he had in tow an unnecessary jerk. The handsome mare gave her black mane a shake in protest, but Jake didn't pay her any attention. Two of his men rode up the trail behind him, one on horseback and the other driving a loaded buckboard. He didn't pay them any attention either.

"Don't touch me."

That had wounded him the most, and got to him—deep

down in a place that he didn't like to go.

Damnit to hell.

Queenie was right to say it, and he knew it. From the first time he set eyes on her, he knew it. She was quality and he was anything but. No way she'd ever want somebody like him, growing up on the streets with no ma and pa or decent place to call home. Yeah, it hurt. It hurt badly. He didn't want to see Queenie again, but there was one thing he needed to do, and then he'd steer clear of her.

Zoe-Esther leaned her head against the rocker, pushed her spectacles down a little on the bridge of her nose so she could see over them, and stared off into the distance. The exercise, she believed, helped her weakened eyes. She searched the far horizon for something to focus on, a point of concentration. She found one all right, and it was coming right up the trail. Unable to see the rider with absolute clarity—She didn't have to. She knew right away who it was.

Unmindful of the fallen basket of half-done linens, Zoe-Esther scrambled out of her chair. Her stomach seized. What little breakfast she'd eaten threatened to come up. Her head pounded, and when she put her hands to her temples to stop the pounding, she almost lost her spectacles. First she pushed them back up, then whipped the wire rims off and set them down, paying little attention as to where. Running nervous fingers over her loosened hair, she fumbled in her skirt pocket for her ribbon and hastily pulled her coppery tresses into a tie at the back of her neck.

Yitzhak came out of his room.

"Star, we have company," he announced, excited, and walked briskly towards the cabin door.

"Papa, don't!"

"What is this?" Yitzhak turned and faced her, his look full of surprise.

Zoe-Esther searched for a reply, anything that might make sense.

"Well, Papa . . . I . . . I just don't think we should throw open our door to strangers until we . . . until we are certain they mean us no harm."

"Harm is it?" Yitzhak's brow wrinkled. He walked over to the open window for another look.

Furious with herself for worrying her papa, she rushed over to him.

"Oh," she said, standing alongside Yitzhak and looking out the window. "Now I see who it is. Yes, I know him. Not to worry, Papa. Not to worry," she reassured him, then rushed to the door and pulled it open. She wished Papa would stay inside so she would have a chance to get rid of their "company," all the while knowing full well that he would not.

"Wait, wait, I come," Yitzhak said, and followed her outside.

Determined to find her composure and keep it, Zoe-Esther put a hand over the butterflies in her stomach. Her headache persisted. Out of habit, she reached in her pocket for her spectacles—not wearing them was often the reason for the pain in her head. When she found her pocket empty, she doubted they would help her now, any way.

Not this time.

The day was cold, but the look she saw on Jake Whiskey's face was colder.

Zoe-Esther wrapped her arms around herself, more for protection from his frosty expression than to keep out any winter chill. The closer he came, the tighter she hugged herself, and the more she realized that she had absolutely no protection against him.

Chapter Twelve

"Good morning, Mr. Whiskey," Zoe-Esther greeted in the best everyday voice she could find, forcing a smile that she didn't feel.

He stopped a few paces away from her, and sat silent and stone-faced on his horse.

Odd, but the day had suddenly turned gray. *It suits him,* she thought, as she studied his dark visage that seemed to blend with the smoky clouds and stirred winds gathering around them. Zoe-Esther remembered being in his arms yesterday. Then, he'd brought her the sun and the moon. Today, he brought shadows, shadows that marked the distance between them.

What else did she expect? Did she really think he actually cared for her? A kiss meant nothing to a man like him. Unbidden, the unfriendly blonde's face materialized in front of Zoe-Esther. *Jake Whiskey can have a woman like her. A man like him wants a woman like her—not like me.*

Zoe-Esther shivered. Jake Whiskey's severe gaze boring into her right now didn't help. All at once the cold seemed unbearable to Zoe-Esther, the cold from him, and from the coming storm. Annoyed with herself all over again for her attraction to him, and equally angry that she harbored jealousy over the blonde woman, Zoe-Esther did her best to shake off the bitter chill—and Jake Whiskey. She wanted to get rid of them both.

Yitzhak coughed beside her. She'd forgotten all about Papa. Immediately, she turned toward him.

"Papa, the weather, you must—"

Jake slid off his horse and had his heavy duster wrapped around her before Zoe-Esther could finish what she had to say to Yitzhak.

"Keep it on this time," Jake scolded in his low drawl, and pulled the edges of the greatcoat together at her front; his hands lingering just long enough to awaken more unwanted stirrings in her already anxious body. Instantly the coat's warmth, his warmth, wrapped around her, and set her nerves to riot even more.

"Thank you, Mr. Whiskey." She didn't look at him, keeping her gaze directed downward. "But I can't—"

The moment she began to slip out of the heavy, black greatcoat, he stopped her.

"Yes," Jake warned. "You can."

She could swear she heard him say some other curse word under his breath, but she kept the coat on. She didn't want to make an issue of it in front of her papa.

"Star," Yitzhak spoke up. "You should let your friend stand here all day and not introduce him to me?"

Again, she'd forgotten her papa.

At once guilty over leaving Yitzhak out in the cold and *farmisht* by Jake Whiskey's indomitable, intrusive presence, Zoe-Esther found it hard to swallow, much less to say anything. Never had she imagined these two meeting, ever! There was no reason for it, none at all. Too late now to prevent such an encounter, she felt scared. She took hold of her papa's arm for comfort; holding onto the very person she had wanted to keep her secret from.

What if Papa finds out what I feel for Jake Whiskey?
She knew the answer.
It would send him to an early grave.
She must not let either one—not Papa or Jake Whiskey—ever find out. When her firm resolve replaced her jittery nerves and weak knees, she let go of Yitzhak's arm. Whatever she said now, whatever she did, she must take great care.

"Of course, Papa." She forced a smile, acting as if no time had passed since her papa had spoken. "This is Mr. Whiskey, Jake Whiskey," she said in a matter-of-fact tone, keeping her eyes on her papa. She needed one more moment, just one more, before she looked up at Jake Whiskey.

Yitzhak took a step forward.

"It is *gut* to meet you, Mr. Whiskey. I am Zoe-Esther's papa, Yitzhak Zundelevich." Yitzhak made his own introduction and held out his hand.

Zoe-Esther watched the two men shake hands, as any two strangers would do under any normal circumstances. And that is just what this meeting between the two would be: normal. She would make sure of it.

"Mr. Whiskey was a patient of mine in Golden City, Papa." Zoe-Esther hurried with her explanation. "He is not from Tent City. He is a business owner. I just happened to be the only doctor in town the day he was hurt."

"Well *gut*, Mr. Whiskey," Yitzhak smiled at him. "Such *mazel* for you. My Star is an excellent doctor. She keeps me *gesundheit, kayn* easy task."

"Papa uses some Yiddish words, Mr. Whiskey," Zoe-Esther was quick to explain. "He speaks of his good health, that is all." Unable to avoid his eyes any longer, she finally looked at Jake.

"Yiddish?" Jake repeated, far more interested in

178

Queenie's soft, sweet mouth than what she actually said.

"Yes, Yiddish, Mr. Whiskey. It is part of the language of our people," she added, uneasy under his scrutiny. She wet her lips.

"Your people," Jake repeated, distracted by the way her tongue slid across her rosy lips. He wanted to cover them with his own. *Damn.* Bad idea coming here. Bad idea.

"We are Jews, Mr. Whiskey," Zoe-Esther said. She would have looked away from him if she could, but she couldn't. Her mouth went dry. She wet her lips again.

"Jews, yeah, I know." Brought back to the moment, he tried to remember everything Mrs. Bartlett told him about Jews. Uncomfortable with any religious talk, he didn't know a damn thing about God. He wasn't raised that way. Hell, he wasn't raised in any way that counted here, and he knew it.

"*Nu*, Mr. Jake Whiskey, you know of our people? This is a *gut* thing," Yitzhak joined in, wanting to kibbitz with the stranger and become better acquainted. "In Amerika, out here in the West, I do not think so many know of us. It is *gut* that you do."

Jake was having a little trouble with the old man's heavy accent. It was harder to understand than Queenie's.

"Say again where is it you're from?" Jake put his question to Queenie's Pa, but only had eyes for her.

"We come from Russia, Mr. Whiskey. We are Russian Jews," Yitzhak replied. "Do you know of Russia?"

"Not much, Mr. Zun . . . dele . . . vich." Jake worked on pronouncing the name right, embarrassed by his lack of schooling but not too ashamed to look the old man straight in the eye.

"Why?" Zoe-Esther quickly broke in. "Why did you come here, Mr. Whiskey?" She needed to change the direction of the conversation, surprised she actually wanted to defend Jake against any more of her papa's questions.

"I came to pay you for your services, Doc," Jake answered through his tight jaw.

"There's no need, Mr. Whiskey." Zoe-Esther didn't expect this or the rush of disappointment when he didn't call her Queenie.

"Course there is, Doc," he said, only this time the corners of his mouth twitched into a lazy grin.

Disarmed by his enticing smile, Zoe-Esther tried to look away, but she failed. She wondered how he could so easily fuel her anger one minute, yet ignite her fervor for him the next. The longer she looked at him, the more certain she was of the reason. He drew her in whenever she was with him. His slate gaze drew her in. His handsome, mustached countenance drew her in. His perfect, muscled body drew her in. But there was something else about him that drew her in—something she couldn't quite put into words. Her heart skipped faster. If only . . . if only he would touch her again, put his arms around her and take her with him, take her with him wherever he wanted. Her eyes closed and she imagined climbing up behind him on his horse and riding off together, her body pressed close against his, holding on tight, one with him and the rugged west—

Feh! Disgusted with herself over her nonsensical daydreaming, Zoe-Esther opened her eyes to face reality. *Just one more error, one more slip, and Papa will know my feelings for Jake Whiskey.* Jake Whiskey had power over her, the kind to be feared—the kind of fear that could break her heart, and her spirit, if he wanted. All these years she had been afraid of this very thing, only she hadn't been able to put a face on it until now. Now she saw it all on Jake Whiskey's handsome face, and the realization that he held such power over her scared her to death. She wished she didn't want Jake Whiskey. She wished she wanted Daniel Stein. Something else scared her. With all her heart, she wished that Jake Whiskey was her Yaakov—the one chosen for her by the *schadchen*—and she wished that Jake Whiskey were a Jew. But what she wanted, Zoe-Esther knew she could never have.

More importantly, there was Papa. Warning bells rang in Zoe-Esther's ears, loud and clear. Yitzhak would never, ever accept somebody like Jake Whiskey for her. This added a guilt that she could not bear. This heartache she could never bring to her papa.

All of this mishegaz *is for nothing,* Zoe-Esther realized. Jake Whiskey didn't want her. He'd never want her. Not really. Maybe for one night, but not for always, not when he had the blonde and, no doubt, countless others. The pain of this fact hurt in ways Zoe-Esther never imagined on all those nights that she'd lain awake dreaming of just who the matchmaker had in mind for her.

Dreams. That's all they were.

This most unwelcome scene right now was all too real.

"Papa," Zoe-Esther insisted, ignoring the odd looks both men were giving her. "You must go inside. I won't have you sick again."

Yitzhak's puzzled expression over his daughter's surprising lapse into silence turned into a smile the moment she began ordering him around again.

"Child, I am the papa and I say when I go or stay. Now be quiet and be nice and accept Mr. Whiskey's *gelt* so he can be on his way before the storm comes."

Exasperated with his stubbornness, Zoe-Esther knew it was useless to argue with her papa. It took a great deal of effort, but she managed to hold out her hand to Jake Whiskey.

"I'll accept your coin, Mr. Whiskey. Thank you," she said, despite feeling as if she were accepting *tzedakah* instead of a fee.

Feh! Charity.

"Hold it right there," Jake told her and reached for the reins of the bay. The mare stood quietly next to Missouri. "Here," he wrapped the leather straps loosely around Zoe-Esther's still outstretched hand. "She's yours."

"But you can't . . . I can't—" In absolute astonishment, Zoe-Esther stared at the cold strapping laid across her fingers, then followed its line with her gaze to the now skittish animal. The horse reared her head up a little. Zoe-Esther gripped the reins to hold her steady.

"Shhh, hush now," she cooed and stepped forward to put her free hand on the bay's nose, gently rubbing it. "See, I won't hurt you."

The horse whinnied, then settled and began to nuzzle Zoe-Esther's fingers.

"You're a beauty," Zoe-Esther clucked. "And you know it." The gray day did nothing to tarnish the sheen of the animal's reddish-brown coat. The wind gusted again. The bay let Zoe-Esther smooth its luxuriant black mane, ruffled by the stiff breezes.

"I reckon you like her," Jake said under his breath, completely fascinated by Queenie's easy way with the mare.

Zoe-Esther heard Jake.

"Like her," she couldn't hide her pleasure. "Mr. Whiskey—"

"Jake."

"Jake," she conceded, and turned away from the bay, and towards him.

Her smile undid Jake, its aim quick and accurate, causing immediate, agonizing, sweet pain—the kind men killed for. And when she said his name, well it never sounded like that on the lips of any other woman. Damn Blue Blazes. He'd thought he had a pretty good handle on this whole thing with Queenie by the time he'd ridden up, but now he knew he didn't. Right now he wanted Queenie so badly, it was all he could do to keep his hands off her.

He better as hell keep his hands off her—especially with her pa standing right next to them both.

"Mr. Whiskey," Yitzhak abruptly stepped in between Jake and Zoe-Esther. "My daughter accepts your payment."

"Papa!" Zoe-Esther was shocked and embarrassed.

"Don't *Papa* me, Star. You need a horse. Here is a horse," Yitzhak pronounced and crossed him arms in front of his chest to emphasize the finality of it.

"Papa," Zoe-Esther tried to sound calm. She didn't want to have words with him, not in front of Jake Whiskey. "Papa," she repeated. "I cannot accept such payment. We don't need charity. Soon I will buy my own horse—"

"Star, you do not see who brings this needed animal to you? It is God who brings this great gift of *toh vaw*, of kindness, not *tzedakah*. You must say yes," Yitzhak resolved.

"Hold on now," Jake intervened, confused by any talk about God. "No sense getting yourselves all riled about payment for work done. It's not kindness or charity," he said and looked straight into Queenie's nut-brown eyes, momentarily distracted by the coppery flecks he saw dancing in them. He saw something else in their luster, the same willful pride he'd had since he was a kid. His chest tightened at this unexpected bond with Queenie. He swallowed hard.

"Mr. Whiskey," Zoe-Esther found it difficult to hold his gaze. "Mr. Whiskey—"

"Jake."

"Jake," she acquiesced. "I will only accept this horse if you let me pay you, over time, that is." The admission embarrassed her but there was truth in what her papa had said. She did need the bay.

"Yeah, fine," Jake muttered, wanting to end this any way he could. He wasn't going to take a penny from her, but he wouldn't let on just now.

"All right then," Zoe-Esther flashed him another smile. "We have a deal."

Jake's chest tightened again with that same, sweet pain that hit him before, and he couldn't smile back.

"Yeah, we have a deal," he nodded.

"Good," she said and held out her hand.

Jake didn't want to shake her hand. He didn't want to take a chance and touch her, but he had no choice. The instant her hand slipped into his, he cradled it with all the gentleness he could hold on to, fighting the impulse to draw her against him.

"My men came along with me. They're back yonder," Jake said, nodding in their direction but keeping her hand in his.

Zoe-Esther didn't look away from Jake at the two men, one on horseback and the other sitting on the driver's seat of a loaded wagon.

Yitzhak did, and quickly stepped away from his daughter and Jake Whiskey, for a better look.

Zoe-Esther and Jake were alone now.

"I figured you'd need a corral and shelter for the horse so we aim to build them," Jake said with no intention of letting her say no.

"You're right, Mr. Whis—Jake," she corrected and tried to focus on their conversation, not the warm clasp of his strong fingers over hers. "I don't have any provision here for a horse, and so I'll accept your offer but only on one—"

"I know, only if you pay me," Jake finished her sentence for her.

"Yes," Zoe-Esther said, trying to keep her concentration on their conversation and not on her hand in his. His sensual touch made her think of every intimate detail of the day before, every intimacy they'd shared. She went all hot inside. Any moment she'd swoon. She couldn't let that happen. She jerked her hand away so fast that she almost lost her footing.

"We'll just get to it then," Jake said icily, and snatched the bay's reins from her. Without another word he led both horses away, leaving her alone.

Hurt by the unexpected change in his tone and his attitude towards her, Zoe-Esther knew it shouldn't matter to her, but it did. Unable to garner the energy needed to return his coat, she slipped it off her shoulders and took it inside the cabin with her.

Four o'clock and soon it would be dark. The threatening storm held off for most of the day, allowing Jake and his men to build the corral and stable for the bay. Zoe-Esther stayed inside and managed to work on her embroidery. She knew she should take Jake's coat out to him, but she didn't. She didn't think she could handle seeing him again, not yet.

Yitzhak had wandered out several times to watch the construction of the corral, and kibbitz with the men. With so few visitors, he wanted to make the most of the company.

The winds picked up again; this time colder; this time ushering in the much-expected snow.

Glad to have the job done before the weather made it impossible, Jake sent his men back down to Golden City.

He'd just say his good-byes to Mr. Zundelevich, who stood nearby, and then head home himself. No need to see Queenie again.

Yitzhak wouldn't hear of it.

"Jake Whiskey, you must stay and take supper with us. How else can we thank you for your kindness? It grows dark and work is over until sunset tomorrow. And the storm comes. Look, it snows now," Yitzhak held out both his hands and let the flakes begin to pile on them. "You cannot travel on such a night. Come, please, Jake Whiskey."

Jake hadn't figured on this. He didn't mix with the kind of folk that took to inviting folks in for a meal. Caught him pure by surprise, the old man had. Well, he would say no; that's for sure. Simple enough thing to do, refusing Queenie's Pa. If Jake left now he'd beat the worst of the storm down the mountain.

"Come, Jake Whiskey." Yitzhak took hold of Jake's elbow. "It is cold and you need some good hot food on such a night."

Starved his whole life for just such an offer of kindness and attention, and overcome now by boyhood memories— Jake saw himself standing outside all those doors again, all those doors to homes with families inside them, and none ever inviting him in. This memory is what spurred him to lead his horse into the new shelter along with the bay, and then to follow the old man inside, even though Queenie waited there. He forgot all about his decision to leave for Golden City.

Zoe-Esther's back was to the cabin door when it opened. Startled, she turned around right away, unmindful of the burst of cold air. Jumpy all afternoon, about a lot of things, she'd been worried about her papa. She told herself that she was worried he might catch a chill, but really she didn't want him to be outside with Jake Whiskey.

"Papa, it's about time you came in," she scolded. "And here it is time to light—" The sight of Jake Whiskey, walking across their threshold behind her papa, shocked her into silence. She couldn't imagine why he was there. It certainly wasn't to see her again. His behavior earlier had been obvious. He'd turned cooler towards her than the harsh winter night, the moment she removed her hand from his. She certainly knew rejection when it walked up and slapped her in the face, which is precisely why she was so *farmisht* that he'd come back.

"Star, I have asked . . . Jake Whiskey to join us . . . for our . . . Shabbas meal," Yitzhak announced, breathless from his outing. "The storm comes fast now. You should see outside, little Star, the snow falls just like in Mother Russia. And you must see the new stable. It is a true *mitzvot* Jake Whiskey has done for us, Star." Yitzhak hurried over to her and placed a cold kiss on Zoe-Esther's cheek, then bent to warm his hands over the blaze in the hearth.

"Papa." Zoe-Esther didn't try to hide her upset. "You are freezing and you should have come in earlier. I should have come and fetched—"

"Child," Yitzhak stood back up. "Enough."

For the moment she forgot all about Jake Whiskey, almost.

"But Pa—"

"Child, you are a good daughter, a dutiful daughter, but I am the papa. You are a good doctor, a brilliant and beautiful doctor, but I am still the papa. You must not make such a *megilla* over me." He placed another kiss on her cheek and took her hands in his. "Little Star, we are all in God's hands. Yours," he raised her fingers to his cheeks, "are meant for many other things in this life besides caring for your old papa."

"Can I worry a *biseleh,* a little, Papa," she teased him, relieved he appeared well.

"Only a *biseleh,*" he chucked her under the chin, and then grew serious. "Such a *brochah* you are, little Star, a true blessing."

"Blessing or not, Papa, if you don't get out of your wet things, I'll have more water on the floor than in my soup," she lightly admonished, and gave him a gentle shove towards the wooden pegs by the door.

She looked at Jake.

But this Jake Whiskey was much changed from the Jake Whiskey who had walked away from her earlier that afternoon. The expression on his handsome features made her heart wrench; he looked like a child, a lost child who had come in from the cold, dripping wet with the shivers. Gone was his cold scrutiny, replaced now by a far-off, inexplicable look.

"Jake." As soon as she spoke his name and began walking towards him, his eyes hooded over and the youth of only moments before disappeared. When she reached him a man, not a boy, waited for her. "Jake," she said again, her nerves now a jumble. "Please go and warm yourself by our fire." With his Stetson off, he still towered over her. "Your clothes are soaked. I will get you one of Papa's shirts until yours is dry."

She thought of how he'd been out all day working, without the benefit of his coat. Instead of feeling guilty over not bringing his coat out to him, all she could think of was how he looked, naked to the waist, when he'd been shot and she'd taken care of him. She remembered every ripple of muscle, every sculpted edge of his powerful shoulders, and the heady feel of prickled downy hair when her fingers accidentally brushed across his chest. And, judging from the knowing look in Jake's eyes right now, she had the awful feeling he read her thoughts.

Before she made more of a fool of herself in front of Jake, she turned around and went to fetch the shirt she'd promised him, her step unsure. Once she was safe inside Yitzhak's room she closed the door, wishing she could close the door on the evening ahead.

"Dear God, how am I to do this?" she whispered, looking heavenward. "Please, if you could just help me keep my feelings for Jake Whiskey a secret on this night. It is for Papa I ask this, for Papa. He cannot know. He cannot." Of course Zoe-Esther didn't want Jake to know either, but she refused to ask God to help her with Jake, too. In utter defeat, she plopped down on Yitzhak's bed.

She heard conversation coming from the next room. It would not do at all to leave the two men alone for long. Up she sprang, snatched up the boiled shirt, and started for the door.

There stood Jake, bold as brass by the fire, soaked garments in hand, and naked to the waist. Only moments ago she'd conjured such an image; no need for her imagination now.

Everything in the cabin blurred. Her heart skipped one beat, then another, and another. She leaned against the doorframe of her papa's room long enough to steady herself and clear her focus. Out of habit, she groped in her pocket for her spectacles and put them on. Better. Much better. She felt a little easier now, a little more in control.

"Here," Zoe-Esther hurried forward and shoved the dry shirt into Jake's free hand, then grabbed his wet clothes from his other hand. "I'll just take these and hang them to dry," she rushed with her words, but where to go? He was by the fire, right where she needed to be. It pained her to do it, but she turned back around. "Yes, well, actually the pegs here will do the job," she mumbled and quickly as she could, arranged the damp things next to the hearth.

Blessedly, by the time she'd finished, Jake had put on the woolen, homespun shirt. Though a snug fit, at least it covered him up. She tried not to keep looking at him, but she couldn't help it.

His eyes held her in their smoky caress. When he smiled at her, his shaggy mustache twitched ever so slightly at the corners of his mouth. She swallowed hard. Confused by him, she tried to make sense of him. One minute he seemed to like her and the next he didn't. One minute he would shut his eyes against her and the next . . . the next . . . he looked like he did now. This was definitely not the same Jake Whiskey from this afternoon.

She had no protection against this Jake Whiskey.

"Star," Yitzhak gently urged. "It grows late and we must begin Shabbas." Rescued from the moment she turned and smiled at her papa, already seated at the table.

"Yes, of course, Papa. Mr. Wh—Jake, please sit." She invited him to take a seat next to Yitzhak, and willed herself to focus on celebrating Shabbas and serving the meal ahead, and not on Jake.

She had to fight her nerves. Right now, she felt just like she did when she had to perform her first surgery in medical school. Nervous, with an audience of professors watching over her shoulder, she thought for sure she would drop the scalpel and kill the patient. She had willed herself to think of her task, and only that, in order to perform a successful operation. Thanks to God, the patient survived.

Zoe-Esther made a quick silent prayer, asking God to help her survive this night.

The table needed another place set. Zoe-Esther quickly

laid out the necessary items in front of Jake and folded a napkin, just so, beside them. Then she set a third glass down on the venerable, white linen tablecloth, reserved only for the Sabbath. Another quick stir of the soup simmering over the hearth and all was ready.

Time now to kindle the Sabbath lights, the Shabbas candles. The thought of ushering in the Sabbath calmed Zoe-Esther—a time of peace and prayer, of rest, of family and home. She returned her wire rims to her pocket and took up her lace scarf from the table, and draped the scarf over her head. The polished silver candlesticks, placed reverently on the table, already sparkled in the firelight. Zoe-Esther moved to stand in front of the Shabbas candles, striking a match to light each of the two candles. Then she made the Sabbath blessing:

"Barukh Atah Adonai, Elohenu Melekh ha-olam, asher kid'shanu b'mitzvotav, v'tzivanu, le had lik ner shel Shabbas. Amen." The moment she'd made the blessing, Zoe-Esther returned to the hearth and scooped up the nearby empty basin, a pitcher of warm water, and a piece of linen toweling. Saying nothing, she walked around the table and set the basin down in between her papa and Jake. Yitzhak held his hands over the basin and Zoe-Esther poured water over his hands. While Yitzhak dried his hands, Jake followed his lead and did the exact same thing. Once the two men finished washing, Zoe-Esther removed her lace head covering and washed her hands.

Then Yitzhak rose, without breaking the silence, and pulled the loaf of *challah* closer and broke off a small piece of the egg bread, saying, *"Barukh Atah Adonai, Elohenu Melekh ha-olam, ha-motzi lechem min ho-aretz. Amen."* He gave a piece of bread to his daughter and then to Jake. Next Yitzhak recentered his yarmulke on his head before he poured a measure of wine into three small glasses on the table. He raised one of the filled glasses and said, *"Barukh Atah Adonai, Elohenu Melekh ha-olam, asher kid'shanu b'mitzvotav, bo reh pre ha gaffen. Amen."* He took a sip of the wine, and watched while their guest did the same.

"We are happy to have you with us on this Shabbas, Jake Whiskey." He patted Jake on the shoulder. "I forget for a moment, you do not know our Hebrew. I apologize for this. A poor *rebbe* I make. We praise the Lord Our God, King of the Universe, for giving us the Sabbath, for bringing forth bread from the earth and fruit from the vine." Yitzhak gave Jake another welcoming pat on the shoulder, then waited for his dutiful daughter to serve the Sabbath meal.

Chapter Thirteen

It wasn't working. Even with the blessings of the Sabbath, it just wasn't working. No amount of resolve could chase Jake's powerful presence from the little cabin. Zoe-Esther wished the meal would end and he would leave. Her chicken soup congealed in her belly. The small bits of *challah* she'd managed to get down threatened to come back up. She couldn't swallow even one spoonful of pudding. How could she, when all she could imagine were Jake's strong arms around her, covering her mouth with his fiery kisses, the sensual feel of his shaggy mustache teasing, thrilling, and their bodies pressed together in passion's embrace.

Yesterday. She'd had that moment with him yesterday, and it would never, ever come again.

For one thing, and one thing only, was she grateful. Jake's visit did a world of good for her papa. Ever the talker, her papa had not kibbitzed with anybody but her in a long while. With their cabin so isolated, they had not had anybody to supper since their move. Yes, for her papa, it was good Jake visited. For her, it most assuredly was not.

When Jake asked for a second helping of soup and another piece of chicken, Zoe-Esther's spirits plummeted even farther. Quite obvious to her now, her presence had not affected his appetite in the least. Worse, he directed all his attention to her papa, and none to her. The only time Jake looked her way, he complimented her on the meal. Disgusted with herself over her hurt feelings, Zoe-Esther abruptly got up from the table and started to clear the dishes. The water in the kettle over the hearth boiled behind her. Sure to soothe, she needed a cup of strong tea. She hurried and set the teapot to brew.

"Thank you, ma'am. The meal was fine."

The cups almost dropped from Zoe-Esther's hands when Jake's gravelly voice resonated behind her.

Ma'am!

She whirled around, shocked at what he called her. Ma'am sounded so cold, so ordinary. Jake's indifferent regard hurt. It shouldn't matter that he didn't call her Queenie, but it did. And the effect that he had on her shouldn't matter to her either, but it did. She glanced at her papa, sitting at the table, smiling at her. He seemed content and unaware of her upset over Jake. Relieved for that at least, she looked at Jake again, who was also still seated. Jake wasn't smiling at her. Unable to read the perplexed look on his handsome features, she was relieved that he didn't draw her in now with his smile. Before she could even finish her thought, Jake started to smile a slow, mesmerizing grin. Steeling herself against him, Zoe-Esther set the cups on the table.

"You're welcome, Jake," she said curtly, finally answering him, and reached for the brewed tea. She filled the cups and sat back down. She watched Jake take several sips, perplexed by him now more than ever.

"Doc. Mr. Zundelevich," Jake put down his cup and nodded, in turn, to them both before he rose from his seat.

"I thank you for your hospitality, but Missouri and I best head back now."

"*Nu,* Jake Whiskey. What you say is *mishegaz.*" Yitzhak stood up, too. "To go out in such a storm is no good. You will stay here tonight," Yitzhak insisted.

Zoe-Esther didn't say a word. She couldn't have spoken, even if she'd wanted to.

Jake said nothing.

Like a captive bird, Zoe-Esther held her breath.

"All right. Just until sunup," Jake capitulated.

Zoe-Esther's heart pounded.

Spend the night? Here? With us?

No! No! No!

She wanted to yell out her protests.

How could Papa have done this? How could he invite such trouble, such tsuris, *to visit?*

Undoubtedly, her papa saw his invitation as a *toh vaw,* a kindness. She did not. Panicked all over again, she was scared she might give something away, some hint of her hidden feelings. So far she'd done well and ignored Jake, hadn't she?

Of course I have.

His smoky glances and rugged good looks left her completely unmoved, she told herself. The subtle twitches of his shaggy mustache barely caused a flutter to her insides. The even set of his broad shoulders and the lazy way he shifted his heavy boots under the table escaped her notice entirely. And it was fatigue, she was certain, only fatigue and anxiety that tingled up and down her spine whenever he spoke in those low, sensual tones.

"*Gut,*" Yitzhak declared and got up from the table. "Now that you stay, Jake Whiskey, better we should all get some rest. Star, you will take the bed tonight and I will sleep out here."

"But, Papa—"

"*Kayn*, Star. Not a word," Yitzhak admonished. "It is late, I am old, and I am tired. Enough."

Zoe-Esther didn't dare cross her papa again, and certainly not in front of Jake.

"Yes, Papa," she relented, fighting for composure. "It is late and you must sleep. I'll just get your thi—"

"*Kayn*, Star. *Nu. Nu. Nu.* I will get everything I need. You sit and keep company with Jake Whiskey," Yitzhak commanded, then shut the bedroom door behind him.

"Star is a real pretty name, Queenie."

Zoe-Esther's insides jumped at Jake's words. Alone with him now she was afraid—afraid to face him—afraid to face what she felt for him. The power he had over her, in his voice and in his touch, scared her from head to toe.

"Queenie, look at me."

Panicked now, despite her efforts not to be afraid, Zoe-Esther wanted to flee, to escape, to be anywhere but sitting in front of the very last person in the world she should be with.

Her head pounded.

The Shabbas candles flickered between Zoe-Esther and Jake; each little flame still danced in celebration of the Sabbath.

Zoe-Esther shifted her regard to the burning tapers. Soon they would be out. Their light would be gone.

Just like Jake will be. And should be.

The painful reality of the moment hurt like an open wound.

"Queenie," Jake spoke in a hoarse whisper. "There are things . . . words that need saying to you. If I don't get them out now—" He stopped and took hold of both her clasped hands across the table.

Unable to look elsewhere Zoe-Esther stared at his strong, warm fingers splayed over hers. Nerves on edge, she began to shiver.

"Queenie." Jake grasped her hands tighter. "I got no right to ask, but—"

She forced her gaze to meet his. What she saw in his penetrating, slate depths broke down all of her hard-fought resolve.

"I didn't plan on this, Queenie, but seeing you again, touching you. Ah hell—" Jake wrenched his hands away from hers and left the table.

In the next moment he had her in his arms.

"Don't be scared, Queenie," he pulled her tremulous frame against him. "I couldn't take it if you were scared of me."

Somewhere in the foggy recesses of her mind, Zoe-Esther expected her papa to come through the door any instant. If Yitzhak found her in Jake's arms, it would be the end of him. Zoe-Esther knew she had little choice. She could not do this to her papa. She must not.

But when Jake's arms tightened around her, her body refused to listen to what she knew was right. Her heart couldn't deny the excitement he stirred in her, the passion he promised with his heated touch. The moment she sank against him, her trembles eased. She nestled her cheek against the rough edges of his shirtfront, then, as if it were the most natural thing in the world, she lifted herself on tiptoe and drew her arms up to encircle his neck, and closed her eyes.

To experience his kiss once again was all she wanted now. All she'd ever dreamed of would be in it.

When Jake's mouth claimed hers, pressing, invading, igniting, Zoe-Esther had no choice but to let go of everything she'd saved up inside since she was nine years old—saved up for her match, her Yaakov.

No! No! No!

Her eyes flew open.

This time Zoe-Esther couldn't stop the clamor of warning bells going off in her head, each bell ringing stronger, louder, and more grating than the last. Cold realization sent a stabbing pain through her heart, its jagged edges shattering her life into pieces. What she was doing now with Jake Whiskey was wrong.

It would always be wrong.

She ripped her mouth from his and yanked her arms away. It hurt too much to look at Jake. She squeezed her lids closed, as if she were a child, desperate to run and hide from what frightened her. More afraid of Jake now than anyone or anything she'd encountered before, Zoe-Esther had never experienced fear like this agony, this impossible heartache. Willing herself to shut Jake out and away from her, Zoe-Esther knew her papa's life and her own depended on it. In numbed silence she waited, as if by some magic Jake would disappear and send this moment into the shadows of faint memory. Anguished moments passed and still Zoe-Esther waited, eyes shuttered, for Jake to drop his arms from her—then she would be safe again, then all would be well.

When Jake at last took his arms away, Zoe-Esther opened her eyes and met his. The sudden chill she felt was nothing compared to his unexpected, icy countenance. The change in him was sobering.

All worry over her own fears drained from her; replaced now by worry over what she read in Jake's steely expression. Her already-broken heart wrenched for him. She'd done this to him. Yesterday she believed this rugged Westerner couldn't possibly return her affection, yet today she learned she might be mistaken. Yesterday she believed she didn't even want his affection. That was a mistake, too. It was her fault that the soft lines of his handsome features had turned to granite; that the passion in his slate gaze had turned to sadness, and then to stone. The cold in the room grew unbearable.

A death knell replaced the earlier warning bells in her head, growing louder just as before, letting Zoe-Esther know with undeniable certainty she would never again know the warmth of Jake Whiskey's embrace. From such a cut, she was also certain, she would never mend.

She wanted to step away from him, but she couldn't. It tortured her to see his features so changed, so deadened to her. The image of the little boy that she'd seen on Jake's face when he first came inside the cabin struck her, and she longed to reach up and touch his cheek to bring some kind of solace. The doctor in her longed to soothe, to heal, but the woman in her dared not.

"I come back now, Star and Jake Whiskey." Yitzhak re-entered the room.

Startled, Zoe-Esther backed away from Jake so fast that she almost landed in the fire still blazing in the hearth. Grateful to have avoided such a calamity, she looked straight at Jake, and not her papa. Jake hadn't moved. He hadn't reached out to help her, either. That hurt worse than any burn she might have gotten.

"I am an old man and so I take an old man's time to do things," Yitzhak smiled as he approached the pair, seemingly oblivious to what had just transpired. "Star, why do you stay so close to the fire? For such a smart daughter, sometimes you act *meshuga*," he chided in a good-natured way.

"Mr. Zundelevich," Jake turned slowly and faced Yitzhak, his voice low and even. "I'm gonna check on the horses and then I'll be back and bed down." Then he removed his greatcoat from its peg, crossed the room, and was out the door before another word was spoken.

Zoe-Esther flinched when Jake reached past her to retrieve his coat, alarmed by the strangeness in his voice. It wasn't what he said but the way he said it. His menacing, level voice unnerved her, and sent unwelcome shivers down her spine. Frightened by his change in tone, she clutched the cold hearthstones even tighter as she watched him leave. She should have been relieved to see him go, but she wasn't. Emotions warred within her and she didn't know what to do, especially with her papa standing next to her giving her such a questioning look.

"Star," Yitzhak spoke first. "*Gavalt,* what is the matter here?"

Oy vey! Papa cannot find out. He just can't.

"I am not so old I cannot see something is wrong. I go out and you are talking nice and I come back, and you are not talking so nice."

"Why Papa," Zoe-Esther labored to sound nonchalant, "nothing is wrong. I was chilled and moved too near the hearth. And Jake, as he said, is worried over the horses in the storm. That is all, Papa," she lied. "Papa, you must not conjure such worries, not even a *biseleh.*"

"All right, little Star, I make a *tzimmes* out of nothing. It is the Shabbas. I will say no more," Yitzhak smiled now.

Grateful he apparently accepted her explanation, and didn't pick up anything in Jake's changed tone, she also hoped her papa wouldn't notice the change in her. She wouldn't give her papa the chance. Any second Jake could return. She needed to act quickly.

"Papa, I will go to bed now," Zoe-Esther announced, not waiting for a reply. She hurried into the bedroom and hastily shut the door behind her. Leaning her back against the closed door, she fought to steady her shattered nerves. This was all awful and it was all her fault, all of it.

She heard the outside door to the cabin reopen. Her heart jumped. She couldn't breathe. What would Jake say to her papa? Much as she didn't want to listen, she had to. Full of dread and unease, she turned her head and put an ear to the rough-hewn wood.

"*Nu*, Jake Whiskey, how bad is the storm?" Yitzhak greeted.

"Dying down," Jake answered.

"*Gut, gut.* Come and warm yourself, and we can have a nice talk."

Sick with fear, Zoe-Esther pressed her ear closer to the cool wood.

"If it's all the same to you, Mr. Zundelevich, I'd like to bed down now."

"Sure, sure. Of course," Yitzhak sounded disappointed.

Relief washed over Zoe-Esther. Jake wasn't going to reveal anything to her papa: anything about what just transpired between her and Jake. Relieved, she moved away from the door and stretched out, face down, on the little iron bed. Her cheek brushed the clean muslin and, blessedly, she could now take in a decent breath. It had been such a day, a day unlike any, ever, in the whole of her life—a day that would change the rest of hers. Fighting weariness, Zoe-Esther needed to sort it all out. She rolled onto her back and stared at the cabin ceiling.

Her wished-for clarity did not come, but only more confusion. So much had happened in such a short span of time. Ever the calm and capable planner, Zoe-Esther didn't really like surprises, and Jake Whiskey had been a surprise to her. Everything had been going along all right until Jake arrived today. Most importantly, her papa's health had improved, which was a true blessing. *A true brochah.*

Other surprises gnawed at Zoe-Esther. She couldn't accept the fact that she'd come to care for someone like Jake Whiskey, and so fast. He was a rake, a gambler, and a *goy.* That she might really want to love, honor, and cherish anyone, least of all him, gnawed at her the most. Until now, until Jake, she'd vowed never to make such a vow, to any man. *And to think of such a vow to Jake Whiskey—when he is not my match, my Yaakov.*

Burdened with this sad reality, Zoe-Esther wanted to escape and forget she'd ever met Jake Whiskey. Turning back onto her belly, she reburied her face in the muslin pillow. Suddenly she was nine years old again in her village and wishing with all her heart that she had never stopped to see the *schadchen,* the matchmaker. If only she'd not given in to girlish fancy. If only she'd never heard Yaakov's name. If only she'd stayed on her usual, practical, disciplined path in life. If only . . . if only . . . if only . . .

Her worries soon sent her into an exhausted, fitful slumber.

"You had to go and do it, didn't you?" Jake mumbled to himself while he guided Missouri down the slippery, snow-covered trail toward Golden City. "You had to play your hand, you stupid son of a bitch." His horse whinnied and twitched its ears at the sound of his words, as if understanding its master's dilemma. Any other time Jake would have laughed, but not now. Not when he'd played out his hand on such a bad hunch—and lost.

The storm had dissipated overnight and the skies had

cleared. Bitter cold now, the day just breaking, Jake was eager to get back to the Golden Gates where he belonged. He wanted to giddy-up Missouri, but icy conditions made travel hazardous. Signaling for his horse to slow, they both needed to go more careful-like. He didn't want to risk any injury to Missouri. Hell, as far as he was concerned about any injury to himself, he didn't give a damn about anything except getting as far away from Queenie as he could. Back in Golden City is where he should be, back with his own kind.

What was he doing thinking somebody like Queenie would ever give him the time of day? Somebody like her who's all respectable and smart and has a real family, shouldn't come near anyone like him. He wasn't worth it and he knew it. It had hurt more than he'd figured when she rejected him.

You stupid son of a bitch. You asked for it and you got it.

Jake wanted a drink so badly it made fists on his insides. A smoke would have to do. When he reached for his to-bacco makings in his coat pocket, he touched the edges of an envelope instead—the letter Queenie's pa asked him to mail. Shoving the envelope out of the way, he felt for his to-bacco pouch. In no time he had a cheroot rolled and lit. A couple of deep draws didn't help to improve his mood. Maybe a good turn at the faro table would. His fingers itched to get hold of a playable hand. He wouldn't make the same mistake again—at the tables or with women.

Zoe-Esther woke with a start and bolted upright in bed. It took a moment for her to clear her head. Dim light pene-trated the oilcloth-covered window, just enough to illumi-nate the inside of the cabin bedroom. The same room, in the same cabin, where she and her papa had lived for months now. Yet, instinctively, Zoe-Esther knew there was nothing the same about this day, this place, or her life any more.

Freezing cold permeated the air but she didn't feel it. From such a difficult night's sleep, her limbs, too, should be stiff and sore, but they were not. Her head didn't pound anymore. Thanks to God. She wasn't in any more pain, but she did feel as if someone had just administered morphia to deaden her senses. She was dead inside. With loneliness and emptiness her companions now, she willed herself to shut Jake Whiskey out of her heart and mind forever. When his image tried to surface, she chased it away. When her breast tightened with grief and loss, she ignored it. When her body ached for his touch, she forced herself to go numb.

Determined to steel herself against any such frivolous, wanton, dangerous emotions ever again, Zoe-Esther got out of bed and straightened her rumpled clothing. Determined also, never again to dream of the one chosen for her by the *schadchen,* she erased all thoughts of any matchmaking, ever, from her future.

Other things mattered in her life, other more important, meaningful things. There was her papa to care for. His wellbeing mattered above all else. Life on the frontier was very hard and she must do much, much more to make her papa's life better, and the lives of others. She wanted to be a doctor in Golden City—not a seamstress. Though grateful to care for the miners and their families in Tent City, despite their lack of payment, Zoe-Esther wished all the townsfolk would welcome her care. It shouldn't matter to her, but it did. Accustomed to prejudice in her life, she longed for acceptance now as a woman, as a doctor, and as a Jew.

I must . . . I will try harder.

In the next room she heard her papa stir. He was up and would be cold and hungry. The fire needed tending. More wood must be brought in. There was breakfast to prepare. Intent on her tasks, Zoe-Esther hurried to the door, giving no thought at all to the possibility their overnight guest might still be there.

Zoe-Esther wished she had a nice piece of whitefish for her papa this morning. She wanted to reward his silence. If he thought anything was amiss about last night, he said nothing. Well, she had no whitefish, or herring, or pike. Instead she warmed a bit of leftover chicken and served beaten biscuits and hot tea along with it. Too bad they couldn't have a chicken coop, giving them fresh eggs every day, but mountain life would never allow for it. If the chickens didn't freeze to death, wild animals would get to them for certain. Trips to the local mercantile in Golden City would ever be a necessity in their lives.

And now I have a beautiful horse on which to make them.

Which, up until this moment, she'd forgotten she had.

"Papa," she shot up from the table and tore off her apron, "I must see to the horse."

"Slow down, daughter," Yitzhak was smiling over his glass of steamy tea. "First, I must give you something." He put down his tea and reached into his shirt pocket.

Zoe-Esther took her hand off the door latch and turned around. Wary now, she took careful steps back across the room.

"Star, Jake Whiskey left this for your horse," Yitzhak intoned mischievously, and placed two fifty-dollar bills on the table.

Zoe-Esther had never seen so much money at one time.

A fortune. She peered hard at it, as if waiting for the bills to vanish before her eyes. Unreal as it seemed, there they were, right in front of her. The moment she reached to touch the unfamiliar bills, reality hit her and she jerked her hand away.

"Papa, we cannot—"

"Little Star, I know what goes on in my daughter's pretty head. You think of this *gelt* as *tzedakah* and it is not charity. Jake Whiskey said you must have this to take care of the horse through the winter. Daughter, you have never had such an animal. You do not know what the costs can be to keep it. I believe what Jake Whiskey says is true. Besides, Star, we have little enough to live on and this will help."

Much as it hurt and as guilty as she already felt over her meager earnings, Zoe-Esther knew accepting the money made sense. She had not considered the cost of what it would take to feed and house a horse. But a hundred dollars? Surely it could not be so much. After quick mental calculations she realized that with such a sum she could provide for her papa, purchase needed warm coats for them both, and care for her horse, with enough left over to restock her medical bag. The money tempted her, reaching out with its promise of a more secure winter.

Now was no time to act the *golem*. She could not be foolish and reject Jake Whiskey's money. Unable to afford the luxury of associating the man with the moment, Zoe-Esther did not hesitate a second longer and scooped up the money, then quickly added it to the nearly empty Mason jar hidden in the wood box by the door. She gave Yitzhak a bright smile, refastened her shawl, and hurried outside.

Warmed only a little by the sunshine, Zoe-Esther tried to stop her teeth from chattering and her body from shivering while she made her way through the fresh snow toward the corral. The bay whinnied from inside the shelter, making Zoe-Esther hurry even more.

"Good morning, my beauty," Zoe-Esther cooed the moment she reached the animal. The bay whinnied again and turned its head towards Zoe-Esther, then turned back and shook its dark mane.

"Well, well," Zoe-Esther laughed. "I've had better greetings before. Never mind, my beauty, you take all the time you need to get to know me." She spoke in soft tones as she reached out and smoothed her hand along the bay's russet back. The animal flinched, but allowed her touch.

Zoe-Esther had never seen a horse more beautiful than this one. "There, there, my *sheyn,*" she soothed. "Such a beautiful animal deserves a beautiful name," she continued. "And so I shall name you Sheyn. It means beautiful in Yiddish, just like you."

The skittish animal turned again to look at Zoe-Esther, this time it bobbed its head only a little, and then calmed.

"Such a good girl, Sheyn. You and I will be great friends. You will see." Zoe-Esther reached out with her other hand to stroke the bay's nose. "You must give me time and be patient with me. I've never had such a gift as you in my life, and I must learn to take proper care of you. I haven't ridden much before and I must learn that, too."

The horse twitched its ears.

Zoe-Esther went on as if the conversation with Sheyn were the most natural in the world.

"I do, however, know how to hitch up a saddle. I learned that coming west. So all is not lost, Sheyn. We will learn together, won't we, my smart beauty?"

The animal bobbed its head as if it understood and agreed with her.

The newly erected stable, though small, was big enough,

Zoe-Esther thought. She glanced around the space, satisfied Sheyn had a good home. Surprised to see bags of feed and bales of hay along one side of the stable, Zoe-Esther refused to let gratitude turn to remorse for having pushed Jake Whiskey away. Sobs welled in her throat, but she choked them back. It could do no good to allow such reflection. No good at all. Forcing herself back to reality and to the moment, she looked around the rest of the stable for some kind of feed bag or pail for Sheyn. Her heart lurched when she spotted full saddle gear hitched over a rail by the entryway.

She hadn't thought about all she would need for Sheyn.

Jake evidently had.

Her chest tightened and she instinctively put both hands over it, to guard against any more unwanted heartache.

Jake Whiskey is nothing to me and I am nothing to him.

Such painful acknowledgement was unwise, unhelpful, and unnecessary, Zoe-Esther silently admonished, and walked over to the hitching rail. She ran her hands over each part of the saddle, inspecting it much as if she were examining a patient. The cool leather felt wonderful and smelled wonderful. After long minutes, convinced everything was in proper order, Zoe-Esther turned around to feed Sheyn, wiping away tears that she didn't realize she'd shed.

Chapter Fourteen

"Easy, Jake," Matthew cautioned from behind the bar.

Jake could see the men approach in the barroom mirror's reflection. He set down his freshly emptied glass of Jack Daniels and slid his gun hand just over his holster, alert to the trouble coming up behind him.

"Jake." Matthew kept his voice low.

Jake heard Matthew but kept his eyes on the men in the mirror.

"I need to tell ya what's been goin' on with Belle since ya left yesterday," the loyal barkeep gulped out in a hurry. "I got a real bad feeling Belle's up to somethin'. She's been mad as a hornet at ya. Every dang time I said somethin' about ya, she flared up again. This has gotta be Belle's doin', all Belle's."

"Son of a bitch," Jake swore under his breath. He'd just come from one bad situation at Queenie's, and hell if he hadn't walked straight into another one. He'd only had enough time to walk inside the Golden Gates and get a drink before the sheriff, four deputies, the mayor, and the head of the Town Council entered his place.

The action in the crowded saloon came to a standstill. Chairs scraped across the wood floor as men got up from their card play. The piano music stopped and so did all conversation. Not one peep out of any of the dancing girls on stage or from the other ladies could be heard throughout the saloon. An eerie quiet settled over the smoke-filled room.

Jake felt all the eyes at his back. His guard raised and his gun hand ready, raw instinct kept everyone in his sights.

Where was Belle?

Goddamn it.

He'd no reason to doubt Matthew's real bad feeling about her now. The truth of it turned his guts.

"Whiskey," The sheriff said, standing six feet behind Jake, and flanked on both sides by his deputies.

"Matthew," Jake kept his eyes to the mirror. "I believe these gents need some drinks. Tell you what, Sheriff," Jake said all easy and agreeable, "I'll have one with you. Matthew, pour me another."

"Whiskey," the sheriff spat out again.

Matthew couldn't hide how dangerous he felt the situation was from Jake. Jake saw it in Matthew's anxious eyes. He sure didn't want Matthew to get hurt. Jake waited for him to finish pouring his drink.

"Go get these gents some more of my fine Tennessee bourbon from the storeroom. We're all out. Now, Matthew," Jake insisted.

Matthew stayed put.

"Ya know, funny thing. I plumb forgot to get more," he leveled at Jake, all the while moving his hand under the bar where his shotgun rested.

Jake gave Matthew a grateful nod.

"You through playing, Whiskey?" the sheriff asked.

Jake turned, slow and careful, and faced the lawman.

"Hell, Sheriff. I'm not the one playing. What's your game coming here?" Jake asked.

"It's no game. Fact is, Whiskey, you're finished. Ain't

210

nothin' left in the cards for you here."

Jake itched to wipe that smirk off the sheriff's face, but first he needed to know what the hell was going on.

"I'm listening." Jake fought hard to keep his trigger finger off his Colt .45.

"Not much explaining necessary, no sir," the sheriff went on. "The deed to this place isn't yours. Seems it never was. Papers weren't right from the start. This property, and everythin' in it, belongs to Belle Bliss, plain and simple. You've got one hour to clear out, Whiskey. Startin' now," the sheriff warned.

Jake had figured Belle might be up to something, but he hadn't figured on this.

"Show me the deed, Sheriff, or by damn I'll shoot you right here and now," Jake threatened.

"Tell him, Mayor," the sheriff ordered, but didn't take his eyes off Jake.

"Yes . . . well . . ." the mayor spoke up, his fear obvious. "I . . . uh . . . you see, Whiskey, the Town Council has the proper deed to this place . . . and . . . well your name isn't signed on it. Belle's is . . . Belle Bliss," he finished, and wiped the perspiration from his brow.

"Belle's is."

The way the mayor said it gave her away.

Goddamn it. Belle had probably slept with the mayor and every sorry, spineless bastard on the Town Council. He figured she probably had something on every one of them, for sure.

"Is that a fact, Mayor?" Jake took a step towards the heavyset, nervous man.

The mayor started backing away, but the tall man next to the mayor grabbed hold of his arm and stopped him.

Henderson.

"What have you got to say about all this?" Jake snarled at the head of the Town Council, an inch shy of Jake's height. Every time Councilman Henderson came into his saloon, the girls scattered. Jake never liked the guy. No one else liked him much either. Except Belle. She'd always dealt with him. Now Jake knew why.

"Mr. Whiskey." Henderson played innocent. "Nothing much at all to say. The proof's in my office and I'd be happy to fetch it. But you see, Mr. Whiskey, all of the papers are under lock and key until Judge Coffee decides to unlock them—"

Henderson didn't finish his sentence.

He didn't have to. Jake didn't miss a trick in the no-good bastard's beady little eyes. He understood the bastard's meaning all right.

"Unfortunately for you," the wiry councilman added, satisfaction written all over his milky, pointed features, "it could take weeks, maybe even months, for the judge to consider your case."

The cards were stacked against Jake for sure. Even the damned judge must be in on it, Jake thought. He wanted to put a bullet through all of these idiots, Henderson most of all. Hell, people had accused Jake of cheating, when he had a whole group of cheats standing right in front of him. Goddamn town officials, all a bunch of crooks, every lying one of them.

"What'll it be?" The sheriff straightened and moved his coat out of the way, just enough to clear his holster.

"Now what the hell do you think it'll be?" Jake leveled back, keeping an eye on them all. "You got five guns ready for me, here in my place, with folks all around. How about we take this outside, Sheriff? Your odds are better than mine, five guns against one—"

"Two," Matthew pronounced from behind the bar.

"Five to two still ain't bad, Sheriff," Jake said.

Jake didn't blink but the sheriff did, and slowly slid his coat back over his holster.

Jake's reputation with a gun might have been the reason.

"Listen, Whiskey, I gotta enforce the law," the sheriff explained. "You gotta clear outta here. These guys have the goods on you."

Jake's gun hand eased the moment the sheriff's did. The sheriff was right. There wasn't anything he could do about this—about Belle—right now. He had to fold, and he knew it. If felt to him like the whole town wanted him out; not just these weasels.

"All right, Sheriff. You and your friends here win this hand. I'll be gone in an hour," Jake fired back and started for his office. He didn't wait for anybody else to speak up, not even Matthew.

The door to his office stood ajar. Suspicious, Jake eased it open. What else could go wrong today? He had his answer the moment he saw his safe wide open: Belle. Couldn't be anybody else. She must have found the combination hidden in his desk. Instead of checking the safe right away, he looked around the room for Belle, as if she'd still be in there, rifling through his life. His guts turned again.

Hell hath no fury like a woman scorned.

Never having Bible learning, Jake had heard more than one customer at his place repeat the phrase over the years. Now he knew what it meant.

Cleaned him out, Jake realized when he examined the contents, or lack of them, of his safe. All his money, his papers, all gone. Angry with himself over his stupidity, he needed to get the hell out of there, and quick. He'd wait to find Belle.

In fifteen minutes time, with his carpetbag in hand, Jake let the doors of the Golden Gates swing shut behind him.

Zoe-Esther tried hard to smile and not feel guilty when Yitzhak presented her with the Hanukkah menorah he'd carved from wood; once again she was reminded of how very much her papa had sacrificed for her. She was the reason their beautiful silver menorah from the old country was gone. One day, when they had money to spare, she would go to Denver City, or wherever she needed to go to find her papa the silver menorah of their traditions.

"Papa, this is wonderful," she said, and cradled the wood carving in her hands. Set on a smooth base, the menorah stemmed up and then out, to form an arc. Within the arc were eight holes in a row, and then one created slightly apart from the rest—meant for the *shamush* candle, used to light the other candles on each of the eight nights of Hanukkah. After quick calculation, she realized the holiday would use up their precious store of tallow. Maybe a great miracle would happen as in ancient times, when the oil in The Temple miraculously stayed lit for eight days when there was only enough to last one. Miracle or not, warmed to thoughts of the holiday of Hanukkah, Zoe-Esther would find a way to make do.

To please her papa, she made latkes, traditional potato pancakes. She had splurged on a small piece of beef brisket for him, too.

Indeed, good fortune smiled down on them, on this the last night of the holiday. Quick to shrug it off, Zoe-Esther refused to think that it was because of Jake Whiskey's generosity that they could enjoy such good fortune.

On each night of the holiday Yitzhak had not failed to

raise the idea of how nice it would be to have *mishpachah,* family and friends, gathered with them. How nice, too, he'd gone on to say, to have *naches,* joy, from children that only a *zayde,* a grandfather, can appreciate.

Zoe-Esther knew what her papa was up to. She remembered the promise she'd made him in Philadelphia—the one to marry Daniel—the one she'd no intention of keeping, even for her beloved papa. Though his health had improved, Papa would never understand her lie. But marriage to Daniel, or anybody else, was out of the question. The notion of her ever wanting to find her match, would remain a secret. Yitzhak didn't know about her folly, and she vowed never to reveal it.

Zoe-Esther made another on-the-spot vow. She'd keep her mind and her purpose on two things, and two things only: her papa and medicine. Together, the two would be enough to fill up the rest of her days, but perhaps not all of the empty nights ahead of her.

Five long weeks since Jake Whiskey had left their cabin. Five, long, miserable weeks.

Zoe-Esther couldn't help but wonder if any of his nights had been lonely, too?

Feh! Likely as not.

Suddenly the overpowering stench of rosewater made Zoe-Esther nauseous. Forbidden images flashed in front of her—images of another woman with Jake, in his bed—the beautiful blonde she'd seen at his place. The blonde's silken hair fell over Jake's bare chest. Her naked body pressed ever closer—

"Feh! Feh! Feh!" Zoe-Esther expressed her disgust with herself, upset at her utter lack of self-control when it came to painful thoughts of a man she must not think about.

"Gavalt? What is this you say, daughter? What upsets

you so on this last night of Hanukkah?" Yitzhak sounded disapproving.

"Oh Papa, I am such a klutz. I almost dropped the hot skillet." She rushed to cover her anxiety with her lie. "Here, the latkes are ready." She served several onto his plate, then quickly turned back to the hearth and took the loaf of braided *challah* bread from the small, cast iron oven.

"Star, take care you should not burn yourself," Yitzhak cautioned, less disagreeable now. "I should make things nicer for you. You should have a proper oven and not such a poor one I make from the old pot belly left out back of the cabin."

"Papa, shush. The oven makes perfect *challah*. You work miracles with your hands, just like our beautiful new menorah," she insisted, then took up a match to light the *shamush* candle. Once all eight candles were illuminated, they made the blessings and sat down to enjoy the festive meal.

Tired from the day and from fighting unwelcome thoughts about Jake Whiskey, Zoe-Esther hoped that tonight she could sleep. A little rest, and all would be well. Maybe if she contrived a more comfortable bed, added more straw to her mattress near the hearth, it would help her sleep.

"Star," Yitzhak interrupted her reverie. "Let us talk a while more before going to sleep."

"Of course, Papa." Though exhausted, she couldn't refuse him. "But even though you are better, you must not push yourself," she advised.

"Push, shush, I only want to *kibbitz* a little," Yitzhak sighed. "Such a *yom tov*. Such a good day we had, daughter," he sighed again and settled into the rocker.

Zoe-Esther resumed her seat at the table and listened

while Yitzhak mused about Hanukkah and memories of the old country.

So busy wallowing in self-pity about her lonely nights, she'd lost sight of how very much her papa missed kibbitzing and schmoozing with everybody, and how lonely he must be. In their village in Russia, and in the city of Philadelphia, there were many to talk to. Here in the mountains there was no one, only her. Necessity had made it so. She'd had to isolate him to treat his tuberculosis. Now, with his symptoms gone, maybe she could do something.

A move to Golden City, even if they had the money, remained out of the question. She refused to risk Yitzhak's health degenerating, since she believed his susceptibility not only to a recurrence of tuberculosis, but to other invasive illnesses, still existed. No, they must stay put.

What to do? What to do?

She thought a moment.

I have it.

Excited over her idea, she pretended to listen to Yitzhak, all the while making plans.

She decided that when the wintry weather allowed her to, she would saddle Sheyn and ride along the same route used by the miners to go back and forth from Golden City to Blackhawk and Central City. The road wasn't far from their cabin. Anxious to re-supply her medical bag and begin making house calls to the townsfolk in nearby Golden City, Zoe-Esther intended, of course, to continue her ministrations to all the impoverished miners and their families in Tent City. When the miners trekked back and forth from the mines, she would simply ask them to stop in on occasion and visit with her papa, certain they would agree.

She hoped her plans would succeed, not just for her papa, but for her medical practice. True, the two doctors in

217

town shut her out, but would all of the townsfolk? If she
called on the townsfolk, making them aware of her skills
and offering her services, wouldn't they welcome her, and
let her in? How she hoped and longed for such acceptance
as a doctor, as a woman, and as a Jew in America. It could
be just like her village in Russia, everyone friendly and hos-
pitable. On second thought, Zoe-Esther realized she would
be better off leaving her religion out of any discussion with
her patients. It would be unwise, she knew, to bring up the
subject. Experience in Russia and in Philadelphia had
taught her as much.

"Matthew," Belle snapped at him the moment she
walked into the room. Early still, there were few customers
in the saloon.

Matthew didn't look up from his task, but kept drying
the glasses he'd just washed.

"Matthew!" she shouted now.

He took his time looking up. He had stayed at the
Golden Gates, but not for Belle—for Jake. When Jake came
back to reclaim what was his and deal with Belle, he'd be
there for him, like always.

"Things are different around here now, Matthew," Belle
threatened. "You gotta listen to me now and you best do it
if you know what's good for you."

"Whatcha gonna do, fire me?" Matthew threatened right
back.

Belle wasn't a stupid woman. Matthew was the best barkeep in all of Golden City. Besides, having him near reminded her of the good times, with Jake.

Damnit. Jake got what was coming to him, didn't he?
Taking up with that redheaded hussy right in front of her.
He deserved to lose it all: the saloon, the furnishings up-

stairs and down, and every cent he had. It was only right.

He should have married me when he had the chance. Well, Jake lost and I won. I have it all now.

But she didn't. She didn't have Jake.

Scared of what might happen when he waltzed back in through the doors of the Golden Gates, Belle felt again for the derringer hidden in her garter. Odd that he hadn't shown up yet. She dreaded the moment, but longed for it, too. Certain she could convince him to come back to her when he did return, Belle hoped he wouldn't put a bullet through her first. Fear made the hairs on the back of her neck stand on end. Suddenly anxious and queasy, she turned her ire onto Matthew.

"Get these tables clean by the time I come back," she insulted more than ordered, and then made a beeline for the saloon office and slammed the door behind her.

My medicine, where is it? I need it, now.

Desperate to find her opium, she pulled open first one desk drawer, then another, letting the drawers and their contents spill onto the floor.

Where is it? Did someone steal it?

In a panic, her hands shook so badly she had trouble opening the last of the drawers. When she did, she found her magic potion and immediately put the little dark bottle of soothing liquid to her lips. One swallow, then another, and her head began to ease, her stomach settle, and her torment fade away.

"Go . . . away," Jake slurred through his closed door at the Bartlett Rooming House. He'd barely come out in weeks, not even for meals, and he sure as hell wasn't coming out this time. Content to drink his liquor and pass into oblivion every day, he didn't need this aggravation.

Mrs. Bartlett rapped several more times.

"Jake Whiskey, you open this door. If I have to knock it clear down, I will."

Her threat wasn't idle, Jake could tell.

"Jake," she said again.

As before, he ignored it.

The fog he'd been living in for the past weeks suited him fine. The liquor was good, the bed comfortable, and the isolation perfect. He downed another shot of whiskey and tried not to think about anything or anyone else on the other side of the locked door. Too drunk to do much else, he fell back onto the bed.

Colors swirled and flashed in front of him. He couldn't shut his eyes against the images taking shape: images of Queenie . . . then Belle . . . one all smiles . . . the other cursing him out.

Hell, both of them had wronged him. He didn't want any part of either of them again. Despite his intoxicated state, he knew what was what. He wasn't good enough for Queenie, and he wouldn't sink low enough for Belle. Caught in the middle of nothing but pure trouble. "It ain't the first time and like as much it ain't the last," Jake muttered under his breath.

He'd been cheated out of his saloon, but that wasn't what stuck in his craw so badly he couldn't get anything but alcohol down. Hell, he didn't even want to pick up a deck of cards anymore, the gambling urge surprisingly gone clean out of him.

Worthless. He felt nothing but worthless now. He'd lost the one thing that had given him some self-respect in life: his money. He was reduced to the homeless kid he used to be, begging for leavings outside local brothels. Not many had cared about him then, apart from some of the prostitutes. Now wasn't much different. No decent folk in town would give him the time of day without his money; nobody but Matthew.

Matthew.

Forced to sober, Jake needed to find his old friend. Likely Matthew was real worried about him. Damnit, how could he have forgotten about Matthew in all this time?

"You sorry son of a bitch," Jake berated himself and got off the bed.

"Jake Whiskey!" Mrs. Bartlett yelled loud enough to wake the dead now.

"I'm coming. I'm coming," Jake answered this time, and opened the door.

"Well that's better," Mrs. Bartlett took her fisted hand down, which had been ready to rap harder still if need be. "I thought I best give you my news before you drink yourself into an early grave," she said sourly.

"Oh yeah?" Jake couldn't help himself, and smiled at her. Liked her despite her nosy ways, always had. "Wh . . . at . . . news?" he yawned and stretched his long arms overhead.

Mrs. Bartlett sat down in a chair by the window and waited for Jake's full attention before she continued.

Moments passed. No one said a word.

Finally Jake understood what she wanted, and sat down on the edge of his bed across from the eccentric landlady.

"That's better, Jake."

She tried to sound miffed with him, but he knew she wasn't really.

"Word on the street is that someone's looking for you, Jake. I've asked around but I don't know who it is. Could be anybody."

Jake got up and searched the room for where he'd

dropped his gun belt. The moment he spotted it in a corner of the room, he grabbed up his holstered Colt .45 and strapped it on.

"Jake," Mrs. Bartlett got up, unable to hide the worry in her voice. "Now don't go rushing out looking for trouble. Maybe it's not."

"Always is," Jake said and found his greatcoat. A letter stuck out of one of its pockets—Queenie's pa's. He pulled his coat on then removed the crinkled envelope.

"Here," he handed the envelope to Mrs. Bartlett. "Mail this for me? Might not get a chance today."

"Of course, Jake," she agreed, in obvious distress over what he'd said.

Jake squared his Stetson on his head, nodded his thanks and a quick goodbye to Mrs. Bartlett, and then strode downstairs, determined to make his presence known and face whoever it was gunning for him.

Jake sat at a table all afternoon in the crowded, noisy Crooked Creek Saloon. Folks shot him looks but nobody came over. Little surprise to him that they didn't. A bottle of whiskey sat next to him but his glass remained empty. He'd yet to pour a drop into it. His gun hand needed to be steady. After weeks of drinking, with his innards still raw and shaky, he focused hard on keeping his fingers still and his aim straight. He pulled the brim of his hat down a little farther on his brow, and kept his eyes locked on the saloon doors.

A lanky well-dressed man entered. Something about the man struck Jake as being familiar, but Jake couldn't make out what it was. His gun ready, Jake didn't take the stranger out of his sights as the man approached.

"Mr. Whiskey?" The stranger stood with hat in hand, all

friendly-like. "I've been a lookin' all over town for you. Bout given up I'd ever find you."

Silas Preston. Jake remembered the craggy, weathered face now as that of the miner who'd lost his claim at the Golden Gates. Sounded the same but sure didn't look the same in his new, fancy duds.

"Can I sit, Mr. Whiskey?"

"Yeah," Jake kicked a chair out for him, surprised the miner was the one searching him out.

"Want a drink, Silas?" Jake offered, and relaxed his gun hand.

"No, sir, Mr. Whiskey." Silas shot him an embarrassed smile, showing an uneven set of yellowing teeth. "But I'm shore happy you 'membered me, yessir."

"Yeah, well, what can I do for you?" Jake asked him.

"More'n likely it's what I can do for you," Silas said and pulled a folded paper out of his jacket pocket. "Here's my claim, the one I done lost an' the one you give me back." He put the claim down on the table in front of Jake.

Jake said nothing, did nothing.

"Take it, Mr. Whiskey. It's yours now," Silas encouraged. "You hepped me when nary a soul would. I'm payin' you back now is all. The claims's up by Blackhawk. Been real good to me and the wife and young'uns, yessir. Paid off good. There's still plenty gold left but the wife wants to clear outta here and go somewheres else. Mebbe out Nevada way or even all the way to San . . . fran . . . cisco. The mine ain't played out yet an' I wanna give it to you, Mr. Whiskey. It's all legal like. I've done been to the Claims Office an' your name's on it, so you got no choice but to take it."

"I can't accept this," Jake told him and started to get up, wanting to leave before Silas could see how much his offer had gotten to him. In all of Jake's sorry life, no one had ever given him a break—until now. Overwhelmed by Silas' offer, Jake needed to hightail it outta there.

"Wait, Mr. Whiskey, please," Silas stood up and took hold of Jake's arm. "You gotta take the claim. It's yours anyhow, fair an' square." Silas picked up the document and shoved it at Jake.

Jake reluctantly took hold of the claim paper, holding it in his hands as if it were the precious ore itself.

"Where the claim is and all is writ down there for you. Up near Blackhawk, just like I said." Silas put his hat back on and smiled at Jake. "I wish you good luck with it, Mr. Whiskey."

Before Jake had a chance to thank him, Silas Preston turned and walked out of the Crooked Creek Saloon.

Matthew.

Jake thought of his old friend.

The two of them together might be able to make a new start. Neither of them knew a damn thing about mining, but hell . . . they could learn.

Chapter Fifteen

Their wood store was dangerously low. Zoe-Esther realized she and her papa would need more to see them through the rest of the winter. She'd had no idea how important firewood would be to them when they first arrived at the cabin. With all her stitch work and practice of medicine, she'd had little time to replenish their store of wood. Besides, she wasn't so handy yet with the ax. Nothing was to be done for it, she knew, and decided to go down the mountain and make arrangements for a wagonload of wood to be delivered to their cabin. She hoped the firewood wouldn't be too expensive, since their budget was already tight and she needed enough money to properly restock her medical supplies.

"Easy Sheyn. Easy girl," Zoe-Esther cautioned, very aware her horse took to the snowy, icy trail far better than she did. She, not her horse, needed encouragement for their tricky descent into Golden City. The sky stayed cloudy. Snow threatened. In need of a warm coat, Zoe-Esther pulled her doubled shawl closer when the wind picked up, and hoped the weather would hold for her day's journey. The trail, Thanks to God, had obviously been kept open by the mining supply wagons. The tenacity of the miners never ceased to amaze Zoe-Esther.

She'd never been to Blackhawk or Central City and couldn't imagine attempting the thirty-five mile trek in the dead of winter. She wished she could do more for the miners and their families. Already resolved to help with their medical needs, she hoped to find a way to help feed and clothe them. Like the *shtetl* of her childhood, their needs were many. Long weeks had passed since she'd been to town. Uneasy over her neglect in her care of the miners, she would not let such time pass between visits to Tent City again. Maybe she could run a clinic there two days a week instead of one? It would take money, extra money she didn't have.

Well, she hoped to have more money, and soon.

Once she visited all of the townsfolk and offered her medical services to them, Zoe-Esther prayed the good citizens of Golden City would welcome her in. Yet to decide what her charges would be, she recalled a partial list of rates back in Philadelphia: house call, two dollars; delivering a baby, ten to thirty dollars; reduction of a fracture, five to ten dollars; and operations, twenty-five to one hundred dollars.

But that was Philadelphia.

This was Golden City.

Zoe-Esther doubted the townsfolk would pay such city prices on the frontier. Of course, she'd make allowances and adjustments. Even with that, her earnings should be adequate and enable her to care for the needy mining families. Another intention seeded in her mind over the winter and turned into a dream: to someday care for invalids with tuberculosis.

The climate in the West, plus her treatment regimen, had helped her beloved papa. Certain other tuberculosis patients could benefit from the same type of care. It had occurred to Zoe-Esther how much patients suffering from the same ailment might benefit from the same care she'd prescribed for her papa. And she knew just how to do it: open a hospital, a hospital for tuberculosis patients. Then she could oversee consumptives throughout all phases of their care and convalescence. Though she'd not visited them, Zoe-Esther had heard about healing mineral springs farther up in the mountains, used by the Indians. Settlers and trappers brought back such tales, and she'd overheard the accounts when she was in town. She wondered if any of them actually partook of the healing waters. Miners in Tent City, too, told her of hot springs near Blackhawk and Central City. Thanks to God, Yitzhak was better, but the idea of curative vapors intrigued Zoe-Esther. One day she wanted to see first hand what potential the waters might hold. For now, she would have to be content with the treatment at hand.

All of Zoe-Esther's hopes and dreams hinged on her acceptance by the residents of Golden City. Filled with *chutzpah* for the task, what she needed was luck, *mazel*, and lots of it. She could use every bit of luck she could find. Once she had enough money, she could realize all of her dreams in medicine. As far as her dreams to find her match, or to ever have a life with Jake Whiskey, she'd already let those dreams fly right out her oilcloth-covered windows. Being a doctor would more than make up for any such silly, romantic dreams.

Certainly it would.

Of course, it would.

If Zoe-Esther told herself this enough, she hoped that maybe one day she would actually believe it. Unfortunately for her so far, no matter how much she thought she was in control of her errant emotions, she'd yet to chase away all images of Jake Whiskey. *One day I will.* For now, she desperately needed to keep both feet planted firmly in reality, and to convince the good townspeople of Golden City to utilize her medical skills, and to pay her for them.

She'd find out soon enough if they would.

Sheyn stumbled slightly, but it was enough to pull Zoe-Esther out of her worries over unfulfilled dreams, personal or otherwise. The sure-footed animal promptly corrected its step. Some of Sheyn's confidence must have rubbed off on her, Zoe-Esther realized, no longer doubtful of her own ability to make it to town on horseback. She eased in the saddle for the remainder of the trip, despite the threat of coming snow.

Zoe-Esther made sure to go into all three frontier apothecary stores, a little surprised at finding three of them. What didn't surprise her was the cool reception she got from the first two apothecaries once she engaged them in conversation. They'd heard about "Doc Zoe. Word gets out." Neither man wanted to bother with her and claimed that no one else in town would either, her "being a woman and a foreigner and all." By foreigner, she knew exactly what the ill-bred men meant. A Jew is what they meant to say. Instead of being upset by the implication, it fired her anger.

"Do you mean, sir," Zoe-Esther struggled to stay polite when she asked both apothecaries, in turn, the same question. "Do you mean, sir, that you will not sell me the goods I need?"

"Yep, that's right," both said.

Zoe-Esther had expected them to be a little suspicious of her, but she hadn't expected this; not complete refusal to help her. It did little good when she pressed her case with either of the bigoted, unreasoning apothecaries. She was shown the door, twice over.

By the time she reached the last apothecary store, dashed hopes had replaced her anger. If she had to send east to get the things she needed, it would take more money than she had. How could she earn the funds she needed if she couldn't get her medical practice going in the first place? Embroidery work certainly wasn't the answer, either.

Feh! Golem! Shlimazels!

Her anger at the two previous apothecaries flared again. Incompetent fools. Likely, neither one of them had ever picked up a *sefer* in the whole of their sorry lives. If they'd read even one book at all, she'd be shocked.

Hit by pungent odors the moment she stepped inside the last apothecary door, Zoe-Esther automatically shut her eyes to better concentrate on the smells. The smells immediately took her back in time to medical school, where she'd found she had the uncanny ability to discern one preparation from another. She forgot her upset over the previous apothecaries' prejudice. Zoe-Esther breathed deeply once, then again, careful to pick out each medicinal smell.

Mercury-Chloride. Calomel. Ether. Iodine. Essence of Peppermint. Rubbing alcohol. Ipecac. Licorice Root. Gentian. Jalap—

"Help you, miss?" the dutiful apothecary greeted, and got up from his warm seat by the iron stove at the rear of his shop. Once behind his crowded counter, covered over with polished, white porcelain jars and rows of wooden boxes with mysterious drawers, the apothecary straightened his vest, reset his watch fob, and checked his latest display, ready for his new customer.

Zoe-Esther didn't look at him. She didn't want to hear what she knew that he would say. No, is what he would say.

To postpone the inevitable, she kept her gaze cast onto the laden counter, and kept silent. More scents wafted in front of her nose.

Camphor. Mustard. Ammonia—

"A-hem," the apothecary cleared his throat. "Like I said, can I help you, miss?"

Certain that he would not help her, she faced him anyway.

There was nothing extraordinary about the man's looks, she thought, scrutinizing him as if he were a new patient. Brown hair parted down the middle. Full mustache and mutton-chop sides. Average height. Average weight. And no discernible health problems.

"Yes, you can help me," Zoe-Esther answered flatly, knowing all the while he would not.

"Well then, good," the apothecary smiled and extended his hand to her. "Name's Henry Guthrie."

Zoe-Esther didn't expect such politeness. It wouldn't last. The moment the amiable man found out who she was—a woman doctor—he'd turn her away just as the others had. She raised her hand to shake his and repeated her name, and waited for the reaction she knew would come.

"So you're Doc Zoe. The miners are always going on about you," he exclaimed and pumped her hand several times. "I'm pleased to finally make your acquaintance."

"You are?" She didn't believe Henry Guthrie.

"Yes, I am. Fact is, I give the miners credit here, all of the time, just like you do. I've heard all about you."

Astonished by Mr. Guthrie's sincerity and obvious kindness, not only to her, but also to the poor miners, Zoe-Esther couldn't think of a thing to say.

Mr. Guthrie took his hand away and placed both of his

palms flat on his counter. "This here is my business," he pronounced, his brown eyes sparkling with pride. "I don't have any quarrel with Jewish folks. Never have. Never will. Been good customers whenever they've passed through these parts."

Amazed he'd said "Jewish" and not "foreigner," Zoe-Esther warmed to Mr. Guthrie's straightforward talk, and to his obvious, perceptive ability.

"I know how folks are around here and I'm sorry for it," he shook his head as if to emphasize his disgust. "And I suspect you're a regular doctor with formal learning; not like Doc Pritchard and Doc James. They've taught themselves pretty good, but there's times I throw them right in there with quacks, faith healers, and charlatans."

Zoe-Esther had suspected as much herself: that neither of the so-called docs had a formal education. What medicine that they practiced, she feared, might be more about payment for services than having anything to do with a high standard of medical care. Certain the two frontier docs treated their share of broken limbs, festering sores, and bouts of ague, she wasn't at all certain about their skills in doing so. Mr. Guthrie's opinion of the two frontier doctors made her even more wary of them.

"Listen, Doc, I like you. And not just because you're the prettiest young woman we've had in these parts in some time," he flattered. "This town needs you, but folks here are so dang bull-headed, it's likely to take a while. And, as you can see from my full stock of preparations here, they like to tend themselves. I don't have all these preserves of nostrums and remedies for nothing. Folks in these parts don't send for a doc until they're real bad off."

Zoe-Esther had already guessed as much. It wouldn't make getting her practice going any easier.

"Mr. Guthrie, how is it you're so modern in your thinking about women doctors . . . about me?"

"I like that," he said, his satisfied smile indicative of his pleasure at her compliment. "A modern thinker. Yep, I am a modern thinker," he repeated. "You see, Doc Zoe, I hail from the East, too. Been out here since '59 and, well, just stayed. Didn't come for the gold and silver. Nope. Just for the adventure of it all. Trained myself in this trade and it's worked out all right up to now. Had to read whatever I could get my hands on about medicine and herbs and such. And I've been able to keep helping out the poor. Just like you."

Like me?

Mr. Guthrie's words made Zoe-Esther feel ashamed of herself for worrying so much about her lack of money, and not worrying enough about finding a way to take care of people in need. Mr. Guthrie was a good person. She warmed to him. It heartened her to know that not everyone in Golden City was a bigot. The miners were not bigots, either. Nor were the Pollards, or Mrs. Bartlett, or—Jake Whiskey.

Not for the first time today, she had to fight back tears.

"So, Doc Zoe. Like I said, what'll it be?" Mr. Guthrie asked.

His question rescued her from the depressing turn her thoughts had taken.

She tossed him a smile, then she took out the careful list she'd made of the items she required, and started at the top.

"Mrs. Bluett, please give me another moment of your time," Zoe-Esther implored. Quick to take advantage of Mrs. Bluett's half-open door, Zoe-Esther pressed herself through it.

"Young woman, I did not invite you in. You are not welcome here," the stern-faced Mrs. Bluett proclaimed and opened the door wider, for Zoe-Esther to leave.

March winds blew across the polished hall, ruffling all in its path, except Zoe-Esther. She wasn't leaving.

Mrs. Bluett, no doubt frustrated with her rude visitor, grudgingly had to shut her door against the bluster outside.

"Young woman, if you persist here, I'll be forced to get the sheriff. No matter to me if you wish to spend time in jail. No matter a'tall." Her jaw set, Mrs. Bluett folded her thin arms and stood firm, much like her unwanted guest.

"I'm a doctor," Zoe-Esther hurried with her plea. "If only you'd try to understand. I want to help you and your family. I want to help everyone in Golden City. Yes, I'm a woman, but our numbers are growing. Back east—"

"All very well and good," Mrs. Bluett interrupted. "You can just take *yourself* back east. We don't want your kind here."

"My kind?" Zoe-Esther understood her meaning, but wanted to make Mrs. Bluett say it.

Mrs. Bluett looked away and said nothing.

Zoe-Esther stared straight at the now-discomfited woman and waited.

"Yes, well . . ." Mrs. Bluett's face suddenly flushed red with anger.

She turned it on Zoe-Esther.

"I'll say it then, young woman. You just keep caring for the poor folks and miners and such and stay away from us. We're respectable citizens. We don't want any Jew, man or woman, taking care of us. We're God-fearing people, all good Christians. Doc Pritchard and Doc James do just fine by us anyways. I don't believe you have decent medical learning like them. I surely do not," Mrs. Bluett finished her tirade and pursed her lips, the hard lines of her face drawn even deeper than when she'd begun.

"I'm sorry for you," Zoe-Esther said, and wished things were different. "I'm sorry that you don't have room in your heart for tolerance and understanding, Mrs. Bluett. I mean you no harm. I'm a healer, a physician. God is in my heart, but I truly wonder if He is in yours."

Zoe-Esther turned away from Mrs. Bluett's shocked expression and reached for the door handle. She had to take a strong hold, as the winds outside still raged. Their rage matched her own, she thought, leaving Mrs. Bluett's and stepping head-on into the tempest.

"Whew. I'm all done in, Matthew," Jake admitted and collapsed onto his bunk.

The older man grinned and gave his stew another couple of stirs. His young friend was tired, but it was a good tired. Jake had worked all day in mud thicker than blackstrap molasses, thanks to the early snowmelt. Spring thaw had started for sure. It would snow again, and could come down on into summer, but it melted fast.

"Ya just rest yourself a bit," Matthew tossed out over his shoulder to Jake. "I'll wake ya when supper's ready, and ya can have it for breakfast," he laughed out loud, knowing full well Jake was already asleep.

"Nathaniel Hill, ya say, Jake?"

"Yep, Nathaniel Hill," Jake repeated. "The surface ore around here is played out. It's all about deep, hard rock mining now, but the stamp mills aren't getting the job done. Hill has started up what's called a smelter. I'm real curious about it, Matthew. Fact is, I'm thinking to meet Hill. Maybe we'll throw in with him."

"Good enough for me, Jake. You've done right well by us so far. I can run things here just fine," Matthew reassured.

"Then it's settled," Jake said and got up from the table to get his gear together. "I'll leave at first light."

"Hang on, Jake. Sit yourself back down a spell, will ya? That Hill fella isn't goin' anywhere."

Jake set his pack on his bunk, and then sat down himself, across the table from Matthew.

"If this is about the new business, don't worry, old pard. I'll make sure to check everything out real good before I invest any of our gold. If you want to come with me, that's fine, too."

"No, Jake. This isn't about any business or any gold," Matthew told him.

Wary now, Jake wasn't sure what Matthew was up to.

"You know, Matthew, if this can wait, I'd like to get on with things," Jake said, and started to get up.

"Well it cain't, Jake. No, sirree," the older man pronounced. "You're gonna sit and you're gonna listen."

Jake didn't like taking orders, even from Matthew, and especially when he didn't know what was coming. But Matthew was family to him now, the only family he'd ever had.

"Have some more coffee," Matthew softened his tone now, and filled both of their mugs with the steamy brew.

"All right then. Let's have it, Matthew." Jake itched to leave.

"Don't get yourself all riled up. I just wanna have a lil' talk is all," Matthew replied, his weathered face the picture of innocence.

Jake leaned against his chair back. His jaw clenched.

"Ya know, Jake. You're a changed man ever since we

come up here to Blackhawk. Good changes, I'd say," Matthew lit up his pipe and puffed on it.

Jake tried to sit still, but he sure as hell didn't want to. The blisters on his callused hands began to smart. His boots felt tight, and his shirt collar rubbed him the wrong way.

"Best of the changes, Jake," Matthew's aged, lignite eyes twinkled now, "is that you're not drinkin' anymore. I'm proud of ya for that, yes, sirree."

Jake listened.

"And ya done gave up the cards," Matthew continued. "Never thought I'd ever see the day."

Jake hoped this was the last of it.

"And no more fancy women, neither."

Jake didn't like the direction this was going.

"Belle's outta your life and I cain't say as I'm unhappy about it. Won't ever understand why ya didn't go after her an' make her pay for what she done to you, but I reckon that's your business."

"I reckon," Jake gritted out.

Matthew kept on. "Now that pretty red-headed filly, Doc Zoe. She was really somethin'."

"That's it, Matthew. This talk is over." Jake scooted his chair out and got up. He wasn't about to listen to any talk about Queenie. He grabbed up his gear. The blood in every single one of his veins began to course.

"Ya can walk away from me, Jake, but ya cain't walk away from the truth." Matthew got up, too.

"Old man, you don't know what you're saying," Jake tried not to get angry.

"The hell ya say," Matthew spat out. "I know for sure what I'm sayin'. You're smitten with the Doc and ya oughta admit it. And ya oughta get yourself down outta these mountains, and snap her up afore another fella does."

"Like I said," Jake spoke through his still-clenched jaw. "You don't know what you're saying, Matthew."

"You're all mixed up about the filly." Matthew wouldn't give up on the subject. "She's got ya goin' six ways from Sunday. But she's right for ya. I know she is. All the changin' goin' on with ya, it's cause of her and ya know it," Matthew insisted.

Sam Hill.

Jake threw his gear back onto his bunk and flopped back down in his chair at the table. He had no words now for what he was feeling.

Matthew sat back down, too.

"Listen, son," Matthew appealed gently. "I know your life ain't been an easy ride, but that's all changin' now. You're makin' it dang good here with the minin' and all. I'm real proud of ya. I'm glad you're all done with Belle, too. But the Doc, son, that Doc Zoe's right for ya. I could tell the first time I seen the two of ya together."

Much as it went against his grain to talk about himself, Jake needed Matthew to understand the truth of it.

"I tried, Matthew. I tried with Queenie but—"

"Go on, son," Matthew encouraged.

Jake swallowed hard. "Fact is she didn't want me. I wanted her, Matthew, but she turned me down flat."

Matthew said nothing. He hurt for Jake. Horse-feathers. Matthew thought the Doc liked Jake.

"I wasn't good enough for her," Jake threw out.

"Did the Doc say that to ya?" Matthew asked, his temper flaring.

"No, Matthew, she didn't have to. I'm not good enough for her and I know it. She's quality, real quality. She has learning and a family, and she is religious-like and all. What

237

do I have to offer someone like her? Nothing, that's what," Jake leveled.

"Hogwash," Matthew's temper died down. He'd suspected all along how Jake felt about himself. Well he didn't feel that way about Jake. Jake had a lot to offer to Doc Zoe. Maybe he couldn't convince Jake of it, but maybe the Doc could. He sure wished things between Jake and the red-headed filly hadn't gone sour.

"You're good enough for the likes of any gal, Jake. Don't ya forget it," Matthew said gruffly and then re-lit his pipe.

Jake wasn't listening to Matthew anymore. Queenie's rejection was as raw now as it had been months ago, when he last saw her. Not a day went by that her words and her rejection didn't hit him in the face. To want somebody so much—somebody who didn't want any part of him— gnawed at his guts. The ache wasn't going away any time soon, and he knew it. He still wanted Queenie all right, so badly that he could taste her creamy skin and rosy lips every time he thought of her.

And what Matthew said. Was it true? It hadn't occurred to Jake until Matthew said so, that he had stopped drinking and card playing. The only reason for it, Jake figured, must be because he'd lost his saloon.

Yeah, lost was the right word for it, all right.

Jake wasn't going to wait for morning. He grabbed up his gear, said his good-byes to Matthew, and shoved open the cabin door, all the while trying to shove away all thoughts of a rusty-haired, freckle-faced beauty from his mind.

Zoe-Esther tossed and turned all night. Too worried to sleep, she had run out of time and she knew it. The hour glass had overturned months ago when she'd tried in vain to get her paying medical practice going, and now the last sands had spilled along with the coming of summer.

Her money was all but gone; spent on food for her papa and medicines for the miners. Thanks to God for the miners and their generosity. With barely enough to take care of their own families, the miners paid her with whatever they had. Usually that meant food or precious kerosene oil, but often the well-intentioned miners promised to pay in gold dust when they could.

With little choice now, Zoe-Esther knew she'd have to risk moving her papa back east where she could find steady work. Daniel had been right all along. She'd failed to make it on the frontier as a doctor.

Daniel.

Zoe-Esther had given him little thought in the past year. Remembering him now made her think of all of her failures, especially her failure to make a living in medicine. Suddenly an even worse failure hit her, one hidden in the recesses of her troubled thoughts: she hadn't found her match, her Yaakov, either.

It's not fair.

Zoe-Esther rolled onto her stomach and banged her pillow with a fist, then pressed her cheek flat against the muslin. So what if she felt like she was nine again. What did it matter?

"It doesn't, not at all," she whispered into the dusky silence. If only she could bury her face in her pillow and make everything wrong in the world, go right. If only her Yaakov were there to help her—to love her.

Fighting tears, Zoe-Esther turned back over and stared at the cabin ceiling. There wasn't much to see in the dark; not even imaginary cracks forming shapes out of her anatomy book. Suddenly she longed to be back in Philadelphia, back in her old apartment, cracks on the ceiling and all. Would she do it all over again and make the same mistake twice?

"No, I would not," she whispered to no one at all. "I should not have stopped to see the *schadchen*. I should have been stronger." Strong. She was so tired of having to be strong for her papa and for the mining families. Just once she longed to be encircled in somebody else's loving arms, safe, secure, and happy. That someone else came to mind. It wasn't Daniel. It wasn't anyone she'd tried to imagine over the years. It was Jake Whiskey, the man she yearned for, the man she loved, but could never have.

"It's not fair," she whispered again into the silent night. "It's cruel and—"

She couldn't go on. Her tears wouldn't let her. They spilled down her cheeks. She didn't have the energy or the inclination to wipe them away.

Chapter Sixteen

"Why didn't you call for me earlier, Mrs. Ingstrum?" Zoe-Esther tried to keep her voice calm and her panic hidden. The stench of excrement and vomitus hung in the sweltering tent's stagnant air, trapped like pond scum in a forgotten water hole.

"Your husband, how long has he been like this?"

"Two days it is, Doc Zoe," Mrs. Ingstrum wrung her hands and began to cry. "I try every-ting I know but nahting I do is helping, Doc."

Zoe-Esther had rushed in the summer heat to Tent City the moment she'd been summoned to see the Swedish immigrant. Perspiration ran down her face and stung her eyes. She put her spectacles on but didn't really need them to see what ailed Mr. Ingstrum. Despite the blistering temperature, a cold, chilling dread washed over Zoe-Esther. She was scared to death now for everybody in Golden City: every man, woman, and child!

Cholera! No examination was necessary for Zoe-Esther to be sure of her diagnosis of the morbid, communicable disease. Mr. Ingstrum's malodorous bed and extreme, gaunt features said it all. Her patient lay prostrate, in a coma, and near certain death. If he'd been ill for two days, that's all the time anyone had. Sometimes patients died after only hours of coming down sick.

Mr. Ingstrum's face was a purplish hue, his eyes and cheeks sunken in from severe fluid loss. His cool skin was dry and non-pliant. His pulse was very weak. Zoe-Esther could barely palpate it. Her heart went out to the dying man, for die he would, and soon.

"Mrs. Ingstrum, please get me a basin of water and let's wash your husband and put a clean cloth to his brow." While the woman rushed to do her bidding, Zoe-Esther realized what must be done. The soiled linen, every single bit used to clean Mr. Ingstrum's diarrhea and vomitus, would have to be destroyed. But polluted water was their worst enemy now. Zoe-Esther quickly called to mind everything she could remember in Dr. John Snow's writings, "On the Mode of the Communication of Cholera." She had read his 1855 British treatise in medical school. Dr. George Wood, a professor of Materia Medica at the University of Pennsylvania, had written on the subject as well.

Cholera was a water-borne illness proven to spread through ingestion of water contaminated by infected feces and other excreta. Physical contact with victims, too, could be deadly. Accepted, successful treatment didn't exist, Zoe-Esther believed. She also believed that the cures prescribed often threatened to kill when the disease did not.

Calomel, a mercury compound, given to induce diarrhea and rid the body of toxins, made fluid loss worse and caused teeth and gums to break down from mercury poisons. Opium was often ordered to moderate diarrhea and relieve pain, but it was absolutely too dangerous for children. Sometimes chalk or a starch enemata was prescribed for the young. Counter-irritation for abdominal cramps often meant applications of mustard plaster or turpentine over the area in question. Treatment remained experimental in Zoe-Esther's opinion, with doctors having to learn by trial and error. Never in all of her schooling did she think that even once she might have to confront this horrible contagion! Now that one looked her in the face, she must contrive the best treatment to try to save the most lives.

Her logical, medical mind turned over plan after plan before she settled on the obvious. With cholera, patients die in cardiovascular collapse very quickly from dehydration and fluid loss due to severe diarrhea, urine loss, and vomitus. Logic told Zoe-Esther that rapid replacement of vital fluids had to be the best answer, rather than harmful drugs. Administration of fluids, isolation of the sick, and destruction of contaminated clothing and linens must be helpful to combat illness. And, of course, scrupulous hand washing. Above all, Zoe-Esther had to find out where folks got their water. Then she could try to prevent its further contamination.

"Mrs. Ingstrum," she spoke gently to the grieving woman. "Your husband will soon be at peace. He won't feel the pain of this world anymore. I wish with all my heart I could work a miracle and save him, but I cannot."

"I know, Doc Zoe, I know," Mrs. Ingstrum said weakly and placed a kiss on her dying husband's forehead. "I jus sit here a spell with my Lars. Ya go on now. Ve'll be fine, Doc Zoe, jus fine . . ." Her voice trailed off. Zoe-Esther left to give the Ingstrums privacy.

Cholera would spread fast through Tent City, and kill fast, Zoe-Esther knew. Who? Who could have been the culprit to bring such torment to them all? It could be any immigrant, anyone from anywhere, so it would do little good to puzzle over who the culprit might be.

By late afternoon Zoe-Esther had all the answers she

needed about the water supply in Golden City, situated at the mouth of Clear Creek. Fed from the creek, a man-made ditch ran from one end of town to the other, with shallow, common wells dotted along the main streets. More than once she saw buckets, filled with goodness knows what, dumped into the watery ditch. Even though there were outside privies used, she shuddered to think how easily the privies could pollute the town ditch.

Exhausted and dreading the next weeks more than anything in the whole of her life, she hurried Sheyn along the trail back to her cabin. Yitzhak would be waiting. Relieved to know he was isolated from harm, with a fresh source of uncontaminated spring water, he must continue to stay away from Golden City. Especially after his battle with tuberculosis, he could not endure even the mildest case of cholera. As for herself, Zoe-Esther would pack what she needed and head back to town early tomorrow morning. She must make people listen and understand what they had to do if any of them were to survive. Offering up a prayer to God for the welfare of all the townspeople, she knew they were in His hands now.

A week went by, with many in Tent City still sick or dying. Many, too, who attended the sick, had succumbed. It would be several more long weeks before the cholera outbreak ran its course. Zoe-Esther knew that she could fall ill any day, and so she hurried that much more with her ministrations to the stricken. Families organized as she had instructed them to do, taking care to destroy contaminated bedding and gather fresh water from upstream in the Clear Creek. No one was to consume any of the water from the common ditch or shallow wells. Likewise, no one could dump any wastes into the nearby waterway. As best they could be, those who became ill were isolated from the rest of the family. Instructions were left to provide water and other healing fluids whenever the patient could swallow them. The only way to fight cholera was with fluids, fluids, and more fluids, Zoe-Esther believed. She worked day and night making rounds to all in need in Tent City. Worse off than the rest were the sick children. It broke her heart to see their innocent little faces wracked with pain and their frail bodies drawn up into a ball, trying to stop the terrible cramping brought on by so much suffering.

Zoe-Esther prayed her remedies were having some effect on preventing needless deaths. She mustn't lose hope. Her patients in Tent City depended on her, and she would be there for them, even if it meant she'd contract the dread disease herself.

"Doc Zoe?"

Someone spoke behind her. How she dreaded hearing about yet another who might perish. Reluctantly, she turned around.

"Doc Zoe, is it?" the stout stranger asked again, perspiration dripping down his face.

The noon rays of the sun beat down mercilessly.

"Yes, I'm Doc Zoe, sir," she answered. She didn't recognize the neatly dressed man. "How can I help you?"

"Well, ma'am . . . Doc, I mean." He took his hat off and nervously turned its brim round and round in his sweaty hands. "My name's Jeb Farley and I . . . my family, I mean to say . . . we need you to come. It's real bad up and down Main Street with the cholera and all. Everyone's sick and Doc Pritchard . . . well . . . he died yesterday."

"I'm very sorry to hear that, Mr. Farley." She hadn't liked the frontier doctor, but certainly never wished him dead. It hit her just then: that for the past week she'd not

245

thought about anybody except her patients in Tent City. True, she'd been busy beyond anything one person could handle, but still she was upset with herself now for not having thought about the rest of Golden City. And now, with Doc Pritchard gone, all the rest of the townsfolk would be in grave need of help.

Suddenly struck by another fearful blow, she thought about Jake for the first time in a very long time. Maybe he hadn't left town as she'd heard! What if he still lived in Golden City!

What if he lay ill and . . . dying! Nauseated with fear, she had to know. She'd comb every house, every saloon, until she found out.

Oh please Dear Lord in Heaven, please do not take Jake from this earth . . . or from me. Not until I tell him—

Never before had Zoe-Esther known such a fear; not even when the soldiers charged down into her village in Russia; not even when she expected the soldiers to kill her.

If Jake dies—

Right now, at this moment, she had to take care of the dying in Golden City, and pray with all her heart that Jake would never be one of them.

"I'll come right away, Mr. Farley," Zoe-Esther assured him. "Just wait a moment while I fetch my medical bag."

"Thank you, Doc," the worried man said, and stayed rooted to the spot.

After she saw to Mr. Farley's wife and child, she knew she had to find Doc James and try to convince him to join forces with her to fight the cholera epidemic, using her treatment plan. Bottles of calomel, rhubarb, castor oil, large quantities of opium, laudanum, and camphor were just making Mr. Farley's family sicker. The medicines did no good at all, making their diarrhea and vomiting worse, the child more at risk than the mother.

Zoe-Esther found Doc James in the last place she thought to find him: his office. He sat at his desk, alone, quiet and stone-faced, with a bottle of liquor uncorked in front of him, and a dirty glass in his hand. Disheveled, with strands of his thinning hair plastered down the sides of his reddened, puffy face, his eyes glazed over, and with his shirtfront soiled and unbuttoned at the neck, she wondered at his mental state.

"Doc James?" she softly called, and came to stand right in front of his slumped posture.

He didn't answer her. He didn't look at her, but seemed to be staring off somewhere in the distance. His thin lips quivered, and he tried to mumble something.

Zoe-Esther couldn't understand what he strained to say.

"Doc James," she pressed, and wished she could get through to him. It was too late, however. No need for her to discuss a plan of treatment for his patients. He needed help himself. Right now she had to leave Doc James and see to the critically ill. Later, when she could, Zoe-Esther would come back and see to the doc.

Before she could think straight about anything or anybody else, she must find out about Jake. Running as fast as her feet would take her, she headed for Mrs. Bartlett's Rooming House. The good-natured landlady had to know. Didn't Mrs. Bartlett know everything about everybody in Golden City? *Dear Lord, what if Mrs. Bartlett is ill . . . or worse!* Zoe-Esther tried not to think at all, and kept on running.

"Zoe-Esther, child, I'm that glad to see you," Mrs. Bartlett threw her arms around Zoe-Esther and hugged her hard. When she let go of Zoe-Esther, she quickly ushered her inside. "Child, we've great need of you, you have to know. I wanted to come for you myself but I know how folks have treated you, and, well, I've been ashamed, too, for not doing more to help you."

"Mrs. Bartlett, don't fret so," Zoe-Esther rushed with her reassurance, at the same time thanking God above that Mrs. Bartlett was alive. "I must ask you something. It's very important." Breathless, her chest hurt. "Is Jake Whis—" She couldn't say his name, scared to death what Mrs. Bartlett might tell her. Her legs wanted to give way, and go out from under her. "Is Jake—"

"Child, child. Come sit down before you swoon." It was Mrs. Bartlett's turn to console.

Zoe-Esther sat down on one of the settees, grateful for the steady seat. Her chest still pained her.

"Mrs. Bartlett, please. Is Jake Whiskey dead or alive?"

"So this is what brings you to me? Jake Whiskey." Mrs. Bartlett sat down next to Zoe-Esther and took up one of her hands, patting it gently. "He is fine, dear. He is very much alive. He left town months ago, and has not come back. Not even once."

Zoe-Esther turned her hand over and clenched Mrs. Bartlett's fingers hard.

"He is? He is alive? You are sure?"

"Of course, child. Of course he is. You must believe me," Mrs. Bartlett said.

Unable to speak, to say a word now, Zoe-Esther's tears said it all. Relief washed through her with such force, she couldn't hold her tears back any longer. She crumpled against Mrs. Bartlett's ample shoulder.

"There, there, now," Mrs. Bartlett soothed. "You just

get it all out, honey. I know how it is with you two."

"But . . . but how could you?" Zoe-Esther sobbed.

"Tish-tosh, my pretty child, never you mind about that. I know these things, that's all that needs saying now," Mrs. Bartlett said, putting her arm around Zoe-Esther's quaking form. "How about I make us both a nice cup of tea? It always soothes," she was quick to add.

Zoe-Esther calmed and her tears began to dry. She pulled herself to sit up straight on the settee.

Mrs. Bartlett left her to make the promised pot of tea.

Thirty minutes later, more relaxed than she'd been in over a week, Zoe-Esther knew she should leave Mrs. Bartlett's and start attending the families in town. She had to try to save as many lives as she could. Spurred into action, she set down her teacup and stood.

"Just where do you think you're going without me?"

"What?" Surprised, Zoe-Esther couldn't imagine what Mrs. Bartlett meant.

"You're going to have your hands full with all the sick folks here, and I mean to help you," Mrs. Bartlett pronounced. "Simple as that."

"But—"

"No ifs, ands, or buts, child. I'm offering my place here, too. You can use my rooms here for the sick."

"Do you know what you're saying, Mrs. Bartlett? You're putting yourself at great risk."

"And you're not, I suppose?" the older woman answered back.

Grateful beyond words for assistance, Zoe-Esther gave Mrs. Bartlett a quick kiss on one of her apple cheeks then turned and snatched up her medical bag. She'd left it in the hallway when she came in earlier. Mrs. Bartlett hurried now, too, and pulled the front door shut behind her.

The two women lost no time in beginning their sickbed rounds.

Exhausted and drained, and against her better judgment, Zoe-Esther used the last of her aromatic powder of chalk to help quiet Mrs. Bluett's youngest son. Yes, there was a tincture of opium in the nostrum, but the little boy's misery needed soothing. If she could ease the child enough so he could drink vital liquids, there was hope for a recovery. As she'd done for days and days, Zoe-Esther offered up a prayer to God for the child.

"I thank you, Doc Zoe, for taking care of my Lester and for speaking to the Lord for us." Mrs. Bluett stood at the bedside and spoke in hushed tones. "Doc Zoe, I want to . . . I need to apologize to you for—"

"Please, Mrs. Bluett, not another word. It's all right. What's important is for you to stick like glue to your child and offer him as much to drink as you can. You know everything else to do. We've talked about it all, I think. I'll be back tomorrow. Send for me at Mrs. Bartlett's if you need me, for anything."

"I'll do that Doc Zoe. God bless you." Mrs. Bluett gave her a grateful smile then bent down to her son.

At the end of three weeks, over a third of the population of Golden City and Tent City, several hundred men, women and children, had died from cholera. The repressive pall of death settling over the whole town left survivors in mourning, and gravely afraid. The daily ritual of wagons trolling the deserted streets for more bodies added to the survivors' burdensome sorrow.

But with no new cases in several days now, Zoe-Esther believed the epidemic had perhaps run its course. A *yom tov,* a good day and reason for joy, if it were true. For some reason she and Mrs. Bartlett had been spared, both working diligently day in and day out to care for the sick and dying. Never in her life would she forget the older woman's dedication and sacrifice. Every day she said a blessing, a *brochah,* for all of Mrs. Bartlett's good deeds, for her true *mitzvot.*

When the following week brought no new cases, Zoe-Esther knew there was reason for joy again in Golden City. Thanks to God, despite countless losses, many survived the dreaded contagion, including Mrs. Bluett's young son and Doc James. For their lives and all the others saved, Zoe-Esther would be eternally grateful.

By the middle of August, with the cholera epidemic behind them, townsfolk began to put the pieces of their shattered lives back together. Important to them all, they needed to prevent, as best they could, a future outbreak of disease. Deeper wells had been dug far away from the old, shallow ones and the city ditch was gone. The Town Council hastened to improve Golden City's water system. They'd listened to Doc Zoe and took her word as gospel now, leaving all prejudice against her buried in the past. In fact the entire remaining population listened to her, and wanted to come to her now for their medical needs, especially with Doc James still incapacitated. Rumor had it he might never hang out his shingle again.

Zoe-Esther, miracle of miracles, had a clinic now thanks to the kindness of Mrs. Bartlett, who insisted Zoe-Esther take over all three floors of her rooming house. Mrs. Bartlett said that she would keep her residence on the main level, and help out with cooking and with whatever else she could.

"I'm very grateful, Mrs. Bartlett," Zoe-Esther said, still shocked by her generosity.

"It is Hester, child. You must call me Hester and no more of this 'Mrs. this' and 'Mrs. that.' All right?"

"Yes, if you like . . . Hester." Zoe-Esther liked her name and thought it sounded Jewish, like the old country. "I must also ask something of you."

"Anything, child."

"I want you to take payment for your kindness. You will lose any future income from potential boarders. Whatever my patients can pay, I will give you a portion."

"Ridiculous. I don't need the money, child. My husband left me with enough to get by, so never you mind about it."

"Well, I do mind, Hester," Zoe-Esther said, determined to have her way. "If you won't accept my offer, I cannot accept yours."

Hester Bartlett smiled at her young friend and finally acquiesced and put out her hand.

"Good," Zoe-Esther returned her smile and shook hands. "Then it's all settled, we're in business."

"Papa, Papa." Zoe-Esther kissed him on both cheeks and hugged him again. "I'm so happy to see you, Papa. You look wonderful and healthy," she exclaimed, elated to see him after six weeks away.

"Star, my little Star. Thanks to God, you are *gesundheit*, in good health. But what are these circles under your eyes and so thin you are," he chided and stood away from her a moment, shaking his head. "I was so worried about my little girl, helping all the sick with no one to help you. Thanks to God," he rasped out and took his beloved daughter in his arms again.

"I'm sorry you worried over me, Papa. I told you I'd

send word if something happened, but this is all behind us now. We are both alive and such a *brochah* is cause for great *simcheh,* great joy." She gave him another quick kiss on his tear-stained cheek and at once set the kettle to brew for tea.

They talked into the night of all that transpired during their absence from one another. Yitzhak talked about how much better he felt and all the wood he had chopped, and Zoe-Esther about her many new friends and, best of all, her new clinic.

"I have everything I want now, Papa," Zoe-Esther beamed at him. "You are in good health and in good spirits and I can work as a doctor and get paid for it now," she said, more lighthearted than she'd felt in a long time. "We both have everything we need now, isn't it wonderful?"

Not so wonderful yet, little Star, Yitzhak opined to himself. *When you are married and a bride, then, then we will both have everything. You will be a* kalah *under the wedding canopy with the man you love and I will be a proud papa. Maybe a* zayde *I will be one day, if God wills you to give me grandchildren. I know how much you must miss your Daniel. Soon, very soon, he will be here.*

With no idea of the unexpected, disastrous turn of her papa's thoughts, Zoe-Esther kept on talking and shared all her hopes for the new clinic in Golden City.

Gone for nearly two months, Jake had just returned to Black Hawk. Nathaniel Hill, with whom he was now in business, had sent him out of the Colorado Territory on business dealing with the new smelter.

"Cholera!" Jake didn't want to believe what he'd just heard Matthew tell him. He didn't want to think of who might not have made it through. "Matthew, I'm saddling back up and heading down to Golden City. Can you keep a watch over everything here a little longer? There's someone I—" He couldn't finish, deathly afraid for Queenie's life.

"Sure can, son," Matthew reassured, certain he knew who the someone was that Jake was so riled up about. Matthew had liked the redheaded filly from the start, her bein' the right one for Jake an' all. Not a praying man, Matthew thought now might be a good time to start.

Busy at her clinic, where patients from Golden City and Tent City were welcome, Zoe-Esther had seen more broken bones, swollen sores, and bouts of ague in the past weeks than during the entire year she'd been on the frontier. Happy to treat such curable maladies, she didn't turn anyone away, no matter the time of day or night. She had been at the clinic for three nights straight. It was long enough to be gone from her papa. Tomorrow she'd head back to their cabin to make sure he fared well. In the morning, before she left Golden City, she would first make a stop at Mr. Guthrie's Apothecary. No doubt he'd lost some of his customers, since many in town came to see her instead of purchasing his nostrums and remedies. True to her promise, she intended to continue to buy what she needed from his store to help compensate his losses. Of course it went without saying that she'd send her patients to Mr. Guthrie for anything she might prescribe for their care.

Since it was unusually warm for a morning in early September, Zoe-Esther wouldn't need her reliable shawl for her errand to Mr. Guthrie's, and instead grabbed up the satchel that she would need.

"Hester," she yelled over her shoulder as she reached out to turn the door handle, "I'll be back to say goodbye before I head home. If anyone needs me, I'll be at Henry Guthrie's pla—" She stopped short when she opened the door and ran right into her papa.

"Papa!" Her heart drummed in her terrified chest. Something horrible must have happened for him to be here. He'd never been away from their cabin before, not since they'd moved in!

Correctly reading the terror in his daughter's eyes, Yitzhak offered her quick reassurance.

"I am *gut*, Star. Not to worry, even a *biseleh*."

"But Papa," she didn't believe him. "You would not be here unless you had good reason. If you are sick, you must tell me," she demanded, fighting her growing fear for his welfare.

"Star, calm yourself. I am not sick and I have a very *gut* reason for coming," Yitzhak smiled mischievously. "I wanted to see for myself the look on my little Star's face when she sees what a surprise I have brought her."

A surprise?

Before Zoe-Esther had even one moment to imagine what her papa meant, out stepped—

Daniel Stein!

Her satchel dropped from her hand onto the floor. Surprise couldn't begin to describe how she felt. She went numb all over. Her brain, her heart, her entire body refused to believe what her eyes told her—that Daniel actually stood, flesh and blood, in front of her, right here, right now!

Zoe-Esther shuddered to think what his sudden appearance could mean.

Chapter Seventeen

"*Nu,* what is this, you two?" Yitzhak stepped forward and put a hand under each of Zoe-Esther and Daniel's respective arms nearest him. "Is this any way for a *kalah* and *chassen* to greet after so long apart?" he teased and tried to pull the pair closer.

There it was. Her papa said it. Bride and groom! Zoe-Esther couldn't speak. She couldn't move, either, and stood frozen to the spot, sorry already for the questioning expression covering Daniel's handsome face. He'd changed little in a year. His dark good looks and strong physiognomy reminded her only of all their times together in medical school and their steadfast friendship—not *mina lieber,* not my love. Daniel's very words, the ones whispered to her back in Philadelphia. How she wished that he were back there still.

Zoe-Esther didn't have to look at her papa to know that he wondered, as did Daniel, what was wrong. His wonder would lead to worry and worry would lead to relapse. She couldn't risk Yitzhak's health. She must not. His happiness far outweighed her own.

"Daniel, I'm so happy to see you," she did her level best to sound excited and threw her arms around his neck. "Forgive me, I just couldn't believe it was you. I was so startled that I couldn't speak. But here you are." She took her arms down and clasped both of his smooth, strong hands in hers, all the while keeping up her brightest smile.

Daniel pulled her hands to his lips and kissed both of them.

"Zoe-Esther, you are beautiful, just as I remembered." He gave each of her hands a squeeze then pulled her against his chest. "I've come to marry you. I love you," he said low against her ear.

Not yet. *I cannot pretend I love him, too! Not yet.*

"Yes, Daniel, I know you've come to marry me and I will marry you as soon as you like." She got her words out fast, and knew she'd never be able to take them back.

"*Nu,* when will you stand under the *chuppah* and join in marriage?" Yitzhak asked, elated, first giving Daniel a slap on his back, then kissing both of his daughter's flushed cheeks. "I think a week from Shabbas, after sundown next Saturday, is a *gut* time," Yitzhak offered, not waiting for either of the couple to speak up. "I know there is a rabbi that arrived on the same wagon train as you, Daniel, a true *brochah* for us all." Yitzhak looked heavenward and paused a moment before continuing. "The Rabbi's family is camped close by and so I go this very day and talk to him," Yitzhak announced. "This is *gut* with you, Star? And you, Daniel?" he asked, at last seeking their approval.

Daniel laughed and Zoe-Esther did, too—at least on the outside.

"*Gut, gut.*" Yitzhak's smile grew broad. He gave his daughter another hug. "You have made your old papa very happy on this day, little Star. Such *naches* I have never known."

"I am glad to bring you joy, Papa," Zoe-Esther whispered against his shoulder, choking back the tears of an-

guish and sorrow that threatened to unleash at any
moment.

"This is Daniel Stein, Hester," Zoe-Esther introduced
him the moment Hester entered the front hallway of their
clinic.

Hester shook the young man's offered hand, then imme-
diately recognized Mr. Zundelevich, who stood behind
Daniel. "Mr. Zundelevich, please come into the parlor."
She stepped right past Daniel and held out her hand to
Zoe-Esther's papa. "I'm thrilled to see you so well, Mr.
Zundelevich," she said and pumped his arm enthusiasti-
cally.

"Please. It is Yitzhak," he said, and warmed right away
to Hester Bartlett's friendliness.

"Come in and sit in our parlor, Yitzhak," Hester directed, not at all bashful about using his first name or
showing her interest in him. The change in him amazed her.
Why she'd no idea a'tall how handsome a gentleman he
was, him being so taken with the consumption before. But
now when she took his measure, her hand went to her
throat to make sure her cameo pin was in place, and to her
hair to straighten it, just so.

Too *farmisht* about what she should tell Hester about the
reason for Daniel's coming, Zoe-Esther missed the sudden
interest developing between her papa and Hester. Zoe-
Esther's thoughts turned inward. She had to control the
conversation so that Hester wouldn't be shocked about her
and Daniel. She was afraid that Hester might express surprise about Daniel, and about his unexpected arrival, in
front of her papa. After all, Hester knew who Zoe-Esther
was in love with, and it was not Daniel.

"Hester, I've . . . we've something to tell you." Zoe-

Esther quickly pulled Daniel to sit next to her on the opposite settee. The moment Hester turned toward her, Zoe-Esther willed her friend to understand and keep her silence. "Hester," Zoe-Esther began again and kept Hester's perplexed gaze. "Daniel and I are betrothed."

Disbelief was written all over Hester's round, usually jolly, face.

Panicked, Zoe-Esther kept talking, trying to find her nerve.

"Daniel and I were in medical school together back in Philadelphia. Why, he's come all the way here now to marry me. It's *Papa's* fervent wish," Zoe-Esther emphasized, hoping against hope that Hester would catch on and read the plea in her eyes. "How can any daughter go against the wishes of her dear papa?"

"Oh . . . I see, child," Hester slowly nodded her head, seeming to grasp the meaning of Zoe-Esther's pointed choice of words. "Why, certainly no daughter must disobey her papa's fervent wishes," Hester reiterated. "So, Daniel," Hester turned her attention toward him now. "Welcome to Golden City. I think you'll find life here a little different than in the East. Do you plan to settle here?" Hester asked.

Zoe-Esther suspected Hester's simple question was due more to her friend's understandable curiosity, than to any attempt at polite conversation.

"Yes, Mrs. Bartlett," Daniel answered courteously. "I plan to settle here, with Zoe-Esther. I hope we are marrying because we love each other, and not just because Yitzhak gives us his blessing," he joked, then took up Zoe-Esther's hand in his and pressed a quick kiss to her fingers.

Zoe-Esther's first response was to pull her hand away, but she dared not do it. When she saw the questioning look on Daniel's face, she knew he waited for her to say something in return.

"Of course, Daniel. We are marrying for love." Zoe-Esther said, grateful beyond words for Hester's quick mind.

"Mrs. Bartlett," Yitzhak joined in now. "I want—"

"Stop right there," she protested. "It's Hester."

"Hester." Yitzhak smiled at her and started over. "Hester, then. I know how *gut* you treat my little Star. This I do not forget. But I must ask more of you."

"Anything," Hester answered before she realized what she'd said. Embarrassed, she stared down at her hands folded in her lap.

This time Zoe-Esther noticed the sparks between her papa and Hester. Why Hester looked absolutely taken! And her papa . . . well, she'd never seen him grin so broadly at anybody before! If not for her own tangle and melancholy over the whole impossible situation with Daniel, she would have given them both more of her attention. Right now, she could not. In fact, content to sit back and let others do the talking, she wasn't even curious about what her papa wanted to ask Hester.

"*Nu,* Hester, what do you say about helping with the children's wedding?" Taken aback by Yitzhak's question, Hester didn't let on that she was. She appeared the very picture of composure. Ambivalent over how she should answer, Hester didn't want to make a mistake. If she said no—Yitzhak would be unhappy with her. If she said yes—Zoe-Esther might never forgive her.

Both women were rescued from their utter discomfort by a sudden knock at the front door. Zoe-Esther and Hester got up at the same time to answer the knock.

"I must see to my patient," Zoe-Esther explained.

"I must help her," Hester mumbled and followed Zoe-Esther out of the parlor.

Yitzhak and Daniel exchanged puzzled looks, but kept silent about the ladies' hasty departure.

"Child, what shall I do?" Hester at last had a chance to ask now that the new patient had been treated and had left Zoe-Esther's office.

Zoe-Esther rubbed her hands over her hot cheeks and shut her tired eyes. Why was it so warm? The air in the room had never been so close. She opened her eyes and poured a glass of water from the pitcher on her desk. Maybe it would cool her and give her nerve for the week ahead. She took a few sips then set her glass down.

"Hester, this is all unfair, to me and to you. But there's nothing to be done for it. Papa wants me to marry Daniel, and marry Daniel I will. Please don't ask me to explain everything now. I can't." Zoe-Esther didn't want to cry. She took another sip of water.

"Child, is there nothing I can do? Can I talk to Yitzhak for you? Does he know about—"

"No!" She hadn't meant to shout, and was thankful her office door remained closed. "No," Zoe-Esther repeated, quieter now. "Papa doesn't know about Jake and he cannot, ever." This time she did cry.

"There, there," Hester consoled, and put her arms around her sobbing little friend. "You just get it all out, child. I can't say as I agree with what you are doing, but if your mind is set to marry Daniel you must have your reasons. I won't say anything to your papa about Jake," she promised.

"Thank you," Zoe-Esther answered weakly, then pulled out of Hester's supportive embrace. "Now we both must go back . . . in . . . to Papa and to Daniel," she sniffed. "They will be worried."

Hester nodded her agreement and followed Zoe-Esther out of the office, worried now more than ever about her little friend.

Jake reached Golden City by mid-morning. It was the worst ride he'd ever had in his life. The ride had nothing to do with the dark of night, and everything to do with him finding out about Queenie. He headed straight for Mrs. Bartlett's Rooming House. *She'll know about Queenie. She's gotta.* Jake wrapped Missouri's reins around the hitching post out front of Mrs. Bartlett's, then charged toward the door and rapped hard, not seeing the sign overhead that read *Medical Clinic.*

"Land sakes, hold on," Hester called from the other side of the door. Zoe-Esther was home with her papa and not at the clinic. If need be, Hester would have to send for Zoe-Esther to return to town. The moment she opened the door and saw Jake, her heart went out to him. Her intuition told her precisely why he'd come, and she wanted to cry for the tragedy of it.

"Come in, come in, Jake Whiskey." Hester greeted with as much cheer as she could muster. "I'm that glad to see you. You look as if you've been riding all night! It's been months and months, Jake. Come into the parlor," she offered and led the way.

Impatient to ask about Queenie, Jake followed her lead and sat down on one of the settees. He didn't waste time letting her know she was right. He had ridden all night. "Mrs. Bartlett, I've come here to ask you about—"

"I know Jake. About the rusty-haired, freckled faced doc. Am I right?"

"Yeah." His insides clenched. He wanted to ask his question but he'd never been so scared.

"Jake, she's fine. Zoe-Esther made it through the cholera just fine. Fact is, she saved a lot of the folks around here. What a brave girl, Jake," Hester added, then wanted to kick herself the moment she said it. None of this was going to do either of them any good. No matter what, Hester refused to be the one to tell him that his love was going to marry someone else in a week's time. It wasn't in her to be that cruel.

"Thank you, Mrs. Bartlett." Jake swallowed hard and felt the blood rush back through him. He let out the breath he'd been holding. Queenie made it! He wanted to hoot and holler, but stifled the urge. Damn. In all his life he couldn't remember a time when he'd felt this good.

Normally Hester would be pleased to see Jake so happy, but this wasn't a normal circumstance. Poor fella would find out soon enough about Zoe-Esther, and then where will all his happiness go?

"How are you, Jake? Really?" Hester softly inquired.

"Oh, me." Jake smiled at her now. "I'm fine, too."

My, what a handsome, strapping young man he is, Hester thought. *What a wonderful, lovely couple he and Zoe-Esther would have made.*

"What have you been up to, Jake, away all these many months?" Hester asked, wanting to steer him away from any questions about Zoe-Esther. She listened as he told her about his mine, and Matthew, and then his work at the smelter in Black Hawk. What a grand thing it was, Jake making such a success of his life after what happened at the Golden Gates. Hester could not have been more proud of him if he were her very own son.

"Are you gonna tell me, Mrs. Bartlett?" Jake interrupted her reverie.

"Tell you what, Jake Whiskey?" she said, even though she knew perfectly well where this question would lead.

"About Queenie . . . uh, I mean about Doc Zoe, Zoe-Esther?" Jake stumbled out.

"What would you like to know about her," Hester stalled for time.

"Mrs. Bartlett, if it's all the same to you, would you just tell me if you've seen her?" Jake said. "How is she? Does she still live up the other side of town with her pa? Are they getting on all right?"

Hester's heart broke yet again for Jake. She could see how much he cared.

"As a matter of fact, Jake, Zoe-Esther stays here with me a lot. Fact is, she runs her clinic here. And you're not to worry about her. She's doing real well with her doctoring and making a decent living. As for Yitzhak, her father's doing real well, too. They still live in their cabin for the most part," Hester finished, and hoped and prayed Jake would be satisfied with what she'd told him.

"Appears there's been some changes since I left," Jake said.

Not all good ones, I'm afraid, Hester wanted to say, but held her tongue.

"Yes, Jake, more than you know," she answered with what truth she could.

"Would you . . . would you do me a favor and tell Queenie . . . I mean Zoe-Esther," he corrected. "Would you tell her that I was by and that I wish her well? I'll be leaving tomorrow for Black Hawk," he said, and then got up from the settee. "I'd be pleased if you'd give Queenie my message." He forgot to say Zoe-Esther.

"Of course, Jake," Hester said and got up too, relieved indeed that he hadn't pressed her for more, though she wondered why. "Will you be stopping by again before you head out?"

"No ma'am, I won't."

"Well, Jake Whiskey, come here and give this old lady a hug," she ordered good-naturedly, not caring what he might think of her motherly request.

When she shut the door after Jake, Hester turned it all over in her mind again and again, and still could not come up with any solution to bring Zoe-Esther and Jake together. *I suppose it's just not meant to be. No match here,* she admitted, feeling every one of her fifty plus years.

"Rabbi Sidovsky is happy to come!" Yitzhak could hardly contain his joy. "He comes here to talk to you and Daniel Friday before Shabbas, Star." Yitzhak gave his daughter a bear hug then released her to go find Daniel, and share his good news.

Happy her papa appeared hale and hearty, now able to make the wagon trip back and forth from their cabin with ease, Zoe-Esther wasn't happy about his news. She moped around the rest of the morning at the clinic, doing her best to come up with a smile for her patients. So far today the clinic had been busy, and for that she was grateful. Less time to dwell on a wedding that she didn't want, to a man she didn't want.

Not a bit hungry, Zoe-Esther dreaded today's mid-day meal. She hadn't been able to get anything but hot tea and a little water into her churning stomach for the past two days. To make things worse, all of them, Papa, Daniel, and Hester, would join her to talk about all of the wedding preparations. She'd given Hester her permission to help her papa with the plans. *If this makes things a little easier for Papa, then all the better,* she'd decided.

"*Nu,* what do you think, Hester? Some chicken, some *kugel,* a little noodle pudding? Some hot potatoes in borscht with a little *tzimmes,* too? Yes, a nice chicken, Hester, this is what we need to make a celebration." Yitzhak settled back in his chair at the mid-day table, a satisfied expression on his face. "And some schnapps, of course, peppermint schnapps," he threw in.

"Yitzhak, excuse me but you don't remember where you are. This is America, not Russia," Hester chided. "Maybe we could make a mix of things, things the folks around here will enjoy. Chicken, yes. Fried chicken and mashed potatoes. And beef, platters of it. And corn, that would be delicious," Hester insisted.

"We cannot at least have a little strudel then?" Yitzhak came back at her. "You know, Hester, you are a nice, smart woman but everything you do not know. I say we have boiled potatoes and not what you say . . . Feh . . . mashed potatoes—"

"Yitzhak," Hester interrupted him, her tone more conciliatory than his. "Yitzhak, let us make a compromise. You have your potatoes and I'll make mine. You have your strudel and I'll make a nice butter cake for the wedding table."

Zoe-Esther listened to her papa and Hester go back and forth, sounding more like a husband and wife of many years rather than new-found friends. In truth, Zoe-Esther didn't care what was served at her wedding. Unable to keep her attention on any of them at the table, she played with her food, and then took a sip of water.

"Zoe-Esther," Daniel spoke quietly, leaving Yitzhak and Hester to talk to one another. "Zoe-Esther, what is it? You can tell me. I know something bothers my beautiful bride-to-be and you must tell me. All day today you've been upset. What is it?" he asked again, even more gentle than before and put his hand over hers.

It's you, Daniel! It's you! She wanted to scream. Right away she was guilt-ridden about having such bad thoughts about Daniel. He didn't deserve this. None of it was his fault. After all, hadn't she led Daniel to believe that she'd marry him one day? Zoe-Esther worked up a smile and turned to look into Daniel's dark, perceptive eyes, all full of questions for which she had no answers. The important thing now, and the only thing she could do now, was to re-assure him.

"It's just . . . I'm just worried for you, Daniel," she hurried with her lie. "It's not right you should give up every-thing back east, your practice and all, and come out here to no man's land. You love the hospital where we trained. I know you do. None of this is fair to you, Daniel," she ex-claimed and withdrew her hand from beneath his. Like ev-erything else about this day and this conversation, his touch only set her nerves on edge.

"Zoe-Esther," Daniel recaptured her hand. "If this is all that bothers you, do not worry. I want to marry you and take care of you for all the rest of our lives. It doesn't matter where we live, where we work. What matters is we will be together, always." He leaned over to kiss her, but she turned away.

"It's something else then, isn't it?" Daniel said, wounded over her rejection. "It's someone else, isn't it, Zoe-Esther?" he gritted out his same question, unwilling now to look at her. "You forget how well I know you. You forget a lot of things . . ." His voice trailed off.

Her heart wrenched. Her head ached. Zoe-Esther had no idea what to do or say to Daniel. To see him so sad and hurt undid her. How could she keep lying to him when his only fault was to be such a good, trusted friend to her? She wrung her hands, thinking it should be her own neck, instead. For one thing only did she feel some bit of relief: her papa and Hester remained engaged in animated discussion with each other. At least neither of them had seen what took place between her and Daniel.

A heavy knock on the front door saved her from the impossible moment. Without a word more for Daniel, Zoe-Esther pushed out her chair and got up to see who it could be.

Jake battled with himself all morning over whether to try to see Queenie or not before leaving town. He hadn't intended on it, but now he needed to, to see in person that she was all right. He almost had himself believing that was the only reason. First he had someone else to see.

He stepped up onto the planked porch outside the Golden Gates. Though early still, the saloon seemed unusually quiet. Jake pushed through the double doors. Time to settle things with Belle. Hell, she could have the whole damn place. It meant little or nothing to him anymore.

What the—

Cobwebs caught him across the face. He wiped them away and stepped inside the deserted saloon.

I'll be damned. There wasn't a soul in sight.

From the looks of things, likely there hadn't been anyone there in some time, Jake realized. He walked over to the empty, scratched, and dusty bar. If he closed his eyes he could hear the piano playing, laughter, cards turning, and drinks on the house of past glory days. Moving away from the cracked, beveled mirror, once a proud fixture of the Golden Gates, Jake started for his old office. Maybe he'd find a clue there about what happened to the place and to Belle.

"Jake Whiskey," a voice from behind stopped him. He turned around and recognized Jim Summers right away. They'd dealt faro together at the Golden Gates for years.

"Jim, good to see you." Jake came forward and put out his hand.

"Same here, Jake," Summers said and shook hands. "I'm danged surprised to see you, Jake. After all that happened to you, here at your place . . . well . . . let's just say, no one gave spit you'd come out all right." Summers shook his head and laughed. "I shoulda known. Hell, we all shoulda known you'd do just fine, like always."

"What in Blue Blazes happened here, Jim?" Jake turned the subject away from himself fast. "Where's Belle?"

"You've been gone a long time, Jake and a whole lot is different. First is, I'm sorry to be the one to tell you, Belle died a while back."

"What?" Jake couldn't believe it. "How? When? Was it the cholera?"

"Nope, not cholera, Jake. Opium, that's what done her in. She couldn't stay away from the stuff and one day, well she just up and died from it."

Jake couldn't say anything. Hard to imagine Belle dead, much less the way she died. He chose to remember another Belle—his beautiful, spirited Golden Girl of Golden City.

"And about the place here," Jim Summers kept on, oblivious to Jake's faltering attention. "The Town Council took over everything after Belle passed, but they couldn't make a go of it, like most other things they try to do around here." Summers smirked. "Anyways, Jake, now that you're back, are you gonna get things up and running again? I bet you could get this place back if you tried. Those council members don't have all their dogs barking, if you know what I mean."

Jake heard some of what the dealer said.

"This business isn't for me anymore, Jim. I'm all done with saloons."

"Too bad. You were good. You were *really* good," Jim Summers reflected and said goodbye to Jake, before he turned and slowly walked out through the creaky, swinging doors of the deserted saloon.

Jake didn't follow him. He needed more time to take it all in.

Chapter Eighteen

Whoever knocked at the clinic door persisted.

Zoe-Esther reached into her skirt pocket and withdrew her spectacles. She put them on and crossed the hall leading to the front entrance, knowing that she'd need her wire rims to examine the patient waiting for her on the other side of the door. Too bad someone had to be ill to give her an excuse to leave the dining table. She wished her headache would go away. Her head would probably pound, just like the persistent patient at the door, for the rest of her natural life.

The doorknob caught. Zoe-Esther turned it harder but still it refused to rotate. "Feh," she muttered her disgust with the unforgiving handle and tried again, this time using all of her strength. The knob gave way, and the door along with it, setting Zoe-Esther off balance and landing her hard against the wall behind the door. The mishap did nothing for her headache. She managed to catch her spectacles before they fell to the floor and shoved them back into her pocket. Grateful she hadn't fallen, Zoe-Esther leaned against the wall for support and shut her eyes, hesitant to show her embarrassed face to the patient on the opposite side of the door that stood ajar between them.

"Look lady, I won't bite. I promised, remember?" A low,

271

salty voice reverberated through the door.

Unmistakable. Zoe-Esther recognized the voice.

Jake!

Her eyes flew open, but the rest of her couldn't move. She easily remembered the very first words he'd said to her, the first time she'd met him, a lifetime ago.

Oh, Jake.

"Queenie, you still afraid of me?" he teased.

She'd heard those words before, too. The fact that he remembered them thrilled her. Powerful emotions rushed at her, too many to sort out at one time. Best of all, he'd said, *Queenie*. How she had missed hearing him say it—more than she'd let herself realize, until this moment.

Is it possible? Is Jake truly here? Zoe-Esther wanted to see for herself, but didn't dare, afraid that he might not be.

Strong, masculine fingers clasped the edge of the door and began to ease it away from her.

Petrified, feeling naked and exposed, Zoe-Esther kept her back glued to the wall and squeezed her eyes shut in self-defense. She heard the front door close, and knew the barrier that stood between them, the barrier that protected her, was gone.

"I'm glad to see you, too," Jake teased in a gravelly whisper.

Frozen, speechless, and utterly defenseless now, Zoe-Esther refused to open her eyes and face the moment.

"Queenie," Jake said again and stepped closer. The tiny cleft in her adorable chin beckoned. He wanted to kiss her chin, her beautiful face, and every other part of her that she'd let him. He put a gentle hand just under her chin.

Zoe-Esther jumped at his tender touch, but couldn't bring herself to open her eyes and meet his slate scrutiny. The clean essence of musk and masculinity, his essence, misted around her. She hadn't forgotten. How could she? His compelling nearness reminded her of so many things she'd trained herself, and failed miserably, to put from her mind. Struck by something else familiar, the sensation of déjà vu, Zoe-Esther remembered the first time she had felt the sensation—the first time she met Jake—and felt as if she had always known him . . . and loved him.

"I said I wouldn't bite, sweetheart," he teased further, more intimately than before.

Sweetheart, he said *sweetheart!*

Ever so slowly, Zoe-Esther opened her eyes.

She drank in his features, every loving detail that she'd dreamed of over the past months, and let her gaze travel from the top of his shaggy, cropped head of hair down past the allure of his smoky mustache, then run free over every inch of his well-proportioned body.

"Well, Queenie, I'd say you missed me all right," Jake said, his muted voice huskier now. He drew his other hand up to join the one he already had under her chin, and rubbed his thumbs in little pulses over and under her alluring chin. His hungry fingers splayed down the curve of her soft throat then came back to her face, to the flush in her cheeks, before he laced his fingers in the sides of her hair. His gentle coaxing easily loosened her coppery tresses from their fastening at her nape. He pulled her close.

"I'm gonna kiss you now—"

The same words, the very same she'd dreamed of hearing from him again. *Yes, Jake. Oh please, Jake. Yes! Yes!* She wanted to cry out, her smoldering passion aroused now. *I love you, Jake—*

His kiss silenced her fevered thoughts.

Urged into immediate submission, Zoe-Esther let him press her back against the wall, his lips at first teaching, then taking what he wanted. At his lead, she opened to him and took from him what she wanted, her ardor matching his.

Time stood still.

The whole world stopped.

Only Jake existed for Zoe-Esther.

Jake's delicious, demanding mouth, the excited brush of his shaggy mustache, the heady scent of musk on his heated skin, his masterful arms setting her to flame wherever they touched, his stirred manhood pressing ever harder against her aching core—only Jake.

Someone rapped loudly on the closed front door.

Jolted back to the present, Zoe-Esther heard the grating, intrusive knock, and evidently Jake did, too. They pulled apart at the same moment, their faces a mirror image of roused passions, both still breathing hard. One difference though: Jake smiled at her. Gripped with utter panic, Zoe-Esther didn't smile back. Her anxious mind raced from one unthinkable scenario to the next, troubled thoughts tumbling and jumbling over each other, each one landing in a tangle!

What if Papa had just come in! Or Daniel! Or both!

She backed away from Jake, as if he were a poison.

What if Papa or Daniel had seen me in Jake's embrace? What would I have said to them?

What could she have said? Her papa might collapse on the spot. If he did, would Yitzhak even want her to save him, after witnessing his daughter break with their Jewish traditions and take up with a *goy!?*

Oh, Jake, there's nothing to be done for it!

She finally turned her attention back to Jake. The way he looked at her now, his eyes in hurtful shadow, his handsome features sullen, his body held taut. What had she just done to him? To let him think, even for a few stolen moments, there could ever be something between them—she had no right, no right at all to put him through this. He didn't deserve it. And deep down inside, she knew she didn't deserve him.

Another rap at the door.

A loud male voice called out through the punishing wood.

"Doc Zoe! Got a delivery for you from Mr. Guthrie!"

Zoe-Esther didn't answer.

"I'll bring it along later, Doc Zoe," the man mumbled to himself.

Zoe-Esther listened while heavy boots walked away.

"So, Doc Zoe," Jake leveled, his tone filled with recrimination. "That's it then. I get it now, the doc part. I'm just a no-account. I sure as hell ain't no doc like you," he accused, his voice conveying all the bitterness and bruising he felt inside. "I'm just plain not good enough, am I?"

This day had gone downhill from the start for Jake. First the sad news about Belle and now Queenie. She was turning away from him, *again*. He sensed it the moment their kiss broke, but he didn't want to believe it. It was his own damned fault for coming, he knew. He should have stayed away from Queenie. If he'd just kept on riding, he'd be close to Black Hawk now instead of standing here in front of a woman he wanted to love, but who didn't want a damned thing to do with him!

Jake took a last look at Queenie, leaning so still and silent against the wall. He wouldn't set his eyes on her ever again.

"Zoe-Esther, who's—" Daniel stopped short when he saw the tall stranger standing too close to her.

"Daniel," she acknowledged, but didn't look at Daniel,

unable to pull her gaze from Jake's hard scrutiny.

Daniel walked up to Zoe-Esther and took her hand in his. "Hello, Mr.—"

When the stranger didn't fill in his name to Daniel, or look at him either, Daniel's suspicions grew. He squeezed Zoe-Esther's hand and pulled it possessively against his chest.

"I'm Daniel Stein, Dr. Daniel Stein." He didn't try to shake hands with the stranger. "I'm Zoe-Esther's *fiancé*." He emphasized the word, suddenly feeling the need to do so.

Zoe-Esther saw the pained expression on Jake's face intensify, and could only imagine what he must be thinking. She tried to pull her hand out of Daniel's, but he wouldn't let go. Frustrated with Daniel, she reached toward Jake with her free hand.

Jake recoiled, and stepped away from her reach.

Oh, Jake. What have I done?

She didn't have much time to contemplate the situation further.

Jake yanked the door open and walked out without a word, the bitter taste of rejection still in his mouth.

"Zoe-Esther?" Daniel wanted answers.

"Not now, Daniel. Not yet," she whispered and jerked her hand from his, not missing the hurt in Daniel's tone.

"All right, but later then? Later you'll tell me all about this?"

"Yes, later—" she sobbed and turned and ran into her office, slamming the door behind her.

"*Nu*, Hester," Yitzhak implored. "What do you know of this *tsuris*? What trouble comes to my little Star that she cannot tell her papa?"

He followed Hester into the parlor and sat down after she did.

The two had just left Daniel, whom they'd discovered only moments before, alone in the front hall. Daniel had no comment for them about Zoe-Esther, other than to say, she'd just had a visitor, and that the visitor was gone, and Zoe-Esther was shut away in her office. Hester, ever the more curious, inquired after the visitor. Daniel's sudden dark mood gave Hester a hint of who had come to call. When Daniel disappeared up the stairs, Hester didn't need to ask him anything else.

Hester, at a momentous crossroads, had to decide now what to say to Yitzhak. If she made the wrong decision, it could forever doom not only Zoe-Esther's future, but also her own as well. Though they had only kindled their friendship in the past days, already Hester was taken with Yitzhak. Her next words could destroy any possibility for a relationship with him. Quick to make her choice, Hester realized that she really didn't have one to make. For his daughter's sake, she had to tell Yitzhak the truth.

"Would you take some water?" Hester encouraged, believing he'd need it for what she was about to say.

"Hester Bartlett," Yitzhak pointed at her. "I think you hide something from me. Water, I do not need. Answers, this is what I need."

"Very well." She took a deep breath then faced him square on. "Yitzhak, there's no other way to say this. Zoe-Esther does not love Daniel." She hesitated before going further, checking Yitzhak's reaction.

Yitzhak shook his head. "This is a bad thing you tell me, Hester." He sat back in his seat. This he did not expect. Unprepared for such news, he kept silent a few moments. "But in time, Hester," he brightened. "In time my little

Star will love her Daniel. I am the papa and I make the match for her own good," he declared.

"What do you mean *for her own good*, Yitzhak Zundelevich? How can that be when she does not love Daniel?"

Yitzhak smiled at her now, as if he held all the answers, and she none.

"Hester, you do not understand our traditions. My Star will make a match with Daniel and come to love him. He is a Jew. She is a Jew. It will be good. I know what is best for my daughter," he pronounced with finality.

"Well this is a fine how-do-you-do!" Hester blurted out and stood up. She began pacing back and forth in front of Yitzhak. "Yitzhak Zundelevich, you do not know what is best for Zoe-Esther. Not about this."

"Please, Hester, sit. You make me dizzy."

Still fuming, she did sit, only this time across from him and not next to him.

"Your daughter loves another. The man, the man who just visited . . . this is the one she loves," Hester tried hard not to get mad again.

"*Nu,* this is true? Another Jew lives here in this place?" Yitzhak was shocked. Now *he* got up and began to pace. "All the time I want little Star to be with nice Daniel. But if she loves another Jew then . . . then I must meet him, and I will see." Yitzhak said emphatically and sat back down.

"The man she loves is not a Jew," Hester informed. There was no way to soften this for Yitzhak.

"*Mishegaz!* What you say is *mishegaz!*" Yitzhak raised his voice. "My little Star would not love a *goy!* This is crazy, what you say!"

He stared holes through Hester.

Uncomfortable, she shifted in her seat. She had more to say.

"Your daughter loves Jake Whiskey. You have met him before, I think."

"Jake Whiskey? Yes, I know Jake . . . but for my daughter—No! No! No! Not for my little Star!" Too agitated now to stay seated, Yitzhak stood.

"And why not for Zoe-Esther?" Hester got up, too.

"Hester, we are Jews. Our traditions keep us alive. If we do not honor our traditions, then we die. Zoe-Esther must marry in our faith. She would never go against me in this. Never!" he resolved.

"But—"

"Do not say another word on this subject to me, Hester Bartlett. You have said enough," Yitzhak said, then turned and strode out the front door of the clinic, leaving the heavy door rattling in its frame.

Zoe-Esther raised her sleepy head from her desk and looked out her office window. It had grown dark. She had no idea how long she'd slept. It didn't matter. Nothing much mattered anymore. All cried out now, she silently renewed her vow to put Jake and Yaakov, and all of her senseless dreams of them, out of her mind from this day forward.

It took effort but she got up, straightened, reset the tie in her hair, and ran a hand over her blouse and skirt, making sure all was tidy. Out of habit Zoe-Esther gave her office a quick once-over, satisfied that it, too, was neat and orderly. Odd, it suddenly struck her that no one had awakened her to see any patients the remainder of the day. Certain Hester would not turn anyone away, Zoe-Esther thought about the reason a moment, and wondered if Daniel had taken care of her patients.

Daniel.

Zoe-Esther hurried out of her office and up the stairs in search of him.

"Daniel, what are you doing?" Zoe-Esther rushed into his room the second he opened the door. "Why . . . you're packing, aren't you?"

"You're surprised?" Daniel answered sharply.

"No," she said, wanting to be honest with him now, about everything. "But Daniel, please, we have to talk."

"I don't want to talk, Zoe-Esther. I want you to leave, so I can," he snapped back.

She was not about to leave, and instead, found the room's only chair and planted herself in it.

"Daniel Stein, I want you to listen to me. Please," she softened now, praying that he would listen.

Daniel set his carpetbag on the bed. He sat down next to the case, then leaned over and lit the kerosene lamp on the bedstead. The little flame brightened the room, but not his spirits.

"Zoe-Esther, we have nothing to say to each other. Nothing," he said, his shoulders slumping along with his mood.

It hurt her that she'd hurt him so. He deserved to know the truth.

"Daniel, the man you met today, Jake Whiskey, is someone I care . . . I cared about," she corrected, and realized she had already broken her promise not to lie. Maybe just this one lie she could allow, for Daniel's sake. "I met Jake when I first came here. I did develop feelings for him, but . . . that's all in the past."

"Zoe-Esther, even so, what does any of this have to do with me?" Daniel spat out angrily.

"Daniel, it has *everything* to do with you." Zoe-Esther rose and came over to the bed and knelt down in front of him. "I . . . this is hard for me to say, Daniel. I still want you to marry me, if you will."

"I don't understand," he said.

"Daniel," she swallowed hard, determined to try again. "It is a good thing, a very good thing that you are here now, with me. This is as it should be. Don't you see? You and I, we belong together. We share so much. We are both Jews. We are both doctors. We both want the same things: a good medical practice, a good family," she flushed a little when she said, "family."

"But Zoe-Esther, you do not love me as I love you. I know you don't," Daniel protested.

"Not yet, Daniel," she met his dark, incredulous eyes. "But I know I will come to love you one day as more than a friend . . . as a husband."

"What of this man, this Jake?" Daniel asked. "You say he is in your past. Is this true, Zoe-Esther?"

"Yes," she told him, pained by the truth of her answer. Tears threatened, but she choked them back, and kept her focus on Daniel. She watched his dark visage change from disbelief to relief, and his warm smile return.

"Zoe-Esther," Daniel stood up, pulling her with him. "What is past then will stay in the past. Only the present and the future matter. If it is in my power to make the present and the future happy for you, I will."

"Thank you, Daniel," she managed, swallowing new tears over his generous, forgiving heart. "And, I promise to make our present and future together as happy for you as is in my power."

He placed a gentle kiss on her forehead.

She let him, then put her head against his chest and her arms around him, grateful beyond words for Daniel's understanding.

★ ★ ★ ★ ★

A welcome calm settled over Zoe-Esther during the night hours, and she awoke in her appointed bedroom at the clinic, a new person. After her talk with Daniel she'd gone straight to bed. And now, miracle of miracles, she had a strange sense things would turn out all right after all.

She and Daniel would marry. Certain that they would find their own happiness, Zoe-Esther was even more certain that Yitzhak would be the happiest of them all. It fell on her to make him so. After all, he'd sacrificed so much for her already, bringing her to America, making sure she had a chance to go to medical school, and coming west at her bidding, nearly dying from tuberculosis. And there was his beloved Sarah. He'd lost his Sarah right after her *ema* gave birth to her. Zoe-Esther owed her papa far more than merely giving him a son-in-law and grandchildren. She owed him her life.

Making up her mind to fill the rest of the days before the wedding with work at the clinic and any necessary preparations, and feeling more light-hearted than she'd imagined she could, given the circumstances, Zoe-Esther hopped out of bed. Yitzhak and Hester would be downstairs at breakfast, her papa also staying in a room at the clinic until the wedding. It occurred to Zoe-Esther that she had not even said good night to Yitzhak last night, or to Hester. *What must they think of me?* She would hurry with her morning toilette so she could join her papa and Hester at breakfast.

"Where is Papa, Hester?"

"Come, sit down child, and have some eggs and biscuits," Hester greeted, all alone at the table. She'd worried all night about Zoe-Esther, wondering what happened be-

282

tween her and Jake yesterday, and what Daniel might have seen.

Zoe-Esther sat down but didn't serve herself, uninterested in food or coffee.

"Hester. Papa?" she insisted.

"Child," Hester put down her cup and leaned back in her chair. First things first, Hester realized she would have to wait to find out about yesterday. As for today, for right now, she already had her little white lie for Zoe-Esther all thought out, believing it wasn't her place to tell Zoe-Esther what had really transpired between herself and Yitzhak.

Hester sighed and began again.

"Child, your father and I had a few words yesterday. He wasn't happy with me and left for awhile, that is all."

"All? What do you mean all? What words did you have? Where is he?" Zoe-Esther anxiously tossed out her questions.

"Calm yourself, child. It is nothing. Really." Hester kept up with her charade, hoping Zoe-Esther would believe her.

"Then tell me, please," Zoe-Esther begged, her heart pumping. "Tell me what this nothing is."

"Well, truth be told," Hester kept her fingers crossed under the table against her lie. "The truth is your father and I don't seem to agree on your wedding plans. He wants things one way and I want the opposite. He wants everything Jewish, absolutely traditional, and me, well I think he should let go of tradition a little and combine some of our western ways in the ceremony and reception." Hester picked up her cup and took another sip of coffee, as if nothing at all were amiss.

"Hester Bartlett," Zoe-Esther charged. "You're trying to tell me that Papa left here because he was angry with you about my wedding?"

"Yes, dear," Hester replied innocently, and put down her cup.

"And you've nothing else to say about it?"

"No, dear."

Frustrated, less anxious now, Zoe-Esther didn't quite believe Hester, yet she did believe that Hester would tell her if something had happened to her papa. She'd developed a great affection for Hester, almost a daughterly affection, and trusted her completely.

"Where do you think Papa is now?" Zoe-Esther gave up on why he'd gone and needed to know where, if she could. God forbid he should get sick again.

"I'm sure he's at the Gilpin House or the Clear Creek Hotel. You're not to worry over him, Zoe-Esther. He's a grown man, a healthy man now, thanks to you, and he can take care of himself once in a while."

Hester was right. Of course she was right, but still Zoe-Esther wouldn't be at peace until her papa returned to the clinic. Any moment now he could walk through the door, and then she'd find out what had really happened between her papa and Hester.

"And so, tell me now what happened with you and Jake and Daniel." Hester asked matter-of-factly. "Something sent Jake out the door, Daniel up the stairs, and you to your office in such a rush."

Amazed that Hester guessed correctly about just who it was that had called the day before, Zoe-Esther wasn't about to tell the intuitive woman anything else.

"Why nothing at all, Hester." Zoe-Esther conjured an innocent smile. "Nothing happened at all. Jake came in and we exchanged hellos. Daniel came in and we all exchanged hellos. Then Jake left. I left. And, Daniel left. That is all."

"Humph." Hester knew a lie when she heard one.

Hadn't she just done the same? *I suppose I'll have to find out on my own,* she mused silently. She admired Zoe-Esther's spunk. *Moxie,* she'd heard Yitzhak describe the word, spunk, before. *Yes, moxie. Zoe-Esther has moxie, just like me.* Hester couldn't keep herself from grinning.

Zoe-Esther smiled now too, but not for the same reason. She didn't miss Hester's note of disapproval and knew how badly Hester wanted to hear more—to kibbitz over every little detail—but Zoe-Esther thought it might do Hester a bit of good to be kept in suspense, for a while at least.

"Good morning, ladies." Daniel greeted them cheerfully as he entered the dining room.

Suspicious, Hester knitted her brows. When Daniel placed a quick kiss on the top of Zoe-Esther's head, and Zoe-Esther warmed to the kiss, whatever troubles existed for the two yesterday, Hester gathered, no longer existed.

"Here, Daniel. Have a nice cup of coffee," Hester offered, and filled the cup in front of him, all the while wondering just what he and Zoe-Esther were up to.

Chapter Nineteen

Yitzhak checked his pocket watch.

Ten o'clock.

Gut. Not so early. Not so late.

Next he checked the bottle of schnapps that he'd tucked away in an inside coat pocket. *Gut, gut,* he thought again. Standing now, outside his room at the Gilpin House, he needed another moment to remind himself exactly what he would say to Jake Whiskey, who was registered in a room on the same hallway. By chance, Yitzhak had seen Jake's name when he went to sign his own name on the hotel registry the night before. Whether it meant *mazel* or *tsuris,* good luck or more trouble—he would soon find out.

All night Yitzhak had been up. Sleep, how could he sleep? Never in his life had he worried so over his daughter. Always he'd thought that she wanted exactly what he wanted for her. He wanted to bring her to safety in Amerika, and she wanted to come. He wanted her to be a doctor, and she wanted to be a doctor. He wanted her to marry Daniel, a Jew like her, and he'd thought she wanted to marry Daniel. How could things have come to this? That his little Star would choose a man not of the fold! This, Yitzhak never thought of. Anything he would do for his little Star, anything in life, but not this. Never could he give his consent.

Never!

And so it went, with Yitzhak pacing back and forth in his room, arguing with himself over what to do. More than once he lifted his gaze heavenward and appealed to God for help.

"Lord, I ask you, what should I do? I love my little Star. I want her to be happy, but to choose for a husband a man who is not a Jew! How is a father to accept such a thing! I cannot."

Yitzhak paced the night through. There was no answer for it except that Star should obey him and marry Daniel Stein. He was the papa and he knew best.

But what if Hester was right? *What if my little Star loves Jake Whiskey, a goy!* Would it be so terrible for her to marry him? Jake was a *mensch*, a nice person yes, but for someone else, not his little Star. She must make a match with Daniel.

Yitzhak was still upset with Hester. *Maybe she makes it all up in her head,* he thought. But then why would she do such a thing and bring such *tsuris* to him and to his daughter? No, Hester would not do such a thing on purpose. Hester just did not know enough of their Jewish traditions and how much they meant to them.

"To lose our traditions is to lose everything," Yitzhak said into the darkness.

Moonlight crept in, giving him barely enough light to walk the length of the room without tripping over its furniture. The bed, when he passed it repeatedly, didn't invite him to sleep. If he climbed into bed, he knew he would only get right back up.

"So why should I bother?"

Dawn approached and still Yitzhak worried over what to do. He refused to leave all of their traditions back in the old country. It did not matter that he and Star lived in Amerika now, not to Yitzhak. Still they must keep their traditions. He thought of the *schadchen*. Always, she did a lively business and always her word stood for law—almost always. For his little Star, the final word belongs to the papa and the mama! And, with his Sarah gone, the decision was up to him.

My Sarah . . . what would my Sarah want for our little girl? Over and over in his befuddled, *farmisht* mind he asked this question, then, at long last, he had the answer he needed.

Jake heard the knock at his door but wasn't interested in answering it. Packed and ready to head back to Black Hawk, he wanted to leave. Hell, he'd already spent enough time in Golden City. "Wasted time," he muttered. Time wasted with Queenie, but maybe not the rest of it.

Jim Summers, the faro dealer he'd run into at the Golden Gates the day before, had sought him out later in the day. Said the Town Council was all in a hullabaloo over what to do with his old saloon property since Belle had died. It seemed that none of the council members could figure how to run the place or get the money needed to do it. "Why, them fellas don't know which end's up, if you ask me, Jake," Jim had volunteered.

Evidently the same mixed-up bunch had sent Jim Summers to find Jake, since word had already spread that he was back in Golden City. Would Jake consider helping them make sense out of the mess his old place was in? Would Jake consider running things again? Jim didn't think Jake owed the idiots one doggoned thing!

Only because Jake hated seeing his saloon in ruins did he agree to see the Town Council. Not sure what he wanted them to do with it, Jake definitely did not want his place back. He had the money to buy it back, but the idea of buying his own saloon was nothing less than the dumbest idea anybody'd ever thought up.

Ah hell, he'd work something out. Maybe he should just give them the money to fix up the Golden Gates and tell the council who they should get to run it. He had some names. It took the rest of the afternoon for Jake to get things settled with the council, and when he'd finished, he returned to the Gilpin House. It was late when he got back to his room. He decided against starting for Black Hawk. It would be dark soon and he'd be better to wait until morning. Dog tired and hungry, he didn't go for any supper but fell into bed instead. Luckily he didn't have time to think about Queenie, since he was asleep the moment his head hit the pillow.

Someone rapped at his door again. Jake was up but didn't want company. Irritated, he charged over and jerked the door open.

Anybody he might have expected to be there, anybody—except Queenie's pa! Dumbfounded, without a clue what to say or do, Jake stood there, silent as the grave.

"Jake Whiskey, what is this? You look like somebody died," Yitzhak tried to joke. "You do not have a nice hello for me after all this time?" Yitzhak said, then slipped past Jake and went into his room.

Jake slowly closed his door, but he didn't turn around.

Yitzhak pulled his flask of schnapps out of his coat pocket and set it down hard on the round, oak table in front of the room's only window.

The sound of it made Jake turn.

"Jake. Come, let us have a little schnapps and a nice talk," Yitzhak invited, then took up two nearby glasses and started to pour them both a drink.

"I don't drink," Jake told him, feeling like an idiot, but not over the alcohol.

Yitzhak threw Jake a friendly, surprised smile. "Well, I do, now," Yitzhak replied and took a sip of his drink. "*Gut*, this is *gut*, Jake Whiskey. Peppermint schnapps, the best," Yitzhak said and finished the rest of the schnapps in his glass.

What Queenie's pa was doing at ten in the morning, belting down alcohol in front of him, Jake couldn't for the life of him imagine.

"*Nu*, Jake, come and sit," Yitzhak directed, and took a seat in one of the chairs at the oak table.

Mutely, Jake obeyed. What else could he do?

He could turn tail and run, was what he wanted to do.

Whatever Mr. Zundelevich came to say to him, Jake didn't want to hear it. Beaten up yesterday by Queenie, he didn't feel like letting her pa pile it on. Jake had lost his Queen of Hearts three times over. He wasn't about to play a fourth hand. Besides, like his drinking, he didn't feel like card games anymore.

"All right, Jake, I get right to it." Yitzhak leaned forward a little.

Here it comes, Jake moaned inwardly. He knew now why Mr. Zundelevich had come. He'd come to tell Jake to stay the hell away from his daughter.

"Jake Whiskey, I want you should marry my Zoe-Esther," Yitzhak said, then settled back in his chair and folded his arms in front of him, meeting Jake's shocked, paralyzed expression head-on.

Shocked wasn't a strong enough word for it.

Jake knew that he must have heard wrong. He shook his head to clear his confusion. Damned if he hadn't really started to lose his mind for sure. Jake stayed silent.

"*Nu*, Jake, what is this?" Yitzhak used a fatherly tone. "You do not understand what it is I say? Jake, tell me?"

"Say . . . again," Jake mumbled.

"I said I want you should marry my Zoe-Esther."

He hadn't heard wrong after all. Jake swallowed hard and sat back against his chair, still at a loss for words.

"Jake Whiskey, listen to me." Yitzhak implored. "I am the papa and I need to know some things, things only you can tell me."

"What things?" Jake rasped.

"My little Star, do you love her?"

In all his years of hard living, even when guns were pointed right at him, Jake had never come up against anything so tough. Queenie's pa sure as hell didn't mince his words.

"I have time, Jake Whiskey." Yitzhak's tired eyes twinkled. "I have nothing but time to wait for you to tell me."

Before Jake even realized what he'd said, he answered. "Yes."

"Yes, this is what you say? *Gut, gut,* Jake." Yitzhak smiled. "You love my daughter and so I make the match and I make the wedding."

Surprised and shocked by his own answer to Queenie's pa just now—that he loved Queenie—Jake tried to follow Mr. Zundelevich's words, accent and all.

Yitzhak's smile faded.

"Jake Whiskey, you do not wish a wedding with my Star?" he sounded hurt.

"Mr. Zundelevich—"

"Call me Yitzhak."

"Yi . . . yitz . . . hak," Jake corrected, for some reason finding his first name harder to pronounce than his last. "I'll only say this once. I love your daughter. I would marry her in a heartbeat, if . . . if she wanted me. Truth is, I don't think she does."

"Sure, sure she does." Yitzhak brightened when Jake was through. "I told you, I am the papa and I make the match. My Star loves you. This I know. My Star wants to marry you."

"Excuse me, Yitz-hak, but I think she already has a husband picked out, and it's not me," Jake said.

Yitzhak thought a moment before he spoke.

"This is true, Jake. Daniel, a nice boy, yes, but she does not love Daniel. This I just found out. So, I say she will not marry nice Daniel, but you, nice Jake Whiskey, instead," Yitzhak declared emphatically.

"I don't understand any of this," Jake replied honestly.

"*Nu*, what is to understand? Just be on the steps of the town hall in two days time, at sunset. You will stand under the *chuppah* as *kalah* and *chassen* and we will make a wedding!"

Jake had no idea what Yitzhak just said, but he was pretty certain about the "wedding" part. Of one thing, though, Jake wasn't certain. He had to ask Yitz-hak, no matter the humiliation.

"I . . . I need to tell you." Jake fumbled for the right words. "I've been a lot of places and done a lot of things I'm not proud of. Let's just say I've lived pretty low. Maybe Queenie shouldn't have someone like me for her husband," he said and looked away, embarrassed and self-conscious.

"Queenie is it, you call my Star? This is very interesting, Jake. Someday we will talk of it," Yitzhak said, uninterested in what else Jake just told him.

"Did you *hear* me?"

"Hear you? Yes, yes, of course, Jake," Yitzhak returned his attention to his future *eydem*. "My son, we, all of us, have bad times. It is not always easy, this special gift we have of life. What is important is to live it the best that you can. I am sure, Jake Whiskey, you have lived your life the best way you knew how. But now, my son, now you can look forward to only good times, as husband to my little Star."

Until Yitzhak called him son, it never occurred to Jake before—what he'd missed out on his entire life. He'd never had a ma and pa to call him son, and he'd never known what it could feel like. It felt good, real good to be called son. Hard to hide his emotions, the ones he'd kept buried ever since he was old enough to know better, Jake couldn't keep the silly, childish grin off his face. He felt accepted in spite of all his flaws and failings. He felt like he was home.

Now Jake could say it, and he wanted to shout from the rooftops! *Yes! Yes! Yes! I'll marry Queenie come Saturday!*

But Yitzhak spoke before Jake had the chance.

"*Nu,* Jake, I will ask you to stay away from Star until the wedding. Such a happy surprise for her this will be, when she sees you waiting for her under the *chuppah!*" Yitzhak clapped his hands together with glee.

"Hold on. You mean Queenie doesn't know about this yet?" Jake's heart sank.

"She does not, Jake Whiskey, and you must not tell her," Yitzhak insisted. "My gift to my daughter on her wedding day is to make for her the right match. Don't make me an unhappy papa and ruin my surprise," he warned good-naturedly.

Jake wasn't about to argue with Yitzhak, but he was uneasy about things. Hell, Queenie might take one look at him, at her pa's *surprise gift* for her, and bolt.

But he'd risk it.

★ ★ ★ ★ ★

Zoe-Esther rushed out of her office the instant she spotted Yitzhak passing by her window.

"Papa, Papa, where have you been?" She tried to sound upset with him, but all she felt was relief when he walked through the front entryway. She threw her arms around him and hugged him hard.

"*Oy vey,* Star. You choke an old man," he teased.

"Old man, my foot," Hester said. Having heard the commotion in the front hall, she'd put down her mending to join in.

"Hello, Hester," Yitzhak greeted, his grin broadening even more.

"Papa, answer me," Zoe-Esther demanded. "Where have you been?"

"Been? Where have I been? This, child, is of no importance. I am back. Now this is all that is important," he chided gently, then brushed past his daughter and took up Hester's hand.

Whichever of the two women registered more shock on their faces at his action, it could not be told.

"Hester, you and me. We have plans to finish. The wedding is in two days and you do nothing about it," Yitzhak said lightly, as if he were continuing in mid-discussion on the subject.

"Nothing about it? What—"

Yitzhak didn't give her a chance to say anything else.

"You and I have plans to make, and many things to get done for the wedding, Hester Bartlett. Time is running out. How can my Star have a wedding with no food, no dress, no wedding guests invited, no plans to make a party after?"

"What—"

Still he didn't let Hester speak.

"Now what we *do* have is a rabbi. The rabbi is coming after Shabbas to perform the ceremony. The rabbi brings his *rebitzin*, his wife, and his sons, his cousins, everybody in his family who is traveling with him on the wagon train. And what *mazel!* One of his sons plays the violin and we will have beautiful wedding music, and laugh, and dance and make such a wonderful party!" Yitzhak exclaimed.

Yet again, before Hester or his daughter could say a word, Yitzhak pulled a baffled Hester behind him toward the kitchen, all the while instructing her on how they must hurry now to get everything ready in time for his little Star's wedding.

Zoe-Esther didn't know whether to laugh or cry. Wanting to do both, she did neither, and wore her stunned expression back into her office. She had two patients due soon and she needed to think about them, and not about her upcoming wedding to Daniel.

"Oh Hester, it's so beautiful," Zoe-Esther marveled at her newly sewn wedding gown, very close to tears. She rushed over to the mirror in her room to have a better look, more to avoid Hester seeing her tears than to admire her image. Zoe-Esther had never seen a gown so lovely! She pulled the white satin dress up against her, lovingly adjusting its lace-trimmed neck against hers, before placing its matching sleeves, just so, over her arms and wrists.

"Here dear. It's missing one thing." Hester had to choke back her own tears at the sight of the lovely young woman in her wedding dress. Ever so gently Hester took the lace veil, stitched around its edges with tiny pearl beads, and placed it over Zoe-Esther's head. It just reached her waist, in the front and back.

Zoe-Esther dared a look at her reflection in her wedding

veil. Never in all her imaginings, had she imagined this! She felt like a princess, just like the ones in all the fairy tales she'd read as a child. Her veil fell so softly over her now that it made her think of puffy little clouds in a soft breeze. Any moment the misted magic of it could blow away. But unlike all the stories of her childhood, her own fairy tale would not end happily ever after. In this beautiful veil and gown she would not marry her Prince Charming, but Daniel, her dear friend and companion.

It will be enough.

She'd made her promise to Daniel and she meant to keep it.

Waking in a frenzy Zoe-Esther realized today was her wedding day. Neither happy nor sad, she did feel a little *farmisht* when she thought about all the events of the day to come. And by day's end, she would be Mrs. Daniel Stein.

She shot up in bed.

Daniel!

Why, she hadn't laid eyes on him since . . . she reflected a moment, since the night Papa returned, two days ago! Guilty from head to foot, she should have thought of Daniel before now. After all, soon he would be her husband. She would not make a very good wife if she already ignored him so.

Zoe-Esther scurried out of bed and threw on her usual skirt and blouse, intent on finding Daniel.

Utterly unsuccessful in locating her soon-to-be husband, Zoe-Esther sought out her papa and Hester. Maybe they knew where Daniel had gone. What a strange week it had been, what with first her papa disappearing, and now Daniel.

"Child, I've no idea about Daniel," Hester said and started out of the parlor, having only just entered it.

Suspicious, Zoe-Esther called her back.

"Hester, surely you know where Daniel is."

"Surely I do not," Hester said and started out of the room once again.

"Hester Bartlett, come back in here. Now," Zoe-Esther commanded, placing her hands on her hips.

"Child, there is still much to do. How am I to get a thing more done if you keep me here any longer?" Hester complained.

More suspicious than before, Zoe-Esther knew Hester hid something from her. Wait. Finally Zoe-Esther thought of where Daniel was.

"Oh Hester, forgive me. My nerves are a little frazzled. I know where Daniel must be," Zoe-Esther smiled forgivingly.

More nervous than Zoe-Esther could have dreamed she was, Hester froze, afraid of what she might hear.

"He's probably worrying over a wedding gift or some other surprise for me," Zoe-Esther felt sure. "I must finish with my surprise for him. I embroidered him special handkerchiefs with his initials," she said. "I hope he likes them. Oh Hester, such a day full of surprises," Zoe-Esther said with as much cheer as she could, then placed a warm kiss on Hester's cheek and hurried back up the stairs to get ready.

"You have no idea of the surprises in store for you, child," Hester whispered under her breath.

The parlor clock chimed five bells.

"Gracious me." With little time until the wedding Hester rushed up the steps, close behind the bride-to-be.

"It's time, child," Hester opened Zoe-Esther's door to

summon her to her wedding.

"I'm ready," Zoe-Esther replied quietly, full of emotion for what was to come. "Where's Papa, Hester? And Daniel? Are they already at the town hall?" she asked as she followed Hester out of her room and down the stairs.

"I'm that sure they are," Hester tossed lightly over her shoulder, and kept on going. Zoe-Esther caught up with her once outside the clinic. The two walked together now, arm in arm, down Main Street toward the town hall.

"So many, Hester!" Zoe-Esther marveled when she saw the crowd gathered before the Town Hall. "I'd no idea you invited all of Golden City to my wedding!" But for the unexpected number of guests, Zoe-Esther thought the warm, mid-September evening just right for the ceremony. She was happier still when she started to recognize all the familiar faces, townsfolk and miners with their families. To have everyone together, side by side, for her wedding to Daniel helped give her needed courage to keep her marriage promise.

Dozens of merry guests parted to allow Zoe-Esther passage. Just above their heads Zoe-Esther could see the top of the *chuppah,* her wedding canopy. Four poles supported the square of white canvas that she would stand under to marry Daniel. Papa would be waiting there for her. She wanted both her papa and Hester to stand under the *chuppah* with her and Daniel.

Glad for her veil, Zoe-Esther hoped no one could see how hard it was for her to hold a smile. Worse, she didn't want Yitzhak to see her misery. Daniel either, of course. With a quick silent prayer to ask God for His blessing, Zoe-Esther shut her eyes a moment to receive His *brochah.*

When she opened her eyes what stood before her wasn't a blessing—but a miracle!

Jake!

Wonderful, passionate, tall, rugged, handsome Jake stood under the wedding canopy, with Daniel nowhere in sight! Zoe-Esther should look for Daniel, but she couldn't take her eyes off Jake. His shadowy scrutiny stayed fixed on hers. Somewhere in the recesses of what rational thought she had left, it dawned on Zoe-Esther that she was about to marry Jake—not Daniel!

Jake's loving hand went out to her, and she took it, as if she no longer held any control over her own body. She let Jake draw her to stand next to him. His warm smile eased her mind and she looked to him, only him.

The rabbi came forward.

Zoe-Esther knew the rabbi spoke, but at first couldn't listen to or even look at the rabbi, so strong was Jake's power over her. Only when she began to hear some of the familiar words of the wedding ceremony did Zoe-Esther switch her gaze to the rabbi.

"Zahava-Esther, do you promise to love, honor, cherish, and obey Yaakov, from this day forward—"

Zoe-Esther stared in absolute astonishment at the rabbi.

He said Yaakov! The rabbi called Jake—Yaakov!

All of a sudden the truth of it hit Zoe-Esther so hard, she had to gasp for breath. She grabbed Jake for support. Her knees buckled. Her head buzzed.

Of course! Jake! Jacob in Hebrew is Yaakov!

It was her only thought before she collapsed in a dead faint.

Chapter Twenty

Jake scooped Queenie up the moment she fell at his feet. He'd seen females faint before, for all sorts of reasons, but not like this. This wasn't a swoon and Queenie didn't have a faint heart! Hell, she might just as well have taken off and run for her life away from him!

It killed him to realize that Queenie didn't want him, didn't love him. Her pa had been wrong, dead wrong. She looked lifeless in his arms just now, with her veil still over her serene, captivating face. He felt as if he were carrying Queenie to her grave, when all the while it was his. As soon as she regained consciousness, he knew she'd run like hell.

Unnamed faces and unknown voices circled around him like buzzards going after prey. He didn't try to pick out what any of the voices were saying. He didn't care what they said. He drew Queenie's body closer, as much for protection against the crowd, as because of the certainty that he'd never hold her in his arms again. Somehow in his emotional fog, Jake headed for the medical clinic, wanting to lay Queenie down where it was safe. He'd get her safely there, and then he'd leave.

"Yaakov?"

Queenie. Her soft voice reached up to him and he immediately loosened his coffin-like hold on her, but kept on walking toward her clinic.

"Yaakov?"

He didn't answer her. He needed to get Queenie to her clinic first. He didn't want to say goodbye to her with so many eyes on them.

"Jake, put me down!"

Forced to now, he stopped.

Zoe-Esther squirmed in his arms.

"Jake Whiskey, you let me go, now!"

Jake didn't want to let go of her, but he had no choice.

Zoe-Esther had no experience waking up in any man's arms, least of all the man of her dreams, her Yaakov—the very reason she'd fainted in the first place. How easy it would be to slip back into her veiled dreams, for dreams they surely must be. How could there be any reality at all to this moment? Since she was nine years old, she had wished for this to happen, but she'd stopped believing that her dreams would ever come true. Should she dare believe now that they had?

Powerful arms held Zoe-Esther, easing her spinning head, warming her, adding strength to her weakened limbs. She didn't want Jake to let go of her, but until he did, she couldn't know if this moment was real, or something she'd conjured to defend her senses against marrying Daniel.

"Jake, put me down," Zoe-Esther said for the third time, and pulled off her veil, all the while hoping that the rabbi really had said what she thought he said: *"Zahava-Esther, do you promise to love, honor, cherish, and obey Yaakov, from this day forward—"*

"I do."

"You do what?" Jake asked, stupefied, and set her on her feet again.

"I do!" Zoe-Esther cried, this time to Jake's face—to her Yaakov. Happier than she'd ever been in the whole of her life, Zoe-Esther knew that the man who'd just held her so masterfully in his arms, was and always would be, her Yaakov, her true and wished-for match. The *schadchen* was right, Zoe-Esther marveled to herself. She kept her ecstatic gaze on Jake's puzzled features. All the time across the ocean, growing up in the East, going to medical school, coming to the frontier; all the time the matchmaker meant to keep her promise to Zoe-Esther—to make her a match with Yaakov!

"Oh Yaakov. I do! I do! I do!" Zoe-Esther exclaimed and threw her arms around him, never, ever intending to let go of him again.

"Hold on, Queenie," Jake rasped, straining to make sense of her. He took hold of her slender arms and pulled them from around his neck, setting her away from him.

Both he and Zoe-Esther remained oblivious to the curious eyes all around.

"I don't know what you mean, Queenie. I don't know what you want."

"Yaakov, I want you. All I've ever wanted is you."

"But—"

She put her shaky fingers to his lips. "Shhh, Yaakov. There are no buts, not anymore," she reassured quietly. "I love you. I want to marry you, only you," she told him, then took her hand down.

"But, Queenie . . . who—"

He stumbled over what he had to ask.

"Who is Yaa-kov?"

"You, Jake. You are Yaakov."

"But—"

She put her fingers over his smooth lips, mustache and all, once more.

"Let's just say it's God's work," Zoe-Esther smiled, knowing the *schadchen* had more than a little something to do with it, too.

Jake took Queenie's fingers away from his lips and then pressed a kiss onto them, thinking that he might have "just gotten religion," after all.

The crowd around them, including Yitzhak and Hester, hurried to follow as the betrothed couple made their way, hand in hand, back to the steps of the town hall, where the ever-patient rabbi still waited.

In five minutes' time everyone stood back in their places, Yitzhak to the right of Jake, and Hester to the left of Zoe-Esther. The rest of the crowd closed in a circle behind them. Everyone was ready, everyone but—

Daniel!

Zoe-Esther shot Yitzhak an anxious look. The instant she read the mischievous glimmer in his eyes, her intuition told her that her papa knew exactly, precisely what happened to Daniel. After she'd made her marriage vows to Yaakov, she would find Daniel, and she hoped with all her heart that he would understand why she could not, in good faith, marry him.

"I now pronounce you husband and wife." The rabbi beamed at the couple then took the glass wrapped in white linen from the step behind him, and placed it at Jake's feet. "Yaakov," he leaned in and instructed quietly, "you must break the glass. This is for luck."

Jake readily stomped on the glass, shattering it to pieces.

Everyone cheered and applauded from behind them, though it could be said that none except for those who came with the rabbi understood why the groom just broke a glass underfoot.

303

"*Mazel tov!*" the rabbi congratulated loudly.

Yitzhak hugged his daughter and his new *eydem,* tears of joy streaming down his face. Hester hugged them, too, and had to wipe away her own unstoppable tears. Already, lively music could be heard over the throng of well-wishers as a violist, the rabbi's son, stepped out of the crowd and approached. At the same moment, another musician, this time a western fiddler, stepped out of the crowd, and played along. Somehow the two fiddlers matched their instruments to the same song and everyone cheered, "Hurrah!"

In fact, no sooner had Zoe-Esther and Jake stepped out from under their wedding canopy, than revelers began to celebrate, tapping their feet and forming their own twosomes to dance in time with the spirited fiddles. Drawn immediately in, Zoe-Esther and Jake joined them, doing their best to keep up.

Tables laden with food framed the large street square marking the celebration. Many of the women in Golden City, with the help of the miners' wives, had prepared a sumptuous feast. Of course, at Yitzhak's instruction, there was also "a little chicken, some nice potatoes, some strudel, and lots of schnapps." Hester made sure, too, that her tiered "butter wedding cake" had a special place in the center of the main table. No one, absolutely guaranteed by the amount of food and drink, was in any danger of leaving the wedding party hungry or thirsty. The warm evening provided a perfect setting for what surely for Zoe-Esther and Jake was the perfect wedding.

Only now did the torches, put in place earlier, need to be lit. And only now did Zoe-Esther and Jake break away for a long desired moment to themselves. But before they could decide where to go to be alone, Yitzhak found them.

In truth, Zoe-Esther was glad.

"Papa," she scolded the moment he'd finished placing another kiss on her forehead. "Tell me now. What happened to Daniel?" She pressed him for an answer, not caring if Jake or anyone else heard her.

"Little Star, it is all right." Yitzhak put a fatherly hand to her cheek. "Daniel and I talked and we decided it is better you should not marry him."

"What, Papa, do you mean by *we* decided?" she asked severely.

He took his hand away from her cheek.

"I mean what I say, Star. You are a *zade*, a married lady now, married to Yaakov and not Daniel," Yitzhak scolded and nodded towards his new *eydem*.

Jake didn't say a word or move a muscle. He didn't want to miss any of this.

By now Hester had spotted the three of them, and she came to stand beside Yitzhak. Like Jake, she was not about to interrupt father and daughter, either.

"Papa, please." Zoe-Esther's tone softened.

"Star, you are not to worry. Daniel is good with this. We talked and I told him I am the papa and I make the match for my daughter. I told him he was a very nice boy, but not for my little girl. He understood, Star," Yitzhak assured her.

"Where—"

"He has already gone," Yitzhak interrupted. "Two days ago Daniel left to go back to Pennsylvania, to his hospital, and his family, and his friends."

Grateful and relieved, Zoe-Esther made a silent prayer that Daniel would be all right, then brushed a quick kiss on Yitzhak's cheek.

"Thank you, Papa, for everything," she said, knowing how hard it must be for him to have let her marry a man outside the fold.

"So, Yitzhak Zundelevich," Hester scolded. "You tell Zoe-Esther you made the match when it was I who made it?"

Zoe-Esther started to laugh. She didn't have the heart to correct her papa or Hester and tell them it was really the *schadchen* from the village of her childhood. It tickled Zoe-Esther that her papa and Hester kibbitzed back and forth with such ease. Maybe, just maybe, there was a match she would make one day, for them.

Jake put his arm around his new wife and whispered in her ear.

"Let's get out of here."

His husky suggestion sent shivers up and down Zoe-Esther's spine.

"Yes, let's," she said, her face turning crimson.

"Star, what is this?" Yitzhak sounded alarmed. "You look all flushed. Are you all right?"

"Yitzhak, of course she is all right." Hester grabbed hold of his arm to lead him away. "Are you so old that you don't remember how it feels to be in love?"

"Yes, I remember." His eyes twinkled and he grinned broadly, ear to ear. "*Nu,* my children," Yitzhak said to Zoe-Esther and Jake. "I say good night to you now. You may go with my blessing." Yitzhak waited with Hester as "his children" walked down the street, then disappeared from sight. He was confident that his new *eydem* would take *gut care* of his little Star. Later, later he would tell everything to Yaakov. He would tell Yaakov that, just like Yitzhak is a patriarch of the Hebrews, so, too is Yaakov, the first the papa of the second. Yes, later he would tell his new son, Yaakov, all about his new, special place, not just in the family, but in their religion.

The sight of his new wife astride her horse, her wedding

dress hiked up past her knees, with her hair all loose and beautiful tumbling down her back in the silvery moonlight, was something Jake never figured on seeing riding up ahead of him. He hadn't figured on ever having a wife, much less one like Queenie.

Although it was hard to keep his concentration on anything but her right now, still Jake tried to think on everything that had happened in the past week, and on this unbelievable day. Feelings he'd been so careful to hide for so long had been freed. Finally he had a family, his own family, all respectable-like. He had a wife to love, and her pa, and maybe one day he and Queenie would have children running underfoot. Jake would never again be on the outside looking in and it felt damned good. He had everything he'd ever wanted now, all because of the turn of one little card: the Queen of Hearts.

Grinning inside and out, Jake realized it wasn't an unlucky card for him after all. Fact is, he didn't have to gamble anymore, with the Queen of Hearts or anything else. He liked what he did for a living now, partnering with Matthew in gold mining and smelting, and truth be known, he liked himself better for doing it. And what he liked the most about himself now was that Queenie had actually accepted him as her husband.

She'd brought him nothing but good luck since the day he met her. He'd been wrong about her from the start. He had a lot of making up to do to her, and he couldn't wait to get started. Jake gave Missouri a quick nudge to spur his horse on and passed his surprised wife on the trail, intent on being the first to reach the isolation of her cabin. They would plan a real honeymoon, but time for that later. Right now, the only thing on Jake's mind was getting his wife in his bed. For tonight, hers would do fine.

★ ★ ★ ★ ★

By the time Zoe-Esther slid off Sheyn and installed her alongside Jake's horse, her nerves had got the better of her. Only a few moments ago she'd been all right, hadn't she? The whole ride up the mountain, she could think of nothing but Yaakov and how excited she was to be with him. That was the part, the to-be-with-him part that set her nerves on end. She'd been absolutely fine until he'd ridden past her, in a rush for what?

Our wedding night, that's what!

She knew he was inside the cabin now, waiting for her, wanting her. Petrified, Zoe-Esther took slow steps, knowing he'd find her wanting all right. Why he was the only man she'd ever kissed, ever even let touch her in any romantic way! The same, she knew, couldn't be said for him. Sure he'd known other women before her, she didn't care. That was then. This was now: a new start for them both.

What did matter, what frazzled her nerves and made her feet drag, was that in all her medical studies, she'd never read one paper, had even one lesson in . . . making love. Of course she knew the how of it and the why of it. She just had no idea if she could *do* it.

Sheyn's whinny from the corral made Zoe-Esther stop and turn around. Funny, she only now remembered that she'd never paid for her horse. In another lifetime she'd promised to pay Jake Whiskey. In this one, she was about to settle everything with her husband. Any other time Zoe-Esther would have appreciated the irony of it, but not now; not with her heart thumping in her chest, every bit of air sucked out of her, and her mouth stuffed dry with cotton. More anxious than she wanted to admit, Zoe-Esther forced herself to turn back around and walk toward the cabin.

Close now to the cabin door, she had only to rotate the latch and go inside. How could such a small act count for so much? How could so much be dependent on which side of a door you stood?

Scared into action by her own inaction, Zoe-Esther turned the latch and slowly pushed open the door, steeling herself against her mounted fears.

"Help you, lady?" Jake teased, standing naked to the waist by the lit fireplace.

The same words again, the very first ones he'd ever said to her. Just as she did, he must remember all of it: all their minutes, hours, and days. All their moments in time together. The possibility that he'd been thinking of her when she thought he couldn't possibly be, made her fall in love with him all over again. Zoe-Esther's fears ebbed while her passions flamed.

No words were needed now, for either of them.

Zoe-Esther pulled the door shut and latched it behind her, all the while meeting her husband's smoky, heated gaze.

He smiled.

She smiled.

He started for her.

She started for him.

Their lips brushed lightly at first, just enough to spark the fire about to break out between them.

Jake laced his fingers in the mass of fiery waves at the back of Zoe-Esther's head and pulled her to him, urging her mouth against his. Hungry for her, he couldn't get close enough, touch her enough, or taste enough. When her sweet tongue explored his mouth and followed his lead, he had to have more. He pulled all of her petite, soft frame against him now, every shapely, comely inch of it, wrapping his arms around any part of her that he could find.

Her desire fanned and ignited, Zoe-Esther luxuriated in the feel of his powerful, muscled chest, shoulders, his back and hips, letting her hands roam free over him. He felt wonderful, smelled wonderful, and tasted delicious. When he urged her closer, she melted in his arms, feeling the liquid heat build in her core. He'd set her on fire and she'd willingly burn for him.

Jake groaned against her lips and pressed her harder against his burgeoning manhood, knowing, despite the annoyance of their clothes, that his wife was almost ready for him.

"This dress is so beautiful," he whispered against her mouth, her cheeks, and her neck. "I don't want . . . to ruin it," he said low and breathy, fumbling over the buttons down its satiny, white front.

Zoe-Esther covered his usually steady hands with her own. "Let me," she panted, then quickly undid her dress.

Jake raised his hands again to her bodice and began loosening the ribbons of her exposed, filmy chemise. This time his fingers worked with steady certainty. Before he untied the ribbons, he moved his hands to the edges of her dress and slipped it off her shoulders.

She helped him.

He loved her for it and for so many, many, other things.

Since it was impossible for him to think now, about anything, Jake let Queenie's dress shimmer to the floor before leading her over to the fireplace, where he'd set bedding earlier. He let go of her, kicked off his boots, and had his pants removed in seconds flat. Grabbing up her hand again, he eased her down, gently, slowly, to lie with him in front of the sparking, spitting flames.

Zoe-Esther's last coherent thought was that she'd come willingly into the fire with Yaakov. She gave in to one pleasurable sensation after the other. Aware only that she lay naked beneath her husband, she arched her feverish hips up to him, impatient, needing a release for her mounted passions. Yaakov . . . only Yaakov . . . only her husband could give her the release her body demanded.

"Yes, yes, yes," she murmured against the moist, hot, savory skin of his neck, his shoulder, his chest, anywhere she could taste him and touch him. "Yes, my love . . . yes!"

Nothing in any of Zoe-Esther's imaginings about a man and a woman together, ever could have prepared her for this—this wonder, this pleasure, this fulfillment of love.

When he entered her a second time, this time more easily, she ached and throbbed, yet wanted more, encouraging him never to let go.

"I love you, Yaakov, I love you, I love you . . ." she whispered before drifting asleep nestled against the warmth of her husband's body, safe in his tender, loving embrace.

"Well, good morning, Mrs. Whiskey." Jake teased Zoe-Esther awake with the gentle brush of his mustached kiss on her soft, parted lips. "I like the sound of it. Do you, my beautiful bride?" He brushed another kiss across her cheek, then nuzzled behind her ear, her neck, her . . .

"Yes, yes, I like it!" she giggled, needing to stop him from tickling and teasing her into oblivion.

"So, is that a yes or a no? I don't think I quite heard you," Jake whispered huskily and continued to rain kisses down past her neck.

"Yes," Zoe-Esther answered dreamily, already giving in to desire. "Yes, Yaakov," she rolled into him, pressing, wanting him so. "I like it very much."

"I like *you* very much, wife," Jake said and made love to her again.

Hours later they got up and dressed, at least partially; she wore the quilt and he tucked a blanket around his waist.

"Really, Yaakov, I am serious." Zoe-Esther wanted to make sure that her husband understood her meaning. This was too important to them both.

"You know, sweetheart, I still can't get used to Yaakov. I've been plain Jake all my life. I'm not sure I can measure up to being Yaakov," he tossed lightly at her.

She could tell he wanted to avoid what she'd brought up only moments before. The subject of money wasn't going to be an easy one, she knew. But things needed to be said.

"Yaakov, I am a doctor with paying patients now . . . some of them at least. The point is that I can take care of us. And Papa, too, of course. Things will be tight, but we can manage. Then, when you get back on your feet in whatever you—"

"Enough, Queenie," Jake couldn't let her go on. "What is all this about?"

"What is this about?" she parroted, incredulous at his question.

"Sweetheart," he implored, "why are you worried about money?"

"I'm not, Yaakov. Well, what I mean—"

"Yes?" he interrupted. "Tell me what you mean." Jake wasn't angry, in fact he was becoming more interested in this conversation by the minute.

Zoe-Esther pulled the quilt closer around her body and walked toward him. As soon as she stood in front of her husband, she softened her tone and began to explain.

"Yaakov, you do not have to worry about the money for

us, for our family. This is what I mean to have you understand. I know. I know about everything. I know that you
lost all you had at the Golden Gates. It is all right, my love.
We will be fine, you will see." She reached up and gently
brushed the strands of salt-and-pepper hair that had fallen
over his forehead.

He clasped her hand so tightly it frightened her. But
when he relaxed, then pressed her fingers to his lips, she relaxed, too.

Jake couldn't believe it.

Queenie married him thinking that he didn't have a
dime. All of his life he'd believed money was his ticket to
everything. After things folded at the Golden Gates, and
after he restarted his bankroll with mining and smelting,
he'd still believed money mattered. He sure as hell thought
it mattered to all women, even Queenie. If he weren't
wealthy now he might not have said yes to her pa's
matching them up. After all, who would want somebody
poor?

Queenie.

Queenie would.

Gripped now with raw emotion, Jake's heart filled with
the love he'd saved up all his life to give . . . to Queenie.

"Yaakov, what is it?" Zoe-Esther was alarmed by his
troubled expression.

Jake's troubled years melted away. He smiled at his precious wife, unable yet to tell her what had been wrong with
his life before he met her, or that she was the one now
making it all go right.

Zoe-Esther warmed to his smile, needing to see it to
make sure that all was well with him. With no idea of the
bright future ahead—that her husband had enough money
to build her another clinic, a tuberculosis hospital, to take

313

care of all the poor in Golden City, and then some—she nestled against his comforting warmth, not caring that her quilt fell to the floor. All she cared about, all that she needed in the world was Yaakov, holding her in his arms, and thanks to the matchmaker, he could.

—Mazel tov—

About the Author

Matchmaker, Matchmaker is Joanne Sundell's first published novel. She holds a B.S. degree in Nursing and is a long-standing member of Romance Writers of America. While she loves reading all types of romance and women's fiction, she enjoys writing historical westerns about heroic women of strong purpose. With her three children grown, Joanne lives in the mountains of Colorado with her husband of thirty-two years and their entourage of felines and huskies. Her e-mail address is sundell@coweblink.net.